DEADLY SECRETS

A.M. ACOSTA

CONTENT WARNING
Deadly Secrets is intended for adult readers only
It contains mature themes and sexually explicit content and is not
intended for readers younger than 18 years old.

Line and Copy Editor: Jenny Sims
Cover Designer: Jani Mapatuna

ISBN (PRINT) 978-84-09-61579-7
ISBN (EPUB) 978-84-09-61593-3

1st Edition 2024

To my strong, independent readers who don't like being told what to do, but also love being manhandled and fucked hard against the wall. Don't let anyone convince you that you cannot be both.

TRIGGER WARNINGS

Deadly Secrets isn't entirely dark but has mildly dark elements.

Your mental health is important to me, but it should be more important to you. A list of potentially triggering themes can be found below. Please read responsibly.

Should you have any inquiries regarding this list, please get in touch with me at amacostaauthor.com or via any of my social media accounts. I primarily use TikTok and Threads, but you can also connect with me on Facebook and Instagram.

- Attempted murder
- Child sexual assault (mentioned but not depicted)
- Death and grief
- Hospitalization
- Kidnapping
- Mild torture
- Murder
- Offensive language
- Poisoning
- Sexually explicit scenes
- Stalking
- Suicide (mentioned but not depicted)
- Underage drinking
- "All I Want for Christmas Is You" by Mariah Carey

CONTENTS

PLAYLIST

Hoobastank—The Reason

John Legend—All of Me

Red Hot Chili Peppers—Under the Bridge

The Ink Spots, Ella Fitzgerald—Into Each Life Some Rain Must Fall

Charli XCX, Rina Sawayama—Beg for You

Billie Eilish, ROSALÍA—Lo Vas A Olvidar

Billie Eilish—when the party's over

Charlie Puth, Selena Gomez—We Don't Talk Anymore

The Weeknd, Kendrick Lamar—Pray For Me

Mariah Carey—All I Want for Christmas Is You

Melrose Avenue—Suffering

Lewis Capaldi—Before You Go

Annie Lennox—I Put A Spell On You

Billie Eilish—Billie Bossa Nova

Zara Larsson—Ain't My Fault

Muse—Stockholm Syndrome

Korn—Take Me

Fall Out Boy—Dance, Dance

Thirty Seconds To Mars—The Kill

EIVISSA VIBES

(Sienna)

I'm never drinking again.

That was all my brain could think as I emptied my stomach contents inside the toilet, and by contents, I meant the little booze that my system refused to process from last night. I couldn't even keep track of how many times I'd told myself the same thing over the past three weeks since Sarah and I landed in Ibiza, but my promises had gone out the window every night I stepped foot inside Pacha.

We'd been planning this vacation since we began our final year at Rubin American Boarding School in Switzerland, and I was certainly testing my limits when it came to partying hard. Every day on the island felt like Groundhog Day. We'd kick-start the day by having breakfast in our villa, then chill at a different *cala*—those hidden beaches with crystal-clear waters that screamed Spanish paradise. When the sun dipped below the horizon, it was time to hit the club, and I'd be ready to hunt for my next prey. This usually meant searching for a cute Spanish guy to sweep me off my feet and help me forget the nightmare waiting for me back home.

Today was our last day on vacation. Sarah would return to England, and I would have to return to New York and face my parents.

When I stepped outside the bathroom, the sunlight blinded me momentarily as I tried to take in my surroundings. My head pounded, and I reeked of vodka.

Collapsing onto the bed, I grabbed my phone from the bedside table and saw it was ten o'clock. I'd barely managed to get three hours of sleep, and the loud snores from my right made my headache even worse.

I tried remembering what had happened the night before, but the last thing I could recall was drinking tequila shots with Pedro—*or was his name Pablo?*—and having one of the most disappointing fucks of my life. He wouldn't have found my clit even if I drew him a map, so I guessed I had put as much energy into remembering his name as he did in making me orgasm.

I gave Pedro—*well, let's call him Pedro*—a nudge in an attempt to wake him up.

"You need to leave." He groaned but continued sleeping, so I kicked him until he opened his eyes.

"What?" He sounded disoriented.

I was being a bitch, but I didn't care. I'd asked him to leave, but at some point, after our unremarkable night, I dozed off, and he'd stuck around.

"I said that you need to leave."

"Are you always this friendly with your lovers?"

A lover? Please, last night could almost qualify as PG-13.

I pinched the bridge of my nose with my fingers to bring some relief. "I have a flight in five hours, and Sarah and I need to check out in two, so please grab your things and go." My mood was souring by the minute. I would be home in less than twenty-four hours, something I wasn't looking forward to.

Mumbling something in Spanish that I couldn't quite make out, Pedro quickly dressed, collected his belongings, and headed for the bedroom door. Just before reaching for the doorknob, he paused and turned around.

"Can I have your number?" he asked.

"What for?" I deadpanned. "I live in the US. I don't see the point."

"Joder cómo se ha levantado la americana...Well, nice meeting you, Sienna. It was fun."

I didn't respond. While he might have had a great night, mine had been anything but below average.

As soon as he left, I wasted no time and made a beeline for the shower. I had less than two hours to pack my things and have breakfast, and given my current condition, it felt like insufficient time.

* * *

I dragged my feet downstairs until I reached the back garden, where Sarah enjoyed breakfast. We'd secured a stunning Mediterranean villa with breathtaking sea views overlooking the pebbly beach at Platja des Codolar. Even after three weeks, the sight continued to leave me breathless.

"Good morning, beautiful," she exclaimed cheerfully. Sarah was in a good mood, which made me suspect that her night had likely been more enjoyable than mine. I wanted so badly to smack that smile off her face...

"Hey," I grunted in response to her happy-go-lucky attitude. Sarah laughed while she poured me a cup of coffee. I sat beside her and arranged some toasted bread on my plate. After drizzling some extra virgin olive oil over it, I added a couple of slices of *jamón serrano*.

God, I love Spanish breakfasts.

"I spotted Pablo heading out about half an hour ago." *So he was Pablo, not Pedro. Oops. My bad.* "He seemed a little upset. What did you say to the poor guy?"

"The poor guy? Worst fuck of my life, good riddance."

I was being unreasonable, but Sarah knew me well enough to realize that Pablo wasn't the issue. I'd been avoiding any conversation related to my summer internship at Cos Pharmaceuticals, the company my dad started five years before I was born. "Shall we grab something to eat on our way to the airport?"

"C'mon, Sienna. Stop deflecting. Tell me what's going on." Sarah sighed. "You've been a bit off the entire trip. You've always been a wild card, but you've never been this careless or insensitive. Have you talked to your parents yet?" Sarah was right, and as much as I was inclined to continue skirting around the topic, my friend happened to be the most determined person on the planet, so I knew she wouldn't let it slide.

"There's nothing to tell. I'm supposed to start my internship in three weeks and go to college in September."

"You don't sound excited." She took a sip of her coffee.

"I'm excited about college, but definitely not the internship." The prospect of working for my father was far from appealing. Our relationship had deteriorated beyond repair when he decided to ship me off to Switzerland at age twelve. The last thing I wanted was to spend more time than necessary with him before I left for Stanford. Don't get me wrong, I was genuinely grateful for meeting Sarah. Without her, my time in Rubin would have been a nightmare. "I'd rather drink piss, but it was a condition he imposed if I wanted him to cover my college tuition and expenses. If enduring a month of working with him means he won't cancel my AmEx Platinum, then I'm willing to make that sacrifice."

"You sound like a brat." Sarah chuckled.

"You know I am." I gently nudged her with my elbow. "My mom has been calling me nonstop, trying to convince me to go on vacation with them, but I can't be bothered. I'd rather spend that time home alone."

"Are you sure?" she pressed.

"Yes. If I must choose between preparing pellets to feed the lab rats or spending some *quality time* with them in Cabo, I'll choose labor over hammocks. It's the least painful option." Sarah knew how I felt about returning home every summer. She could count with her two hands the number of times I had traveled back to New York in the past six years or how many times I had faked not being disappointed when my mother had called me saying they couldn't visit because of my father's demanding work schedule. His company had always been his priority, and as much as I didn't want it to affect me, it did.

"Miles texted me," Sarah added.

Miles and I dated for six months until I broke up with him a month ago. I could lie and say it was because I was going back to the US while he was heading to Australia, but the truth was that I'd grown tired of his stupid ass.

"What does he want now?"

"He said you're not answering his texts."

"Maybe Miles should take the hint and stop messaging me." I'd been avoiding his texts for the past two weeks. He insisted on us staying friends and that he would come and visit me as soon as he could…

I hope he doesn't show up in California because he won't like the sound of my door hitting his tanned Aussie face.

We stayed silent for a few more minutes as we finished our breakfast, savoring our last moments of peace under the Spanish sun. An hour later, we were both packed and waiting for our local taxi driver to arrive.

Sarah would fly to London via Madrid, where we would say our goodbyes before I boarded my connecting flight to New York.

* * *

After an uneventful flight and several champagne glasses, I arrived at JFK International Airport eight hours later. As soon as the arrivals doors swung open, I immediately spotted my mom holding a bouquet. I took a deep breath and summoned my warmest smile as I approached her.

"My dear Sienna! I've missed you so much." She squeezed me tightly as tears streamed down her face. Marie Moore stood at just five-three, but her strength more than made up for her petite stature. Her light brown hair was shorter than I remembered.

"You've cut your hair!" I beamed.

"Yeah, do you think it suits me? Your father insists it makes me look younger," she remarked. Fortunately, I'd inherited my mom's features—her cute nose, full lips, and sun-kissed complexion. With her short hair, she could easily pass for my older sister.

"You look fantastic. Speaking of the devil, where's Dad?" She anxiously nibbled on her lower lip before replying to my question, yet even before she uttered a word, I could already anticipate the answer.

"I know he promised he would come too, but you know your father. Something urgent came up. He wanted me to tell you how sorry he is." Her voice carried a tone of disappointment, but we both understood that disappointment was a recurring theme for Edward Moore. "Let's go home. I'm eager to hear all about your trip to Ibiza."

THE BASEMENT

(Sienna)

I only had three weeks of freedom left before starting my internship at Cos Pharma, so I decided to make the most of it and have fun exploring what the city had to offer.

A few days after I got home, I texted Caroline. We hadn't been particularly close friends, but she knew how to have a good time, and I needed that precise diversion to avoid being under my parents' scrutiny at home. Our paths crossed three years ago during one of my summer visits. Caroline was employed as a bartender at Port Chester Country Club and had connections to all the trendiest clubs and bars in the city. We hit it off right away, but our friendship never fully blossomed since our time together was restricted to just five weeks each year. We didn't share many common interests either, except for our mutual love for parties and alcohol.

Caroline

> We'll pick you up at 7. Wear jeans, nothing fancy.

> And put something on that shows skin. I want to introduce you to a friend *wink emoji*

> I don't date, but if he's hot, I might make an exception…

Caroline

> I've shown him a picture of you.

> Believe me when I say he has other plans for you that are not dating *taco emoji* *eggplant emoji*

Her last text made me chuckle. She was nothing like the people I'd met during my time at boarding school. Rubin American Boarding School was full of arrogant, entitled pricks who believed they were superior to everyone else. Half of them hailed from European royal families, while the other half were either offspring of political figures or rock stars. Sarah was, in fact, the only normal person. Her father, Tim Afolami, was the CEO of a very successful water treatment company in the UK, and she intended to follow in his footsteps by pursuing a degree in chemical engineering and biotechnology at the University of Cambridge. Money, beauty, and brains—a killer combination.

After spending what might have been an overly long time in the shower, I moisturized my body with vanilla-scented body milk and blow-dried my hair until it had a naturally styled look. Everyone knew that when Caroline said "casual," she meant we were headed to an underground bar where all you could smell was whiskey, sweat, and tobacco, so I made sure I looked good without overdoing it. I wore my favorite pair of jeans and a red tank showcasing my curves and finished the look with black military boots and red lipstick.

I headed downstairs to the living room, where my parents were having dinner. About an hour ago, my mom knocked on my door and asked me if I wanted to join them, but whenever it was just the three of us, I felt super awkward. During the infrequent moments we shared together, my father often stressed my obligations as part of the Moore family and emphasized the importance of how I portrayed myself to the world. I politely declined the invitation, which clearly displeased her. Judging by the expression on my father's face, he wasn't thrilled either.

"Hey, Dad, Mom. I'm going out with Caroline. I might be back late. I just wanted to give you a heads-up," I informed them. The clattering of my dad's cutlery against his plate startled my mom. He pressed his lips tightly together, and his eyes gave the impression he was about to snap.

"Sweetheart, not now," my mother whispered softly as she tenderly laid her hand on my father's wrist. Throughout my life, she'd always shielded me from him. She would craft last-minute excuses to justify his absence when visiting me in Switzerland or his disinterest in my personal life. The only thing that really interested Edward Moore was how well I did in school, just so I could go to an Ivy League college and play my part in maintaining his public image, like a pawn on a chessboard. His grand plan was for me to eventually join him in managing the company, but he failed to understand that the last thing I wanted was to work for him at Cos Pharmaceuticals.

He looked at me, then extended his index finger, directing it toward me. "I'm away on business next week until Wednesday, but I expect you to meet me in my office on Thursday morning at 9 a.m. sharp. We need to discuss your internship before we leave for Cabo."

"Are you sure you don't want to join us?" my mom interjected. She still hoped that I would change my mind, but as appealing as Cabo sounded, I preferred to stay home.

"Mom, I'd rather stay here. We've already had this conversation. I want to make the most of my time here before heading to Stanford in a few months." I approached the table and kissed my mom on the cheek before heading to the front door.

Mrs. Bishop, our housekeeper, was already there waiting for me and holding the door open. "Good night, Miss Moore. Enjoy your evening."

Caroline waited outside, leaning on the passenger door with a smirk. She wore black shorts, a Metallica T-shirt, and comfy Converse shoes. With a nod toward the vintage black Cadillac parked in my front yard, she playfully beckoned me. "Jump in, cutie. The night is young."

*   *   *

Seated in the back of the car, I couldn't help but notice that Jake, Caroline's friend, kept gazing at me through the rearview mirror. She introduced us as soon as I hopped in the car, and he'd barely focused on the road since we left Moore Manor.

"See something you like?" I challenged. Jake was very attractive, had an infectious laugh, and it seemed he also had excellent taste in music. "The Reason" by Hoobastank blasted through the car's speakers while my eyes roamed Jake's tattooed arms and how his black T-shirt accentuated his well-defined biceps. His hair, dark and slightly longer at the front, almost grazed his eyes, which were the most striking shade of green I had ever seen. The way he would touch his short stubble made me wonder how it would feel between my legs.

Why am I always this horny?

"We'll be there in ten minutes," Caroline announced. It turned out we weren't hitting the city tonight but going to a private party at one of Jake's friend's houses. Caroline and I made small talk while Jake drove us to Greenwich, a town in southwestern Fairfield County, Connecticut. By the time we arrived, the party was in full swing, and dozens of cars surrounded what looked like a country house. Jake struggled for a few minutes to find a parking spot, so he ended up leaving the car in front of someone else's truck.

"Don't worry, it's my friend's car. If she wants to leave, she'll text me," Jake said when he noticed my hesitation.

The moment we entered the house, all eyes in the living room turned in our direction. At first, I thought they looked at me because I was an outsider, but then a horde of girls came running toward Jake to say hi. It was evident that he was popular with the opposite sex.

Using this diversion to my advantage, I ventured into the kitchen area in search of a beer.

During the entire evening, Caroline kept introducing me to people. I seamlessly joined their conversations, which mainly involved topics such as football, the latest movie releases, and some drama involving a girl named Mandy and her boyfriend, Marcus.

I made my way around the party, looking for Caroline. It wasn't the first time she had ditched me for dick, so I decided to find Jake to make sure he would give me a ride home. It took me a solid ten minutes to locate him casually leaning against a doorframe in the living room, beer in hand, engaged in conversation with another guy who soon wandered off, leaving him alone by the time I reached him.

"Hey, have you seen Caroline?"

He looked me up and down, his stare making all the butterflies in my stomach come alive. "No. I haven't seen her in a while. Maybe she's fucking someone in one of the rooms."

I rolled my eyes, making Jake chuckle.

"Caroline mentioned you studied in Europe. Is that true?" he asked.

"Yes. I went to a co-ed boarding school in Switzerland."

"Nice," he responded, taking a sip from the bottle. "How was it? Did you have to wear one of those tiny uniforms with a skirt and a tie?"

"It wasn't tiny, but you're right. I had a uniform: Knee-high socks, skirt, shirt, tie, blazer…"

"Hmm. I bet you looked good in one of those. You still have it?"

The thought of Jake brushing his fingers on my skin and pushing his hand below my skirt made me clench my thighs.

"You've watched too much porn, Jake," I retorted.

"You can't blame me for picturing you wearing one," he replied. "I bet you had all the guys wrapped around your finger."

"Not really."

Jake arched an eyebrow and brought his lips to my ear, whispering, "I find that hard to believe. If it had been me, I would have been on my knees asking you on a date…and maybe doing other things too."

Holy shit.

Jake's deep voice was alluring, and the only thing that came from my lips was some incoherent and awkward humming.

He pushed my hair to one side and added, "I want to show you something." Jake must have found my expression amusing as he laughed and leaned backward. "I didn't mean that. Caroline told me you play the piano, and my friend's dad works for a producer. He has a grand piano downstairs. He soundproofed the basement. I thought I could show you."

I was sure he had ulterior motives, but having a soundproof room in the house piqued my interest. He grabbed my hand and guided me toward the staircase leading to the basement while a few girls looked at me with a hint of jealousy. As we reached the bottom, Jake swung open the door and invited me inside. I let out a surprised gasp.

"Wow, Jake, this is beautiful!" I walked toward the grand piano in the corner of the room. On the opposite side was a tiny home studio for voice recording and several monitors.

"My friend's dad likes to compose. He had this installed so he could work from home, too."

I caressed the Steinway & Sons black grand piano and lifted the fall board as I sat on the bench. Some sheet music was piled on top of it, but I decided to play something lighter than Mozart or Debussy. I placed my fingers on the keys, my feet on the pedals, and started to play "All of Me" by John Legend.

"You're good!" Jake exclaimed. He stood next to me while I got lost in the music. It was one of my favorite songs. The lyrics and how the melody went straight to my soul always spoke to me.

Once I finished the song, I looked at Jake, who was smiling. It was the first genuine smile he gave me instead of a smirk since we met. I liked it.

"Do you want me to teach you? Maybe you can use my lesson to seduce some of the hyperventilating women up there?" I said, pointing my head upstairs.

"Sure. But I'm not interested in any of them."

"Are you sure?" I smirked.

"I'm here with you, am I not?" Jake took my hand and pulled me to my feet.

"Are we leaving?" I asked, confused.

"No, but you need to sit on my lap so I can get a good view of your hands."

"Are you sure a view of my hands is what you want?" I teased.

Jake didn't respond to my flirtatious comment but moved me to the side so he could sit on the bench and pull me onto his lap.

"Place your hands on top of mine and follow my lead," I instructed. I would teach him just a few notes, but how his body was pressed to my back kept distracting me.

After a few minutes of trying my best to show him how to play

"Under the Bridge" by Red Hot Chili Peppers with just four chords, he moved his hands away and placed them on my upper arms. I wasn't sure if he'd just grown tired of my lesson until he gently trailed his fingers up my arms toward my shoulders and pushed my hair to one side. He ran his tongue along the side of my neck, and a sweet shiver traveled down my spine as I noticed the bulge pressing against my ass. He grabbed a fistful of my hair, turned my face, and ran his tongue against my lower lip, gently tugging it with his teeth. My pussy throbbed, and something in me snapped. I bent my arm around his neck until our kiss became more demanding, more savage. I pulled back, but I wasn't nearly done with him. I wanted more.

I knew sex and alcohol were my coping mechanisms when I didn't want to face my feelings, and since I came back to Port Chester, I felt way too much. I just wanted to drown in another feeling that didn't hurt that much.

I turned around until I straddled him. He cupped my face with both hands and crushed his lips to mine. I opened my mouth, our tongues touching, and it felt like my whole body was set on fire. Jake was an excellent kisser, and I wondered what other things he'd mastered with his tongue.

There's only one way to find out.

I grabbed the bottom of my top and pulled it over my head, dropping the fabric onto the floor.

"Fuck, you're gorgeous." Jake continued kissing my neck, biting my skin in a delicious and torturous way. His mouth traveled down my neck toward my collarbone. Bringing one hand to my back, he skillfully unclasped my black lace bra and pushed it down my arms until I was completely naked from the waist up. He gazed at me, taking in every inch of my bare skin while his eyes darkened. "The things I'm gonna do to you." He rested his hand against my chest and gently pushed me so my back curved against the keyboard. When he was happy with my new position, he bent over and tugged on one of my hard nipples with his teeth while his fingers played with the other one. My eyes shut, and a moan escaped my lips when he flicked his tongue and sucked it into his mouth. My hips moved of their own accord, seeking all the friction I could get from his hard-on.

"Are you wet for me, Sienna?"

I regretted wearing jeans, and all I wished at that moment was that he would rip them off and fucked me good on the piano. With a swift movement, he grabbed my hips and stood, placing me on the floor in front of him. Jake continued to kiss me as he unbuttoned my jeans and pulled them down to my feet together with my underwear.

I was completely exposed while he still had all his clothes on. "Take off your clothes," I demanded. He followed my commands, and the moment he took his pants off, my mouth dropped.

"See anything you like?" He had a smug expression, throwing my earlier words back at me.

"It's what you can do with it that matters."

Jake grabbed my hair with his right hand, jerking up my head to face him, and brought his lips closer to my mouth before saying, "Be careful what you wish for. I'm not sure you can take it."

I circled my hand around his hard length, making his thick cock twitch with my sudden grip. I stroked him twice, with just enough pressure.

"Do your worst."

Jake walked me to the small couch against the wall just outside the tiny studio.

"Sit down, Sienna."

I looked at the leather sofa and then at Jake.

"I don't want to ruin it."

"I don't like repeating myself, sweetheart. Sit down before I make you."

Did I like being treated like a child? No. Did I enjoy the way Jake commanded me to sit and basically shut the fuck up? Hell yes.

Jake knelt in front of me. Spreading my legs wider, he took a good look at my pussy before he dove in and licked my slit. "Hmm, you taste good," he exclaimed. "Now let me see you come on my face." Each one of his strokes was slow and precise, switching between licking, sucking, and flicking my bundle of nerves with the tip of his tongue, but when I lifted my hips, seeking more pressure, he changed the tempo. Sweat covered my body, and I could feel my wetness coating the couch. Jake's hands dug into the side of my thighs as he continued devouring me like I was his last meal. I was close, so close, that when the pressure built in my lower stomach, I knew I was getting to the point of no return.

"Jake, I'm coming." A scream ripped from my throat as I writhed and clamped his head with my legs. Jake didn't stop.

"That's it. Come for me. Let me hear your pretty screams."

When I reached my climax, he continued licking my pussy, my walls clenching as my orgasm rolled through me again and again until I couldn't take it anymore and pushed on his forehead. Jake allowed me only a moment to catch my breath while he grabbed a condom from his wallet and rolled it down his shaft. He lifted me and bent me over the arm of the couch. "Spread your legs wider." He placed his cock at my entrance and pushed only the tip a few inches. "Fuck. I'm gonna come just by seeing you like this."

Jake took my hips with both hands and buried his dick inside me. He started to fuck me with slow movements, which drove me crazy. I knew he did it just to make me beg, and he succeeded.

"Please, Jake. Harder. Faster."

He chuckled.

"Hold on tight to the couch." After his warning, Jake slammed into me with deep and hard thrusts.

"Oh my God," I screamed.

While he continued to fuck me mercilessly, he placed one hand on my lower back and tugged my hair with the other one until my head tilted backward. I panted, and my body kept sliding forward with the force he used to slam into me over and over again. Jake bent over and moved his free hand around my waist until he rubbed my clit with circling strokes.

"Yes," I groaned. "Jake, I'm close." My body was on fire, hot lava running through my veins, and beads of sweat covered my chest, too.

"Come for me again, sweetheart."

My second orgasm hit me as I came apart on the leather couch. Seconds later, Jake followed me over the edge, his moans filling the room.

I'd never been so grateful for being in a soundproofed basement. Over a hundred people were probably at this party, and the walk of shame would have been dreadful.

We stayed in the same position momentarily, trying to catch our breath.

"You're something else, Sienna. Fucking hell."

"Fucking hell, indeed."

TURNING POINT

(Sienna)

"You're late." My father, who had been waiting for me since 9 a.m., had his jaw clenched and nostrils flared. His gaze was so intense it could melt ice, and the way he clutched the arms of his chair suggested he was on the verge of losing his patience.

Last night, I went out again with Jake and Caroline and arrived home around 5 a.m. I had barely slept for a few hours when I woke to the sun blazing through my window. I had completely forgotten to close the curtains and set the alarm.

Jake stayed over, just like he'd been doing every night since we met last week, but when I opened my eyes this morning, my bed was empty.

Did he leave just after I fell asleep?

I liked Jake, but we both knew we were just friends with benefits. It worked for me and, apparently, for him too—a perfect match. I'd be leaving for Stanford soon, so getting attached to him wasn't an option. Truth be told, I was having a good time, so I'd decided to keep hanging out with him until I left, as long as he was okay with that. The last thing I wanted was for him to start catching feelings, so I needed to limit our interactions and follow my go-to rules. No dates. No flowers. Nothing. Parties, enjoying the outdoor pool, and good sex. That was all I wanted for my summer. I wasn't asking for too much. Was I?

"I'm sorry. I went out last night and didn't hear the alarm on my phone. Sorry," I lied.

"Your mom told me you've been going out every night since you returned. Is that all you're going to do this summer?" I could hear the reproach in his voice.

"Well, that and the internship," I replied.

"I trust you're taking this internship with the seriousness it deserves. Many people would kill for this opportunity. I won't tolerate you showing up late at the lab or smelling like a cellar. Do you understand me?" His voice was calm, but it carried a heavy warning I couldn't ignore.

"Of course. I wouldn't want to ruin your reputation, *Father*." I emphasized the word "father" more than necessary, but at this point, I didn't care for his approval. He lost his right to care the moment he forbade me from hanging out with my best friend and shipped me off to Europe without a single warning.

He sighed.

"Sit down," he said, pointing at the chair he'd placed next to his. "Let me walk you through the program I designed for you."

Over the next two hours, he explained the four-week plan he'd prepared for my time in the lab. He'd organized a rotation of tasks across various departments at Cos Pharmaceuticals, intending to provide me with some level of experience before starting college. I wondered if he'd noticed how little I was interested in working for him. Since I arrived, he never bothered to ask me about my final exams or my trip with Sarah. When I mentioned going to Ibiza with her for three weeks, he stayed quiet and said nothing about it. I knew he liked Sarah and thought she was a good influence even though she was the troublemaker between us.

"I want you to go through everything, and I want you on Tuesday at nine o'clock, not nine thirty or ten, in my office to go through any questions you might have. Your mom and I are leaving for Cabo next Friday morning, so you'll be on your own until we return. Peter will be available via email if you have further questions while we're away."

"Sure thing. Would you prefer that I email my questions before our meeting? I've heard it's a standard business practice."

"Don't be a smart-mouth, Sienna. My patience is limited." I was well aware that I pushed boundaries by speaking to my father in such a way, but I couldn't help it. Sarah often claimed that I enjoyed challenging him to gain his attention. Even if that were the case, it had never worked.

"I'll see you on Tuesday then."

I walked toward the door and pushed it open.

"And Sienna." I turned around. "It's the last time I see someone sneaking out of your room in the middle of the night. This isn't that kind of house. Understood?"

I slammed the door on my way out.

* * *

It was Friday morning.

My parents would be leaving in half an hour, and I had grand plans for the weekend. With them gone, I would have the house to myself. I'd already arranged for Caroline to invite a group of friends over on Saturday, including Jake, obviously. I was determined to host an unforgettable party that would be the talk of Port Chester. All I had left to do was purchase the alcohol, pick up some snacks, and curate the perfect Spotify playlist.

Footsteps approached the living room, where I sat enjoying breakfast. Mrs. Bishop had thoughtfully made a plate of scrambled eggs and bacon and two slices of sourdough toast topped with avocado. She knew of my love for coffee and had gone the extra mile to procure some capsules for my favorite drink, pumpkin spice latte. Her thoughtfulness had always been remarkable. In this household, she appeared to be the only individual who genuinely cared about my preferences and had the keen attention to detail required to recognize when I craved Starbucks. It wasn't like that before. I had a fantastic childhood, but everything changed six years ago.

"We're leaving, darling. Our flight to Cabo is in about an hour. Are you sure you don't want to come with us?" My mom had pushed me daily to change my mind about going on vacation with them to no avail.

"No. I'm good. Caroline might come over tomorrow with some friends." Mrs. Bishop would probably tell my parents anyway, so it was better to give them a heads-up.

"Is the boy I saw this morning leaving the house through the back door coming too? I thought I was clear last week about having boys over?"

My cheeks turned pink, and I opened and closed my mouth, unable to respond to him. I told Jake to be careful, but apparently, my father didn't sleep or instructed the staff to keep an eye on me constantly. As expected, my father carried on lecturing me.

"You've shown a lack of respect toward your mother and me since you arrived. You choose to have your meals alone and avoid spending time with us. You stay in your room throughout the day until the evening, then disappear to who knows where. On top of that, your lack of decorum concerns me, as you keep bringing that tattooed boy into our home. The neighbors are already whispering things. Do you want to become the talk of the town? Things can't continue down this path. You have responsibilities to fulfill."

I sat there, paralyzed. The words had cut through the air like a sharp blade and hung heavy between us. It contrasted with the man I had known growing up, a father who had always been gentle and kind. My mind raced back to my childhood when my father and I were inseparable. We would go on long hikes, and he would even tell me bedtime stories he had made up on the spot. Those were the days when I felt truly loved and cherished by him. Not anymore. Everything changed when they sent me to Europe. It was a decision that took me by surprise, and I never understood why he did it, and he never offered a decent explanation. He became distant and emotionally detached, and it felt like he was pushing me away. The pain of abandonment had been overwhelming, and I often cried myself to sleep, wondering what I had done to deserve such treatment. Then Sarah and I became best friends. She was my rock.

As my father's words hung in the air, I felt my anger building. I met his gaze and furiously replied, "I don't give a flying fuck what the neighbors think. That tattooed boy has a name, Jake, and don't you dare judge him just because of his tattoos."

"Watch your mouth, Sienna," he reprimanded. "We're going to sit down and talk when we return from our vacation. We've already spent way too much time on this nonsense, and now we're running late.

"Meanwhile, I'm going to freeze all your cards. It would be best if you understood that as long as you live under my roof, you will do what I say. Clear?"

I stood, causing the chair to screech loudly against the wooden floor. I moved so quickly that the chair toppled backward, colliding with the windowsill.

"You can't just freeze my cards!"

"Oh, trust me, I'm more than capable, and I'm going to," he snapped, shifting his posture toward my mother and gripping her by the elbow. As usual, my mom remained silent. No matter the situation, it always frustrated me how she consistently sided with him. I could never be sure if it was because she genuinely shared his views or if she simply avoided disagreeing with or opposing him. She never dared to contradict him, and this occasion was no exception.

"I hate you. I'm counting down the days until I can leave for California and put miles between us, away from this place and away from you. I'm fed up with all of this. You haven't cared about me or how I felt for the past six years. You shipped me across the Atlantic without giving me an explanation, for fuck's sake. And now, out of the blue, you want to be the doting parent, setting boundaries and expressing concern about my reputation?" I began to laugh, not because it was funny, but because the situation was ridiculous, and I was pissed. He never cared about me. Why now? Was it to prove a point? That he had control over me?

"I know I've given you plenty of reasons to be mad at me, but I can't just stand by and watch you sabotage yourself." He sighed. "You think I don't love you, but I have my reasons for sending you to Switzerland. I just hoped you'd eventually forgive me for sending you to Europe after all this time. Holding that resentment will only poison your soul, Sienna. I hope one day you'll find it in your heart to forgive me." Evidently, my words had deeply affected him, and a small part of me wished to take them back. But I was stubborn. I would never be the first to yield in an argument. "We must go. We'll talk when we get back."

As the front door shut behind them, I remained in the living room, still shaken by my father's words.

I wish I'd said something, anything at all.

I should've told them I loved them even though I was still upset about them sending me away. They were my parents. Deep down,

I knew everything they did was because they cared about me. I just wished they'd shown their affection by spending time with me, not by flashing their cash.

Life doesn't come with a warning. You never know when it's going to be the last time you'll see someone you love.

And that was precisely what happened.

That was the last day I saw my parents alive.

A BETTER PLACE

(Sienna)

Fuck my life.

Father Wakefield was saying something to me. I was pretty sure it was one of those transcendental phrases—you know, something like "they are in a better place" or my personal favorite, "one day you'll meet them again." People usually don't know what to say at funerals, but honestly, I couldn't care less about his words. Nothing he said would make the grief go away. I couldn't even focus on his words. I was just lost.

I felt everything and nothing at the same time. It was like my body had shut down, unable to process everything that had happened since last Friday.

Jerry, my father's personal assistant, showed up uninvited at eleven in the evening at Moore Manor. His face was pale, and his eyes were full of pain when Mrs. Bishop announced his arrival and welcomed him into the living room.

"I know it's late, Sienna, but I must speak with you. May I sit?"

My curiosity transformed into concern at the exhausted look on his face. I pressed pause on the remote, put the popcorn down on the coffee table, and extended my hand, inviting Jerry to sit on the opposite couch from where I was sitting.

"Please, have a seat," I said.

Despite how late it was, he still wore his suit, and looking at the dark circles under his eyes, I could tell he'd had a rough day. Jerry Payne would only come to the house when there was a pressing matter or my father would summon him, but my parents left today to spend a week in Cabo, so I had no idea why he came to the house. He'd been working for my dad since I was a child. Jerry sometimes came with us during vacation, and I liked to think of him as a detached uncle. He wouldn't smile often, but his current facial expression had me on edge.

"Before I say anything, I need you to know that I'm here for you, that you can count on me like your father always did." He was tense. I could see how shaken he was, and at that moment, when he said those words, I knew something terrible had happened.

"Did? What is it, Jerry? Has something happened? Are my parents okay?" Something stuck in my throat, like I was trying to swallow words that hadn't been said yet.

"Sienna, there was an accident. Your parents' private jet…" He paused. "They're gone. I'm so sorry, kid."

I knew Jerry said something else, but the ringing in my ears blocked everything out, and I felt sick, just like now. Still, before I could make a scene in the middle of St. Mary's Church and throw up like I did on my mother's favorite Persian rug, I excused myself from Father Wakefield with a forced smile and ran to the closest restroom. After I emptied my stomach—not that it was full whatsoever, as I hadn't been able to keep anything down the past few days—I sat on the floor for what felt like an eternity until I heard a knock on the door.

"Miss Moore, it's Mrs. Bishop. I saw you come in here a while ago. Are you feeling alright, darling? Can I do anything for you? Would you like me to fetch some water?"

I rose to my feet, attempting to force down the overwhelming lump that had formed in my throat. Still, as I braced myself for the flood of tears, they remained stubbornly absent, which only added to the weight of despair I carried, making me feel even more broken and empty inside.

I had to face the music again. The church was full of people, and everyone expected to see me, shake my hand, and give me their condolences.

"I'm coming out, Mrs. Bishop. Just give me two minutes."

"Okay, darling," she responded.

I walked to the closest sink, washed my mouth and hands, and checked myself in the mirror. My eyes didn't look like mine anymore. When I was a kid, my father always told me I had the prettiest eyes; "Like honey," he would say. "That's why you're so sweet." Now, they looked empty, clouded, and a bit swollen. Honestly, I looked like shit. I hadn't been able to sleep for the past six days, mainly surviving on lattes with extra espresso shots. Someone could think by the look on my face that I'd cried myself to sleep every night since the accident, but the truth was that I hadn't been able to shed a single tear.

Not once.

I googled it because I was getting worried that I wasn't grieving as one would expect after the sudden death of both parents. Apparently, it happened frequently, and it was said online that it could be linked with a type of grief called "inhibited grief" due to suppressed emotions. I guessed everyone dealt with loss in their own way. I wondered when the gates would open, and this overwhelming feeling came crashing down, hitting me.

During the service, Mrs. Bishop held my hand the whole time. I felt utterly isolated, surrounded either by strangers or by staff employed by my parents. Sarah kept checking on me every day, but yesterday evening, she called me to say her flight got canceled, and she wouldn't make it on time. Despite trying to find an alternative one, everything was fully booked, so I suggested she stay in London.

I took a deep breath.

Here we go, Sienna. You can do this.

SEX AND THE CITY

(Sienna)

It'd been three weeks.

I still hadn't cried.

The only things that seemed to help with the numbness were my friends *gin* and *tonic*. I'd been drinking myself to sleep because it was the only way I managed to get some rest. Otherwise, the nights were full of nightmares.

But today, the house felt too heavy. I couldn't bear to exist between these walls.

Tomorrow, I would meet with the family's lawyer—my lawyer, I guessed—and with the executor of my parents' will. The whole thing made me nauseous.

I needed to leave this house and have a drink, maybe several.

I hopped into the shower quickly, threw on the first summer dress I found in my closet, and slipped into my beloved Hermès Oran sandals. After that, I booked an Uber that dropped me off at some bar on Murray Street. I didn't usually hang out on this side of town, but the online reviews were good enough that I figured it would be worth a try. Nobody really knew me in this area, and I sure didn't want anyone pitying me right now.

As I entered the bar, I realized I had chosen a great place to drown my thoughts. The bar was beautiful: dark walls and wooden floors, teal velvet curtains, dimmed yellow lights, dark leather stools, and, most importantly, barely crowded. "Into Each Life Some Rain Must Fall" by Ella Fitzgerald and The Ink Spots played in the background.

How appropriate.

I took it as a sign and walked toward the barman. He kindly asked for my ID, so I showed him the fake one Caroline gifted me last Christmas.

I was on my third drink when someone sat next to me. I looked at him from the corner of my eye and noticed that he was staring at me. When I turned my head to face my new drinking buddy, I thought he was probably one of the most beautiful men I'd ever seen. He had short dark hair, a bit curly at the ends and the front partially covering his eyebrows, black eyes, and a sharp jawline. He wore a black shirt and trousers, and his jacket rested on another stool.

"I've observed you for the past twenty minutes, and it looks like your day was shittier than mine."

My body stiffened in response to his voice. It was deep, alluring, and full of warmth.

"I don't know how shitty your day was, but I can assure you that mine probably takes the cake," I replied.

"My mother just got engaged," he blurted out without blinking.

"I can't see why that's a terrible thing."

"My dad died in a car accident three years ago." He paused. "She met this guy and got engaged in less than ten months. I know she deserves to be happy, but it feels too soon." He sighed. "It looks like she couldn't wait to move on." He gulped his drink and continued. "I left the engagement party because I couldn't stand the happiness floating around the room. It seems like everybody wants to forget. I can't. I just couldn't breathe." He exhaled and asked, "What about you?"

I didn't know what to tell him. I didn't know the guy. The only thing I knew about him was what he'd just told me and that he really needed a drink. He'd just finished a glass of what looked like whiskey in one gulp and was currently ordering a second one. I didn't understand why he was opening up like this, but I figured sometimes it was easier to spill your guts to a stranger than a friend. Based on his words, he'd been in this bar for at least twenty minutes, so who knew how many drinks he'd had so far?

Enveloped in the depths of his gaze for a moment, I hesitated. Shall I tell him the truth? Would it scare him away?

Fuck it. I'm probably never seeing him again.

"My parents died almost four weeks ago in an accident. I haven't been able to cry since then, which is starting to scare the shit out of me. Also, I'm meeting with the executor of the will tomorrow. It's like there's this big empty hole inside me, and some days I feel like I'm about to have a mental breakdown." There. I said it.

The silence stretched between us for a few seconds before he responded. "Fuck me…well, that definitely takes the cake for sure. I'm sorry about your parents."

"I'm sorry about your father, too."

"Do you live here in the city?" he asked.

"No. I live in Port Chester. It's about fifty minutes from here."

"Yes, I've been there before. My soon-to-be stepfather owns a house in Rye, and my mother and I are moving there next weekend. I spent a lot of time there before my dad passed away, so I'm quite familiar with the area."

"Oh really? Maybe we've met before."

"Believe me, if I'd met you before, I'd remember." He couldn't take his eyes off me, but then his attention shifted to my mouth, and his eyes darkened. I could feel my heart racing. I didn't know if it was the drinks or how he looked at me, but he noticed, and the corner of his mouth turned up, giving me a smirk that made my hands sweaty and my heart beat faster. He was definitely my type. If we had met under different circumstances, I would have made a move on him. In fact, I still had to restrain myself from flirting with him when I only wanted to know how good his hands would feel on my skin. Old habits died hard.

My mouth suddenly felt dry, like I had licked sandpaper. I took a sip of my drink, meeting his gaze. Something about him made me nervous, but at the same time, I felt comfortable around him.

He could totally be a serial killer, Sienna.

We spent the following hour talking about the music we liked, our favorite spots in the city, and sharing our favorite restaurants in Manhattan, but then his face dropped, and the air between us shifted.

"Penny for your thoughts," I said.

"It's nothing," he answered cryptically, clenching his jaw.

I checked my phone and noticed it was 10:36 p.m.

"Shit. I should get going. The meeting with my lawyer is quite early, and I need to get some sleep. It's gonna be a challenging day."

He didn't say anything; he just kept looking at me. I took his silence as my cue to leave and said, "It was nice meeting you. Good luck with everything." I turned around toward the women's restroom. There was no way I could manage an hour's ride to Port Chester when I desperately needed to pee.

Once I finished, I exited the toilet stall, and my heart missed a beat. He stood before me, leaning against the sink with his hands resting on the black marble on both sides of his body and his right ankle crossed over his left foot. He was taller than I expected, and his black shirt showed every outline of his arms and muscles. I couldn't move. My legs had decided they didn't respond to my commands anymore, and heat rushed up my body and burned my cheeks. I was almost a hundred percent sure I was blushing.

In one smooth movement, he pushed himself off the sink and walked toward where I stood. It was clear to me at that moment that he was a predator, and I was nothing more than prey. A different girl might have felt intimidated or maybe even scared, but the way he towered over me just thrilled my inner whore with anticipation.

Closing the space between us, he dropped his head and whispered, "I have realized I don't know your name." His voice was husky and dark.

I panted, trying to catch my breath.

What the hell is happening?

"Sienna." I sighed.

"Sienna," he repeated as his mouth traveled down the left side of my neck, his lips barely touching my skin. He was so close that I could smell his breath filled with spice and caramel notes. His left hand slowly caressed my right arm as it made its way upward, my nipples peaking through my dress in response to his touch.

"What do you want?" I trembled.

"What I want…is something I've fantasized about since you entered this bar, Sienna. I want to fuck you until you come all over my cock."

I released a trembling exhale.

He cupped my face, and our eyes locked, but when his focus shifted to my lips, I dropped my purse and crashed my mouth into his. Hard. He opened his mouth, and his tongue collided with mine. Nothing about this kiss was sweet and tender; it was full of lust and an insatiable hunger. He moved us toward the far end of the restroom until my back hit the wall. He never stopped kissing me as my hands began exploring his chest, holding his face, and kissing him harder. His mouth traveled to my neck, nibbling and teasing the sensitive spot beneath my earlobe. Just as I was about to reach for his belt, his left hand seized my wrists and held them firmly above my head.

"So eager."

His right hand started drifting down from my neck, over my breast, to the hem of my dress, to the inside of my thighs, and as I shifted my legs farther apart, he gave me a teasing smile. He knew I wanted this as much as he said he wanted it. I could feel his hand playing with my underwear, but when his fingers slid down inside my panties and started circling my clit with gentle strokes, a soft moan escaped my lips.

"You're already so wet, Sienna."

I loved how he said my name in a desperate whisper.

I continued kissing him, tasting him, when he suddenly sank one finger and then a second one inside my pussy. It clenched.

"Oh my God," I hissed as his fingers started moving in and out of me.

My body shuddered while his hand fucked me, and my hips moved to the pace he set. My climax built, but he took his fingers out as soon as he noticed. *Seriously?*

"Not yet, Sienna. I want you to come with me buried inside you," he said to me playfully. He brought his fingers to his mouth and licked my wetness, muttering, "You taste so fucking sweet."

I was panting, and a trickle of sweat glided down the back of my neck.

After releasing my hands, he bent down to remove my underwear and placed my panties inside his back pocket. He unbuckled his belt and tugged his zipper down. My mouth dropped when his cock sprang free. I'd had my fair share of lovers but had never been fucked by someone this big and never in a public place where anyone could walk in. It was exhilarating.

He placed his left hand on the wall next to my face and wrapped his hardness with his right fist. "I have a condom in my wallet," he told me, pointing with his head to his front pocket, and without one drop of hesitation, I took it.

I held his face with both hands and kept on kissing him, our tongues dancing desperately, while he put it on. I wanted him inside me, bringing me to oblivion. I wanted more. I wanted to feel everything.

With one swift movement, he grabbed the back of my knees and lifted me against the wall.

"What if someone comes in?" I asked with concern, not because I didn't want someone seeing me like this—at this point, I didn't fucking care about being caught— but because I didn't want anyone cock-blocking me.

"It's locked from the inside. I gave a generous tip to the bartender in exchange for the master key." He winked at me, and I snorted a laugh.

He lined up his tip at my entrance, and a shiver ran through my spine, his eyes on me glittering like the apparent predator he was. He pushed in only an inch and hesitated, but I moved my hips, demanding more.

"I don't want to hurt you," he confessed.

"I don't care. You said you wanted to fuck me. I want you to. Hard. Don't hold back."

He still didn't move.

"Please," I begged.

Then he did what I asked. With one swift movement, his hips flexed, and he was all the way in. A groan escaped my throat. It was a mixture of pain and pleasure, and as soon as he retreated, he slammed his body against mine again. And again. And again. And again. I wrapped my legs around his waist, locking my ankles together and digging my nails into his shoulders to get a better balance.

He leaned down to kiss me, drinking every moan directly from my mouth, both hands now gripping my ass. I cried out, moving my hips to meet his thrusts while I lost all track of time.

The sounds that filled the restroom were obscene.

"Do you feel it? Do you feel how your pussy enjoys being destroyed by my cock?"

As soon as he said those words, he hit that sweet spot inside me that made me arch my back and sent me to my climax, screaming loud enough that everyone in the bar must now be aware that two people were fucking in this restroom.

He continued to fuck me with an intensity that I thought we would collapse on the floor.

"Fuck, I'm gonna come too." A few moments later, he let out a groan and slowed his movements. He stayed buried inside me for a little longer, our foreheads against each other as we tried to catch our breath.

"I have to say, I never expected my day to end like this," I said with a smile plastered on my face. It was probably the first smile in a long time.

"Me neither," he replied with a wicked smile.

He gently helped me place my feet back on the floor and threw the condom in the trash can to my right before tucking his dick inside his pants. I leaned down to grab my purse when I heard him unlock the door with the master key. I suddenly felt a bit embarrassed. It seemed he couldn't get away from me quickly enough.

"Hey! You didn't tell me your name," I shouted.

He stopped and turned his head, looking over his left shoulder.

"My name is Zayn." And just like that, he was gone.

Zayn.

It was hard to believe that I'd just fucked a stranger in a public restroom. But then, as I replayed the whole thing in my mind, my stomach sank.

Zayn just left with my panties in his back pocket.

I broke into a hysterical laugh and felt less numb for the first time in weeks.

THE WILL

(Sienna)

My phone started ringing. I lifted my head from the pillow and checked the screen.

"It's too early…" I complained while pressing the answer button. "Hey, Sarah." I yawned.

"Morning, gorgeous," Sarah said with way too much energy. It was 5:40 a.m. She kept forgetting the five-hour time difference between New York and London, and I kept forgetting to silence my phone when I went to bed.

"I have something to tell you, but promise me you won't try to talk me out of it," she warned me.

"It's five in the morning, Sarah! Can this wait? I have a meeting with my lawyer at eight thirty, and I'm exhausted. I got home late last night and need more sleep; the gin hasn't left my system yet."

"Uh, you went out last night? Spill the tea, girl."

Sarah had been my ray of sunshine since we met when we were twelve, and I missed her terribly. The distance would be our worst enemy. I couldn't picture my days without her laughter or her positive energy. Especially now.

"I promise I'll call you later and tell you about it, okay? Wait till you hear it, girl. You're gonna FLIP." I chuckled.

"Well, why don't you tell me about it tomorrow when I land in New York?"

"WHAT!?" I screamed.

"I feel terrible that I couldn't come to your parents' funeral, and I want to support you as much as I can as your best friend, soooo…I've booked a flight. I land tomorrow morning at JFK and will stay for a couple of weeks so I can help you move to California. Would you like that?"

My chest tightened.

"I'd love that," I said, tears welling in my eyes.

"Alright. Let me send you my flight details. No need to come pick me up; I'll grab a cab. Considering everything you're handling now, you must be knackered."

She was so British.

"Okay, babe. Text me when you land."

"Good luck today, Sienna. It's going to be a tough morning, but you got this. Love you."

"Love you too. Bye."

*   *   *

Mr. Lehman, my lawyer, stood outside the building holding two cups of coffee. He wore an expensive suit and a golden Rolex, but that didn't surprise me as he was one of the founders and the principal partner at the Lehman & Sakkas Law Firm. It was one of the best firms in the country, and he'd been on my father's payroll for almost seven years. Although we'd only met twice, I immediately recognized him as I crossed the street.

"Good morning, Miss Moore. I took the liberty of ordering you a latte," he said, handing me a Starbucks venti cup.

I took a sip, and its rich flavor exploded in my taste buds.

"Thank you, Mr. Lehman. I'm a Starbucks junkie, glad you remembered. I'm incapable of saying no to a pumpkin spice latte. It's my favorite," I responded.

"I just wanted to go over what will happen today quickly. As I said over the phone, Mr. Lawrence was your father's right hand at Cos Pharmaceuticals, as you very well know, and the executor of the will. Your father appointed him. He'll read your parents' will today and inform you, as their sole heiress and relative, of its content and how everything they owned will be distributed based on their wishes. However, if you don't agree with something stated, we can discuss the next steps in my office tomorrow."

My father was a prestigious businessman, so I already knew he took the time to write that will with my mother. Edward Moore wasn't the kind of man who would trust someone else to do the dirty work. He would carefully read every contract, even the small print, and wouldn't sign anything without knowing what each page said.

"It's okay. I'll respect my parents' wishes. I'm sure they've left me enough not to worry about my future."

We took the elevator to the forty-third floor. When the doors opened, a woman in her mid-thirties was already waiting for us. "Welcome, Miss Moore, Mr. Lehman. I'm Laura, the office manager. Please follow me. Mr. Lawrence is already waiting for you in our conference room." She was pretty. Laura wore a dark gray pencil skirt, a cream blouse with a bow on her neck and padded shoulders, and a beautiful pair of Manolo Blahnik's Campari Mary Jane pumps in black. I made a mental note to myself. I needed those shoes.

It'd been three years since I last visited this office. I used to spend a lot of time here when I was in school, but since I moved to Switzerland, I'd barely come. It looked like my father renovated it. It had a light gray industrial floor, wooden panels, an open-office style, and eight glass conference rooms on the right side. An open kitchen at the end had fruit bowls, cookies, croissants, and *pain au chocolat*.

"My father never told me the office was renovated." I wasn't surprised he hadn't mentioned it to me. After all, why would he? We stopped discussing what was going on in our lives quite a while ago.

"The work was completed about a year ago. Your father said it needed a facelift, that young minds now prefer to work in open spaces with billiard tables and free coffee," she said, turning her face to meet my eyes. "He was a great man and an amazing boss. I'm truly sorry for your loss."

I said nothing but kept walking beside her, Mr. Lehman slightly behind us. Laura opened the glass door to the last conference room. Peter Lawrence, Cos Pharmaceuticals' Chief Operating Officer and one of my father's closest friends, stood from where he sat and came to meet us.

"Thank you for coming, Miss Moore. Mr. Lehman." He shook my hand, and Mr. Lehman extended his arm to greet my father's colleague as well.

"Please, call me Sienna. There's no need for formalities. You've known me forever," I told him.

I sat at the table next to my lawyer and opposite Peter. After placing a bottle and a glass of water in front of each of us, Laura walked out of the room.

"Before we start, I want to offer you my condolences again. I respected your father a lot as the CEO of this company and as a board member, but on a more personal level, he and your mother were just great people and close friends."

I figured he was at the funeral but didn't recall talking to him. I was pretty sure I did, but I was mostly zoned out that day.

"Let's begin," he said, opening the envelope in front of him. "Your father appointed me as the executor of their will. As such, I'm responsible for administering your parents' estate and carrying out their wishes as established in this document. All their assets, such as financial holdings, real estate, direct investments, or collectibles like art, will be distributed to the intended beneficiaries. Do you have any questions before I proceed to read their last wishes?" he asked.

"No, I'm good. Please continue."

Peter read the will, and it was nothing I didn't expect. I was the sole beneficiary of most of the stuff he listed. I didn't have any relatives. Both of my parents were only children with no siblings, and my grandparents died a long time ago. Some of the charities my parents worked for would receive a substantial amount of money, and I would fulfill their role and serve on the board in a couple of them.

"Last item. Cos Pharmaceuticals." Peter hesitated. He looked at me as if trying to say, *brace yourself.* "Miss Sienna Marie Moore will inherit Cos Pharmaceuticals Inc., the business, and its assets. Mr. Edward Louis Moore's shares will be transferred to Miss Sienna Marie Moore; these account for 51% of the company's stock. Mr. Peter James Lawrence, Chief Operating Officer at Cos Pharmaceutical, will continue to oversee the ongoing business operations within the company until the Board of Directors appoints a new Chief Executive Officer."

A knot built in my stomach, my pulse began to race, and my hands started shaking.

"What does it mean? Don't get me wrong, I know what it means, but...what is expected from me?" I asked.

"It means you own the company, Sienna," Peter responded.

"You will control the board, and you will have the last word for every single decision. Until a new CEO is appointed, I'll continue to oversee the business. You don't have to worry about the company's day-to-day operations, but I can train you in the role and bring you to key meetings so you can learn about the company, the business, and how to become a great leader like your father. You're now the major shareholder and president. I understand this is a significant responsibility for someone your age, but you have our full support to ensure this new role doesn't affect your studies."

The major shareholder? President? I was eighteen, for fuck's sake. I still struggled to choose the toppings I wanted on my pizza.

"You obviously need time to digest the amount of information I've unloaded on your shoulders, but it would be great if we could sit down and draw up a plan before you leave for college. Your father would want you to focus on your studies, so I will help as much as possible to keep this from becoming an additional burden."

It was a lot to take in, and there was so much to unpack.

"That's all, Sienna. I've prepared a copy of the will," he added, handing Mr. Lehman a manila envelope. "My assistant will call you to arrange a meeting next week once you've had the opportunity to go through everything in more detail."

We all stood, and Peter walked us to the elevators. I noticed that everyone in the office was looking at me as I strolled past their desks on the main floor. Were they looking at me because they felt sorry for me or because they knew I was their new boss?

The whole thing was ridiculous.

Peter noticed and said, "They don't know anything yet. Our PR department is currently in conversation with our investors and the board to see how we should announce it internally and to the press. I'll send you the final communication to announce your name as the major shareholder and president for your approval. I think the announcement is scheduled for the end of September, in about four weeks."

Peter escorted us to the lobby, where we stopped in front of the elevators.

"Thanks, Peter," I said, mustering a strained smile. "I suppose I'll see you again soon."

"Take care, Sienna," Peter replied, giving me a brief but warm hug before he turned around and left.

Mr. Lehman and I entered the elevator, and he pushed the button for the ground floor. We stayed silent for about twenty floors, and then he turned his face to me and said, "You've done well. You've listened and kept yourself together. Let me summarize the contents of the will and see if I need your signature before you leave for college. When do you leave?" he asked.

"On the eighth. Classes don't start until September sixteenth, but I want to explore campus and settle in my apartment before then."

I couldn't believe I would be moving across the country in less than two weeks. With everything that had happened, I wasn't as excited as I was two months ago. I'd procrastinated packing since the funeral, but the task seemed less terrifying now that Sarah would be staying with me to help me move.

Mr. Lehman and I said our goodbyes, and I picked up the phone from my handbag. There was a text from Sarah.

Sarah

> Hello, gorgeous. My flight leaves from LHR at 8:55 a.m., and I arrive at 12:15 p.m. JFK local time. I'm traveling with Virgin.

> Can't wait to see you! Hope the meeting goes well.

PS I have sent a little something to your
house. It should be there by now. Love
ya. xxx

During the ride home, I kept staring out the car window, wondering what it would be like to live a different life. Mine had always been easy since everything was handed to me on a silver platter. But man, I'd trade all the money in the world for just one more day with my parents. Wasn't the saying, "You never miss the water until the well runs dry"? Facts.

When I got home, Mrs. Bishop handed me a box. Sarah had sent me a bottle of Dom Perignon Vintage 2012, my favorite, with a note.

I'm sure today was tough, but I'm proud of you. Have a bubble bath and drink the whole thing while listening to some Billie Eilish in the background. By the time you wake up tomorrow, I'll be there. Love, Sarah.

She was indeed the best.

A GHOST FROM THE PAST

(Sienna)

"I'm here, darling!" Sarah yelled from the foyer, dropping her luggage on the floor. I hurried downstairs and threw myself in her arms, all while Mrs. Bishop excused herself to give us some privacy. We stayed like that, holding each other for a few minutes. Sarah held my shoulders with her hands and took one step back to get a good look at me. Her brows furrowed slightly, and her eyes widened.

"You look like shit, Sienna."

I'd lost some weight but didn't think I looked that bad. Did I?

I stayed quiet, but tears stung my eyes. I hugged her back tightly, sobbing like a little girl. The pain in my chest consumed me. I knew this was bound to happen. I'd been holding my tears back for some time now, and it only took one look from Sarah to unleash everything I kept inside.

"Oh, it's okay, Sienna. I'm here now. Everything will be alright, I promise," Sarah murmured into my ear, her gentle touch gliding through my hair.

But I did feel alone. I only had my parents, and she lived across the world. I had a few friends at boarding school, but only a couple of them texted me when the news of the crash got to Europe. *A text.*

They didn't call. Ultimately, they turned out not to be the good friends I believed they were. But Sarah was here, and that was all that mattered.

When I composed myself, I showed Sarah to one of the guest rooms. She stopped in the middle of the hallway and exclaimed, "Hell no. I'm sleeping with you. I want to spend every minute of the day with you until I have to leave. Let's go to your room," she commanded, seizing my hand.

Sarah had always been extremely bossy. "I'm a type 8 in the enneagram, remember?" she frequently said as a way of justifying her *don't mess with me* front and being a stubborn bitch.

She started unpacking her luggage in my room while telling me all about her new boyfriend, James, and her fantastic sex life. She was not leaving any tiny detail out of the conversation. I was so glad she came. She'd always been good at making me laugh. Sarah had a habit of bouncing from one guy to the next, and even though she seemed pretty into James, I could tell she was holding out for her next crush to come along.

"I'm sorry, Sienna. I'm being an insensitive bitch. Here I am, talking about my sex life after all you've been through in the past few weeks," she said with a sad smile.

"I don't mind. It helps distract me from all the noise in my head." I bit my lower lip. "And not everything has been negative. Recall when I mentioned going out two days ago?"

She gave me a curious look.

"Don't tell me you started using Bumble, Tinder, or any of those apps, Sienna."

I glanced at the window and considered how much I wanted to tell her. I knew she wouldn't judge me.

"I fucked a stranger in a bar. In the restroom, to be more specific."

"SHUT. THE. FUCK. UP." She let the three dresses she was holding fall to the floor, and with two quick leaps, she landed on my bed, on her knees, facing me as I reclined against the headboard. Her eyes widened, resembling those of an owl. "Sienna, I need you to fucking tell me all the details. I want to know everything. His name, how big his dick was, how many times he made you come, and when you are seeing him again. Was he good?"

I couldn't hide my laugh. I loved Sarah. She lived for gossip and drama, but she usually had the juicier stories.

"His name is Zayn. I don't know how old he is—maybe a couple of years older—I don't know anything about him, and I don't have his number. We met at a bar and talked for a while, then he followed me to the restroom," I told her.

"I need more details, Sienna. Keep talking."

"He fucked me against the wall. It wasn't a quick fuck, but we couldn't take our time, you know...we were in a public place. It probably was the best orgasm of my life. He knew what he was doing. And his voice...oh my God, his voice. I could have just come by how he said my name."

I couldn't get his voice out of my head, his mouth, the way he touched me.

Do you feel it? Do you feel how your pussy enjoys being destroyed by my cock?

The memory made me shiver.

"I initially regretted not asking him for his number, but he didn't ask for mine either and left in a hurry...But anyway, I'm leaving for Stanford in less than two weeks, so I guess it worked out for the best."

"I'm so jealous right now, Sienna. I can't believe you fucked a stranger in a public restroom."

"I know. The things one must do to entertain you."

* * *

Sarah and I spent the following days shopping, exploring the city, and packing my things for Stanford. She also came with me to visit my family's mausoleum so I could place some flowers in front of my parents' crypt. My mother loved lilies, so we stopped at a local flower shop to buy a bouquet for her.

"Are you ready?" she asked.

The moving company was scheduled to collect all my boxes in just thirty minutes. We were set to catch a flight to San Francisco in the morning, and Sarah would be staying with me for a couple of days before her return to the UK on Saturday. The idea of her departure weighed heavily on me. It had been so lovely having her around that the prospect of putting thousands of miles between us left me with a heavy heart and a tight feeling in my chest.

"Not even remotely," I replied, looking at everything on my bed. "Most of my stuff is in the boxes. I'm taking some clothes with me for a few days while I unpack everything, plus the laptop, my phone, chargers, toiletry bag, and makeup…"

"Condoms…"

"Sarah!" I shrieked. "Anyway, I have everything I need, plus my ID. I think I'm all set—not ready, but set. Have you finished packing?"

"I'm almost done. I only need to close this bloody suitcase." Sarah was currently sitting on top of her suitcase and bouncing her ass up and down. She bought too many clothes during our shopping spree and couldn't close her luggage.

The company arrived an hour later, and all my things were on their way to California. We spent our last night at Moore Manor gossiping and drinking wine. I can tell she was very excited about studying at Cambridge. She claimed that living at Christ's College was the fulfillment of her Harry Potter childhood dreams.

"I'm a Dumblewhore who just needs to find the perfect wand," she joked.

"Are you going to keep seeing James?"

"You know me. I don't do long distance," she said with a wink.

"Are you gonna tell him?" I asked.

"I'll do it before I leave London. Gosh, I hope he doesn't cry like the last one. Have you seen Jake since the funeral?"

Jake and Caroline had contacted me multiple times, but I'd been actively dodging their calls throughout the summer. In one of his recent texts, Jake told me he was heading Upstate for work until the end of the year and suggested we meet. However, I had isolated myself within the walls of Moore Manor ever since the funeral, and the thought of seeing them and potentially having an uncomfortable conversation weighed heavily on my mind.

"No, I haven't. I've been ignoring his messages since the service," I confessed.

"What a shame... He did seem like a good guy, but I understand." Sarah sympathized.

"Yeah, I know, but I'll be leaving soon, and the last thing I want is to add more complications to my already complex life," I explained.

Little did I suspect that California had its own set of complications waiting for me.

* * *

Sarah left almost a week ago.

I'd almost finished unpacking, and after buying new furniture, my apartment at Aster Hall finally felt cozy. I liked my accommodation. Aster Hall was mixed-gender housing, and most units were one-bed apartments with an en suite bathroom. Each one had a small living room and a kitchen. I could afford to rent my own apartment, but then I would miss college life. I was so used to sharing space with other students at boarding school that I preferred seeing people my age rather than oldies with Chanel sunglasses holding Pomeranians in the elevator.

While my mood had certainly improved since Sarah arrived, I still cried myself to sleep almost every night. I was fully aware that I couldn't continue down this road and began considering booking an appointment with a counselor or a therapist. The last thing I wanted was to fall into a depression.

It was Friday, and my classes wouldn't start until Monday. My teachers had uploaded their syllabi on the intranet, so I made a list of the books I needed to buy and updated my Microsoft Outlook calendar with key dates and my weekly schedule. According to Google Maps, an academic text bookstore was in the area, just a ten-minute walk from my dorm. It seemed like a good idea to take a break from all the cleaning and organizing I'd done to leave the apartment and get some fresh air.

The moment I set foot in the bookstore, I knew I needed help. The store had multiple floors, and I couldn't even see its full extent from my position by the counter. Realizing I wouldn't locate the books on my list without some guidance, I approached one of their employees and asked for directions. He kindly pointed me to a section at the back of the store.

I was looking for a specific book on one of the shelves when someone spoke from behind me.

"Do you need any help?"

I spun around and was greeted by a guy flashing me a warm smile. Towering at an impressive height of around six-two, he appeared to be a giant compared to my five-four frame. He had Asian features, black hair, dark eyes, a cute nose, and perfect teeth. I smiled back at him.

"Yes, thank you. I'm looking for this book," I said, pointing at my list. He looked at the piece of paper, and without hesitation, he extended his right arm and reached for a book behind me. His whole body practically pressed against mine, and I blushed. I took a step back, but I hit the bookshelf.

"Let me guess, you're a freshman majoring in a science field?" he said, holding the book before me.

"Is it that obvious?"

"Yeah, a little. I assumed, based on your list. My best friend is a sophomore majoring in bioengineering, and he had a similar list last year."

Why is he so handsome, and why can't I stop staring at his killer smile?

"Are you coming to the party tonight?" he asked me.

"What party?"

"Every year, all the seniors from economics organize a freshman party at Banbury Hall. It starts at ten o'clock. You have to come. If you don't know anyone, you could look for me," he said with a wink. "Give me your phone," he demanded. "I'll give you my number, and you can text me when you get there. By the way, my name is Noah. What's your name?"

"Sienna," I told him while handing him my phone.

"Nice to meet you, Sienna."

While he typed his number, I observed him in more detail. His arms were well-defined under his white T-shirt. He had broad shoulders and strong hands. His hair looked messy but purposely messy, quite sexy, like *just-got-fucked* hair. I wasn't a fool…great hair, a beautiful smile, good social skills, and that body…he was definitely a fuckboy, and I was his next victim.

"I've sent myself a text, so I have your number too. I'll see you tonight." We parted ways after he gave me back my phone and gifted me with another flirty smile. Once I exited the store, I looked down at my screen, noticing he'd saved his number as Noah and a heart emoji. He had already sent me a text.

Noah

> I can't wait to see you tonight. I hope you come ;)

I had the feeling that the text had a double meaning.

* * *

I didn't know why I was so nervous. I'd changed my outfit twice before deciding on a sleek black knit dress with an open back that snugly embraced my figure, featuring a straight neckline and delicate straps. My hair was down with loose, beachy waves. I finished my look with natural but glossy makeup, my favorite Gucci T-Strap block heel sandals in black, and a small black leather hobo handbag. First impressions were always important, and I wanted to look my best to feel extra confident tonight.

Looking at myself in the mirror, I couldn't help but notice how much I looked like my mother. I guessed I had never stopped to think about it too much, but after my parents' tragic death, all I could think about was the many moments like this one that I would have loved to share with her and get her advice. I stopped my train of thought, or I would otherwise ruin my makeup.

I left my apartment around ten-thirty with the goal of being fashionably late. It was a fifteen-minute walk from Aster Hall to Banbury Hall, so I took my AirPods out of my bag and played music from one of my Spotify playlists. "Beg for You" by Charli XCX feat. Rina Sawayama was playing when I arrived at the party—that song always put me in the right mood.

The place looked amazing, and it was packed. Balloons were everywhere, and disco lights illuminated the space. I could feel the music in my chest. The dance floor was full of students, and a huge sign said, "Welcome to Stanford." Everyone seemed to be having a great time.

I wasn't going to text Noah yet because I didn't want to look desperate, so my best option was to get a drink. I made my way through the crowd and hit the bar, but as much as I tried to get the attention of any of the servers, none of them looked my way while I stood there waving my hand like an idiot. It looked like all of them ignored me on purpose.

"I think they proactively ignore you unless you have a dick between your legs. I've been standing here for five minutes longer than you, and nothing. That guy arrived one minute ago and is already holding a whiskey and Coke."

The voice came from the girl standing to my right. She was slightly taller than me, with long blond hair, bright baby-blue eyes, and a doll's face. She was stunning—showstopping pretty.

"HEY PRINCESS, CAN WE ORDER OUR DRINKS NOW?" she called out to a brunette server flirting with two guys. She was loud and reminded me of Sarah. I liked her already.

"I'm Sienna Moore. What's your name?"

"Maggie Towerby. Nice to meet you, Sienna." We shook hands.

When Maggie finally got our drinks—gin and tonic for me, of course, and rum and Coke for her—we headed to a place at the back of the party where we could talk.

"Are you a freshman, too?" Maggie asked.

"Yes. I arrived a few days ago. I haven't done much aside from decorating my dorm. I'm staying at Aster Hall. And you?"

"I arrived two days ago. I'm at Greenhill Hall, which is the only one I could afford with my budget because I'm on a scholarship. It's across campus, but it's super nice and clean."

"Wow! A scholarship. You must be super smart. That's awesome," I beamed.

We spent a good forty-five minutes talking about Stanford and the lives we just left behind. I didn't tell her much because I didn't want to kill the vibe with my drama, but I told her that I was from New York, that I was currently living at Aster Hall, and my major. Maggie mentioned that she was actually from Queens and a freshman pursuing a major in chemical engineering. Although we had different schedules with only one lecture in common, it was a relief to have at least a familiar face around on Wednesdays. The more we talked, the more I realized we had a lot of things in common. She was very easy to talk to. She was telling me all about her first couple of days at Stanford when I saw Noah approaching us. He wore blue jeans and a military green shirt; the sleeves were rolled up just below his elbows, showing off some muscle. I couldn't take my eyes off him, and as he got closer to us, all I could think about was how much I wanted to thread my fingers through his *just-got-fucked* hair.

"Should I feel offended that you didn't text me?" he mocked, placing his right hand on my exposed lower back and bringing his mouth to my ear. "You look fantastic, Sienna. I have been thinking about you the whole day."

I felt my cheeks flush.

I didn't know how to respond, so I opted for the easiest way out.

"This is Maggie; we've just met. Maggie, this is Noah…we met this morning at Bluebird Book Shop. He invited me to the party."

From the moment I made the introduction, Maggie unleashed an unstoppable torrent of questions upon Noah. I knew nothing about him, so witnessing her intense questioning was an unexpected delight.

"So you're originally from Chicago, but your mother was born and raised in Washington, and your dad is from Tokyo?" Maggie was on a mission.

"Yes, your honor," Noah replied.

It seemed that love had blossomed between his parents during one of his father's business trips to the United States, and the rest, as they say, was history. Noah, a sophomore, aspired to graduate with a political science major.

I smothered a few giggles at his uncomfortable expression. Clearly, he hadn't anticipated such a thorough interrogation. Noah was funny and charming, cracking jokes and answering all of Maggie's questions.

"Do you want to ask me about my favorite sex position too?"

I snorted, spitting out half of my drink through my nose.

Noah leaned in closer and whispered, "Do you find the question funny, princess? I hope you're not too attached to this dress because before the night is over, I'm ripping it off you and bending you over. So yes, you've guessed right. Doggy style is my favorite position."

My heart began to beat like crazy inside my chest, and all the blood from my body rushed to my face. The room suddenly felt too hot. Maggie noticed and frowned. I prayed she hadn't heard what he'd said to me, but the subtle smirk beginning to form on her lips hinted that she might have an inkling. The three of us kept talking for about half an hour when Noah suddenly yelled at someone behind me.

"Hey, Ander! Come here, man. I want to introduce you to someone."

I stiffened.

A wave of anxiety washed over me, and my breathing became uneven. *Ander.*

It just couldn't be. *There must be a thousand Anders in the US*, I told myself. I turned my head so fast that I thought I would get neck whiplash. Then our eyes locked, and the room started spinning. He WAS that Ander. *My Ander.* He was clearly not *my Ander* anymore. I last saw him six years ago, and we lost contact when I moved to Switzerland. I was twelve, and he was thirteen. We'd known each other since we were babies because his father, William Scott, and my father were partners at Cos Pharmaceuticals, but when my dad bought him out of the business, Ander and I stopped hanging out. I assumed something big had gone down between our parents, but whenever I asked my dad why I couldn't hang out at Ander's house anymore, he would say they had a fight and that it was grown-up stuff I shouldn't worry about.

"Ander, let me introduce you to Maggie and—"

"Sienna." Ander interrupted, finishing Noah's sentence.

"Oh," Noah exclaimed. "You already know her?" Noah looked surprised.

"Yes," he snapped. Ander kept staring at me. I couldn't read his facial expression, although one would say that he didn't look happy to see me at all.

"Hi, Ander. I wasn't expecting to find you here, but I'm glad to see you again." I was being sincere. A part of me always missed him while I was growing up, all because of the stupid way we lost contact. I remembered it as if it was yesterday.

"Sienna, I don't want you to see Ander anymore. You're too young to understand. One day, I'll explain everything to you, but for now, I forbid you to have any contact with any member of the Scott family. I'm dead serious."

"You can't stop me from seeing my best friend, Dad. I don't know what his father did to you, but it's not his fault!" I ran to my room and slammed the door shut.

The next thing I knew, my dad had enrolled me at Rubin American School. He said it was the best education he could provide for me, but

I always suspected that my father just wanted to put miles between our friendship. There had been times when I was curious and checked his name online, but I never found him on social media. He didn't look like the sweet boy I remembered, yet he looked like *my* Ander.

I need to stop calling him that in my head.

His dark blond hair was shorter, but his blue eyes could still pierce my soul like they did when I was twelve. Even now, I couldn't shake off the effect his eyes had on me.

"I wish I could say the same."

If the music hadn't been that loud, everyone would have probably heard my heart breaking into a million pieces.

I knew we hadn't talked or seen each other in a while, and it wasn't like I expected a hug from him or something. But this? I never anticipated the hatred in his voice. Maybe he was resentful that I didn't fight hard enough to stay friends, but he didn't try to contact me all this time either. Life happened—our parents happened, actually—and we were just kids.

I felt tears at the edges of my eyes, so I stepped away without saying a single word. I didn't want to burst into tears in front of them. I barely knew Noah and didn't want to give Ander the satisfaction of seeing how his words had upset me. His intention was clearly to hurt my feelings. Much to my regret, he had succeeded. He looked and smelled like him, but he was definitely not *my* Ander anymore. That boy I remembered would never have treated me like that.

Just as I was about to leave the building, Maggie caught up with me and grabbed my arm.

"Hey, are you okay?"

"I'm fine." I sniffed. "I'm sorry. I shouldn't have stormed away without saying goodbye, but I couldn't stay there for another second."

"I understand. He was an asshole. Do you want me to walk you back to Aster Hall? I know I talk a lot, but I'm good at listening, too." She gave me a kind smile.

"Thank you, but I prefer to be alone right now."

Maggie looked disappointed, probably because her only friend was ditching the party.

"Do you wanna get some coffee tomorrow?" I asked.

Her face lit up.

"I'd love that. Do you want to go to Starbucks? I'm a pumpkin spice latte whore, and it's been back on the menu since last Tuesday."

I really liked this girl.

THE NOTEBOOK

(Ander)

"What the fuck, man?" Noah exclaimed, swiftly turning around with his hands raised in the air.

The blond girl just went after Sienna, who clearly left upset. Good. I hadn't seen her in over six years, and although I had moved on, some wounds apparently never closed. Seeing her again brought back some memories I wished I had forgotten. She stood there with a big smile and doe eyes, and all I could think about was how much I hated myself for falling for her.

"What?" I shrugged.

"Look. I don't know what happened between you two, but you obviously have an issue with her. Did you date her or something?"

"No. I didn't date her. We used to be friends, but not anymore."

"Oh, did she break your heart?" Noah mocked, putting his hand on his chest.

"Drop it. I'm serious." My words were sharp. I didn't want to dwell on what happened years ago. The past was the past, but it seemed like the universe had another plan and a fucked-up sense of humor.

"Okay, okay. I'll drop it. But just so I'm clear, there isn't an issue if I, let's say, want to make a move on her? I mean...if you say there's never been anything between you two…"

I didn't know why Noah's interest in Sienna pissed me off so much, but it did. Yet should I disclose what happened to him, he might assume I still harbored feelings for her, which was far from the truth. No. Those emotions were long gone. I might have been a fool as a kid, but I learned my lesson and will never make the same mistake twice.

"You wanna fuck the girl? Don't mind me. I don't fucking care, but the less time I have to spend around her, the better."

* * *

"Good morning, son."

It didn't happen often that my father called me. He was the kind of businessman who would ask his assistant to call me rather than do it himself, so the moment I picked up the phone, I knew he was either calling to tell me how disappointed he was or to ask me to do something for him.

"Hey, Dad. What do you need?" I deadpanned.

"Is that a way to greet your father? Where are your manners?"

I sighed.

"Dad, I'm busy. Is there something you need, or are you just checking on me?"

I began pacing around my bedroom like those pigeons in Central Park, just going in circles. Whenever I talked to my dad, it always got me anxious. I paused in front of one of the mahogany shelving units and started meticulously organizing each book and DVD until I came across *The Notebook*.

My parents spent the whole afternoon shouting at each other. It had been their daily routine for the past year, and I sometimes wished they'd get a divorce. Things hadn't been good lately. My father spent most days away from home, traveling or at the office, and the time he was at home, he would either yell at me or my mother for the tiniest shit.

"The Notebook *or* Pride & Prejudice, *your choice,"* Sienna said, holding *two DVDs in front of me. She came to my house almost every day since our classes finished a couple of weeks ago, and every day, we would pick a different movie. It was Sienna's turn today, and she was determined to choose a romantic drama. She lived for romance, for happily ever afters, and Ryan Gosling.*

"Do I have to choose between those two shitty movies?" I really enjoyed pissing her off, and I couldn't help myself.

"You've made me watch all the Star Wars *movies. Be happy that I haven't picked a* Harry Potter *movie yet."*

She'd been one of my best friends since I could remember, and I'd always considered her like a little sister, but in the past year, she'd physically changed a lot, and I must admit that I'd surprised myself by staring at her more than once and maybe for too long. Last week, Sienna invited me to her house to spend the day at the swimming pool, and when she took her dress off, my mouth dropped. I hadn't seen her in a bathing suit since last summer, and the last thing I expected was to see her wearing a Quicksilver bikini that barely covered her chest and round ass. I couldn't take my eyes off her, and every time she got closer, I couldn't think straight.

By the time we finished watching The Notebook, *Sienna hugged a pillow and silently cried at the screen. I'd watched her for most of the movie and hoped she hadn't noticed.*

"Hey, Son. Are you listening?"

I quickly realized I hadn't heard a single word my father said over the phone.

"Sorry, I got distracted."

That was what Sienna was—a distraction. Out of all the colleges in the world, even in the US, it was just my luck that she got accepted into Stanford. This was my place, my little kingdom, to rule away from my father's claws. He always ruined everything I wanted, and now her presence also threatened my peace.

"I was saying that Claudia needs your schedule to book an appointment with the tailor within the next four weeks. Email her your details ASAP so she'll stop bugging me."

My father didn't sound particularly excited about his upcoming wedding. I kept wondering why the hell he proposed to her, especially considering how his marriage with my mom ended. By now, I would have thought he'd hate the idea of "till death do us part." They managed to achieve a civilized co-parenting arrangement a year after my mom filed for divorce, but the moment I turned eighteen, she limited her interactions with my father as much as she could.

"I saw Sienna last night." I didn't know why the words came out of my mouth like vomit. The silence stretched for a few seconds, which seemed like an eternity.

"Sienna Moore?" he asked.

"Yes. She's studying at Stanford, and I bumped into her at a party."

"I don't have time to hear about your little reunion. Don't forget to send the info to Claudia." And with that, he hung up. It wasn't like I was going to tell him shit, but the way he ended our conversation left me seething, mainly because he was one of the reasons Sienna and I never saw each other again after that summer.

A BIRTHDAY INVITATION

(Sienna)

My phone pinged with an incoming text from Noah.

Noah

> I don't usually apologize for other people's behavior, but Ander was an asshole last night, and I'm sorry.

> If you're in the mood for me to do some groveling on his behalf, I have a few ideas in mind ;)

> Do you have any plans for today?

"Is that Noah?" Maggie asked, widening her big blue eyes and taking a sip of her pumpkin spice latte. The Starbucks on campus was just a mere five-minute stroll from Aster Hall, and I prayed that my love for coffee, especially lattes, wouldn't transform into a crippling addiction before I got my degree.

"Yes. He's asking me if I have any plans today, but I'm not sure I should see him again, considering he's friends with Ander. I don't want things to get complicated."

I didn't know why Ander was such a dick to me last night.

He was clearly not happy to see me, and the more I tried to think about why, the less it made any sense. When I arrived at Rubin, I wrote to him a couple of times, excitedly sharing stories about my classes and telling him about Sarah. However, disappointingly, he never responded to any of my letters. If anyone had the right to feel angry, it was me. I'd believed him to be one of my closest friends, my best friend, yet the moment I left Port Chester, he chose to ignore me completely.

"Look, based on the little you've told me today, I can see you have a history with Ander, but Noah clearly likes you, and you like him, right? He's the one who should worry about Ander, not you. You don't owe Ander anything, and if Noah texts you, it's because he doesn't care or has his friend's blessing. So please, text him back, and when you fuck him, call me, and tell me all the sordid details."

I couldn't hide my smile. Maggie had a point. I didn't owe Ander a thing, and my undeniable chemistry with Noah was apparent. Last night when he whispered in my ear about wanting to rip my dress off, my pussy throbbed between my legs.

"Okay, I'll text him, I promise. Just not today. Our classes start tomorrow, and I would rather have a drama-free Sunday."

By the time I reached my dorm, it was already almost two o'clock. However, I wasn't hungry, so I changed into something cozy and switched on my laptop. When I opened my email account, I saw an email from Peter. He'd sent me the first draft of the press release about becoming the major shareholder of Cos Pharmaceuticals.

RE: Press release – Miss Moore
Peter Lawrence <peter.lawrence@cospharma.com>
To <sienna.moore@cospharma.com>
Cc <prcos@cospharma.com>

Dear Sienna,

Please find below the text the PR department drafted for the press release. I have attached a picture of you to accompany the statement. The press release will be published on the website on Friday, September 20th, so I would appreciate it if you could send back your suggested changes before the end of business on Tuesday.

Best wishes,

Peter

PS I hope you're all settled and enjoying your time in college. I will call you once the announcement has been published.

Friday, September 20th – 10:00 a.m.

Effective September 12th, Sienna Moore becomes the major shareholder at Cos Pharmaceuticals Inc.

NEW YORK—(BUSINESS WIRE)—*Cos Pharmaceuticals Inc. (NYSE: COS) would like to announce that Sienna Moore, daughter and sole heiress of the late Edward Moore, Founder & CEO, has assumed the role of major shareholder in our esteemed company, effective September 12th.*

Until the Board of Directors appoints a new CEO, Peter Lawrence, COO at Cos Pharmaceuticals, will continue to oversee the business's day-to-day administrative and operational functions.

"I feel very honored by the trust that my father placed upon me. My commitment to the company he built when I was a child is absolute, and with Peter Lawrence as my mentor and interim CEO, I have full confidence that my father's legacy is in good hands," Miss Moore commented.

Upon reading the announcement, I felt my palms grow sweaty and my breathing become shallow. Was I having a panic attack? I was overwhelmed because it all felt so painfully real that I felt like drowning. In the past three months, I'd endured the fallout of a nasty breakup and the death of both of my parents in a plane accident. Now, I had the massive responsibility of taking over my dad's multimillion-dollar business. While I should have been excited about starting college, it got soured by my childhood best friend insulting me. Honestly, I was on the brink of a breakdown.

I hit reply and told Peter and the PR team that the text was perfect and that I didn't wish to make any changes. The photo was okay. It was not my best picture, but at least I looked professional.

* * *

As I entered the Biochemistry & Molecular Biology class, I quickly spotted Maggie comfortably seated in the fifth row. It was our third day of college, and I was enjoying all my classes so far. The first day was a roller coaster of emotions. There were moments throughout the day when I wanted to call my mother and tell her all about my classes, my new apartment on campus, and my run-in with Ander. Sometimes, I would catch myself looking at my mobile screen with my thumb over her name on the agenda. I still kept their numbers active, as if deleting them or canceling their contracts would feel like admitting that they'll never be able to answer my calls anymore. They were just numbers, but I kept telling myself the day would come when I felt strong enough to delete them. Until then, who cared?

Maggie and I were chatting when Professor James Reed entered the classroom. He was in his early thirties and quite attractive. I was sure more than one girl in this room wouldn't mind doing *special assignments* to improve their grades. Don't get me wrong, I got it. If all professors looked like him, absenteeism and illiteracy would be extinct.

"Good morning, everyone. I hope you have enjoyed your first two days because you may regret taking my course by the end of this class."

A murmur broke out among the class as a result of his greeting, but he turned on the projector and continued presenting.

"Today, I'll introduce proteins, their structure, function, synthesis, and degradation, so unless you have a question, I want silence and your full attention on the screen."

Reed spent the next fifty-five minutes going through the basics, and by the end of the hour, he handed out a stack of papers to one of the students at the front. The guy picked one up and passed the entire stack to the next person to his right. When I got the chance to grab one for myself, I saw a list of questions. Fifty, to be more precise.

He stood in front of the class with his back to the table, his hands locked behind him.

"I want you to work on those questions and return your answers by the end of the week. I won't accept assignments after 5 p.m. on Friday, so you have two days to work on them. I want short and concise answers. If you cannot reach the point quickly, I'll mark your response invalid. Don't waste my time," he said sternly. After that, the class was dismissed.

The day went by quickly, and once I finished my last lecture, Vector Calculus for Engineers, I went straight to the campus library. My plan was to work until late tonight on Reed's assignment and take Thursday and Friday to review my answers and work on being succinct. When I approached Maggie and invited her to join me, she declined, stating that she was weary and preferred to work from the comfort of her room, clad in her cozy pajamas. I couldn't blame her. These first few days had proven to be draining for both of us. While the idea of studying from the convenience of my apartment seemed attractive, I couldn't ignore the temptation that a nearby fridge posed as a potential distraction. I often found myself standing before the open refrigerator door, gazing into the void, unable to make up my mind. Frozen yogurt, cheese, or perhaps a satisfying sandwich?

Maggie had agreed to meet me tomorrow evening at my place to review our responses and offer suggestions for improvement, so I guessed tonight it was just me, myself, and I…and fifty questions to work through.

It was around midnight when I decided to call it a day and retreat to the solace of my apartment. It became evident that completing the assignment in its entirety tonight was an unattainable task, and to be frank, I was utterly drained both mentally and physically. I'd been yawning nonstop for the past half an hour, and I needed a shower and a bed. After I placed everything in my laptop bag and my phone in my back pocket, I walked through the expansive library aisles. The place was huge. During the day, it was full of students, but I didn't think I had seen a single soul in the past hour. Given that it was only the first week of classes, it seemed people weren't in study mode yet. But me? I'd forever been the student known for achieving excellent grades, never missing a deadline, and eagerly participating in class discussions.

Only my footsteps echoed softly through the library as I mentally reviewed the classes I had tomorrow. Suddenly, a faint sound of steps reached my ears from somewhere behind me. I instinctively glanced over my shoulder, but no one came into view. An anxious knot formed in the pit of my stomach. Perhaps it was the residual effect of having watched one too many horror movies, for this moment eerily mirrored those scenes where the unsuspecting blonde meets her untimely demise. But she shouldn't have gone into the basement…should she? The voice in my head told me to get the fuck out.

Don't be as stupid as the chicks in horror movies, Sienna.

As I reached the end of one aisle and turned right, I hit a wall. But it wasn't a wall…it was someone's chest. A startled scream escaped my lips, causing my bag to slip from my grasp and crash to the floor. My eyes darted upward, ready to face my murderer.

Noah.

"Sorry. Did I scare you, Sienna?" he said, raising one eyebrow with a mischievous smile.

I thought my heart was going to jump out of my chest.

"No," I lied.

"Why are you here so late, by yourself?" he asked.

"I was working on an assignment. And you?"

"Actually, I was looking for you. We haven't talked since Saturday, and I've been dying to see you." His eyes darkened as he closed the gap between us, leaving me sandwiched between him and a bookshelf. He laid his hands on each side of my head and lowered his face only a few inches from mine, our noses almost touching. I could smell his scent, like coffee and sandalwood, with a hint of jasmine. I could feel his warmth all over me. It was intoxicating. I knew I should be scared. We were alone, and I didn't know him well enough. We had only met a couple of times, and although my instincts told me to run, his presence overwhelmed all my senses. He knew the effect he had on me.

"Are you avoiding me, Sienna?" His voice was low and seductive.

"No. I've been busy," I breathed.

He tsked.

"Too busy to answer a simple text? Tell me the truth."

I nibbled on my lower lip, prompting him to shift his focus to my mouth. The tension between us was tangible.

"Look, I don't think it's a good idea for us to be friends, Noah. You know…because of Ander," I responded.

"But that's where you're wrong." He brushed his lips against my jaw and neck. "I want something else from you. I don't want to be your *friend*. I want more. I want to be the one you think about when you touch yourself. I want to be the name you moan every time you come," he whispered in my ear. Then he nipped my earlobe.

Fuck.

I whimpered.

I could feel my nipples tightening behind my top, my body aching for his touch, but when I thought he was about to kiss me, he backed off.

"Hey, I get it. I'm sorry if I came on too strong, but I genuinely like you, and it's hard for me to keep my distance. But we can be friends, right? Let me prove it to you. It's my birthday on Saturday, and I'll be hosting a party. As my *friend*, I want you to come," he said.

Can I be friends with Noah? Things were complicated with Ander in the mix, but all I could think about was how Noah's lips would feel on mine.

"Is that an invitation or a promise?"

His eyes widened by my sudden burst of sassiness. Did I really say that out loud? I blamed it on the adrenaline coursing through me, amplified by his proximity and the intoxicating effect of his words.

"I guess you'll have to find out."

*   *   *

"Do you have any plans on Saturday evening?" I asked Maggie. With Reed's assignment nearly complete, we'd decided to take a break and satisfy our hunger with a well-deserved dinner. Opting for convenience, I ordered chow mein, spring rolls, and sweet and sour pork from a nearby Chinese restaurant. Knowing my lack of cooking skills, I assured Maggie that relying on Uber Eats was the safest and most practical choice. The idea of making a real meal had never crossed my mind, mainly because there was no reason for it. I had spent my teenage years in boarding school, where the kitchen staff handled everything, or at home in Port Chester with Gloria and Mrs. Bishop. Gloria, our cook, always said I was a kitchen liability. I guessed putting a bag of popcorn in the microwave or a pizza in the oven didn't count as cooking. If I wanted to survive five years at Stanford, I might need to buy a cookbook or enroll in cooking classes. *Maybe I can hire a new Gloria?*

"I don't, why?"

"Noah ambushed me yesterday in the library and told me that his birthday is on Saturday. He's hosting a party at The Cave and invited us. Wanna be my plus-one?"

"The Cave?" Maggie asked, totally excited. "I'm *ABSO-FUCKING-LUTELY* going with you. That club is the best one in a thirty-mile radius, and you can't get in unless you're *on the list.*"

When Noah sent me the details of the party today, I hesitated. I was sure Ander would be there, but perhaps Maggie was right the other day when she said that maybe he was okay with me seeing Noah. Otherwise, Noah wouldn't invite me to his birthday party, would he?

It'd been a week since I bumped into Ander, and I was still trying to wrap my head around what he'd said. He looked angry, but I hadn't seen him in six years, so why would he be angry with me? I thought that our friendship meant something to him, but in truth, he was the one who failed to follow through on his promises to stay in touch. The thought of visiting him during the first Christmas break had once flickered through my mind, but my father was very clear when he said, "I forbid you to go to the Scotts. I'm serious, Sienna. William and I stopped being partners for a reason, and the apple never falls far from the tree."

I remember being very upset when he made that comment because Alexander Scott was nothing like his father. He was Ander, the grumpy, caring, protective, but sometimes annoying friend who always knew how to make me laugh, and that thought upset me even more. He didn't care about me; he never wrote to me like he promised. Maybe I scared him. Perhaps I shouldn't have kissed him. He returned my kiss, but what if he regretted it the moment I left? Maybe I went too far and broke what we had. I wasn't a kid anymore, but I had some pride. I liked Noah, and my past would not influence my future.

"Good. Tomorrow after classes we'll go shopping. I need a dress that makes Noah want to rip it off, so your advice is required," I said with determination.

"That's my girl," Maggie replied, but then her face shifted to a sympathetic expression. "How are you feeling? And I mean aside from all the boys' drama. Since you told me about your parents the other day, I've been meaning to ask you because, in a way, I understand how you feel."

"What do you mean?" I asked, intrigued.

"I haven't told you much about my past, but my mom died from cancer when I was thirteen. My dad couldn't face living without her and took his own life."

Her confession left me speechless.

"I didn't have other relatives, so I entered the foster care system. The first year, I felt really lonely. Especially since I was consistently moving from one house to another." She paused and swallowed. "So what I'm trying to say is that I know you may feel you have no one, but I'm here for you if you allow me to."

A lump formed in my throat, and tears welled up in my eyes. It had only been a week since our paths crossed, yet our shared connection felt incredibly profound, almost as if it were destined. Perhaps, I mused, this was the very reason for our instant bond. We were two young women who intimately understood the pain of losing both parents and the ache of navigating life's challenges without the guiding presence of a beloved figure. I threw my arms around Maggie's neck and gave her a hug that I felt within my bones. She hugged me back, and we started sobbing while holding each other tight. We stayed like that for about five minutes until Maggie broke the magic.

"I'm not gay, but this is kind of turning me on."

I smacked her arm, and we both started laughing. I wiped tears from beneath my eyes. I felt lighter, a weight easing from my chest. I had not only made a friend but a friend who understood what I was going through. In that sense, I felt lucky.

"I'm feeling better, but some days are hard. There are so many things in my day-to-day life that I'd love to share with my parents. They studied here too, so they were very excited when I received my admissions letter. I could feel they were proud although my dad's ambition was for me to attend an Ivy League college."

"I'm glad you didn't. What did your parents do for a living? I've seen the shoes and the clothes you wear to class, so I'm assuming that you're either a European princess studying incognito in America or the heiress to an oil empire…" she said with amusement.

"My dad owns…well, owned a pharmaceutical company, and my mom was the founder and director of a non-profit charity," I explained.

"Is that why you want to do bioengineering? So you can work at your father's company?" Maggie asked.

"Well, that's the funny thing. I have just inherited fifty-one percent of the shares, making me the major shareholder, so I technically own the company."

"WHAT?" Her voice was so high-pitched that I was sure she woke up the entire building, maybe even the dead.

"In fact, the PR team will publish an announcement tomorrow."

As soon as I told Maggie, I realized that I felt excited and scared in equal measure. Just a few months ago, the thought of working at my father's company and following in his footsteps filled me with dread, but now things were different. I wanted my parents to be proud of me. I didn't know what the future held, but something told me I was on the right path.

"Now, let's finish the assignment so we can watch *La La Land*."

"It sounds like a plan."

THE CAVE

(Sienna)

"He's gonna go mental when he sees you in that dress," Maggie said while I stood in front of the full-length mirror that sat on the wall in my bedroom. I'd bought a few dresses but finally settled on a royal-blue silk midi dress with spaghetti straps. Elegant but sexy. Although I'd contemplated different pairs of shoes, Maggie persuasively insisted that the Giuseppe Zanotti flashato leather wrap sandals in argento would be the perfect choice if I wanted Noah at my feet tonight. I had styled my golden-brown hair in a messy low bun with some strands of hair loosened at the front. The only jewelry I wore were the white gold and diamond mini hoop earrings my parents bought me when I turned eighteen last February. I'd done my makeup heavier than usual: smoky eyes, long black eyelashes, and peachy nude lips with a glossy finish.

"If he doesn't make a move tonight, probably half of the club will."

"You look amazing, too, Maggie."

"Don't deflect my compliment. It's true. You're beautiful. Own it, grab your purse, and let's get an Uber. I'm dying to see if The Cave lives up to the rumors I've heard."

"What do you mean?" I was curious about the club because there were no pictures or info online, which I found weird. But I have to say, everything she'd talked about so far had piqued my interest.

"Nobody knows what the club looks like unless you've been inside. All mobile devices, including purses, are left in a locker because photos and videos aren't allowed. Haven't you noticed that there are no pictures of the club on Instagram? Matt from algebra told me that when you get to the front desk, they give you a bracelet with a QR code, which they link to your locker and debit or credit card so you can pay for all the drinks by just showing your bracelet. So if you drop or lose it, report it before you go from Beyoncé-rich into bankruptcy in less than an hour."

The Cave sounded mysterious, and I was getting increasingly excited by the minute.

We called an Uber, and I texted Noah to say we were coming.

Me

Hey, birthday boy. We're on our way, and we'll be there in 15 minutes.

Instantly, I saw three dots dancing on my screen.

Noah

Your name and Maggie's are on my birthday guest list, Noah Nakamura; no need to wait in line. BTW, I can't stop thinking about you. I hope you like to dance.

Me

Are you a good dancer?

Noah

I'm good at so many things, but as I said...you'll have to find out *wink emoji*

As we neared our destination, a surge of anxiety coursed through me, causing the inside of my thighs to grow increasingly sweaty. Uncertainty hung in the air. I had no clear expectations for what lay ahead tonight, but a part of me hoped that my underwear ended up on Noah's bedroom floor.

Upon exiting the Uber, my heart pounding, Maggie took charge and confidently approached the bouncers stationed at the main entrance. To the left, a line of approximately thirty people patiently waited their turn. Still, it seemed there was a privilege list within the guest list because the moment she said we were on Noah Nakamura's birthday list and gave out our full names, one of the security guys removed the red velvet rope and invited us in.

"We're in!" Maggie screamed with excitement as we walked toward the front desk.

Standing behind it were two beautiful women dressed in sleek black dresses that exuded an air of sophistication. Their dark chestnut hair was meticulously styled into a tight, high ponytail, and their plump lips were painted with a vibrant shade of red lipstick. They looked highly polished as if they could work for Christian Grey.

We gave them our names, and immediately, they handed us out two bracelets with a QR code, just like Maggie said. However, when I showed her my credit card and asked her to link Maggie's bracelet to my card, the one to my left declined it with a smile.

"Mr. Nakamura has linked all his guests' bracelets to his card. My colleague Blake will walk you to the VIP table. Please enjoy the evening, and welcome to The Cave."

Was Noah paying for everything? VIP table? I didn't know Noah came from a wealthy background, but the truth was that I knew very little about him. Given his aspirations to pursue a major in political science, I wondered if his family had ties to politics.

Blake, the second hostess, started walking us through the club and explaining the areas where we could find various music styles, such as house, R&B, Latin music, electronic, and commercial. There were five caves, as she called them, with a bar in each and several restrooms distributed throughout the premises. But it wasn't what she was saying that caught my attention. All the walls and the high ceilings were made of stone, like the club was carved inside a rock, and we were actually underground—*The Cave*. As we entered the main dance floor, pink and blue lights illuminated the space, and house music filled the air.

"In addition to the caves that I've mentioned, there are several tunnels that lead to some empty alcoves for more private conversations," she said with a suggestive smile. "There's a reason electronic devices are not allowed. We have a very selective clientele, and we like to offer a level of discretion that other clubs don't."

When I turned my face toward Maggie, she grinned at me. She didn't have to open her mouth for me to know what was going through her filthy mind.

Above the dance floor were three VIP tables with glass panels resembling balconies. Noah had booked the first one. There were two low tables in the middle with several ice buckets. In one glance, I could see that at least one of them had two bottles of champagne. A long, U-shaped white leather couch surrounded the space where at least fifteen people sat and the others stood.

"You're finally here," Noah shouted from behind. He wore navy trousers and a light blue striped shirt. He looked like a model straight out of *GQ* magazine, and I couldn't contain the smile on my face or the butterflies in my stomach.

"Thank you for inviting us, Noah," Maggie said. "This place is fucking amazing!" She was thrilled, and her excitement was contagious.

"I'm glad you like it," he replied without averting his gaze from me.

"You didn't have to link our bracelets to your card. I can pay for my own drinks, you know."

"I know you can, but it's my birthday, and I like to *please my friends.*" He winked at me, and my cheeks turned pink. "I need to say hi to some people, but please drink, dance, and enjoy the music. I'll find you in a minute."

As soon as he disappeared into the crowd, Maggie took my hand and dragged me to the closest bar.

"Let's get a tequila shot first, then we can go and dance our asses off."

Maggie and I had been dancing for about twenty minutes when someone grabbed my waist with both hands. I knew it was Noah because I could smell his scent. His front was pressed against my back, his breath next to my ear.

"You missed me?"

My skin tingled.

I lifted my right hand and placed it behind his neck. I closed my eyes and lost myself to the music. My entire body buzzed with raw desire, my blood thrumming faster. Noah turned me to face him, and I put my hands around his neck while I held his gaze. I could see the hunger in his eyes, and his grip on my hips tightened as he pulled me closer. I could feel the tension building until some idiot decided to burst our bubble.

"Sorry for interrupting, Noah, but Conrad got into a fight, and security wants to kick him out. He asked me to find you. They're holding him in one of the control rooms."

Noah held my face with both hands and said, "Stay here. I promise it won't take me long."

"That's okay. I'll stay with Maggie."

MAGGIE. I had completely forgotten about her. We were dancing together when Noah arrived unannounced, and I got pulled into his arms. She couldn't have gone far. I started looking for her around the dance floor but couldn't see her, so I headed toward the bar. Maybe she went to get another drink, but when I reached the counter, she wasn't there either. I felt like a horrible friend. She probably got sick of watching me dancing with Noah. I checked the VIP area without luck, and with our phones sitting in a locker, my only option was to head to the closest restroom.

Maybe she went to explore other caves or met a guy. I'm probably overreacting.

After approximately thirty minutes of walking through various tunnels and caves, I realized I was lost. Attempting to retrace my steps, I found myself disoriented, unable to recognize my way back to the main dance floor. Amid my confusion, just as I was about to turn left, someone yanked me forcefully to the right. Before I could react, I was swiftly pushed into an empty alcove, my heart pounding with fear.

What the hell?

"Looking for me?"

I collided with Noah's body, his hands instinctively finding their place on my lower back as mine rested against his chest. We were in a tiny alcove, with a couple of designer armchairs at the end but nothing else.

"I was looking for Maggie but haven't found her." I swallowed.

"Well, I'm glad I found you first."

"I need to go find her. She must be worried about me."

"She's fine. Last time I checked, she was talking to a guy in the VIP section next to ours."

I let out a sigh of relief.

"Want me to tell you a little secret?" His left hand traveled up, fisting my hair, his fingers intertwined with my low bun, gently yanking my head back until a small cry came out from my throat. "I've been wondering since I met you how you taste," Noah said, his mouth only a few inches from mine. His tongue licked my lower and upper lip in one smooth movement, and I slightly opened my mouth for him, an invitation for what I'd been craving since we were on the dance floor. Noah laughed softly, and when I fisted my hands on his shirt, he surged forward and kissed me with a force that knocked me back a few steps until my back hit the stone wall. His kiss was desperate and full of passion. Noah claimed my mouth like he couldn't get enough of me. My hands roamed over his muscled chest, desperate for his touch. He held me still with his left hand, keeping a stronghold of my hair, and his right hand cupped my breast. The moment the tip of his thumb circled my peaked nipple, I let out a soft moan into his mouth, which was his undoing. Noah yanked the thin strap of my dress down my arm, his head dipping and his mouth wrapping around my bare breast, licking, sucking, his teeth grazing and biting. I arched my back, my head tilting backward as waves of pleasure electrified every corner of my body. I needed him, all of him.

"Noah, please. You're killing me."

"I still haven't tasted you enough," he said in a guttural voice that sent shivers all over my skin as he pulled away and knelt before me. I couldn't stop watching how his hands traveled up between my thighs until they were lost underneath my dress. "You're so wet, Sienna," he breathed as his fingers grazed the material of my underwear. "I like that you're so wet for me."

I was panting, my head cloudy. I wanted him inside me, to feel every inch of him. But Noah had other plans. He lifted my dress with one hand and pulled aside my underwear with the other. My blood sang with anticipation. Before I could beg him to fuck me, his mouth was all over my pussy. He licked my entrance, circling his tongue around the apex of my thighs and teasing me with slow and long strokes. My moans filled the cave. Part of me was completely aware that anyone could enter and discover us. It'd only take someone wandering around to find this room. But I didn't want him to stop. The gentle strokes of his tongue became more demanding, devouring every inch of me. I could feel myself getting closer to the edge.

"Oh my God, Noah," I said between breaths. One hand clasped firmly onto his shoulder while the fingers of my other hand clenched tightly around his silken hair. "Please, I need you inside me," I begged.

"I'm not done with you yet, princess." He chuckled.

I could feel the orgasm building up as he continued to lick my wetness, feasting on me with his tongue, his teeth, and his lips. When I thought it couldn't get any better, he slid two fingers inside me, pumping them in and out while he continued stroking my clit with his tongue. My legs were about to give out when I reached my climax, my screams echoing through the alcove and my pussy clenching around Noah's fingers. He didn't stop until my orgasm faded away, and I felt my body was going to collapse, my legs still shaking.

He stood in front of me, and holding my gaze, he licked both fingers.

"Fuck Sienna. You taste so good," he said. "I still want to fuck you, but I want to take my time. Stay with me tonight. After all, it's my birthday."

"What if I say no...maybe I just got everything I wanted from you," I teased, stroking my index finger up and down his chest.

"Princess...this was just the appetizer. I told you before. I want you to scream my name every time you come, and I plan on doing that the entire night." He stepped closer, pinning me against the wall, and his hardness pressed against my thigh. "But if you don't want to come to my place...I guess I'll just fuck you here."

I giggled. "Okay. If you insist…I'll stay with you tonight," I agreed, biting my lip.

He pressed a soft kiss on my lips.

"Good girl."

*   *   *

When we arrived at the main cave, I saw Maggie stampeding across the dance floor like a woman on a mission.

"Where the fuck have you been? I've been worried sick about you. I thought you'd been kidnapped or something." Her eyes dropped to our hands, and the realization of where I had been hit her.

"I see…" she said, cracking a smile. "Well, let's go get some champagne. I want to introduce you to someone," she said, pointing at the VIP section.

When I looked up, I quickly recognized Ander leaning forward with his forearms resting on the glass structure and his right hand holding a glass of what looked like champagne. His eyes were fixed on me, a sneer on his face. I knew I was going to see him today—he was Noah's friend, after all—but a part of me thought that maybe he'd warmed up to the idea of seeing me around. Apparently not. I had a knot in my stomach, considering I was about to face him, and the last thing I wanted was for him to fuck with my head again.

We headed toward the VIP area, and when we reached the last step of the stairs, Ander was already waiting for us. Noah kept holding my hand the whole time.

"The man of the hour. Where have you been? Everyone was looking for you," Ander said to Noah, squeezing his shoulder twice with his hand.

"Sorry, I got distracted." Noah flashed a flirtatious smile. "Ander, you already know Sienna, but I don't know if you remember Maggie,

Sienna's friend."

"Nice to meet you again, Maggie."

"I wished I could say the same," Maggie blurted.

"Maggie!" I yelled at her. I was beginning to realize Maggie had some balls, but at this very moment, I just wanted the earth to swallow me.

"Sorry, Ander. She didn't mean to say that. Right, Maggie?" If looks could kill, Maggie would already be dead. I knew she was trying to protect me, but I didn't need anyone to fight my battles.

"I take no offense, Maggie, but since you're Sienna's guard dog, here's a piece of advice. Don't get too attached; she'll dump you at the first opportunity. And the same goes for you, Noah. You can enjoy that little pussy of hers as much as you want, but when she gets tired of you, she'll move on and leave you behind."

SMACK

I slapped Ander across the face. How could someone who had been such an important part of my childhood disrespect me like that? Ander's words hit me like a train out of control. Stabbing me in the heart would have hurt less. Fuck him.

Noah stepped in front of me, facing Ander, and slightly pushed him on the chest with one hand. "What is your fucking problem?"

Suddenly, another guy walked up between them, placing a hand on their chests. "Hey, what the fuck, guys!? I leave you alone for one hour, and you start fighting each other. Did I miss something?"

"Ander thought it was okay to disrespect *my girl* to my fucking face," Noah replied.

The guy turned his face toward where I stood, just behind Noah, and when I saw him, I choked. My soul left my body, and I couldn't move.

Zayn.

How is this possible?

When he recognized me, a line appeared between his brows. "What are you doing here?" His hands dropped to the sides of his body.

"Do you know her?" Noah questioned, utterly shocked.

"We met roughly a month ago in a bar in Tribeca," I responded.

"Of course he knows her," Ander huffed, rolling his eyes. "She is THE girl he fucked in the restroom."

My face turned red with embarrassment.

"Fuck you, Ander," Zayn snapped.

"Well, I guess you got a secondhand present for your birthday."

Oh God.

In the blink of an eye, Noah reared back his arm and delivered a solid punch straight to Ander's face, catching him off guard. Ander stumbled backward and ended up sprawled on the floor. Ander's hand shot up to his nose, his fingers probing cautiously as he winced. He pulled them away, half expecting to see blood.

"What the fuck, Noah? It was a joke."

Zayn immediately held Noah back, who didn't want to stop the fight. But as I said, I didn't like anyone fighting my battles. I walked over to where Ander stood, brushing his pants off.

"Listen to me, you fucking piece of shit. I don't know what your fucking problem is, but I'm sick of your insults. Yes, we were friends long ago, but you're a completely different person from the Ander I loved. Stay away from me and leave me the fuck alone!" I screamed, pointing a finger at him.

As soon as I said those words, I turned around and ran toward the exit. I couldn't stay there any longer, and tears started streaming down my cheeks the moment I reached the VIP stairs. I only wanted to get home, curl in my bed, and cry my eyes out. I hated crying in public, but Ander's words got under my skin. No one had ever made me feel so dirty.

Before I could get to the reception, Noah sprinted past me and stopped in front of me.

"Hey, are you OK?"

"I'm fine," I replied, my gaze fixed on the floor.

Noah gently lifted my chin, urging me to meet his gaze.

"Look at me, gorgeous," he said. "He's not worth your tears."

My lips trembled, tears flowing from my eyes. Noah grabbed me and pulled me close to his chest, and I just fell apart. He didn't say anything. He just held me tight, stroking my hair gently with one hand while he wrapped the other around me.

"I'm making a mess of your shirt with my makeup and my stupid tears," I murmured between sobs.

"I don't care about my shirt. I care about you. Ander obviously resents you for something from your past, but that doesn't excuse his behavior."

"I'm sorry I ruined your birthday," I sobbed.

He held my face with both hands and planted a sweet kiss on my lips.

"Sorry? You're the highlight of my birthday, and Ander doesn't have that much power over me to ruin my evening.

"Let's grab your stuff and go to my apartment. You can text Maggie from the Uber; she's fine. I left her shouting at Ander."

"Are you sure you don't want to stay? It's your birthday, and people have come to see you."

"I don't know, Sienna…between waking up next to you in the morning and hearing you scream my name for the next twenty-four hours or going back to the party…I don't think anyone in their right mind would choose option B."

I cracked a smile.

Once we grabbed my purse, Noah's wallet, and our mobile phones from the lockers, we exited the club and called an Uber. I pulled out my phone from my bag and texted Maggie as we entered the car.

Me

> Hey, I'm okay. I'm leaving with Noah. I'm sorry for ditching you like this because of Ander. Again. I'll make it up to you. I promise.

"So you're the Tribeca girl..."

"I wondered when you would bring that up," I replied. "How is it even possible? Sometimes I think the universe saw that I had an easy life and said, 'Hold my beer,'" I finished with a chuckle.

"Can I be honest with you?" Noah asked.

"Always."

"I was already a little worried about you sharing a past with Ander, but now...knowing what happened between you and Zayn...I don't know, Sienna. I'm not good at this."

"At what?" I asked.

"At complications," he responded cryptically.

"Am I a complication?"

Noah shifted in his seat, turning to face me. He reached out and cupped my cheek, gently stroking it with his thumb.

"You are the most stunning, smartest, and sexiest complication I've ever met in my life. Maybe I should stay away from you..." he whispered. "But I can't."

Noah's hard but slow kiss was something out of a romance book. It was both sweet and passionate, causing my heart to skip a beat every time he slid his tongue into my mouth and moaned.

After a ten-minute drive, during which we spent most of the time making out, we arrived at his place. He lived off campus, and the beautiful high-rise exuded money. The property had a brick facade with limestone trim and a doorman who kindly opened the door as we walked into the lobby. Noah lived on the highest floor, of course, and although the decoration was relatively modern and sexy, it still felt cozy and warm. Just like him.

Noah didn't release my hand until we reached his bedroom. His room was dark and masculine, with gray concrete walls and a bed so large it could have quickly passed for a regulation-size basketball court. To the right was an en suite bathroom with a modern bathtub, a stunning all-glass walk-in shower, and floor-to-ceiling marble walls.

"Go ahead and take a shower while I search for some clothes for you. I'll have the staff clean your dress and underwear, so they'll be ready by the time you're allowed to leave my bed."

I wrapped my arms around his waist and tilted my head back to look into his eyes. "Is that so? Do I need your permission now?" I cracked a half smile.

Noah grazed my cheek with his thumb. I was positive I looked like shit, but the way he looked at me made me feel like I was the most beautiful girl in the world.

"By the time I'm done with you, you won't have the strength to leave my bed." He kissed my forehead and left in search of something comfortable for me to wear.

Before I took my clothes off, I checked myself in the mirror. My eyes and cheeks were smeared with black eye shadow, my hair fashioning a different concept of a messy bun, and my lips were swollen, probably from all the kissing and crying. I took my heels off, then my silk dress and underwear, and placed them on an olive-green velvet Carnaby footstool.

I entered the shower and let the hot water run all over my body, hair, and face. Five minutes later, every muscle in my body finally relaxed.

I had become a ball of tension since we returned from the alcove and saw Ander. *Fucking Ander.* He wasn't worth another moment of my time wondering what went wrong and when.

I was facing the shower wall, running my fingers through my hair, when Noah's strong hands tightened on my hips, pulling me closer to him. He pressed his hard cock against my ass and his lips on my neck. As I tilted my head to the side, offering him better access, he kissed and nibbled my skin, covering my entire body in goose bumps. He turned me around to face him and kissed me, sweet but deep, his tongue stroking mine as he grabbed my ass with both hands and lifted me.

"I need you in my bed now."

With one arm holding me and my legs wrapped around his waist, he picked up a towel and carried me to his bed. Noah lowered me to the floor and proceeded to dry us off with the towel, his gaze lingering on my body as I stood in front of him. I swallowed hard when I saw the size of his length. With chiseled abs, well-defined arms and chest, and smooth skin, Noah's body looked like the gods themselves had sculpted it.

"I owe you a birthday present," I said, breaking the silence.

"I don't need or want any presents. You in my bed tonight is the only thing I want."

"That's a shame. I was going to return the favor," I said suggestively.

His eyes widened as he took in my words.

With one gentle push from my hand, Noah dropped and sat on the mattress, and I came down on my knees between his legs. His nostrils flared as I fisted his cock with my right hand, gently stroking him as he watched me play with him.

"Fuck, Sienna, you're so beautiful."

I leaned in and licked the tip of his cock without breaking eye contact.

"Fuck," he murmured on an exhale.

I ran my tongue along the side of his length, from the base to the top, before I parted my lips and swallowed him whole. I continued licking and sucking while I moved my hand up and down, making sure I applied enough pressure until his cock throbbed with pleasure. Gripping my wet hair tightly, Noah increased the pace, pushing and pulling my head up and down as I took him deeper. He pushed me farther down until he was buried to the hilt, and tears coated my eyes.

"You're being such a good girl for me."

I almost couldn't breathe, but every second was worth it, especially when he praised me.

"Stop. If you keep sucking like that, I'm gonna end up coming down your throat, and I really need to feel your pussy around my cock tonight."

I stood, and he shifted, snatching the navy trousers lying on the floor. He took a condom out of his wallet. After he finished putting it on, he seized the back of my thighs and drew me closer to him, positioning me with both knees on either side of his legs, effectively straddling him. Noah grabbed my wet hair with both hands and kissed me, his tongue clashing with mine. I moved my hand between our bodies and placed the tip of his cock at my entrance, and slowly, very slowly, I started moving my hips up and down until every inch of him was inside me, and a heavy moan erupted from Noah's throat.

"Holy shit. You're so tight, Sienna."

I rolled my hips back and forth in a steady rhythm. Noah grazed one of my nipples with his teeth while his other hand played with my other breast. My clit throbbed with every flick of his tongue.

"I hope you're ready because I'm gonna fuck this pussy until you can't take it anymore."

Noah stood while lifting me in his strong arms and gently placed me atop the mattress. All while still buried inside me. With both hands on either side of my head, he slammed into me forcefully, causing the headboard to hit the wall. He pulled back once more, then thrust into me again, my nails digging into his back.

"Yes. That's it. Just like that," I encouraged him.

"Sienna, eyes on me, princess," Noah said, his mouth drinking each of my moans.

I was so lost in the moment that I didn't realize my eyes were closed. I opened them and stared into his eyes.

My God. He was so beautiful.

"So the princess likes it rough. Do you like it when I fuck you like my little slut? Look at you, taking my cock so well."

His dirty words drove me into a frenzied state. My feminism was going out the window with every word he said, but I didn't care. I loved the way he called me "his little slut." I'd gladly take those words and shove them down my throat alongside his cock.

"Yes. Fuck me, Noah. Keep going," I moaned.

He thrust into me relentlessly, causing the headboard to hit the wall every single time.

"I've imagined fucking you in every position since I saw you at that bookstore," Noah confessed. "Turn around. On your fours."

I shifted my position, placing my hands in front of me and bringing my knees together on the bed.

"One day, I'm gonna claim this ass," he promised, circling my butthole with his thumb. "But today, let me take care of your pussy." Noah gripped my hips, and in one swift movement, he was fully inside me once more.

"Yes, yes! Just like that," I screamed as he thrust into me with such force that I had to steady myself by placing a hand on the headboard.

"Touch yourself. I want to see how you make yourself come," he demanded.

I started circling my clit while he continued fucking me so hard that my vision blurred. My stomach tightened, and I couldn't control the building orgasm.

"Oh my God, Noah. I can't…" My body exploded while the burst of pleasure kept intensifying and coming back in multiple waves. Noah followed me seconds after with a roar that sent shivers across my skin. It took me some time to realize what the fuck just happened. I'd never had multiple orgasms, but *holy shit*…this was good—more than good.

"I love how you scream my name," he whispered in my ear.

Noah pulled out, and I turned over, lying on my back.

"That was incredible," I confessed, pushing my wet hair away from my face.

Noah placed himself on top of me, between my legs, and started caressing my face with his fingers and gently kissing my cheeks, the corners of my mouth, and my jawline. He was gentle and sweet. Very different from the man who was literally fucking me like a beast a minute ago. Noah was a complex guy with different masks, and I kind of liked that about him. It was as if he had these contrasting personalities—the golden boy and the bad boy—sometimes gentle, other times untamed. With Miles, everything was so boring and dull: always had the same plans, the same conversations, and the same boring sex. The chase and the thrill were fun in the beginning, but after a few months, I stopped feeling wanted. And we were seventeen! At seventeen, all he should have wanted was to rip my clothes off, like any horny teenager. His indifference sometimes made me wonder if I was the problem, that maybe I wasn't sexy or exciting enough. When I broke up with him, I felt liberated. The moment I started getting more comfortable in my own skin, I started sleeping around and indulging in casual sex. That was when I realized I was not the problem. Miles probably didn't like me that much.

It was different with Noah. He took what he wanted and was very clear from the beginning that he wanted me.

Miles - 0

Noah - 1

What the hell, I'll give Noah a 10…he just made me come multiple times.

* * *

Just like he promised, we didn't get enough sleep last night.

Noah walked me to my apartment and kissed me goodbye. He promised to call me this week to take me on a proper date.

As soon as I entered my apartment, I went to my room to change into my favorite sweatpants and a T-shirt that said, "I don't have a resting bitch face. I'm only a bitch that needs resting." Sarah bought me this T-shirt in London. Her parents had invited me to spend a few days at their house in Marylebone, and we had the best time. I'd been to London before, but it was the first time I wasn't there with my parents, so we did all the things girls at the age of fifteen would do: shopping in Bond Street, going to the cinema, eating burgers at Five Guys and wandering around Shoreditch, Camden, and other cool neighborhoods.

I texted Maggie to let her know I was home.

Me

Hey. I just got home. I'm fine :) I'll tell you everything tomorrow. How was your night? xxx

Maggie

Morning, gorgeous. I was worried about you. Glad to hear you're okay.

Ander is a dick, BTW. Coffee tomorrow?
I need a debrief about your night *wink
emoji*

Me

Instead of coffee, would you like to have
lunch with me at Gino's? I only have one
class, so I'm free anytime after 1 p.m.

Maggie

I don't know…I need to be careful with
my budget. My scholarship covers my
groceries and some personal expenses…
Maybe another time?

Me

Don't worry about that. I'll pay. It's a good
deal. You listen to my bullshit for 2 hours,
and I feed you good food.

Maggie

You're the sweetest, Sienna, but I don't
want to become a burden.

Me

Look. I have money, but I like to spend
it making people happy. That makes me
happy. And I like you. You're now my
friend, so let me spoil you.

Maggie

You're the best. See you at Gino's at 1:15
p.m.

Me

Cool. I'll reserve us a table. See you
tomorrow!

Meeting Maggie had been one of the highlights of the month. She was funny, intelligent, bold, and fucking resilient. I wondered how her life during those years in foster care had been. Was she happy? She definitely broke the statistics because I was sure not many kids with that background would be able to rise and achieve what she had accomplished so far. Stanford University might not be an Ivy League college, but it is one of the most prestigious schools in the country, so receiving a scholarship was a strong achievement.

I opened my Instagram account. Noah had sent me a request to connect. His profile was open with over six hundred photos and reels—he definitely was a social butterfly and loved the attention. I scrolled down through his feed because this might not be the real Noah, but it was the Noah he wanted to portray in front of the world, which can also say a lot about a person. There were plenty of pictures of nights out, snowboarding, and surfing. None of the photographs were curated, so I guessed he liked to be seen as a fun person who was wild and carefree. My eyes stopped, and I clicked on one specific post. He was laughing with Ander, and Zayn looked intensely at the camera. The three of them were sitting on a sandy beach, Ander and Noah with their knees bent to their chest and Zayn lying back on his elbows. I couldn't believe they were friends, a twisted coincidence.

She is THE girl he fucked in the restroom.

That was what Ander had said. I wondered how much Zayn had told them about me. It was all a fucking mess. I had kissed and or fucked the three of them. Great stuff, Sienna.

I closed the app, and there it was on my home screen: a picture of me with my parents from last Christmas staring back at me. My stomach sank, a dreadful feeling rising in my chest—shame on me. Here I was, going out, laughing, being happy, meeting guys at bars, and enjoying life. I shouldn't feel like that, right? Was I a horrible person? After all, my parents had just died a couple of months ago.

The guilt overtook every fiber of my body, and I started crying. The guilt of being happy without them because happiness shouldn't be part of the equation. I'd lost the two people I loved the most, my only family, and I should have felt broken. I didn't deserve to feel like I did when I woke up in Noah's arms. And I cried and cried, holding a pillow, sinking my face in it. I was a horrible person, a selfish bitch.

Perhaps it would be wise to take a break from seeing Noah for a while and redirect my focus toward my studies. I was sure my parents would want me happy, but it felt like I was moving on too quickly. The weight of guilt pressed heavily upon me, filling me with self-loathing. Right now, I was simply too exhausted to contemplate what lay ahead. With a heavy sigh, I closed my eyes, allowing the guilt to consume me as sleep claimed me. That night, my dreams were haunted by memories of my parents, and upon awakening the following day, the guilt still lingered, refusing to release its grip.

STAY THE FUCK AWAY

(Noah)

I was standing outside Aster Hall.

Sienna hadn't replied to any of my texts all week, and I was beginning to feel anxious. Despite having only met a few times before spending the night at my apartment, I felt strangely comfortable around her. She was constantly on my mind, but I knew I needed to give her space. Perhaps she was feeling guilty about our hookup and was having second thoughts.

I'd been playing our night together over and over again. She felt amazing. My cock twitched inside my jeans just thinking about her smell, her mouth, her pussy, and her soft skin. I needed to see her again. I needed her in my bed again. Soon.

Zayn hadn't brought her up in our conversations, but I knew we needed to discuss the fact that Sienna was the *Tribeca girl* at some point. I didn't know how he felt about her now that he knew she was at Stanford, but I wanted to be very clear with him. Sienna was mine. It wasn't like we hadn't shared girls before, sometimes even at the same time, but with Sienna, it felt different. I only wanted her for myself and wasn't open to sharing her with Zayn.

He better stay the fuck away.

I would talk to him, but I just needed to find a moment when Ander wasn't in the room. He behaved like a complete asshole on my birthday, and I wasn't willing to put up with his shit anymore. I'd been ignoring his calls all week. Ander was probably calling me to apologize, but he was never genuinely sorry when he fucked up, so his apologies were usually wrapped up around two tickets to the Los Angeles Lakers. He said he didn't care if I fucked Sienna, but he did because no one who didn't give a shit would react the way he did when he saw us together. I wondered what happened between them...I didn't want to poke the bear, but I might ask Sienna.

Aster Hall's main door opened, and Sienna walked out the door.

"Hello, princess. I feel a bit hurt. You've been ignoring me all week," I said, crossing my arms over my chest.

"Hi, Noah. I'm sorry. I swear I haven't been ignoring you. It's just..."

"Try again. You're a terrible liar."

She sighed.

"Look. I know I owe you an explanation, but can we please not do this here?"

"Have dinner with me tonight."

"Are you asking me on a date? I don't know, Noah..."

"It wasn't a question. What time do you want me to pick you up?"

Sienna paused for a moment before replying, "Okay. Pick me up at seven o'clock. But you better take me somewhere with amazing food, or you'll regret it."

"Anything for you," I told her, kissing her cheek. I wanted to kiss her lips, but I didn't know where she stood about me, about us. I'd find out tonight.

"I know the perfect place. Nothing fancy, so no need to dress up. I hope you like Mexican food."

Her face lit up with a wide smile. "Yes, I do."

* * *

Zayn and I were seated in the main cafeteria when Ander approached us carrying a tray filled with food. While discussing the imminent start date of the NHL season, we tactfully avoided addressing the elephant in the room. Apparently, not for too long.

"Why have you been avoiding my calls? I've been calling you nonstop," Ander exclaimed as he sat in front of us.

"Take a guess." If he was going to play the stupid card with me, he should have picked another day. I wasn't willing to tolerate any more of his bullshit today.

"Look, I'm sorry. I don't know what came over me."

Zayn sniggered.

"If you want to get something off your chest, go ahead and say it," Ander said.

With a raised eyebrow, Zayn bit into his pizza and remarked, "I don't think it's Noah to whom you owe an apology."

"You fuck the girl once, and now you are her knight in shining armor, or what?" Ander blurted.

I placed my sandwich back on the plate and stared at him.

"Why are you such an asshole? If I didn't know any better, I'd think you're jealous…"

Ander grinned tightly, clenching his jaw.

"Did she do something to you?" Zayn asked.

Ander stayed silent, looking down at his tray and moving the food around with the fork.

"Alright, if you're not up for sharing what happened, that's on you. But she's with me now, and Zayn, the same rule applies to you. Stay the fuck away," I stated.

Zayn flashed me a sly smile.

I knew he always loved a challenge, and dread filled my stomach for some reason. I knew that he had become fixated on the girl he met in New York the moment he couldn't stop talking about her. He went on and on for days. But he was my friend, right? He wouldn't go after her, would he?

I stood, lifting my bag from the floor.

"I mean it, Zayn. Forget about her. She's mine."

THE BREAK-IN

(Sienna)

As Reed dismissed the class, I began to gather my belongings. Maggie had left in a rush, already being late for her next class. Just as I was about to exit the classroom, Reed's voice called out, catching my attention.

"Miss Moore. Can you stay for a minute? I'd like to have a word with you."

"Sure," I responded.

He knew my name. Was that a good or a bad thing?

"I was quite impressed with your answers to my assignment."

"Good impressed or bad impressed?" I asked.

"Actually, in a good way. I've reviewed eighty percent of all assignments, and yours is the best so far."

Despite being used to receiving compliments about my grades, I blushed. I had a GPA of 3.8, but it felt terrific coming from someone with his reputation. He was apparently a genius, having worked in the pharmaceutical industry since he was twenty-four and becoming the youngest lecturer ever at Columbia University at twenty-nine. It didn't help the fact that he was hot.

"I'm looking for a couple of students who want to join my research team and earn extra credits. I thought it might interest you."

"Why me? I'm just a freshman."

He reclined his chair and put both hands behind his head, looking relaxed and casual.

"I saw an article about you the other day. I didn't realize you were *that* Sienna Moore, so I thought my offer might interest you. Are you going to pursue a career at Cos Pharmaceuticals?"

"Well…yes. But I'm not sure clinical research is what I want. I've entertained the idea before, but things are now different."

"You don't need to decide anything today. Just think about my offer and let me know before the end of next week. You can give it a try to see if this is a path you'd like to pursue. You won't know unless you try."

Reed was right. I still didn't know if I wanted to major in business or be more involved in the research side of things, so I guessed his offer could be an excellent opportunity to find out.

"Okay, I'll think about it. Thanks for thinking of me. It's an amazing opportunity. So really, thank you," I said with a smile.

"Come to my office when you have an answer. I do hope you say yes."

I walked to my apartment thinking about Reed's offer and his reference to "*that Sienna Moore.*" Did he know my father? I assumed that if he moved in the same circles, there was a chance he had already met my father. The industry may seem like a big ocean full of fish, but in reality, it was more like a pond.

I put my key in and turned it, but the door was strangely opened. *What the fuck.* I was pretty sure I locked the door when I left this morning.

I shut the door behind me and looked around the living room.

"Hello?"

No answer.

I walked around the living room and the kitchen, but everything looked normal, and nothing was out of place. But when I reached my bedroom, the realization that someone had been in my room hit me. A black dahlia was on top of my bed with a small note beside it. I started to panic, looking around because someone could still be inside my apartment. I ran to the kitchen, grabbed a knife from the block on the counter, and scrolled through my recent calls. I pressed on the first familiar name that showed up on the screen. Maggie. One ring, two rings, three rings…she wasn't fucking answering the phone. Maybe she was still in class, and her phone was on silent inside her purse. I was hyperventilating. Perhaps I should call the cops. Maybe it was Noah. Could it be Noah? I returned to my bedroom and checked the bathroom first, just in case. I picked up the note.

You can't escape fate.

Fucking Noah.

The card was not signed, but I was pretty sure this was his doing. Noah must have paid someone at the reception to give him access to my room so he could leave the black dahlia and the note. Although I'd always felt comfortable around him, Noah had clearly shown a lack of boundaries so far: at the library, The Cave, and waiting for me outside Aster Hall once he felt ignored. He had a gentle and caring side but could also be quite possessive. While I enjoyed being dominated and controlled in the bedroom, I wasn't keen on being told what to do outside of it. I needed to have a word with him. I almost had a heart attack. Shit, I might still be having one. My heart was pumping a thousand beats an hour.

Half an hour later, Maggie called me.

"Hey, sorry. I didn't see your call. All good?" she asked.

"Not fucking close."

"What's wrong?"

"I think Noah broke into my apartment and left me a black dahlia with a note. I almost shat my pants."

"Do you want me to come over? You sound like you're panicking."

"No. I'm okay, just fucking furious. I'm having dinner with him tonight, so I'll tell him that it might have looked romantic in his head, but he scared the shit out of me. Not cool."

"Okay. Let me know if you want me to come over later tonight. I could stay with you if you don't want to be alone in your apartment. And ask security to change your lock."

"Yes, I will. Thanks, Maggie. Talk later."

* * *

Noah picked me up in his car at seven o'clock. He owned a convertible Mercedes-Benz SL in dark gray with black leather seats. It was a beautiful car and very comfy. "Lo Vas A Olvidar" by Billie Eilish and Rosalía played in the background.

"I love this song. I'm a big Rosalía fan, and I love Billie Eilish," I said, putting my seat belt on. "She makes me feel things that no other artist can."

"I guess we have that in common. I love Billie Eilish too. "When the party's over" is one of my favorite songs. Are you hungry?"

"Yes. I'm starving. How was your day?"

"Average. But now that you are here with me, my day's starting to look better." Noah placed a hand over my left thigh and squeezed. "How was yours? Did you have many classes today?"

"I did. My Biochemistry & Molecular Biology professor asked me to join his research team, but I'm still thinking about it," I told Noah.

"Why?"

"Because I'm not sure if I want to do that. Everyone keeps telling me that the first year at college is the most important. I don't want to commit to it and have it take away time to focus on my studies."

We continued chatting about college until Noah stopped the car near Stanford EVGR Pod at Off the Grid market. Food trucks were located around the open area: Thai food, Spanish tapas, Burgers, and a Mexican truck. I used to love street food in Manhattan, so I was glad he brought me here. Once we sat on a small picnic bench, Noah pointed out a few starters and mains from the menu that he'd tried before and recommended. While I decided what I wanted, he ordered our drinks—one classic margarita and a michelada.

"What's that? I always order margaritas, but that looks amazing. Does it taste like a Bloody Mary? It looks like it."

"Do you wanna try it?" he asked. Before I was able to reply, he leaned forward and kissed me. His kiss tasted like a mix of beer, something spicy, probably tabasco or chili, and something citrusy.

"Mmm. I like how you taste."

"I like how you taste, too," he replied, giving me a quick peck on the lips and a wink.

We ordered some chilaquiles, birria and cochinita pibil tacos, and some chicken quesadillas. The food was delicious. I hadn't been to Mexico yet, but after dinner, I might start planning a trip with Sarah. Maybe I could invite Maggie too if she didn't mind me paying for the trip.

I wanted to get to know Noah better, so I asked him a lot of questions, including what his parents did for a living.

"My dad's name is Hiroshi. He's the president of one of the world's largest telecom companies, and my mom, Martha, is a United States senator for Massachusetts and a member of the Democratic Party. Maybe you know her. Does the name Martha Robinson ring any bells?"

"Not really. I've been out of the country too long, but I can name you most royal families in Europe!" I replied. "Robinson? Didn't she switch her last name to Nakamura after getting married?"

"She kept her maiden name since she already had a career when she met my dad. She always says she didn't want to lose her sense of identity," Noah said.

"Your mom sounds pretty awesome," I responded, nodding in agreement.

"Yes, she's pretty cool. I hope I'm not making you feel weird by talking about my folks. I can imagine it might be tough to talk about yours, but I'd love to hear more about your fam."

It was very sweet of him to consider how the conversation might affect me.

"I'm good. Okay, where do I start?

"I had a nice childhood. My parents always spoiled me, and everything was great as far as I can remember. Life at boarding school was rough at first, but then I met Sarah. She's from England, and we clicked right away. Many things changed when I moved to Europe, especially my relationship with my parents. I'd only see them a couple of times a year, and most of the time, when I video-called my mom, my dad would disappear after a few minutes. The conversations were the basic how's school and when are you coming home?"

"Why the sudden change?" Noah asked.

"Not a clue. But I struggled a lot. I always enjoyed stirring up trouble...Sarah used to say I did it to get attention from the wrong crowd. Maybe she was right."

Noah and I continued chatting for an hour about our childhoods and life at boarding school when he steered the conversation to my relationship with Ander.

"How long have you known Ander?" he asked.

"Since we were babies. Our parents founded Cos Pharmaceuticals from scratch. But they weren't just partners; they were best friends. Something happened between them six years ago because William left the company, and my father bought his shares. My dad never told me what happened but forbade me from seeing Ander. We used to spend weekends and holidays together, but when my parents sent me to Switzerland, we lost contact."

"Why does he hate you so much?" he probed.

"Honestly? I don't know. You'll have to ask Ander."

"Well...he definitely crossed the line the other night. We briefly talked about what went down at my birthday party this morning, but he kept dodging the issue about why he's acting like a jerk."

"Now that you talk about crossing lines...Look. Maybe you thought it was a romantic gesture, but it wasn't. So maybe we need to set some boundaries. If you want to buy me flowers, just do what every other guy does and get them delivered to my dorm. But please, don't break in again because it almost gave me a heart attack. That shit is only romantic in books and movies."

His brows drew together, his jaw tightened, and his mouth set in a hard line.

"What are you talking about?" he replied.

"You know, the black dahlia and the note you left on my bed," I explained.

"That wasn't me. I've never been inside your apartment. I don't even know what a black dahlia looks like."

A wave of terror overtook my body. If Noah didn't break into my apartment...*who the hell did?* I was so sure it was him that I never called security. I couldn't stop shaking. Someone touched my bed sheets, my things. Maybe they went through my drawers and touched my underwear.

Oh God.

Shaking my head, I exclaimed, "Noah, I'm dead serious. Promise me it wasn't you."

"I swear to God, Sienna, I don't know what the fuck you're talking about," he insisted.

"Someone was in my apartment today. When I got there, my door was unlocked. Shit, shit, shit." A tingling sensation began in my shaking hands, followed by palpitations.

Sensing my unease, Noah stood, held out his hand, and said, "Okay. Let's go. We'll call security on our way to campus and get an emergency locksmith to change your door lock. I'll stay over tonight."

* * *

"I don't want you to leave." Ander looked frustrated.

"I don't want to either, but my father won't change his mind. He says I should stay away from you and your family."

Ander and I had secretly met at Jay Estate Gardens. I was leaving in three days, and every time I had asked my father to drive me to the Scotts' house to say goodbye to Ander, he refused.

He looked sad, but so did I. I didn't want to move to Switzerland.

"This sucks."

"Are you going to miss me?" I asked.

I wasn't sure if he would miss me, but I was certain I would. He'd been a constant in my life since we were babies, and although we didn't go to the same school, I saw him almost every week.

"You'll probably forget about me. You'll make new friends, and you won't remember me."

"How can you say that? You know how important you are to me," I responded.

My feelings for Ander were strong, but they'd morphed from an innocent friendship into something different. His jokes were now more flirtatious, and I'd noticed how he looked at me when we were alone. How he was looking at me now.

"You're important to me too, Sienna. I… I…"

"You what?"

"I'll write to you. I promise."

"I'd love that."

The sun was setting, and I knew our goodbye was approaching.

Ander approached where I sat and held my hand with his, my cheeks turning pink.

"Ander…"

"Yeah?" He turned his face to look at me. Time stood still. He made me feel things. Things I didn't want to say to him because I didn't want to feel rejected. He was already popular with the girls in Rye, and I was just the twelve-year-old girl who once puked on his lap when he dared me to ride the roller coaster with him at a birthday party after eating a double cheeseburger and french fries. I didn't know at what point he became more than a friend to me, but I wasn't sure if he reciprocated my feelings.

He held my gaze for minutes, but I decided that if this was the last time I was going to see Ander, I would make it count. I closed the distance between us and kissed him. I wanted him to be my first kiss. To my surprise, he kissed me back.

We didn't discuss that kiss on the way to the bus stop or what it meant. I just made him promise me again that he would write to me.

"You've promised," I said as I stepped inside the bus. And the doors closed. That little girl didn't know it was the last time she would see Ander's smile.

I woke up drenched in sweat. It wasn't the first time this had occurred. I'd experienced it before—a memory disguised as a bad dream. A memory of something that happened six years ago. The day Ander promised to write to me. But he never did.

I opened my eyes and saw Noah lying next to me on his side, a hand over my waist. He was still sleeping with a peaceful expression on his face. I stared at him for minutes, memorizing every freckle, the curve of his lips, his perfect nose, and eyelashes. He stayed with me last night, and we talked until 3 a.m. Noah was witty and sweet. He thought the flower and the note could be part of a hazing prank, which apparently is very common at Stanford, and I thought he might be right, but it scared me nonetheless. I hated pranks.

I turned around to pick up my phone from my bedside table to order breakfast, but Noah tightened his hold on my waist and drew me closer.

"Good morning, little princess. Where do you think you're going?"

I giggled.

"I was going to order some breakfast, but we can go out if you prefer."

"Nah, I'd rather have you for myself a bit longer before we go to class." He was clearly a possessive guy, but I loved it. "You looked like you had a nightmare last night; you wouldn't stop moving your legs."

He'd noticed my distress.

"It wasn't a nightmare, more like a memory replaying," I clarified.

"What was it about?"

"It's quite personal, and I don't know you well enough to embarrass myself in front of you yet," I responded, forcing a smile.

"I don't care. You could wear the most ridiculous outfit or tell me the most absurd story, and I'd still think you are the most devastatingly beautiful and incredible girl on campus."

"Only on campus? Rude," I said mockingly.

We lingered in bed for another thirty minutes while waiting for Uber Eats to deliver our breakfast. We finished our almond croissants and coffee—an Americano for Noah and a pumpkin spice latte for me, of course—and headed out. He went to his side of campus, and I went to my Organic Chemistry I class. I slipped on my headphones and hit shuffle on my favorite playlist. "We Don't Talk Anymore" came on, and the lyrics hit too close to home.

✳   ✳   ✳

After carefully thinking and discussing it with Peter, I decided to take up Reed's offer. Peter was right. This was an excellent opportunity to find out if I actually enjoyed research and also a great line in my curriculum.

I knocked on Reed's door twice. Despite the office door being open, I didn't cross the threshold until his voice from inside invited me to enter.

"Good morning, Miss Moore. I assume you're here because you've reached a decision."

"Yes," I answered. "I've decided to accept your offer. It's a great opportunity, and I'm honored that you've invited me to be part of your research team."

"Great. You can meet the rest of the team this afternoon after your classes at 4 p.m. Ideally, I would like you to come every day for an hour, but I can be flexible if you have exams or other commitments. Just let me know in advance. I'll tell you more this afternoon. The lab is in this building, room L-56," he explained.

"I'll see you later, then."

Later that day, once all my classes were done, I headed toward the lab. I quickened my steps with anticipation, my heart pounding faster and faster with each stride.

One Christmas, my father bought me a microscope, some beakers, flasks, and a white lab coat. I loved playing the scientist with him. We would imagine that we were about to discover the cure for an extremely dangerous disease that was turning people into zombies. He would pretend to get infected and would chase me around the house, trying to bite me and infect me, too. Sometimes I played along and started chasing my mom around the kitchen. It was one of the best memories I had with him. He loved making me laugh, and as an only child, I really appreciated the time he gave me. My father was always extremely busy with work but always found time for me. Many of my friends at school had siblings, but I didn't. The closest thing I had to a brother was Ander.

I entered lab L-56, and Reed greeted me.

"Welcome, Miss Moore. Please grab a seat over there. Your lab partner will arrive any second. In the meantime, please read the notes I left beside the Bunsen burner. I'll walk by in a second to make sure you don't have any questions."

The notes included some background information on the project: cell and tissue engineering. Something about establishing new paradigms in stem cell aging and regulation; it sounded important. There were instructions on the different stages of the research, the materials we would need, and the scope of our research for this week and next.

"What are you doing here?" a familiar voice asked me.

Oh Lord.

I lifted my head, and there he was—Ander. Both hands were inside his jeans pockets, and his forehead was creased.

"Professor Reed has invited me to be part of his research team. And you?"

"You shouldn't be here. You're a freshman."

His arrogance had no limits.

"Mr. Scott. Welcome back. Let me introduce you to your new partner, Miss Sienna Moore."

"We already know each other," I said.

"Oh great, that's good. Have a seat."

Reed didn't know that pairing us together was a bad idea.
There was a high chance that Ander would sabotage my work to kick me out of the lab. That thought infuriated me because I knew that he was now capable of such things. The Ander from the past would have been thrilled to work with me.

We sat in silence for the entire hour, not a single word between us. When the hour passed, he grabbed his things and left the room. A few minutes later, I picked up my bag from the floor and left. I turned left at the end of the hallway and bumped into Ander. He was waiting for me.

"Listen to me. You're going to tell Reed that you have changed your mind, and you're gonna leave the research team," he ordered me.

"I will do no such thing." I snorted.

Ander approached me and cornered me against the wall. He was a good foot taller than me, with a broad back and muscled arms. His scent was making me lightheaded. He smelled of bergamot and pepper, earthy with mandarin notes. My heart started racing, but I wasn't sure whether it was because I was now scared of him and what he could do to me or because of his proximity, his chest almost touching mine.

"I'm warning you, Sienna. I'm not the same boy you met years ago. I won't hesitate to make your life a living hell."

"Are you threatening me?" I spoke, lifting my chin in defiance.

"I'm just giving you a warning. Take it as you wish," he said and walked away.

Ander clearly thought he could tell me what to do, but he was wrong. I'd never quit. If he thought for a second that I was scared of his threats, he was going to be shocked because I wouldn't allow him, or anyone else for that matter, to bully me into submission. I'd never been a pushover and wouldn't start now. I was genuinely excited about the opportunity Reed had given me.

I would make the best of the situation, even if it meant working alongside Ander.

DEVIL'S NIGHT

(Sienna)

The week flew by, and Ander continued to ignore me with each passing hour we spent together in the lab. Reed had noticed that we weren't working as a team, but he gave us some space, perhaps hoping that the situation would naturally improve over time. I didn't see it happening anytime soon. The tension between us was so thick you could practically cut it with a knife.

As soon as the hour ended, Ander took his things and left the lab without saying goodbye. Rude.

I grabbed my phone to text Maggie about our plans for tonight, but I noticed a message from Noah.

Noah
> Are you ready for tonight?

Me
> I still don't know what you'll be wearing.

Noah
> It's a surprise.

Me
> Okay…I'll see you later at the fair.

Noah

See you later, princess.

Today was Halloween, and Noah invited Maggie and me to join him and his friends at the Annual Devil's Night Fair on campus. Stanford's Social Events Committee organizes a horror festival every year, and this year, they set up a house of mirrors, a Ferris wheel, a fortune teller, and a haunted house. The pamphlet I took from the reception at Aster Hall showed that there were also several stands selling food and drinks.

I loved dressing up, so Halloween was the perfect distraction after an intense week of classes, homework, and the stress from working in the lab. Maggie opted for a Harley Quinn costume, while I dressed up as a fallen angel for the occasion. I wore black leather pants, a tight black crop top with long sleeves, Saint Laurent Jane over-the-knee black leather boots, and a pair of black feather wings. I styled my hair down in waves and complemented the final look with smoky black eyes and black lips.

Someone knocked at the door when I was about to leave my apartment. I didn't expect anyone because we had agreed to meet at the front of the fortune teller attraction. I swung my door open, and a delivery guy stood on the other side with a black dahlia and a note.

Shit.

"Miss Moore. Urgent delivery." He handed me both items and left.

As I looked at the dahlia and the note, my blood ran cold. The note said:

They won't be able to protect you. You can't run away from me.

Maybe it was me, but that note didn't feel like a hazing prank. It felt personal. Someone had been stalking me. I threw the flower and the note in the trash and left the apartment. On my way out, I spoke with security, who advised me to call the cops. I planned on calling them in the morning. Maybe if they talked to the flower company, they could trace who had delivered them. Perhaps it was Ander trying to scare me so that I would leave the research team. But on the other hand, it didn't make any sense. Why would he send a black dahlia with a note? The other one I found on my bed was placed there even before I accepted Reed's offer.

When I arrived at the Devil's Night Fair, I made my way to the fortune teller tent. Noah, Zayn, Ander, and Maggie were already there, plus some people I recognized from Noah's birthday party. Maggie looked amazing in her costume. Noah was dressed as a samurai, Zayn as a Viking, and Ander as the devil.

"It suits you," I said to Ander.

He snorted.

"You look hot, girl," Maggie exclaimed.

"Yes, you do," Noah said, kissing my cheek sweetly.

"I want to go inside the house of mirrors, but I'd like to visit the fortune teller first. Sienna, wanna come with me?" Maggie asked.

I had never been to a fortune teller before but always believed they were a scam. However, I let Maggie guide me inside the tent. She liked anything related to zodiac signs, numbers, and signs sent from the universe. I didn't believe in those things, but she quickly guessed I was an Aquarius when we met. Not sure if there was any truth to it, but I was kind of surprised.

The old lady welcomed us, inviting us to sit on chairs across a round table. A crystal ball was placed in the middle, and she held a deck of tarot cards between her hands. The whole setup made me laugh, but I went along just to please Maggie.

"Welcome, dears. Please have a seat, and let's begin. Who wants to go first?"

"I'll go first," Maggie responded excitedly.

The old lady shuffled the cards and asked Maggie to cut the deck. She picked three cards and placed them on top of the red velvet tablecloth, pointing at the first card.

"The Wheel of Fortune. Reversed. It means that what goes up must come down. Karma might come calling, my dear." She pulled a second card from the deck. "The Hanged Man. It would be best to put your plans on hold until you get a better perspective. Take it as a non-action period. It's wise and necessary for you to step back and look at the big picture." The last card was the Page of Wands. "I think the message is pretty clear, my child. You're heading down the wrong path. Karma always finds us, and if you don't put a stop to it, it will be over for you."

Maggie sat there in silence, absorbing everything the woman said to her. She looked pale as if she really understood what the fortune teller was saying.

Then it was my turn. She shuffled the cards, and I cut the deck, placing a few cards to my right. She then picked three cards, put them on the table, and turned the first one—Nine of Wands.

"Watch your back," the lady said. "There will be challenges thrown in your way."

The second card showed the Moon. The Moon foreshadowed a problematic, unclear path ahead.

"Things may not be what they seem. Therefore, you must proceed cautiously." A danger ahead, watching my back. How much did she get paid for all this bullshit?

And finally, the last card: the Two of Cups.

"Love is in the air. It looks like you'll meet someone soon who will turn your world upside down," she claimed.

"That's Noah for sure," Maggie interjected.

"Well. I think I've heard enough…thank you, but we need to leave." I grabbed Maggie's hand and dragged her toward the exit. Definitely a waste of money.

"How was it?" Noah asked.

"A lot of bullshit."

Noah and Maggie laughed while she gave him a summary of everything the fortune teller had told us. I was eighteen; of course, I would fall in love with someone eventually. I didn't need a fortune teller to tell me that. The whole thing was ridiculous.

On our way to the house of mirrors, I noticed that Zayn was staring at me. We hadn't had a chance to talk since I discovered at The Cave that he was friends with Ander and Noah. There wasn't much to talk about. We hooked up, and that was the end of the story, but at least it would be good to clear the air between us. You know, rip off the Band-Aid. Still, I couldn't get him or the moment we shared in New York out of my head. The way his fingers curled inside me. I could still feel his hands gripping my ass while he fucked me against the wall.

I bought tickets for all of us, but we were separated into two groups. Maggie and I entered with the first group; the boys joined the second one except for Ander, who decided to skip the attraction. He said he would wait for us at the exit so we could all go to the haunted house together.

It had been quite a while since I ventured into a house of mirrors, but this one differed from the ones I remembered from my childhood. It was set with a Halloween theme. Spiderwebs were draped in every corner, and screams echoed from the speakers hung around the space. The flashing lights switched in no particular order from bright blue to bloody red and dark green.

At some point, a group of people pushed us, and by the time I stopped spinning, Maggie's grip on my hand had slipped.

"MAGGIE!?" I shouted. She was nowhere to be seen.

I kept moving forward, sometimes walking into a mirror and smacking myself in the head. It could have been over five minutes when I saw someone's reflection in one of them. I quickly turned around, trying to see where it came from. Seeing their face or where they were with all the changing lights was impossible. The figure stood only a few steps away from me, hidden in the shadows. The stranger was wearing a black hoodie, black trousers, and a mask, very similar to the ones from the movie *The Purge*.

"Hi. Sorry. Have you seen a girl dressed as Harley Quinn?" They didn't respond. In fact, they didn't move an inch, their body eerily still.

I initially thought they might have entered with my group, as there were fifteen of us, but I didn't recall anyone dressed in black. Maybe the stranger was part of the show, an actor, although something was frightening about the way they stood still, not answering my question.

"Thank you anyway. She'll probably be waiting for me at the exit."

I stepped back, accidentally bumping into a mirror. Simultaneously, they advanced, the red lights reflecting off something they held in their hand.

A fucking knife.

All my senses told me to run, and I obeyed. I kept running and turning at every corner, trying to find the fucking exit. I could hear them getting closer, their boots hitting the ground.

Fuck. Fuck. Fuck.

Suddenly, I saw the exit. I ran out of the attraction like I'd seen the devil to jump straight into the arms of another one. I crashed into Ander's chest with such force that he dropped his phone.

"What the fuck, Sienna! Since when has a house of mirrors been scary?"

"Oh my God. Someone was chasing me with a knife!" I yelled at him. I was shaking.

"Calm the fuck down. It was probably an actor. *Jesus*. You're having a panic attack."

I couldn't breathe, my ears were clogged, and my mouth tasted like metal.

Ander held me while moving us away from the exit.

"Let me know if you're going to throw up. I wouldn't want to end up covered in your vomit again."

It took me a few seconds to process what he said, but I couldn't help but let out a nervous laugh when I did. Suddenly, the panic and fear I'd felt just moments ago slipped away, if only for a minute. He still remembered what happened when we were kids, but I guessed it was one of those experiences burned into your memory. Ander didn't have a change of clothes, so he spent the rest of the day smelling like sour milk.

"Maggie came out a few minutes ago. She went to the bathroom but will meet us at the haunted house. I told her I'd wait for you and the guys to come out."

I held Ander's arm while he comforted me. It felt really good. We stayed like that while my heartbeat slowed to a steady pace, enjoying our closeness with my eyes shut tight. It reminded me of the many afternoons I rested my head on Ander's lap while we watched a movie, and he caressed my hair.

Noah and Zayn came out together from the house of mirrors, suddenly breaking the spell.

"What are you doing?" Noah asked. One look at his face, and I was sure that he was pissed seeing me holding Ander.

Ander noticed and, pushing me away, said, "Someone scared the shit out of *your girl* in the house of mirrors. Sienna came out screaming and shaking like a tiny kitten."

His words triggered a surge of anger within me, and I snapped, "Obviously, I was scared! That person had a fucking knife!"

"Well, I'm sure he was just an actor. Shall we go to the haunted house, or are you too scared to join us?" Ander raised one eyebrow, challenging me with a mocking smile.

I fixed my gaze on him, lips pressed tightly together.

"Lead the way." I was scared, but I would never back down from a challenge.

We all walked toward the haunted house, where Maggie stood waiting for us. I was still shaken by what had happened at the house of mirrors, but I relaxed when Maggie told me she'd also seen them once I described to her how they looked.

"I thought it was pretty scary, too!" She giggled.

We all got our tickets and headed toward the main entrance, where a guy dressed as Michael Myers welcomed us. He went through the safety rules, with particular emphasis on the rule, "Do not touch the actors." We started walking through the different rooms, hearing the screams of other people who had entered before us. It was dark. I was second to last, with Zayn following me and Noah in front of me. We were in the third room, which looked like Regan's room from the movie *The Exorcist*—minus the possessed girl on the bed.

At that moment, Zayn whispered in my ear, "We need to talk."

I looked around, meeting his eyes with surprise.

"This is neither the place nor the time, Zayn."

"Yes, it is. This can't wait any longer." And he yanked me backward, placing a hand on my mouth and moving us to the room we just came from. He closed the door and pinned me to the wall.

"What do you think you're doing?" I whispered when he removed his hand.

"I want to talk to you. I was going to do it at the end of the night, but I can't wait any longer."

I gave him a confused look. What couldn't wait? It had been a few weeks since we met at The Cave, and he'd had plenty of opportunities to sit down and talk to me. Why now? What had changed?

And out of the blue, he kissed me. Liquid heat ran through my body as I returned the kiss because as much as I wanted to deny the truth, I really liked Zayn from the moment I met him in New York. Something dark about him kept pulling me toward him every time I was in his presence. It was very frustrating to be around him and Noah at the same time because I liked them both. Everything was getting fucking complicated. Did Zayn have no boundaries?

I broke the kiss, and without hesitating, I slapped him.

"What the fuck is wrong with you?" I said in disbelief. "For fuck's sake, Noah's your best friend!"

"I don't know, Sienna. I hate seeing you with him so much that it's driving me crazy. You were mine first."

The audacity.

"Let me be very clear. I'm not yours, and I'm not Noah's. I'm not a car or a book you possess." I was fuming. "I can't fucking believe this. First, you left that restroom and didn't even think about asking for my number. And now I'm yours? Fuck you, Zayn."

Zayn's eyes glittered with anger, but his gaze involuntarily flicked down to my lips.

"I thought I'd never see you again, but the last thing I could have imagined was that you'd be here too. And now I have to fucking see you with Noah around campus when all I want to do is kiss you."

He raised a valid point. I was leaving New York, too, but seeing him again before I had to leave would have been nice. No strings attached. And now I was fucking confused. I really liked him, but now the magic of that moment was gone, and we had to face the reality. I was seeing Noah, and even though we hadn't talked about being exclusive, Zayn was one of his closest friends. Feeling guilty enough about returning his kiss, I said, "I guess you'll have to get used to it." The last thing I wanted was to become the type of girl who came between two friends. I turned around and walked away, looking for the rest of the group.

Zayn didn't follow me.

Everything was dark, no screams, no ambient sound...*weird.* I moved at a quick pace, the hairs on my arms up as I kept crossing every room...but there were no actors. *Where the fuck is everyone?* No Jason Vorhees from *Friday the 13th*, Pennywise from *It*, or Freddy Krueger from *A Nightmare on Elm Street...Had they closed the attraction?*

The floor creaked a few feet behind me. Maybe Zayn decided to join me after all. Perhaps he wanted to apologize for the kiss...although I had kissed him as well. However, as I turned around, I screamed at the top of my lungs. It was the same stranger I saw at the house of mirrors, and terror took over my body. I started running, unable to find the exit, jumping from one set to the next, hitting tables, pushing chairs, and opening doors.

Help.

"SOMEONE HELP ME!" I screamed, nearly tearing my throat out. But there was no one; I was alone, hunted by a creep.

My legs ached. The sound of heavy boots approaching from behind caused me to hyperventilate. After what felt like an eternity, I finally saw the green letters "EXIT" above a door. I sprinted toward it with everything I had, my legs nearly giving out. Just before I was able to push the bar, everything went dark. Strong arms held me in place while someone else placed masking tape over my mouth and adjusted a sack over my head. Immediately after, my hands and ankles were bound with rope. My panic intensified. I fought back, but they overpowered me. I wiggled and kicked my legs so hard that I feared I would snap my ankles.

"Please, please stop," I begged. But no one seemed to hear my pleas behind the tape.

I heard someone start a car—the roar of an engine drawing nearer. My body hit a hard surface, and the sound of a door closing above me reached my ears. Moving my hands, I tried to recognize where I was when I hit metal—the trunk. Someone had put me in the trunk of a car. *Oh God. Are they going to kill me? Are they going to ask for a ransom?* I couldn't stop crying, and the tears kept rolling over my wet cheeks, my throat raw from all the screaming.

The car was moving, driving me somewhere. It couldn't be too far from the Devil's Night Festival because it only took a few minutes for the vehicle to come to a halt. I heard footsteps and the driver's door closing.

Please, please God. Don't let me die today.

Someone opened the trunk and grabbed my hands and legs. Two people. Two people were carrying me somewhere. I screamed for help, hoping anyone in the area could hear me. I was on my knees on the floor when I noticed I wasn't the only person screaming and crying; there was also one to my right and another to my left.

"Take the sacks off their heads," someone shouted.

As my eyes adapted to the sudden light, a room full of people came into view. Some of them were faces I recognized: Ander, Zayn, and Noah.

"Welcome to Stanford. Let the initiation begin!" a man with a shaved head exclaimed. Everyone roared in unison as if it were a Fourth of July celebration.

What the hell?

Noah approached me, and with a butterfly knife, he swiftly cut the ropes from my feet and my hands. I immediately removed the tape from my mouth.

"You are fucking dead! I'm gonna fucking kill the three of you!" I yelled.

Ander started laughing, and I lost it. I threw a punch to his face, but he easily dodged it.

"I thought I was being kidnapped, you *sonofabitch*."

"That was the whole point. I assumed you'd heard about Stanford initiations. It was hilarious seeing you thrust and kick your legs like you had a chance," Ander said, laughing like a fucking psycho.

"I tried telling them it was a bad idea, but they didn't listen. I'm so sorry, princess." Noah said as he tenderly kissed each wrist. Meanwhile, Ander remained in the background, smiling as if genuinely enjoying my suffering.

"Fuck you, Ander. The creep with the knife already scared me enough. When someone put the bag on my head, I thought it was them trying to skin me alive!"

Noah gave me a confused look.

"Don't be a drama queen. The guy with the knife in the house of mirrors was probably an actor," Ander explained.

"The same psycho from the house of mirrors was in the haunted house!"

"What do you mean? The Delta Kappa president paid the actors so you and Stacey over there would be alone. There was no one else in the haunted house," Zayn interjected.

"Why do they think I came running and screaming toward the exit if we were alone? Did they think I feared the ambience and decorations? They were fucking chasing me!" I stood to face them, and they exchanged worried looks.

I knew what I saw.

"Look. You're fine. Why don't we all go inside and talk to Nate? He's the president of Delta Kappa. The knife act might be a new thing planned to spice things up from the traditional stunt they did last year," Ander suggested.

I was going to have a word with Nate because I almost died from a stroke. It didn't feel like a prank.

My worries didn't settle after having a chat with *dearest* Nate. He confirmed that *The Purge* act was not something that the Delta Kappa committee had planned. He dismissed it as someone attempting to frighten me or perhaps an actor overly immersed in their role. But why would an actor move from one attraction to the next one to scare me? Did I know the psycho? A shiver ran down my spine at the thought that it could be the same person who had sent me the dahlias with the notes.

"What are you gonna do?" Zayn asked.

"I'm calling the cops. Noah, can you drive me home?"

"I'll drive you home, and I'll stay. There's no fucking way I'm leaving you alone tonight."

MISSING LETTERS

(Sienna)

The police had just left my building.

Noah stayed with me last night, and I called them as soon as we woke up. My wrists were still sore from the prank Delta Kappa had pulled last night.

I told the cops everything. I informed them about the flowers and the notes, that someone had broken into my apartment, and about the stranger with the mask and a knife chasing me at Devil's Night Festival. I couldn't give them a very detailed description because I hadn't seen their face or their hair, just that they wore black sweatpants, a black hoodie, and a mask. They asked me to show them a picture on Google because they had no idea what a 'Purge' mask was. When they saw my wrists, they asked what had happened and if they had been physical with me, so I told them about the Kappa Delta initiation. The moment I opened my stupid big mouth, they blamed the fraternity, of course. "It was probably part of the joke," they said, but I insisted that Nathaniel Martin had already confirmed it was not part of the hazing. They completely ignored my comments because they'd clearly made up their minds.

I was lying on my bed, hugging my pillow between my arms, when my phone pinged.

Zayn

> Sorry about last night. I had a couple of
> drinks before you arrived, and I fucked
> up. Also, about the Delta Kappa stuff.
> Can we meet?

I left Zayn on read.

"I cannot deal with this shit now," I muttered.

My mind kept going back to the stranger who chased me, how close they felt, and how I thought I was going to die. Part of me wanted to believe it was all a joke, but there was something about how that moment felt that, deep down, I knew it wasn't a prank. That the knife was a hundred percent real.

I needed to change my locks again. I didn't feel safe enough.

Last night was a mess not only because of the life-and-death experience but because of Zayn's kiss and how it felt to be so close to Ander again for the briefest moment. Once upon a time, I always felt like that. Cared for and protected. He was always a great friend, and it hit me hard when I realized that things would never be as they used to be. It felt like there was a gaping hole in my chest. Part of me wanted to confront Ander and ask him why he was so angry with me, but the way he'd been ignoring me in the lab told me that he wouldn't give me a straight answer. I was going to confront him, just not yet.

My phone pinged again.

Maggie

> Hey, babe. How are you? Have the cops
> left?

Me

> I'm still on edge. Yes, they left.

Me

Wanna come over and watch a movie?

Maggie

I'll be there in 5.

I needed a distraction, and a movie with Maggie sounded like a great plan.

*   *   *

During the next couple of weeks, my routine kept me distracted and busy. I hadn't received any more flowers or notes from my "secret admirer." Since our little Halloween moment, Ander and I had begun to work almost like a team in the lab.

Almost.

Reed was pleased with our work, and our results were promising. His words, not mine.

However, Ander was in a bad mood today. I could feel it. He'd been huffing and puffing every five minutes, and I feared opening my mouth around him for anything that didn't have to do with the task Reed had given us.

"If you wanna say something, say it. I can see you watching me from the corner of my eye," Ander blurted.

I'd tried starting a conversation with him several times, like every single day, but he'd completely ignored every one of my foolish attempts, so for the past twenty minutes, I'd been burning the side of his face with my stare while Reed explained a protocol to the entire lab.

"Nothing in particular. You look upset, but I guess that is your go-to mood." I was getting a bit annoyed with his attitude today. He wouldn't talk to me unless it was to provide instructions or to point out when I was doing something wrong.

Everyone had already exited the lab when Ander turned around.

"I don't know why you care now. You never did."

"I don't know what you mean. I always cared for you, and you know it. You were my best friend," I said.

"Yeah, sure thing, Sienna. You always did." The sarcasm filled his voice, shooting me like an arrow.

"Fucking say it. Whatever is eating you alive. Say it!" I yelled at him.

He dropped his backpack and stampeded across the room until he faced me. Ander looked furious with fire in his eyes.

"You fucking ditched me! You ignored me for a fucking year! For fuck's sake, Sienna. I wrote to you every single month for a year. Do you know how many fucking letters? Twelve fucking letters. Twelve! All of them telling you how much I missed you, asking you why you didn't write back. I wondered every time I checked the mailbox why you would give me the cold shoulder. It drove me insane! But you know what was the worst thing? You sending your father's errand boy asking me to put an end to it. You didn't have the balls to even tell me yourself!"

My mouth dropped.

"What the fuck are you talking about? I never received a fucking letter from you! I was the one who actually wrote to you twice. I even sneaked out from my house to come over and see you during the first summer break, even though my father had expressly forbidden me to see you. But the moment I walked around your yard, there you were, in the swimming pool with Silvia's arms around your neck and a smile from ear to ear. She was thrilled from being in your arms." I was out of breath, tears burning behind my eyes. "You had clearly moved on, and I wasn't gonna stay and humiliate myself over a guy who had forgotten me. I felt betrayed. I thought we had something special, and you ruined it!"

We didn't say a word for a minute. Our breathing accelerated from the heated argument. Ander closed the small distance between us. I could feel his body almost pressed to mine, his breath caressing my lips, and my eyes dropped to his mouth. His eyes kept darting back and forth between my mouth and my eyes. Was he going to kiss me? He hesitated and took a step back. My heart shattered once more.

"Tell yourself all the lies you need to hear, love, but the truth is, you didn't care. And now I don't." Ander turned and stormed out of the lab, slamming the door behind him.

I couldn't breathe. I needed air.

So then, did he write to me after all? He says he did, but I didn't receive any letters. Or was he just lying?

You sending your father's errand boy asking me to put an end to it.

Then it clicked.

I took my phone out of my back pocket and dialed the only person who would know about this.

Could it be true? I had to know.

"Hi, Sienna. Good to hear from you. Everything alright?" Jerry greeted me as soon as he answered the phone.

"Hi, Jerry. All good, thanks. Something very weird just happened, and you might be the only person who might know what happened." I tried calming my breathing to avoid sounding like an angry pit bull.

"Hmm, okay."

"Alexander Scott is studying at Stanford. You remember him, right? William Scott's son. He just said he wrote to me while I was in Switzerland and that you knew something about it. But I never received any letters from him, so I'm a bit confused…care to explain?"

Silence stretched for a few seconds, but I heard him sigh at the other end of the line.

"It was for your own good. Your father gave me clear instructions to intercept any communications from the Scotts, so I obliged."

So it was true. Ander wrote to me as he promised. He never forgot about me.

"How could you?" A single tear trickled down my cheek. "You know how much I cared about him. How could you?" Before he could respond, I hung up the phone. I wasn't willing to hear any apologies from his mouth although I doubted he would apologize. He did what my father had asked of him, and like Ander said, he was always the most loyal assistant to my father. More tears streamed down my face as I struggled to take shallow breaths, feeling a heavy pressure on my chest. I felt humiliated and betrayed. No wonder Ander was so mad at me. I had disappointed him; I'd broken his heart, and my dad had broken mine. I loved him, more than a friend, and now I wondered what would have happened if I had received those letters.

What had he written in them? Did he feel the same way I felt when I left him at the bus stop? But then I remembered what I saw: him and Silvia Tucker almost kissing each other in the swimming pool. No, he never loved me. He might have missed me, but only as a friend. Otherwise, he would have reached out after he had found my letters. He would have found a way.

I was upset, mostly with myself, for entertaining the thought of kissing him back if he had kissed me and for how I felt when he comforted me after the house of mirrors incident. The reality of my feelings scared me because what I had come to realize in the past few weeks was that I still had feelings for Ander. And I knew I had to put an end to it.

I took my things and headed home, but one thing he said kept creeping into my mind.

I wrote to you every single month for a year.

THE UGLY TRUTH

(Ander)

I hated myself for telling Sienna why I was furious with her. She didn't deserve to know how painful it was that she never wrote back to me. She looked surprised when I mentioned the letters, but it could have just been an act.

It had to be, right?

We arrived at Smith's Tailoring at 3 p.m., just like Claudia, Zayn's mom and my future stepmother, had told us. We flew to New York from San Francisco on a red-eye flight, and although he asked me several times what was bothering me, I didn't tell him anything. I knew I'd been in a horrible mood lately since I found out that Sienna was also studying at Stanford. I hated that she still had such power over my feelings.

I hated her.

Zayn entered the shop ahead of me. The bell on top of the door chimed, announcing our arrival. The shop was old, the smell of leather filling my nose. Behind the counter was an old lady who welcomed us with a warm smile.

"Welcome to Smith's Tailoring. How may I assist you?" she asked.

"We have a three o'clock appointment for the Scotts' wedding," I replied.

Claudia had booked an appointment so we could try on the

tuxedos we would wear to our parents' wedding in March. Claudia and my father got engaged during a trip to St. Tropez this summer. They met at a charity event at the end of last year, and since then, they have become inseparable. She was a widow, and if it weren't for the money she had inherited from her husband, I would have thought she was a gold digger because who could truly love my father?

I was already acquainted with Zayn because we had frequented the same circles in Rye. We had some friends in common back in high school, but we didn't become friends until our parents started dating. I knew he was at Stanford because I had seen him at some sports events, but this year, we decided it made sense for us to share an apartment since we were about to become family.

I liked Zayn. We had spent a lot of time together since we now lived at Montgomery Hall; he's a bit quiet, but that was a good thing. I would have hated sharing an apartment with someone who wouldn't give me some space, but Zayn was alright. He did his thing, and I did mine. I must admit it hit me hard when I found out that Sienna was the girl he fucked in that restroom. Jealousy. A feeling that apparently took root the moment I knew Noah had also fucked her on his birthday.

The old lady looked at the book resting on the counter in front of her, searching for our names on the agenda.

"Oh yes. Mr. Scott and Mr. Siegel, please follow me. Your father is already in the back trying on his tuxedo."

The lady walked us to the back of the store where a man, probably a hundred years old, was taking some measurements and deep in conversation with my father.

"Father," I greeted him.

"Hello, Alexander. Hello, Zayn. Thanks for coming. Mr. Smith, are we done? I need to return to my office. I have an appointment scheduled with my lawyer in thirty minutes."

"Yes, Mr. Scott. We're done. You can take the tuxedo off, and I'll make the alterations as soon as possible. Let me check my appointments so I can book a new fitting for you. I'll be back in a second." Mr. Smith disappeared to the front of the shop, leaving the three of us alone for a few minutes.

I'd been thinking about what Sienna said the other day, that she'd also written to me a couple of times. Something in my gut told me my father knew about it, so I decided to take this trip as an opportunity to confront him face-to-face.

"Father, before you go…I need to ask you something."

"Be quick. I need to leave in five minutes." My dad and I rarely talked these days. He was always busy running his business, and most of the time when I was back in Rye, he was either traveling or avoiding me.

I wasn't going to beat around the bush, so I got straight to the point.

"You remember I told you that Sienna Moore was studying at Stanford, right? She mentioned the other day that she wrote to me a couple of times when she moved to Switzerland, but I never received a letter…is she lying? Is there something I should know? Please tell me the truth."

My father looked at me, his poker face not giving a hint of what was going on inside his head. He'd always been an excellent poker player, so I was never surprised that he was good at hiding what he thought about everything and everyone.

"No, she's not lying." *There you go.* "She did write to you. You should thank me for taking care of them. You kept writing to her every month, and it was pathetic to see a thirteen-year-old boy falling in love with the girl whose family had attempted to ruin ours and my career. Does that answer your question?"

Bile rose in my throat, my mouth tasted bitter, and my hands fisted at both sides of my body. Zayn stood next to me, and one of his hands gently grabbed my elbow, sensing that shit was about to hit the fan.

"You're a piece of shit." I was fucking fuming.

"Watch your tongue. I won't tolerate your insolence, boy."

"Stop calling me a boy!" I yelled at him.

"Then stop behaving like one. I did it because that girl clouded your judgment. Don't you think I saw how you looked at her? She had you by the balls, and I wasn't going to allow you to wreck your future for a brat whose father almost ruined our lives."

The message was loud and clear. I was a little boy back then, but I wasn't going to tolerate that bullshit from him anymore.

"I'm paying for your tuition, apartment, car, and expensive parties. I own you, and you will do what I tell you to do. Do you understand? Stay away from her. That's an order."

I stayed quiet. I wasn't a kid anymore. He wasn't going to tell me what to do.

He fisted my shirt by the collar and looked at me with a snarl on his face. "Do you fucking understand?" he shouted, pushing me toward Zayn. We both kept our mouths shut. "Good," he said while grabbing his jacket and his mobile phone.

My father left the shop without saying another word, and Zayn and I stood there in silence for a couple of minutes before Mr. Smith strolled in again.

"Mr. Scott, Mr. Siegel, please try on the tuxedos. I'll get some measurements, and you can then leave. I won't take much of your time."

On our way back to my house, Zayn broke the uncomfortable silence.

"You said she meant nothing to you. Why didn't you say you were in love with her?"

Was I? I cared for her and truly missed her when she left, but what did a thirteen-year-old know about love?

"I didn't love her."

Liar.

"Well. It sounded like you did, Ander."

I still remember that kiss. It tormented me for months to know that she was miles away from Rye and the fact that I was just someone for her to use and dispose of. Did she care about our friendship? But now that I knew she'd sent me two letters, everything I believed until a few days ago felt like a lie. I'd been holding on to that anger toward her for years, and once I saw her at the freshers' party, all those feelings intensified.

She did write to me.

I pushed those feelings aside and started packing my stuff. I knew it was time to have a real talk with her. I just had to pick the right moment.

THIRD TIME ISN'T A CHARM

(Sienna)

"You've been very quiet today, Miss Moore." Reed's voice shook me out of my trance.

Ander had not been in the lab for the past couple of days, and all I'd done in the past twenty minutes was stare at the empty stool next to me. In the beginning, I thought he was avoiding me, but then Reed said he had some family business to attend to back home. I felt guilty about missing him despite our recent fight. I still couldn't believe my father asked Jerry to stop Ander from contacting me. He didn't have the right to keep me away from him.

I thought about telling Ander that I had confronted him, that now I knew he'd written to me, but that wasn't the kind of conversation to have over the phone. He should be back today, so I planned to speak with him tomorrow.

I looked at Reed, who was standing next to me, and said, "You can call me Sienna, and yes, I've been a bit distracted. Sorry." To my surprise, I was truly enjoying working in the lab with him, and until now, he'd proven to be an excellent mentor. He'd taken the time to patiently explain everything to me and answer my questions. Reed was by far one of the best professors I'd had, probably the best one, including those from boarding school. He cared for his students, treating us respectfully and like adults.

"Are you happy you joined my team?" he asked.

"Yes, very happy. I'm learning a lot. I want to thank you for your patience, especially considering how difficult it must have been trying to get Ander and me to work as a team. We haven't been easy on you, have we?" I laughed.

"Yes, I've noticed. You knew him before you arrived at Stanford, right?"

"Yes. Our parents used to work together, so I've known Ander since we were kids. Our relationship is complicated."

"I can see that." He gave me a comforting smile. "If Ander keeps bothering you, please come to my office. I can speak with him if his attitude affects your work."

"Thank you," I replied. "I might take you up on that offer, but I don't think it'll be necessary for now. I can handle him."

"I'm sure you can," he remarked with a knowing smirk. Sometimes I forgot he was a professor because he looked so young, and talking to him was so easy. I wondered if there was a Mrs. Reed in the picture.

I gave him a forced smile before he left to help Summer, who was calling him from the other side of the room.

My phone pinged.

Sarah

Hi, darling! How's college? Miss you xxx

Me

Hello, gorgeous. I'm good. How's Cambridge?

Sarah

It's going great. I've met two gorgeous guys; one is Scottish, and the other one is Norwegian. He fucks like a Viking *wink emoji*

Me

PMSL. You'll never change.

Sarah

How's everything? Now tell me the truth.

Me

It's a fucking mess. Noah, Zayn, Ander...and the stalker. The police are doing nothing.

Sarah

Girl, your life should be a fucking soap opera. I'd watch that shit.

Me

I have to go, but let's FaceTime again this week, okay?

Sarah

Cool. Speak soon, love. Take care of yourself. xxx

Me

Love you too. Xxx

* * *

The day was almost over when I reached Aster Hall and saw Noah leaning against the wall of the building, one leg propped up and his hands in the pockets of his jeans. He looked edible. I bit my bottom lip, and he gave me the sexiest smile I'd ever seen. What was it with these gorgeous boys that kept tormenting me?

"Hello, princess. Did you have a good day?" He leaned over and kissed me, both of his hands cupping my face. "Mmm. I've missed you," he said against my lips. My entire body shivered, and a wave of pleasure traveled between my thighs.

"Wanna come inside?"

"Always," he joked. I loved our little flirtatious moments when everything seemed to have a double meaning with him. I held his hand until we were inside the apartment, but as soon as I closed the door, he pinned me against the wall and kissed the hell out of me. He'd clearly missed me. His hands traveled up and down my body, his tongue swirling with mine. My pussy throbbed every time he tugged on my lower lip.

"I wanna play a game with you," he taunted.

"What kind of game?" I asked playfully.

"One you'll like, I promise."

He put his right hand in one of his pockets and took out a red silk scarf. After moving us toward the dining room, he instructed me to sit just by the edge of the table. He grabbed the silk scarf and placed it over my eyes, blinding me. The room immediately went dark. He lifted my skirt and removed my underwear. My heart was beating faster, and my breathing was quickening. I was unsure of what he was doing when I suddenly heard a chair dragged against the floor before me.

"Spread your legs for me, Sienna. I didn't have lunch today, and I'm starving."

I did as I was told.

"Good girl," he praised.

A second later, his mouth was between my legs, licking my entrance. A moan escaped my lips. He was very good at it. Very good. He ate me out like I was his favorite meal. At first, he licked me with long and slow movements, circling and flicking his tongue on my clit or sucking lightly. But when I started grinding against his face, his pace changed. More demanding. He gripped my hips with both hands, pushing me closer to him. I fisted both hands in his hair, forcing him against my pussy, my orgasm building.

"Noah…please. Oh my God." My pussy clenched as I rode my climax, screaming his name.

"Bend over the table. I'm not done with you yet." He removed the blindfold and used it to tie my hands behind my back.

"Look at you. You are so beautiful," he said, running his hands over my back until he reached my ass and spanked me.

I let out a small cry of pleasure.

"Do you like being tied up and at my mercy?"

"I love this side of you, Noah. Love when you go all feral on me."

He unbuttoned his jeans and dropped them and his boxers down to his ankles. With my upper body completely laid over the table, Noah spread my legs a little wider while rolling a condom down his length. It was hard and ready. He held me in place with one hand on my lower back while he lined up the tip of his cock.

"I'm going to fuck your pussy until you scream my name over and over again. I want the entire building to hear that you're *mine*." With one deep thrust, he shoved his dick inside me. "Fuck, Sienna, you feel so good." His hold on my hips tightened, ensuring I'd wake up with bruises in the morning. He started pounding hard and fast, his cock pushing in and out rhythmically. Noah wasn't a sweet lover. He was wild, and his groans filled the entire apartment. Reaching down between my legs, he pressed his two middle fingers on my clit, circling my bundle of nerves with firm and fast movements while he continued fucking me against the table.

"That's it. Look at me, Sienna," he demanded. "Look at me when I'm fucking you."

I turned my face to meet his eyes. "Oh my God, Noah." Every inch of my body felt alive as I pushed back my hips to meet each of his thrusts. "Noah…"

"Yes. Scream my name, princess. Let everyone know who owns you."

The second orgasm was sharp, like something exploded deep down in my core. I closed my eyes from the intensity that came from both his cock hitting that sweet spot and from his fingers working the apex between my thighs. It didn't take long for him to climax, too. Driving himself deep and hard, he suddenly growled, slowing the pace until his body collapsed on top of me.

"I don't want your ego to get any bigger, but that was probably the best orgasm of my life. I know I keep saying that, but fucking hell…" I stated. "Let me know next time you want to play more games because I'm all in."

Noah laughed while he pulled out and threw the condom in the trash can. He gently removed the scarf from my wrists, put it back in his pocket, and yanked my underwear from the floor.

"I don't know about you, but all these games make me hungry. Wanna order some pizza? We can play more games later," he proposed with a wink.

"Pepperoni, please, classic crust. I'm going to take a shower, but make yourself at home." I walked to my bedroom, took a pair of leggings and a baggy T-shirt from the first drawer, and placed them on the toilet seat.

The warm water was incredibly soothing. Apparently, great sex, a warm and relaxing shower, and the prospect of eating pizza were all I needed to turn around a very stressful day at college. It took me about half an hour to wash my hair, exfoliate my skin, and apply my favorite shea butter body milk. The fact that Noah was probably bored waiting in the living room didn't bother me because sometimes a girl just needed a bit of pampering to feel like herself again.

The doorbell rang. I grabbed a towel, wrapped it around my body, and slightly opened the door. Sticking my head out, I yelled, "Can you open the door? I have some cash in my purse if you haven't paid online."

I put my clothes on and dried my hair with the towel until it was damp. When I opened the bathroom door, Noah sat on my bed holding a black dahlia and a note.

"How many of these have you received?" he asked.

I froze on the spot, unsure of how to approach the conversation. I'd considered telling Noah about the one I received on Halloween, but I'd come to accept that it might have been part of the hazing. Apparently, I was wrong.

"Two," I replied. "This is the third one."

"When did you receive the second one, and why didn't you tell me?"

"On Halloween, but I thought it was part of the hazing after what happened that night. That's why I didn't tell you. I didn't want you to worry about me."

"Of course, I'll worry about you. I care about you, Sienna, and that includes your safety."

"What does the note say?" I asked, intrigued.

He handed me the note, which he had clearly read.

You think you're better than everyone else, but you are not special. You bleed like everybody.

I felt sick.

"I'm calling the police. Someone is clearly obsessed with you, and I don't like leaving you alone in your apartment. Whoever wrote these notes knows where you live."

"I already did, Noah. I told them everything, but they kept telling me that it was possibly part of the hazing," I blurted, my voice filled with despair.

"This weekend is Thanksgiving. What are your plans? Are you going back to New York?"

"I was planning on catching up on some homework. It's my first Thanksgiving without my parents, so I'd rather stay here at Stanford and order a turkey sandwich." I usually spent Thanksgiving at boarding school, but I would video-call with my parents every year. Well, my mom. Half of the time, my father only showed his face for about ten seconds and then disappeared.

"Since my parents will be attending a private event, Ander has kindly invited me to his house in Rye. Let me talk to him. I won't leave you alone here with this creep skulking around. I'll see if you can come with us. If not, I'm staying right here with you."

I snorted.

"Yes, sure. As if spending the weekend at the Scotts' didn't sound like a nightmare. I think I'll pass; I would rather face a creep than the Scott family. I doubt Ander's dad would be thrilled to have me there anyway."

"Leave it to me."

Noah was on the phone for about five minutes while I dried my hair. I wasn't particularly thrilled about spending the whole weekend with Ander and his family, but the thought of being alone in my apartment did concern me a little. Maybe I could just go to my house in Port Chester or buy a ticket to Hawaii. That sounded like a better plan, anyway.

"Ander says he's cool with you coming. He'll let Claudia know."

"Who's Claudia?" I asked.

"Zayn's mom."

That was right. I remember the night we met. He was escaping his mom's engagement party. It was weird to think about Zayn and Ander becoming stepbrothers.

"When's the wedding? Zayn told me his mom was getting married when I met him," I explained.

"Yeah. I still remember you already *knew* him before we met... They'll be getting married in March." I didn't miss the sharp comment. Was Noah jealous? "Do you talk to Zayn a lot?"

Yes. He was jealous.

"We talked on Halloween, but that's all."

"What did you talk about?" Noah clenched his jaw.

"Well...nothing happened if that's what you're asking." The lie tasted like rotten meat in my mouth. "He just wanted to know where we stood with each other."

"And where is that?"

"Umm, Mr. Nakamura, are you jealous?" I said in a mocking tone as I approached him. I stood between his legs, stroking his beautiful and soft hair with one hand.

"Jealous of Zayn? Never. We've shared girls before, but I'm not sure I want to have that kind of arrangement with you. I like you too much to share."

Sharing girls? Did he imply dating them sequentially, or did he mean being with a girl at the same time? A chill ran through my body as I imagined that second scenario. Zayn and Noah together with a girl. The funny thing was that, in my head, that girl had my face, and that image turned me on more than I was willing to admit.

DON'T HOLD BACK

(Sienna)

I was on the phone with Maggie all morning while preparing my luggage. She would be helping the local homeless shelter during Thanksgiving, so her plan was to stay at Stanford and watch as many horror movies as she could. I told her to get some ideas on how to avoid being an easy prey to my stalker, to which she replied that my sense of humor was fucked up. I knew it was not funny, but I tended to make jokes during stressful times.

The guys would pick me up in five minutes, and we would head directly to the San Francisco airport to catch our flight. Before leaving the apartment, I quickly went through all my things to ensure I didn't forget anything.

In true gentlemanly fashion, Noah held the car door open for me, so when the driver put my luggage in the trunk, I jumped in the back of the car. I sat in the middle, between Zayn and Noah. Ander sat in the passenger's seat. Silence filled the Uber on our way to the airport, and it stretched until we were at the gate.

"What seat did you get?" Zayn asked me.

"I have 9B," I answered.

Zayn showed me his ticket. "I have 9A. We're sitting together."

Noah and Ander, who slept for most of the flight, were behind us in row 10. Zayn and I didn't talk much, but he asked me some questions about college and my time in the lab with Ander.

I found it awkward to think that I had sex with two of them. I enjoyed spending time with Noah, but there was this rush of excitement every time Zayn would brush my hand with his or every time I would catch him staring at me from his seat. I remember the word he used when he cornered me in the haunted house. *Mine.* I also wondered why that simple word would drive the most insane and dangerous thoughts every time I was near him. My mind would drift to that evening we spent together in Manhattan, and it drove me mad to think about his body between my legs.

"I need to go to the bathroom." Rather than walk toward the front of the plane, I chose the one at the back.

When I closed the door, I immediately reached for the tap. I cooled down my hot cheeks with water until the tightness in my chest eased. I remained in the toilet for a few minutes, gathering all my strength because God knew how much I needed for the weekend that lay ahead.

I opened the door, but Zayn blocked the exit.

"What…" Before I could finish the sentence, Zayn pushed us inside the small aircraft lavatory and clicked the door shut behind him.

"What is it with you and restrooms?"

He grabbed my chin to face him, taking my mouth in a sensual but filthy kiss that drove me slowly fucking insane. His kiss took me off guard, but I kissed him back. I twisted my fingers into his black T-shirt and pulled him closer. I knew how wrong it was to kiss this beautiful man while Noah sat only a few feet away from us. But I couldn't help it.

He pulled away, giving me a soft grin, and then he turned and stepped outside but not before saying, "It's gonna be an interesting weekend."

My face was heated, but I recovered quickly enough so no one would notice that I'd been out of my seat for a long time. When I returned to 9B, Noah and Ander were still sleeping, so I thanked my guardian angel for not making the situation more difficult than it already was.

We landed in New York half an hour later. Mr. Scott had sent his driver to pick us up from the airport, so after collecting our luggage from the belt, we headed toward the parking lot.

It had only been a couple of months since I left New York, but I was mesmerized by the orange and red colors that filled the city. Autumn was one of my favorite seasons. The colors that covered the trees felt bold and homey, and a sense of peace filled my heart. I always loved the chilly wind on my face first thing in the morning. I remembered those days when I would sit at the back of Moore Manor reading a Harry Potter book or playing cards with Ander while the sun set and vibrant hues of red layered the sky. I loved this city in autumn.

It took approximately an hour to get to Rye, and I felt anxious as we approached the Scotts' driveway. It had been over six years since the last time I set foot in this house, and all the memories that this place held were stuck in my throat. I tried to swallow the feelings that rushed over me as soon as the car stopped.

Ander came over to where I stood, grabbed my wrist, and turned me to look at him with a harsh movement.

"I don't think it is necessary for me to tell you that my father won't be pleased that you're here. I've invited you over because Noah told me about the notes, so don't get the wrong idea."

I stood still for a few seconds, thinking about how to answer him. It seemed he didn't want me here, and neither did his father, which wasn't a surprise.

"Don't worry, Alexander. I'm fully aware of how little you care about me. You were very clear last time we spoke." I yanked my wrist out of his hold and grabbed my bag. Before we reached the main entrance, the door opened. A woman came toward us, holding her arms open with a kind smile.

"Zayn, oh my boy. I've missed you!" she said. Her movements were graceful and delicate, like those of a ballerina who knew only how to float with ethereal steps. Her black midi hair, pale skin, and plump red lips only heightened her beautiful features. Her long-sleeve DVF wrap dress beautifully accentuated her body's curves. I could recognize that pattern and design anywhere.

Once she finished hugging Zayn and placed a kiss on his cheek, she moved on to greet Ander and Noah. Then she turned to face me.

"You must be Sienna. I've heard a lot about you. It's a pleasure to meet you finally, darling. I'm Claudia, Zayn's mom." Claudia held my waist and pushed me closer to her, giving me a delicate side hug. I couldn't do anything but smile at the kind gesture.

"Let me show you to your room so you can freshen up before we have dinner. Traveling is always exhausting, so take your time. Dinner won't be served until seven," Claudia informed us.

She walked me to one of the rooms on the first floor, which I quickly recognized. It was in front of Ander's room when we were kids, but I wasn't sure if it still was his room or if he'd moved to the other side of the house, perhaps the third floor.

After I hung up all my clothes, I lay on the king-size bed and stared at the ceiling. I wondered if Ander remembered all the nights I had stayed over to watch movies and eat ice cream. Or about those nights when we would grab our lanterns and explore the garden hunting for monsters.

Curiosity hit me. I stood and walked toward the door. I held the doorknob and slowly opened the door to make sure the hallway was empty. I stood in front of Ander's room, trying to hear anything from the other side of the door before I knocked twice and waited for a response. Nothing. I opened the door and entered the room, closing the door behind me. Everything remained the same as I remembered. A king-size bed placed in the middle of the room with only one bedside table, a desk with tightly organized stationery—far away from the messy chaos that reigned when he lived here—a chaise lounge couch with a cinema-like TV, and wall-to-wall shelves filled with books and DVDs. I stared at some of the DVDs and how something so simple as a movie could bring up memories of some of the best days of my life.

"I knew you couldn't resist."

I turned around to face Ander, who leaned against the doorframe with his hands inside his pockets. I didn't hear him coming in.

"I was just curious. I wondered if you kept it the same," I responded.

"I only changed a few things, like the TV and the bedding. Marvel theme sheets are not cool anymore when you start to bring girls over."

I snorted a laugh.

"I did like them, and as far as I remember, I was the first one."

"Not that kind of sleepover."

I stood there in awkward silence for a moment, gathering all my strength to start the pending conversation between us.

"You know…I spoke with Jerry. Did you know my dad asked him to intercept any calls and letters from you while I was at boarding school?"

Ander didn't respond, keeping the same expressionless face, so I continued, "I'm sorry, Ander. You will never know how sorry I am. You must have thought I didn't care about you, but that's far from the truth. When we kissed—" Before I could finish, Ander interrupted me.

"Don't dwell in the past, Sienna. I try not to. What's done is done, and we can't change the past. And I don't need your apologies. You could have called when you didn't receive any of my letters. I promised you I'd write to you. But you didn't try contacting me, and that was a choice you made."

My blood boiled.

"But that's not true!" I yelled while storming toward Ander. "I wrote to you too, and I came to see you as soon as I was back in Port Chester the next summer. I've already told you what happened when I went to your place.

"And what about my letters, Ander? Because I wrote to you too. You're a hypocrite and a piece of shit." Suddenly, Ander grabbed me and pulled me against his chest, his face just a few inches from mine.

"Watch your mouth, Sienna. You blame me, but you were the one who left and never came back. You weren't there when my parents got divorced, and I needed you. You have no idea what I went through, and you weren't there. I lov…" His gaze dropped to my mouth. "You didn't try hard enough."

Guilt took over my body, thinking about his parents' divorce and how it could have affected him. I wasn't there to comfort him as a friend, and I felt guilty for not trying harder.

Ander loosened his grip on my arm with an apology.

"I'm sorry you had to go through all that, but you weren't the only one who struggled. I missed you too, Ander. Every fucking day."

I walked toward my room, tears burning at the back of my eyes. I knew the situation was fucked up, and the lack of communication between us was not making things easier. He was clearly affected by me coming back into his life, but he shouldn't blame me for all the things that had happened because I'd also been kept in the dark. Now, he knew the truth. If he wanted to continue hating me because he needed to hold on to that anger, he could be my guest. I was done.

I took a shower to clean away all my built-up emotions and dressed in a pair of black leggings and an oversized dark gray sweater. Nobody had told me it was going to be a fancy dinner, so I didn't expect anyone to comment on my sense of fashion.

I headed downstairs a few minutes before seven and strolled through the corridors until I stumbled upon the entrance to the dining room. Voices echoed from the inside, so I assumed everyone was probably already there. When I pushed the double doors, everyone stopped talking, and one particular pair of eyes landed on me. William.

"Good evening, Mr. Scott. Thank you for having me; your house looks just as beautiful as I remember."

"Good evening, Miss Moore; it's lovely to see you again after all these years." His words were kind, but his facial expression made it evident that he wasn't exactly excited about my presence.

"Let's eat, shall we?" Claudia exclaimed with false excitement, her eyes darting between us.

The service delivered a wonderful dinner, I must say. It had been quite a while since I'd enjoyed homemade food around a table. Everyone jumped into casual conversation, Zayn and Noah talking about their work in college and how the year was unfolding at Stanford. They talked about a few of the parties they had attended, and Ander shared some anecdotes from our days in the lab with Professor Reed. It almost seemed like a normal family dinner, yet every now and then, I could feel a lingering tension in the air that kept me on guard throughout the entire evening.

"Sienna, I recently heard that you have been named the major shareholder at Cos Pharmaceuticals. Is that right? Aren't you a bit young and inexperienced to lead the company?" William posed the question in a nonchalant manner, but I couldn't help but detect a touch of disdain in his voice. I didn't appreciate the hostility.

"Yes, that's correct, *William*." If he was going to address me on a first-name basis, I sure could play that game. "We still are in the process of appointing a new CEO, but hopefully, that means I can focus on my studies and leave someone with experience to take care of the business while I'm at Stanford."

"It was an amazing journey to set up the company with your father. I have very fond memories of my time at Cos Pharma."

"Why did you leave then?" I asked. It was a simple question, yet my tone was cold and distant. "Or was that not a choice you actually made?"

William's expression darkened, and his hands clutched the cutlery as if he intended to melt them in his grasp.

"Your father and I disagreed on how things were dealt with in the last year before I left the company. We could not reach an agreement on how to move forward, so I left."

"Is that so?" I challenged him as I lifted my fork and slowly drove a carrot into my mouth.

"Make it as you wish. Some things are better left in the past because it would be very painful to see the image you have of your father turn into something too twisted for you to handle after his death. I don't wish to taint the memory of the dead, especially because the truth wouldn't do any good at this point," he stated with the iciest tone.

"What do you mean?" I asked, confused.

"I mean what I mean." He paused. "I've had enough of this shit show. I'm going to my office. Claudia, don't wait up for me." Everyone stilled, and as soon as William left the room, Noah tried to crack a joke to lighten the mood with little success. I looked around the table. Everyone visibly felt uncomfortable after our exchange, but my head kept spinning about what he'd said.

It would be very painful to see the image you have of your father turn into something too twisted for you to handle after his death.

Was there something awful that my father kept hidden from me, something that drove William to resign? After all, he was one of the founders, and I believed that knowing how stubborn he'd always been, it wouldn't have been easy for him to leave Cos Pharmaceuticals.

"I'm going to bed," I announced. "Claudia, thank you for the dinner. Would you like me to help you tomorrow with the Thanksgiving preparations?" Offering my help was the minimum I could do for a woman who was clearly delusional for marrying that jerk.

"Oh, that'd be lovely. Thank you, my dear!"

* * *

I excused myself to my room and swapped my leggings and sweater for a comfortable set of silk pajamas. I kind of regretted coming to this place, which was plagued with bittersweet memories.

I dozed off pretty fast, but I instinctively woke up during my sleep. I switched my bedside table lamp on and checked my phone; it was 3:46 a.m.

Curiosity got the best of me, so I left my room and explored the house. Maybe I could eat some of that dessert I didn't get the chance to taste during dinner. I headed downstairs, but as soon as I reached the ground floor, I noticed a faint light coming out of the kitchen. I walked toward it, wondering who might be struggling to sleep. Maybe they also had the same idea about getting a bite of that wonderful chocolate cake.

When the fridge door shut, Zayn's figure emerged from behind it. The dim light above the stove cast shadows on his well-toned body. He stood there, holding a piece of chocolate cake on a plate while sporting only a pair of pajama pants and nothing else. My eyes hungrily traced each chiseled muscle, from his arms and shoulders down to his abs. He had one arm and part of his right chest covered with black ink, and it looked like there was a spider tattoo on his hip, just peeking out from his pants.

Jesus Christ.

"Trouble sleeping?" I said as soon as he spotted me by the door.

"Yes. I was tired of tossing and turning when I remembered we hadn't finished all the cake. Wanna have some? I can share," he offered.

I made my way over to the kitchen island and perched myself on top of it. Zayn stood in front of me, setting his body between my legs. He grabbed a small piece of the cake and placed it between my lips. I took a bite, and a borderline sexual moan escaped my mouth.

"What is the verdict?" Zayn asked mischievously.

"Excellent."

"I like your pajamas."

"Thank you," I replied. "I like your tattoos. What's your favorite one?" My eyes roamed his chest and arm, studying every design. I quickly recognized the face of a wolf, a compass, and a human skull.

"This one," he said, pointing at a tiny lion on his chest.

"Is that Simba from *The Lion King*?"

"Yes." He laughed. "My dad used to call me 'cub.' He often said I had the fierceness of a lion."

"I like it," I replied, running my fingers along the lines of the tattoo. "Can I have more cake? I'm still hungry."

Zayn licked his lips.

"Beg."

"You're delusional," I answered. I reached out for a piece from the counter, but Zayn swiftly caught my hands and pinned them behind my back.

"I know how much you want it, but I want to hear you say it."

"Please," I said without breaking eye contact.

Were we still talking about the cake?

He picked a small portion, but he ate the whole piece before he offered it to me.

"Hey! That was mine," I cried.

"Come for it."

I hesitated for a second, if not for a millisecond, and I planted a kiss on his lips. The instant our lips met, a surge of electricity coursed through my spine. Our attraction seemed inevitable, and the only thing that clouded my mind was how good it felt to be under his spell. He parted his lips, his tongue colliding with mine while his hands tightened their grip on my hips. It was consuming. This man was going to be the end of me. Our kiss deepened, and my hands started roaming his chest and his hair. It wasn't enough. I wanted his cock buried inside me and his name on my lips as I came.

"I want to fuck you so badly. It's the only thing I can think about lately," he said between kisses.

"Then stop wishing and do it."

Zayn ripped my blouse in one swift movement, baring my breasts to him. He took one of my nipples in his mouth, and the entire world disappeared around me. My body was burning, and all my senses came alive as he switched to my other nipple. I lifted my body so Zayn could remove both my pants and underwear. Then he took his pajama bottoms off. I was so lost in the moment that I didn't care about using a condom. He grabbed my legs, parted them wider, and pushed my body toward him. He pushed the tip of his cock against my soaking pussy and started pushing and pulling in small movements until his full length was inside me. A groan escaped his lips as he slowly picked up the pace until we were both sweating and moving at the same rhythm.

"Oh my God, Zayn. Please don't stop," I begged quietly, not wanting to wake up the entire household. The only sound in the kitchen was the one our bodies made every time they came together. Zayn continued fucking me and biting my shoulder and my neck.

"Fuck. Your cock feels so good. Right there…yes…keep doing that. Oh God."

Zayn covered my mouth with his hand to muffle my moans, which were getting increasingly louder.

"Come for me, babe, don't hold back."

He slammed into me a few more times until I couldn't control my body anymore, and my orgasm detonated. Waves of pleasure ebbed and flowed throughout my body. Zayn followed me a few thrusts after, spilling his seed inside me. We remained in that position, our bodies intertwined, for a few moments. However, when I glanced up, I noticed Noah standing at the kitchen door, his arms rigidly positioned on either side, his fists clenched, and his gaze piercing mine. I had no idea how long he'd been standing there, but it was long enough for him to realize that I'd just fucked his best friend.

"Noah…" I breathed. Zayn quickly turned around, picking our clothes from the floor and handing them back to me.

As Noah turned away, I leaped off the kitchen island, intending to go after him. However, Zayn caught hold of my arm and whispered, "Leave him be. He won't be in the mood to talk to us right now."

I was so caught up in my feelings toward Zayn that I hadn't considered Noah's feelings. We had never discussed being exclusive, but hooking up with his best friend felt like a betrayal.

"What have I done…?"

"You mean 'what have WE done.' And it wasn't the first time. We met first," he responded.

"You and your fucking habit of calling dibs. This has nothing to do with it. I'm seeing Noah. This was clearly a mistake."

"Is that what I am? A mistake?" His voice was full of hurt.

"I didn't mean it like that."

"What did you mean, Sienna? Because as far as I know, this thing we started in New York didn't end there, and I don't want to end it now either. Noah is my friend, but I can't fucking get you out of my head. Is that what you want to hear? That you've become an obsession, and all I can think about is you?" Zayn raised his voice quietly.

"I like you too, Zayn. Very much. You must know that by now… but I also like Noah. So please don't make me choose between the two of you because I can't. I need time to process this. This is too much."

Zayn stayed silent for a few seconds.

"I'll give you space to figure things out."

He left me there in the kitchen, the walls closing in on me and making it very difficult for me to breathe.

I dressed and walked to my room—the walk of shame. I paused outside Noah's room, contemplating whether to knock. However, I had a gut feeling that if I didn't give him some time to cool off, whatever was happening between us would end abruptly tonight, and that was something I didn't want to let happen.

HARD FEELINGS

(Noah)

I didn't expect to see what I saw last night. I was aware that Zayn still had feelings for Sienna, but I never anticipated that he would act on them, nor did I expect she was still interested in him. I was clearly a delusional asshole who didn't see it coming.

For a second, my heart was crushed by the possibility that Sienna didn't want me anymore, but after the shock was over, I couldn't stop watching. I should have left when I saw Zayn between her legs and heard Sienna's moans, but my feet were glued to that spot, and my breathing picked up. Seeing them gave me a hard-on, something I didn't see coming.

The image of them fucking kept replaying in my mind. I even considered taking the matter into my own hands. My right hand, to be more specific. But I just couldn't do it. It felt wrong jerking off to the memory of my best friend pounding into my girl while she moaned with every thrust…so I spent the rest of the night in my room, tossing and turning in my bed with the worst erection of my life. I was angry, worried, and horny. All at the same time.

Sienna texted me this morning saying that we needed to talk, but I skipped breakfast, cowardly hiding in my room and planning what I wanted to say to my girl.

Yes, she was still my girl until further notice.

All I knew was that I still wanted to see her, but I had no clue if she felt the same or if it was the right move. I could have any girl I wanted, but the only one I truly craved was Sienna. Would she pick Zayn over me? Could I really let go and forgive what went down in that kitchen if she chose me?

Before I found myself spiraling, I made the choice to go for a run to clear my mind. I changed into my sports clothes, slipped into my trainers, grabbed my AirPods and iPhone, and ventured out of my room. As soon as I exited the manor, I was greeted by a refreshing crispness in the air. The atmosphere was filled with a serene silence, interrupted only by the soft rustling of leaves under my feet. The tranquility of the surroundings enveloped me, creating a sense of solitude and peace. "Pray For Me" by The Weeknd and Kendrick Lamar played as I kept running around Scott Manor. My legs were screaming, and my entire body ached. I bent over, my hands resting on top of my knees and my lungs about to explode, but my mind was as clear as the sky. I wasn't going down without a fight because that girl belonged to me. If Zayn believed for a second that I'd let her go, he was sorely mistaken.

I was walking with a steady and resolute pace toward Ander's house when I saw Sienna sitting on the steps by the main door. She was clearly waiting for me, so I picked up my pace and kept my emotions in check. I didn't want her to catch a glimpse of how hurt I was, so I slapped on the poker face my mom had taught me, which came in handy during political shenanigans. I stopped in front of her but stayed silent. I wanted to hear what she had to say before I even considered opening my mouth.

"Can we talk?" Sienna asked.

I began making my way back toward the trees, motioning with my head to signal her to follow me. A few feet into the row of trees, I halted, allowing her to initiate the conversation.

"I can explain. I know it's a typical thing to say, but it's true. I want...I need to explain myself to you. I owe you that much," she said.

"I'm all ears."

"When I met Zayn in New York, I felt this connection with him that I had never felt before. It wasn't only the sex but also how easy it was to talk to him in that bar. I never expected to see him again, and then you came into the picture. I really like you, Noah. You're funny, exciting, smart, and the sex is amazing...mind-blowing amazing—"

"I can sense a 'but.'"

Sienna sighed.

"But when Zayn showed up in my life again, I couldn't stop those feelings from returning. I mean, I still like you, but I also have feelings for him. It's fucked up, I know...but it's the truth. And now I'm fucking confused."

"What are you confused about? It was clear to me last night that you prefer his dick."

"Don't be an asshole!" She ran her fingers through her hair, sighing in defeat. "I don't want you over him or him over you. I'm just confused because I don't know what to do...I want to be with you," she said, tears gathering in her eyes. "But I understand if you don't want to see me again. I get it." Sienna's voice carried a broken tone as if the mere thought of me ending whatever the fuck we had would be too much for her to bear.

"Look. I'm going to be completely honest. Seeing you last night with him was really painful, and I know we never talked about seeing other people. I love Zayn like a brother, but I don't know exactly what you're asking me. Do you want to be with both of us? Do you need time to decide? What do you want? Because I really want you, but I don't like feeling like a fool like I felt last night." I was raw and honest. A part of me didn't want to end things with her, but I wasn't sure I felt comfortable sharing her with him. "I need time to think about what I want, too," I said. "Maybe in that time, you can think about what you want because if you don't, you will only end up hurting both of us. And I won't tolerate it."

She nodded.

"Good. Let's go back to the manor. We need to get ready for Thanksgiving."

She turned around but hesitated.

"Can I ask you a favor?" she said. "Can you not mention what happened to Ander? I don't want to stir more shit between us, and that would be unavoidable if he finds out."

"No worries, but make sure Zayn also keeps his mouth shut. He enjoys provoking Ander, and he'll exploit this situation at the slightest chance he gets."

SPILLING THE TEA

(Zayn)

Part of me felt like a dick, but the truth was that I didn't regret it. Not in the slightest. I'd struggled to suppress my feelings for Sienna for the past two months, but I couldn't resist when she kissed me last night. I tried talking to Noah this morning when he came from his run, but he told me to give him some space and that he would talk to me when he was ready.

My mom had been decorating the living room and dining room all morning with Rosita, our housekeeper. I'd never seen her this excited since my dad passed away three years ago. Seeing her with another man was hard, but I was glad she was at least finding some happiness with someone.

"Are we allowed to have wine? I need a drink." Sienna's voice came from behind me. When I turned around, my mouth dropped. She looked stunning. She wore an off-the-shoulder dark blue dress that clung to her curves, reaching just above her knees and black high heels. Her long brunette hair flowed in waves, gracefully cascading around her shoulders. She looked like a goddess.

"Please, help yourself," my mom replied to Sienna.

"Can I help you, Mom?"

"No worries, darling. Rosita and I can manage, right, Rosita?"

"Sí, señora," Rosita said in Spanish. She was born in Mexico but raised in Miami. She'd been William's housekeeper since he divorced Nora, Ander's mom, five years ago.

"Can we talk a minute, Sienna?" I asked her.

"Of course, let's go outside." She grabbed my hand and led me to the back porch. Feeling her touch once more felt incredible as images from last night rushed into my mind like unstoppable waves. It felt so good to be inside her, finally appeasing the burning flame that consumed me. But last night wasn't enough—not even close. I yearned to feel her body once more, to have her all to myself in a room for an entire weekend without any interruptions.

We settled on a couch tucked away in the corner, which offered direct views of the swimming pool and the forest surrounding the manor.

"I talked to Noah and want to have a similar conversation with you."

"What did you two talk about?" I questioned in a quavering voice.

"About last night. Zayn, I do like you. Like a lot. But I also have feelings for Noah. I'm not exactly sure what that means. Maybe you think that last night signified the end of my relationship with Noah, but honestly, I'm unsure if that's what I truly want. I don't want to let him go, but dammit, I also want you. Whenever I'm around you, I feel a pull that I just can't resist. I've told him I need some space and want to ask you for the same. Could you give me that? Some space until I figure things out?"

I hesitated for a few seconds, unsure if I wanted to give her space. I was a selfish bastard who wanted to spend more time with her and make her mine. But I also suspected that if I didn't give her the space she clearly needed and pushed her to decide now, I would lose her forever.

I moved nearer to her, gently grasping her face with my hands and peering deep into the depths of her eyes. "Done. I'll give you the space you need, but let me tell you one thing, babe. If, when you make up your mind, you come to the conclusion that you want to be with me, I expect you to come back to me on your knees and show me how much you want me. Then I shall decide your punishment for making me wait this long. Trust me, you will hate it, but you'll also love it in equal measure." I kissed her fiercely, ensuring she would remember how good it felt when we were together.

*   *   *

Thanksgiving lunch was surprisingly pleasant. William behaved for the most part of our lunch, making uncomfortable comments here and there, but aside from those moments, I truly enjoyed it.

Sienna told us over lunch about that one time when William decided they needed to sacrifice a real turkey for Thanksgiving. Apparently, having heard the conversation, Ander decided to hide the turkey in his wardrobe with the aim of sparing its life. The turkey ended up shitting on all his sneakers, and Sienna couldn't stop laughing while she told us the story. I loved her laughter. Ander insisted that she was exaggerating, and for a fleeting moment, I could envision the friendship they once had right before my eyes. I wondered whether they could ever regain that friendship, but unless Ander chose to let go of all his bullshit, I found it hard to believe such a reconciliation was possible.

Ander hadn't told us why he was still upset with Sienna even though it was his father's fault rather than hers. But given the secrets that Noah and I were keeping, I wasn't in a position to demand anything from him.

"Are you going to tell us about the stalker, Sienna? Or shall I ask Noah, who apparently is the only one being kept in the loop?" Ander asked.

We were seated on the living room floor, facing the crackling fireplace that cast a warm glow. My mom and William had gone for a walk, so it was just the four of us and Rosita. She had kindly prepared popcorn and mulled wine for us, and as I reclined there with a satisfied stomach after a delightful meal, a protective sensation swelled in my chest, knowing that Sienna was dealing with a creep.

"Well, there's not much to tell. Someone broke into my apartment over a month ago and left a black dahlia and a note. It sounded romantic at the beginning, like a gesture. But I got pretty scared when I later found out that Noah had not delivered the note. I've received a few more notes and dahlias, and the intensity of the messages has escalated," Sienna explained.

"What do the notes say?" I asked her. She mentioned they were kind of romantic, so I started to think that maybe we were facing a guy who had clearly become obsessed with her in a very unhealthy way.

"It went from a 'you can't escape your fate' kind of thing to 'you're not special and can bleed like everybody else.'"

"I would say your pussy is pretty special," Noah deadpanned.

"It's not funny, asshole," Ander said, smacking Noah on the arm and spilling some wine on the carpet.

"ANDER! Your dad's gonna have my head for this, you idiot." Noah jittered, clearly influenced by the mulled wine.

"What are we gonna do about it?" I inquired. "About the stalker, I mean. Not about the carpet."

"We?" Sienna asked, raising her eyebrows. "It's my problem, not yours."

"Well, that's not true. I won't leave you all alone at Aster Hall. Who knows what this freak is capable of? When we return tomorrow, you'll pack a few things and stay in our apartment until we catch the stalker. Right, Ander?"

Ander almost choked on his drink, the unexpected comment catching him off guard.

"She can stay with me," Noah suggested in a clear attempt to keep her all to himself. I wasn't gonna let him have an advantage at wooing her.

"We have a spare bedroom, so she can have privacy. You live in a one-bedroom apartment, and as far as I know, we have both agreed to give her some space."

Shit.

I wanted to retract my words as quickly as I spilled them.

"What did you just say?" Ander asked.

I hoped he hadn't listened to what I blurted, but he clearly did. I could see in his eyes how his mind raced through different scenarios where that comment could easily fit until it all clicked. Suddenly, he rose from his seat, placed his cup on the coffee table, and abruptly exited the room.

"Well played, Zayn. Well fucking played," Sienna retorted in response and trailed Ander.

I hadn't done it intentionally, so much I could swear. My big mouth couldn't help but blurt it all out after a few drinks despite having promised her, just a few hours ago, that I would keep the secret.

"Keep doing that, and I won't even have to fight for her attention," Noah said with a smirk plastered on his face.

AN OLIVE BRANCH

(Ander)

I could hear her footsteps right behind me, but I didn't stop until I was in my bedroom. I pushed the door shut, but she stopped it from closing with her hand. In an effort to avoid her gaze, I redirected my steps toward the window. It shouldn't have affected me that much when Zayn clearly insinuated that they were both pursuing her. I didn't want to read between the lines about the implications of those words. Did Sienna hook up with Zayn again? Was she sleeping with both of my friends? The mere thought made my blood boil, but I had no right to feel that way. She meant nothing to me—just an old friendship I had no desire to revive.

Liar.

And now, Zayn was offering her a place to stay in our apartment.

"Talk to me," she whispered softly.

"I couldn't care less. It's your life, your decisions," I replied dismissively.

"I do care about you, Ander. About us. I want us to be friends again. Please, talk to me," she begged.

My mind was spiraling, my breathing becoming more frantic because as much as I wanted to lie to myself about my feelings for her, I fucking missed her, and I hadn't even realized how much until I saw her at the freshmen's party. She'd been a constant in my life until I was thirteen, my best friend. And now I wasn't sure what she was. A part of me still harbored resentment toward her, holding on to the belief that she'd forgotten about us. Another part of me longed for her friendship, yet another piece of me craved something more than just being friends. That part of me scared me the most now that I knew she clearly had feelings for both Noah and Zayn.

I was lying to myself. I wasn't this angry because of what happened with the letters. Now, I knew that our parents were the ones to blame. I was furious because I wanted her when I shouldn't, a desire I couldn't entertain. She was with Noah, and who knows what was going on between her and Zayn. Still, all I could think about every minute of every day was her. Her smile, her laugh, her eyes, the way my body burned every time I touched her skin.

"I feel there's this huge gap, like a big abyss, between us, but I want to bridge it. I want to work bit by bit to be your friend again. Don't you want that? Don't you miss what we had?" she asked.

Her relentlessness was admirable. After how badly I had treated her for the past months, she still offered me an olive branch. She wanted our friendship back, and all I wanted was that and more. So much more.

I hesitated.

Could I be friends with her? Would I be able to put a stop to these feelings in check when all I wanted was to kiss her and feel her body beneath mine? She should have been my first time.

Who was I kidding? I couldn't just be friends with her. She wasn't mine, but I couldn't stay away from her either. I wanted...No, I needed her back in my life. My life was worse when she wasn't in it.

"Okay," I said, turning around to look at her.

"Just like that? Okay?"

"Yes, I do miss our friendship." I couldn't deny her anymore. "But on one condition." I was fully aware that I was stepping into deep waters, but I also knew that, as a *friend*, it was the best thing to do based on the circumstances. "You'll move in with us until we catch the stalker." Sienna's eyes widened, clearly surprised by my request for her to stay with us. She looked like she was considering our offer, and I wished I knew what was going on in her mind.

She opened her mouth and closed it, hesitating for a few seconds before she finally said, "I'll stay with you. But we start working on our friendship now." I could feel an idea starting to take shape as soon as she threw a smile at me.

That fucking smile.

"I'll pick a movie and we'll watch it downstairs, like old times. But with Zayn and Noah."

"Are you gonna make me watch *Pride & Prejudice* again? Why don't you just tell me now that you hate me, and we're done?" She laughed, and oh my…I had missed that laugh, particularly if I was the cause of it. I could see how she was already peeling back each one of the many layers that I'd built around me when she left New York.

"You secretly love that movie…don't lie to me."

It wasn't the movie that I liked; it was what it represented, but I wasn't gonna tell her that.

We spent the whole evening bingeing movies, starting with *Pride & Prejudice*, followed by *The Devil Wears Prada*. She was so engrossed in the TV screen that she barely noticed the occasional glances Noah, Zayn, and I exchanged. This girl had re-entered my life like a tornado, and all I could do was hope that she wouldn't leave a trail of wreckage behind.

A NEW ROOMMATE

(Sienna)

Maggie helped me pack the few things I would bring to Zayn's and Ander's apartment. I was leaving most of my stuff at Aster Hall, and I would come and go to pick things up when needed. Plus, I didn't want to come across as imposing and getting too comfortable when truth be told, I was only going to be there for a few days, maybe a week or two at most.

The moment I stepped into my apartment, I dialed Sarah's number. She didn't believe me at the beginning when I told her all that had happened during our Thanksgiving break. She went mental when I spilled all the details, including the fact that Noah had found Zayn and me having sex in the kitchen. Maggie's reaction was similar to Sarah's although she said she had seen it coming.

"Are you going to pick Zayn over Noah? Girl, let me tell you something. I'm very jealous of you right now. Noah is hot as fuck, and Zayn…oh my God. He looks like a sex god. Please tell me he made you come several times?"

"Maggie!" I screamed. "Don't be rude. A lady never tells…" She held my gaze for a minute, and we both burst into laughter.

"You're no lady, Sienna. Of that, I'm sure."

It was difficult explaining to Maggie my feelings for both guys. They were very different, and I felt like each one held a piece of me. It was confusing because I wasn't sure I could pick one. It was unfair. Noah texted me a couple of times, trying to convince me to stay with him. But I knew that staying in his apartment wasn't an option. It would only make things more confusing and difficult until I had made my decision. I had a lot of things on my plate, and this was just the cherry on top.

"I have a call with Peter this week. Apparently, he has a potential candidate for the CEO position and wants to talk to me about it." It was great news. Things had been chaotic since my father had passed away, and filling the role would mean more stability at Cos Pharmaceuticals; I was sure Peter would be relieved to take back his previous role.

"Do you know who the candidate is?" Maggie asked.

"No. He said he wanted to discuss it with me personally because, in the end, it would be my decision to give him or her the role." I had asked him to send me the profile, but his hesitation to share any details with me in advance made me a bit suspicious.

"Well, I'm sure if Peter has shortlisted that candidate, it's because he or she is a good option, at least on paper."

"I guess," I replied. "How are things with you anyway? How was your break?" While I finished packing, Maggie told me all the things she'd done at the homeless shelter, and I felt really proud of her for spending her free time with those in need. I felt kind of selfish for ditching her and hanging out with the boys for the weekend, but at least something good came out of my trip to New York. Ander and I were on the same page now, and I was thrilled to rekindle our friendship.

As if Maggie could read my mind, she asked, "Are things with Ander good now?"

"Yes, they're better. It'll probably take some time to reach where we left off, but I'm determined to get there." My mind immediately traveled to our first kiss. Deep down, I knew we couldn't get back to how things were left off…not really.

"Just be careful. He was a dick with you at the beginning, so remember your worth and don't take any shit from him. Okay?"

I loved how protective Maggie was. I was lucky to find such a good friend at Stanford, especially since I missed Sarah so much. I promised to call her soon and introduce her to Maggie. I was sure she'd love her too.

* * *

Maggie and I arrived at Montgomery Hall an hour later. Zayn was waiting for us downstairs to welcome us. The building was very similar to Aster Hall. Montgomery Hall was also a mixed dorm, but in addition to all the perks mine had, this one had its own library, a gym with a sauna and steam room, and I was told that their food at the cafeteria was the best one on campus.

The building looked as if it belonged to the Victorian era, and the front looked like something straight out of a fairy tale, with all these elaborate carvings and amazing details you don't see in modern buildings. It felt like you were actually living inside a piece of history but with all the modern comforts. Maybe the fancy-ass architect who designed the building was trying to replicate an old state in the English countryside. Who knew?

"Good day, ladies," Zayn said while gracefully bending over in a courteous bow. I snorted.

"I didn't peg you for a gentleman," Maggie responded.

"Of course, I'm a gentleman." He smirked. "Let me help you carry the luggage upstairs, and I'll show you the apartment."

Maggie and I said goodbye, and she promised to call me later.

She had a tutoring appointment with one of her teachers and was running late. Zayn grabbed my bags and headed to the elevator. Their apartment was on the fifth floor. Buildings weren't that tall inside campus, but the view was outstanding. The living room windows faced west, and as the sun started setting behind the other buildings, the whole room lit up with an amazing golden glow. It was like pure magic. The way the sunlight streamed through the windows created this dreamy atmosphere that made the apartment feel cozy and welcoming. It was hands down the best spot to hang out with a book and soak in the beauty of the sunset every day.

"You like it?" Zayn asked.

"It's beautiful. Will you show me the rest of the apartment?"

Zayn grabbed my hand, linking our fingers, and started walking toward the corridor. It was a small gesture, but the contact of his skin against mine gave me goose bumps; it was evident the electric connection we had. There were three bedrooms, two to the left and one to the right, and a generously sized bathroom.

"Your room's the first to the left, and we've made some space in the bathroom so you can put your things there."

"You share a bathroom?" I asked, confused. I would have never imagined Ander and Zayn were the kind of guys who would share space. I suddenly felt extremely lucky that I was able to get a one-bedroom apartment with an en suite bathroom.

"Yes, we do. So be mindful of the time you spend in the shower, or I might have to share the space with you just so I'm not late to class," he said as he lifted his hand and tucked a strand of hair behind my ear.

Whenever Zayn touched me, I had this urge to squeeze my thighs, and my heart would race to a dangerously fast beat. Knowing that he would be sleeping just a few steps away from me every night made my head spin.

"Are you hungry?" Zayn asked, pulling me out of my daydreaming state.

"Do you want us to order something? Is Ander coming for dinner?"

"Yes, he'll be home soon. I was actually thinking about cooking one of my favorite homemade pasta dishes."

Did I hear that correctly? This man who looked like a fallen angel with the ability to bring you to your knees knew how to cook?

"Are you telling me that you cook?" I asked, my expression a mix of surprise and curiosity.

He started laughing like it was a ridiculous idea to think otherwise.

Taking a seat on one of the barstools thoughtfully arranged in front of the small kitchen peninsula, I couldn't help but feel a sense of excitement. Zayn poured two glasses of velvety red wine, placing one of them before me with a captivating smile. As I sipped the wine, he retrieved a few fresh ingredients from the fridge. He skillfully sliced the onions with precision and chopped the basil leaves and garlic, then finished by cutting cherry tomatoes in half. I was so captivated watching him work in the kitchen that I didn't even notice Ander entering the room.

"If I catch you fucking in the kitchen, I won't be such a good sport like Noah. I'm warning you," he yelled from the door.

Zayn laughed, but Ander's comment made me feel a bit uneasy. Neither Zayn nor Noah had told me he knew. I tried brushing the awkwardness aside and concentrating on how effortlessly Zayn moved around in the kitchen.

"Don't be an asshole, Ander. We're just cooking dinner," Zayn responded.

"Well, Zayn's cooking. I'm just sampling the wine and cheering him on."

Zayn grabbed a baking tray and started tossing in all the ingredients.

He drenched everything with extra virgin olive oil and gave it a nice dusting of salt and black pepper before popping the tray into the oven and setting the timer.

Ander had gone to take a shower, so while Zayn finished preparing dinner, I made my way to the bedroom and tackled the task of unpacking my luggage. The room was tastefully decorated, adorned with varying shades of whites and grays. Positioned at the center was a comfortable queen-size bed flanked by two nightstands and a closet on the opposite side of the room. Several abstract paintings decorated the walls. The entire apartment screamed interior designer paid by the parents, and *yes, we have a maid.*

"Do you like your room?"

When I turned around, my eyes widened at the unexpected sight. Ander casually leaned on the doorframe, wearing just a white towel around his waist. His dark blond hair was wet. Water droplets cascaded down his tattooed chest and abs, highlighting his muscular frame. My gaze hungrily traced every curve of his body. Only a few tattoos adorned his defined arms. Among them, I identified a snake, an angel with outstretched wings, and two koi fish, but my stomach suddenly dropped as I caught sight of the Aquarius symbol inked above his heart. My steps were slow and deliberate as I made my way toward Ander, my gaze fixated on that tattoo.

"You're not Aquarius; you're Taurus," I said while I traced my fingers over the lines.

Ander gently took hold of my chin, lifting it so that our eyes met.

"Ask me the question, Sienna."

My heart raced, and the world around me seemed to fade away. I nervously bit my lower lip, and Ander's gaze instinctively dropped to my mouth. I was afraid to ask if that tattoo meant my zodiac sign.

I wasn't ready for any of the two possibilities. It would hurt to know that it wasn't because of me, and he was just fooling around with my head, but I wasn't sure I was ready to hear the alternative answer. That I was the reason he had gotten it in the first place. I took a step back and put some distance between us.

"I need to finish unpacking. And yes, I like my room. Thanks for letting me stay here."

Ander's expression became somber, yet he managed to force a smile and replied, "Of course." Without saying another word, he turned on his heels and left to get dressed.

*   *   *

"I think we should start discussing how we're going to unmask this stalker," Ander suggested.

We sat in the dining room, eating the lovely dinner Zayn had cooked.

"What can you tell us about the notes?" Zayn asked.

I took a deep breath and explained everything between the first note I received and the last event before Thanksgiving.

"Do you think they might attend the same classes as you?" Ander asked.

"It would make sense, but they could be anyone." I shrugged, expressing my uncertainty. "They must have been following me to figure out my schedule." The notes exuded jealousy, and it got me thinking—maybe some girl wasn't too happy about me getting cozy with these guys. "Do you think it could be a girl obsessed with any of you? Maybe she doesn't like that I'm hanging out with you three?"

"It is a possibility. I think you shouldn't be alone at any point during the next few days. If you're right, she's not gonna like it when she realizes you're living with us."

Zayn was right. I was a bit scared about how the creep would react when they discovered I was staying in their apartment. The idea of being nannied didn't sit well with me, but I recognized the risks of being alone on campus.

"Bring your schedule, and we can work something out," Ander proposed.

We spent the next two hours going through my calendar and activities until we made sure someone was with me at all times, whether it was Maggie or any of them.

THE ATTACK

(Sienna)

As Maggie and I made our way out of the Biochemistry & Molecular Biology class and headed toward the cafeteria, my phone began to ring. The screen illuminated, displaying Peter's name on the caller ID.

"I'll catch you in a bit," I told Maggie.

"Are you sure? Ander will kill me if he knows I left you alone."

"It's four o'clock on a Wednesday. I think I'll be fine. I need to pick up this call. I'll see you in the cafeteria." As Maggie walked away, I pressed the green button.

"Hello, Peter."

"Hello, Sienna, how are things over there? Are you enjoying college?" Seeking a quieter spot, I scanned my surroundings and found an empty classroom to my left. I slipped inside and settled into one of the tables at the front of the class.

"Yes, I'm truly enjoying my time here, and I've made some friends. So far, it's been good. I guess you're calling me about the candidate for the CEO position, right?"

The line went quiet for a few seconds, and I checked the screen to make sure Peter was still connected to the call.

"Yes. We've received a couple of requests for the CEO position, but one of the candidates seems like the right choice. However, knowing he has a past with the company and your father, I wanted to make sure you had all the information from me before I could send you over the details."

In that instant, my mind connected all the dots, and I recognized the name behind the request even before Peter spoke a word.

"William Scott has applied for the position, and I think he's the best fit for the role."

Before he could say anything else, I replied, "No."

"Just hear me out," Peter continued, "I know things went south between William and your father, but if you take a step back and look at the role, he's our best option. He knows how things are done at Cos Pharmaceuticals; he knows everyone on the board, the company pipeline, and the work culture. He has continued to work in the business since he left the company and has contacts with many investors who could put money into our R&D department. He's the best candidate, Sienna; please consider it before you make any rash decision."

Peter was asking too much of me. He'd already decided since he strongly advocated for William Scott to take the role. However, a nagging feeling in my gut urged me to resist his proposal and seek an alternative.

My father exiled William for a reason, and accepting him as the new CEO felt like betraying my father and throwing away all the work and progress he'd made since William left Cos Pharma. If I at least knew what had happened between them, I could make an informed decision in the best interest of the company.

Maybe if I had a word with him…If he were to tell me why he and my dad broke their friendship, which not only affected their relationship but mine with Ander, maybe I could consider him for the position.

"I don't know, Peter. I won't give you an answer today. Could you give me at least a few days to think about it?" I asked.

"Of course, Sienna. You're the major shareholder, so we need your vote in order to move forward and put an offer in front of him—if that is what you end up deciding."

"Who's voting in favor?" I questioned.

"Everyone wants William back. But the final decision is only up to you. I'm sure you will make the right choice by Cos Pharmaceuticals. Call me when you have reached a decision."

"I will, Peter. Thanks for calling me." I hung up the phone and put it in my back pocket.

A million thoughts clouded my mind. I just knew I needed more information because the unknown was too big, and I worried that I would fuck up just two months after inheriting the company.

Approaching the door, I reached for the handle, only to realize it was locked. Did someone lock me in without realizing I was inside? I mean, I was on the phone, definitely not whispering, and sitting in the front row...so it wasn't as if no one would have spotted me if they happened to glance through the door window.

A sharp scratching noise behind me caught my attention, and a shiver ran through my body. I twisted around only to find a figure dressed in all-black, wearing a Purge mask, standing ominously at the far end of the classroom. They wielded a knife that methodically cut through the wooden panels on the wall as they walked down the steps. My lungs released a piercing scream as I swiftly turned around and tried to open the door. Despite my repeated attempts, the door wouldn't give in. My desperate cries for help echoed through the empty corridors, but no one came to my aid. I was utterly alone and at the mercy of a twisted psycho. I bolted through the rows of seats, trying to get as far as I could from the masked freak, but they continued to chase me across the classroom. I could taste my fear in my mouth, the adrenaline pumping through my veins.

I was fucked.

As I frantically checked my surroundings, I saw a small door that seemed to connect with another part of the building, maybe another classroom. It dawned on me that the psycho might have entered through there. Despite a part of me worrying that this door could be closed as well, I realized I didn't have many options. The psycho was steadily closing the space between us, and the thought of falling into their clutches terrified me. Observing the figure, it didn't seem like a grown man, but rather someone slightly taller than me, possibly a skinny college-age boy. The adrenaline pumping through my veins urged me to take the chance with the smaller door, hoping it could be my escape route. I lunged for the handle, my heart pounding with fear and uncertainty.

To my immense relief, the door budged, and I managed to slip into the adjoining amphitheater classroom just in the nick of time. My trembling hands hurriedly closed the door behind me, hoping it would buy me a few moments of safety. I glanced around the new room, searching for another way out or anything to help me defend myself. My thoughts raced as I considered my next move, knowing that every decision I made in this situation could be the difference between life and death. I ran down the stairs toward the main door. The door behind me cracked open.

"HELP!!!!" I shouted at the top of my lungs.

With a knot in my stomach, I turned the handle and, with a triumphant "YES!" I yanked the door open. As I stepped into the corridor, my body collided with someone. My lungs released a blood-curdling scream as two strong hands tightly gripped my shoulders, holding me in place.

To my surprise and relief, I recognized Professor Reed's face, though my panic was still palpable. It took a few seconds for my mind to process that he had grabbed me.

"Miss Moore, what's wrong?" he inquired, clearly alarmed by my distress.

Tears streamed down my face as I struggled to find the words. "We need to run. They're gonna kill me!" I managed to cry out, my voice trembling with fear.

Confusion etched across Professor Reed's face as he tried to make sense of my frantic plea. "Kill you? Who? What are you talking about?" he questioned urgently.

Desperate to break free from his grip and continue running, I tugged at his hands, but he held firm. I knew that if I couldn't escape, both of us might face grave danger. My mind raced, trying to come up with a plan to protect myself and get Professor Reed to safety as well.

"Calm down. No one is trying to kill you."

"Please, listen to me, James. Someone is back in that room with a knife, and they're trying to kill me again!"

His eyebrows rose in surprise as I mentioned his first name, but with death lurking around the corner, literally, there was no room for formalities.

"Again? Miss Moore, stay here. Let me check the room."

"No, please. Don't go in there. They'll kill you too!" I tried stopping Reed, but he strode resolutely toward the classroom I had just fled, leaving my warning lingering in the air.

He stepped into the room, glancing in all directions, only to find it empty. Closing the door behind him, he purposely walked down the hall to check the adjacent class. Also empty.

What the fuck? Where did the psycho go?

"Miss Moore, it seems you're running from a ghost."

I knew he wouldn't believe me. Why would he? I just hoped that he didn't mistake my behavior for drug use. Perhaps the psycho had made a discreet exit through a window—quite a reasonable assumption, considering we were on the ground floor.

"Let's go to my office, and I'll call campus security."

We walked in silence, my skin feeling cold since the adrenaline rush had left my body. It was the second time they'd tried to kill me, or at least it seemed like that was their plan, and I had felt utterly powerless both times. A little girl cornered without a single ounce of fight in her.

"Here, sit. I'll make some tea."

I sat on the leather couch against the office wall to the left and grabbed a blanket to cover my legs. Professor Reed quickly prepared two chamomile teas, handing one of the mugs over to me while wisps of steam playfully danced in the air.

I told him everything, from the notes to the black dahlias to the Devil's Night Fair incident. I felt like a broken record, repeating myself over and over again, asking anyone to listen and do something about it. The cops wouldn't open an investigation, and campus security was a joke. I even suggested hiring a bodyguard, but Professor Reed insisted on speaking with the security team first to request any available camera recordings that might at least lend weight to my concerns when taken to the police station. When I started calming down, I took my phone out of my back pocket and dialed the one person I needed to see to feel safe again. After two rings, he picked up.

"What's up?" Ander responded.

"Hey, could you come to Professor Reed's office? I'm with him. It's about the psycho... they've tried to..." My throat tightened, making it hard to finish the sentence, but it didn't matter.

Ander read between the lines and replied swiftly, "I'll be there in ten minutes. Don't move," before ending the call.

True to his word, Ander burst through the door after precisely eight minutes, his accelerated breathing revealing he'd rushed from wherever he was when I called him. Leaping from the couch, I clung to Ander, wrapping my arms around his neck. He circled his arms around my waist, pulling me closer, his entire body pressed against mine. A sob broke free from my lips, and Ander held me even tighter, whispering soothing words in my ear.

"I'm here, love. I'm here. You're safe now."

His voice soothed me in a way I couldn't describe.

"I won't let anything happen to you. I promise."

Professor Reed cleared his throat a couple of times, interrupting our hug in a not-very-subtle way. He was visibly uncomfortable.

"So shall I assume this means no more conflicts in my lab?"

I gave him a timid smile before I locked eyes with Ander.

"Yes, Professor. We talked over the break, and there won't be any more issues in the lab from now on," Ander said.

I was relieved to hear those words from him because they gave me hope—hope that we were on the path to healing our friendship.

"Thank you for your help. I don't know what would have happened if I hadn't stumbled into you."

* * *

Ander and I left Professor Reed's office and headed toward the cafeteria, where Maggie should have been waiting for me. She probably wondered where the fuck I was.

She was checking her phone, completely oblivious to everything that had happened. Maggie lifted her head when she noticed someone approaching the table.

"Finally! It took you ages. I guess that's why you were so late,"

Maggie exclaimed, pointing her finger toward Ander. She frowned when she noticed that I was still shaking. "What's wrong?" she asked.

"We just came from Reed's office. The psycho showed up when I finished my call with Peter and almost killed me. They had a knife. I nearly escaped before running into Professor Reed, but the freak disappeared without a trace."

Maggie seemed pretty shocked. "I never should've left you alone," she admitted, extending her hand and grasping mine.

"There was a reason we agreed never to leave Sienna's side. This was the fucking reason. She could have been killed," he ranted. "Could you have lived with yourself if something had happened to her?"

Maggie's lips quivered slightly, and her eyes glistened with unshed tears as she struggled to keep them at bay. "I'm sorry, Sienna. I don't know what else to say."

"It's not your fault, Maggie. Who says they wouldn't have tried attacking me with you there?" I turned to face Ander and placed my hand on his thigh. "Don't be so hard on Maggie. She only left because I told her to. You know how much I hate this 'bodyguard situation.'"

Ander gave my arm a reassuring squeeze, offering some comfort.

"I'm gonna go back to Ander's apartment. Rain check?"

"Of course. I'll call you later."

As Ander and I walked back to his apartment, I couldn't stop thinking about my stalker. I didn't understand why someone would want to kill me simply for being friends with Noah, Zayn, and Ander. It didn't seem like a valid reason to trigger such a violent response, but I guessed that if they were obsessed with me or them, in addition to being mentally unstable, anything I did to piss them off could be reason enough. I just hoped the police would hear me out this time. Maybe next time, I wouldn't be so lucky.

CONFESSION TIME

(Ander)

Sienna spent the rest of the afternoon locked in her bedroom. I gave her some space because she clearly needed it, but several hours had passed since we last spoke. I was desperate to talk to her, so I knocked on her door twice. After a few long seconds, she replied, "Come in."

She was lying on the bed, rolled in a blanket like a human burrito. Her eyes were red, and her lips swollen from crying, which told me that she'd probably spent a large part of the past few hours crying on her own.

"Can I join you?" I asked.

She nodded.

I lay on my side, facing her, and remained silent for a while. I simply observed her. Her eyes were slightly greener, bringing back memories of our childhood when she used to cry at the slightest things, causing her eyes to shift from honey to a greener hue. It always fascinated me. Her perky nose was red on the tip, and her cheeks were covered in dried tears. I reached out and gently traced my thumb along her jawline. Her eyebrows shot up as if she hadn't expected my gentle gesture.

"I hate seeing you like this. I hate seeing you upset," I exclaimed.

"Not long ago, you were the one upsetting me. Why do you

suddenly care? What has changed?" she asked.

I considered for a moment confessing my true feelings for her and admitting my foolishness in thinking she'd forgotten about our friendship, but something stopped me from doing it. I didn't know whether it was because of Zayn and Noah or if my fear of her rejection held me back.

"Everything and nothing," I replied. "Have you been able to rest?" I decided to change the subject.

She moved closer to me, her scent a mixture of vanilla and fresh flowers. It was intoxicating.

"No," she answered, shaking her head. "But I need to tell you something."

I remained silent, waiting for her to say whatever she needed to say.

"Before the incident, I was on the phone with Peter. He is the COO at Cos Pharma. He called me to discuss giving the CEO position to one of the candidates with me."

I wasn't sure where she was going with this or why she was telling me, but the look on her face told me it was important. "Go on," I encouraged her to continue.

She took a deep breath before she told me the last thing I expected. "Your father has made himself a candidate for the role. Were you aware of his intentions? I'm only asking because I need to know if our *new friendship* has anything to do with this."

Wait, what?

"What do you mean? Do you truly think I knew about this? You're unbelievable."

I shifted, attempting to stand, but Sienna grabbed my arm and said, "Please stay. Talk to me." I was usually the last person my dad would talk to about his business ventures or anything, but I couldn't contain the hurt in my voice. I guessed that after all the cold treatment Sienna had been receiving from me for the past two months, I shouldn't really take offense at her words of doubt. But I did.

"I didn't know, Sienna. I swear."

"I believe you," she quickly responded.

"And what did you say to Peter?" My father was a great poker player, and I was sure this meant more to him than just a new business opportunity. I didn't want to express my concerns to Sienna. I had no proof, but maybe her reappearance in my life wasn't coincidental. Was he already in conversations with Cos Pharma during Thanksgiving? He probably was, and he'd kept his cards close to his chest this entire time.

"I told him that I needed some time to think about it, but I'll have to give him a response soon," she explained.

"Let me talk to him before you make any decisions. I'll fly to New York this weekend and see if I can find out anything about his true intentions." It was the least I could do. Cos Pharma was part of Sienna's inheritance, and the last thing I wanted was for my father to fuck with her father's legacy. Especially since there was a huge mystery about why he had left the company.

"Thank you, Ander." Before I could say anything else, she kissed me.

It was just a sweet peck on my lips, but my entire body froze. Before I could even consider returning the kiss, she stood and headed to the bathroom. Sienna left me in her room with a boner and my mind running a hundred miles per hour.

* * *

Zayn came home an hour later and went ballistic when Sienna told him about the stalker. I could see murder in his eyes.

"I swear I'm gonna kill the fucker if they try to lay a hand on you again." Zayn looked possessed, and I honestly thought he meant what he said.

"I'm looking into hiring private security, but I think I want to join a self-defense class," Sienna blurted.

"Are you sure?" I asked.

"Yes. Every time I've faced this psycho, I've felt terrified and helpless. I don't want to feel like this anymore. I want to know that if I ever come face-to-face with them again, I'll be able to defend myself. Only if it means buying me a couple of seconds to run the fuck away and avoid being attacked."

Zayn and I looked at each other, and the moment he broke eye contact with me, I knew what he was about to say.

"I'll teach you."

"What?" Sienna clearly looked surprised by Zayn's offer.

"I'm a black/red belt in jujitsu. I can teach you the basics."

I knew Zayn was a pro. I'd witnessed him in several tournaments where he'd consistently secured the first and second positions. If anyone could teach Sienna some self-defense moves, it would be him.

"I think it's a great idea," I added.

I could see Sienna pondering on the offer. She wasn't aware of Zayn's abilities on the mat, but he was a skilled motherfucker.

"Okay. Thanks," she said in a hushed tone.

The doorbell rang, and Zayn stood from the couch and headed toward the door. Seconds later, an angry Noah stormed into the apartment, demanding, "What the hell, Sienna? Why must I learn from Ander that the stalker came after you today?" His face turned red, and the vein in his neck was on the verge of popping. Sienna dropped her eyes to her hands and curled them on her lap.

"I'm sorry. I should have told you sooner, but I've been in shock all afternoon and haven't checked my phone. I don't even remember where I put it."

Noah sighed and rubbed his hands over his face.

"Give her a break, Noah. You know she hasn't done it on purpose," I responded. He nodded in agreement. His eyes roved over Sienna's delicate form, and his features softened as he noticed the fear across her face.

Sienna spent the rest of the evening curled on the couch, her head on Noah's lap while he caressed her hair and her feet on Zayn's legs. I sat on the opposite sofa, glancing at her occasionally. Since I saw her at the freshers' party, I hadn't stopped thinking about her. In the beginning, I was consumed with rage as all the feelings I had once felt for her resurfaced. She'd always lingered on my mind to the point that every time I saw a Jane Austen book or someone mentioning *The Notebook* or *Pride & Prejudice*, all I saw was her face. But now, everything was different. I was facing the ghosts of my past, and every minute I spent in her company only fueled my growing desire to get closer to her.

A few *Modern Family* episodes later, she fell asleep. I wrapped her in my arms and took her to her room, gently settling her into bed. After tucking her in, I kissed her forehead and said, "Sweet dreams, Sienna."

As I turned to leave, she whispered, "I've really missed you."

Me too, Sienna. Me too.

IT WAS A MATTER OF TIME

(Sienna)

Ander and I finally started working as a team in the lab. We'd made good progress in our research, and Professor Reed was pleased with the change in our attitude. He approached our working station and took my notepad to check my notes.

"How are you, Miss Moore? Were you able to speak with the police department?" Reed had shared the recordings from a couple of cameras with them, but the police informed me that the quality was very poor, and there wasn't much they could do since the stalker's face was covered. However, this time, they took the investigation more seriously. I imagined that witnessing a figure wielding a knife and running toward me provided the proof they needed to believe me. They had requested a list of all the subjects I was enrolled in at Stanford so they could investigate some names. Nevertheless, they cautioned me not to get my hopes up as it could be someone from my past or someone not associated with any of my classes.

"Yes, but I haven't heard from them since I spoke to Officer Johnson. He's leading the investigation. I asked my lawyer to make some calls, and now it seems the police department is more invested in the case, knowing that my parents kept some friends in the FBI."

A flicker of disgust crossed his face, but he swiftly masked his expression, leaving me unsure if I had imagined it.

"Nothing works like having good contacts in this world," he said with a smile that didn't reach his eyes. "I'm glad that at least they're looking into it. Let me know if there's anything I can do to help you."

"Sure. Thanks."

"You're welcome. Since we're finished for the day, feel free to head home once you're done with these calculations. I'll see both of you tomorrow," Professor Reed announced.

After tidying up our workstation, I took my gym bag and headed to the bathroom at the end of the corridor.

"I'll wait for you outside. Be quick." Ander had offered to walk me to one of the local gyms where I was supposed to take my first self-defense lesson with Zayn. I opted for black leggings, a black crop top, and my favorite sneakers, tying my hair in a high ponytail. I was unsure if my outfit fit the exercises we would be doing, but at least I looked good in it. I wondered if Zayn would like it.

Ander's eyes lit up when I exited the bathroom, and he saw me wearing my sports clothes.

"You like it?" I inquired with a cheeky smile.

His eyes roamed my entire body, and heat built between my thighs from the way he looked at me. "Zayn is gonna struggle to focus with you wearing that. That much I know," he replied with a strained expression, narrowing his eyes.

After Ander left me for my class, I walked into the gym. The receptionist greeted me with a warm smile.

"Hi. Welcome to The Dragon Den. Can I help you?" she asked.

"Hi, I have a private lesson booked. Zayn Siegel made the booking."

She clicked the mouse and began typing on the computer.

"He has booked the second room to the left. Here," she said, handing me a towel and opening the barrier. I thanked her for the towel and quickened my pace until I located the room Zayn had reserved for us. He was shirtless and in the middle of doing push-ups. Dropping my bag on the floor, I leaned against the doorframe, taking my time to appreciate the sculpted muscles of his back glistening with sweat.

"Are you gonna come in, or are you going to keep eye-fucking me?" His growl sent tingles coursing through my body.

"Who says that I'm eye-fucking you?" I responded, holding my head high and closing the door behind me.

"Okay," he said while he finished his last push-up and stood.

"First, take your shoes off. They are not allowed on the mat."

I took my sneakers off and placed them next to my sports bag, then I stepped on the wrestling mat and waited for Zayn's instructions.

"Before we practice any self-defense moves, I want to teach you some basic maneuvers," he explained.

Over the next hour or so, he taught me some fundamental movements, such as how to escape from someone's grip or how to use the base of my palm to target and break an assailant's nose. We repeated all the exercises until I was exhausted, and my entire body ached.

His T-shirt hugged every muscle of his torso, arms, shoulders, and back.

Why did men look so fuckable with a black T-shirt and gray sweatpants?

"Okay. Now we're gonna practice a real-life scenario."

"What do I need to do?" I asked, biting my lower lip.

"I'm going to throw an attack your way, and I want you to show me how you would counteract an opponent my size using the techniques I've shown you."

Great.

Before I could seek further guidance from him, Zayn lunged at me, pulling me closer with his right arm. He secured both of my hands and pressed them against my chest while his front pressed firmly against my back. I let out a scream. Desperately, I attempted to free myself from his grip, but no matter how hard I struggled, his hold on me only grew stronger, thwarting my every attempt to break free. I pushed my ass back against him, and I shivered with the groan that escaped his lips right in my ear. I could feel his hardness as I kept grinding my hips against him.

As he loosened his hold on me, I linked my right foot behind his right leg, taking the opportunity to fight him back. With a swift movement, I pushed backward, causing both of us to tumble onto the mat. In an instant, Zayn rolled over me, positioning his entire body atop mine, with his hips nestled between my legs. Securing both of my hands, he firmly placed them above my head, rendering me wholly immobilized in under three seconds.

"Is that how you plan on defending yourself from an attacker? By begging him to fuck you?" He pushed his hips forward, clearly showing me how hard he was for me. My only answer was a quiet whimper.

"I knew you were trouble from the moment I met you, beautiful," he said before his mouth collided with mine in a hungry and devastating kiss. Our tongues clashed desperately while each nerve in my body came alive with every thrust from his hips. I wanted him to rip my clothes off so he could take me here on this mat.

"Please," I begged. It wasn't clear from my plea if I was begging him to stop or to continue. He suddenly shifted one of his hands so he could keep a tight hold of both of my wrists simultaneously. He didn't break the kiss, but his other hand traveled to one of my breasts, pinching my nipple over the fabric. "Zayn," I moaned, my voice full of lust as he pushed his free hand under my leggings. He shoved my underwear to one side and sank two fingers into my wetness as I tried to quiet my cries of pleasure.

"I love how wet you are for me, babe."

He steadily continued with his sweet torture, moving both fingers in an angle that kept hitting the right spot every single time he pushed them in and out. I lifted my hips, seeking more pressure in an attempt to reach that peak that would throw me over the edge. His mouth continued to devour me, our breathing becoming more and more frantic. I was close, so close, but he suddenly broke our kiss and sat back on his knees. Before I could make any complaints, he pushed my leggings and underwear down until my bottom half was completely naked.

Well, I still had my socks on.

"I've fucked you twice already, but I haven't tasted you yet. I'm going to eat your pussy now, and you're going to come on my face. But you need to be quiet. Can you do that for me, babe?"

I nodded, furrowing my eyebrows with my mouth slightly open.

He dropped his head between my thighs, and with one stroke, he licked my entire wetness.

"Mmm, your pussy tastes better than I imagined." Zayn continued licking me as I used both of my hands to thread my fingers in his thick black hair. I was at the mercy of his tongue, and every time he circled my bundle of nerves, my body arched, seeking more friction. Each stroke ignited every cell in my body, and my moans became louder when he pushed two fingers inside me while he sucked on my clit. Every torturous movement of his fingers and tongue brought me closer to fucking Nirvana, and each time I pulled his hair, Zayn's response was to finger fuck me harder and lick faster.

It didn't take me long to reach my climax, but he kept stroking and sucking relentlessly to prolong my orgasm.

When I came down from my high, Zayn grabbed my clothes and passed them to me. I threw on my clothes while he fixed up his sweatpants. He raised my bag from the ground and motioned for me to come closer. Gently, he lifted my chin and planted a soft kiss on my lips.

"You've done a good job today. Let's go home; I'll cook dinner. We can continue our training in a couple of days."

I circled his waist with my arms, planting another kiss on his lips before saying, "Knows how to cook, an excellent personal-defense instructor, and exceptional at giving head. What have I done to deserve you?"

A half smile graced the corner of his mouth as he looked at me.

"You deserved to be worshipped, Sienna. Since I met you at that bar in Tribeca, I haven't stopped thinking about you, and the more I get to know you, the more I know that I want you in my life. I know you care about Noah, so I won't push on this matter any further, but please know that I'm here for you no matter what and that the only way this psycho will get to you is over my dead body." His words were filled with a silent promise. A promise that said that I wasn't alone in this.

"Let's go home, Cobra Kai," I replied, trying to lighten the mood. Zayn burst into laughter, the sound resonating deeply in my chest. He didn't laugh as often as I'd liked, but I understood better than anyone where his darkness came from. I understood that he was my dark warrior with a damaged soul, and I was more than happy to bring light to his life and surrender to his shadows.

CONFIDENTIAL

(Ander)

Claudia welcomed me home with open arms. She always had a smile on her face, and I wondered about two things. First, how could someone so cheerful give birth to someone who always seemed to wear a sour expression, and second, how my dad had managed to seduce a woman like her. Don't get me wrong; my dad was still very good-looking and in great shape for his age, but he always looked angry, as if someone was constantly pissing on his shoes.

"Oh, Ander, I'm so glad you came to visit us. It's a shame that my son couldn't make it. Anyway, I've asked Rosita to prepare your favorite food for lunch."

I kissed her cheek quickly and handed my small bag to Gordon, our butler. I had packed light and planned to stay in New York for only one night. Though I could have had this conversation with my father over the phone, I understood the significance of looking into his eyes to detect any lies. I mean, he had proved over and over again that he was a fucking good liar, but I hoped that he would at least give me a half truth if we had this conversation face-to-face rather than over the phone.

"Where's my father?" I asked her as I removed my coat and my scarf. I also handed them to Gordon, indicating he could put them in my bedroom with my bag.

"He's in his office. I believe he's in the middle of an important meeting, but he told me he was having lunch with us, so he should be finishing up soon."

"I'll wait for him outside of his office. I'll be quick."

Claudia gave me a concerned look, but she knew me well enough to know by now that I was as stubborn as my father.

I headed down the hall and turned left before I reached the stairs. My father's office was to the far left of the house, the last door to the right. I positioned myself with my back against the wall opposite his office door, crossing my arms while waiting for him to end his call. Although I could hear him talking, I couldn't make out any words that would reveal the identity of the person he was speaking to or what they were talking about. After a few minutes of prolonged silence, I presumed the call had ended, so I pushed myself off the wall and knocked on the door three times before opening it. My father was comfortably seated on his luxurious leather chair, positioned regally behind a mahogany desk with stacks of papers placed on top of it.

"Hello, son. How was your trip?"

"It was okay. Thanks for asking. Can we talk?"

"Have a seat." I crossed the room and sat opposite him in one of the two chairs. "You got me all intrigued after your call. What do you want to talk about that couldn't be discussed over the phone?"

I knew his tactics well enough to realize that he was already privy to the reason behind my sudden visit. He only asked the question to coax me into spelling it out so he could feign surprise.

"Sienna told me." I didn't want to say anything else. He was the one who needed to do the talking.

"I see," he responded. "Well, I thought it was a great business opportunity when one of the members of the board called me about the opening. That's all."

I leaned forward, placing both elbows on top of my thighs. "I know you, Father. I find it difficult to believe that this opportunity just opened up out of the blue. If at least you were honest with me and Sienna about the reasons that made you leave Cos Pharmaceuticals, maybe, only maybe, she wouldn't have second thoughts about giving you the position."

He hesitated, probably remembering that the final decision was in Sienna's hands.

"Things are not black and white, Son. Since you were a kid and your mom and I got divorced, you've painted me as this big bad wolf who only does things to punish you. But you have no idea what I had to give up for this family or the sacrifices I had to make. I paid my price and did so willingly, but now I'm here to collect," he spat out, venom lacing his words.

His phone started ringing. He looked at the screen with a frown. My father rose and strode purposely toward the door, saying, "Stay here. We're not done with this conversation."

I slumped on the chair and checked my social media and email accounts. I also texted Sienna to let her know that I'd arrived home. After a few minutes of scrolling through my phone, I got bored, so I started going through the documents on the table. Most were reports about prospective investment opportunities with charts and financial statements. I picked up a folder from the pile to my left, and my eyes widened as I read the label on the cover: "Cos Pharmaceuticals Inc. CONFIDENTIAL. Edward L. Moore." Why did my father have a folder labeled with Sienna's dad's name? With trembling hands, I opened the folder, adrenaline coursing through my veins at the mere thought of my father returning to his office and catching me going through his private stuff. Curiosity overpowered any sense of caution, and I just hoped I didn't end up like the cat in the old saying. Dead. Hanged by one of my dad's expensive ties.

The folder contained many documents, from email printouts and balance sheets to reports and contracts. Uncertain if the contents held valuable information, I did the only thing that came to mind. I took my phone and started taking pictures of every single page. Once I was done, I returned everything to the desk and reclined in my chair like nothing had happened. My heart was about to come out of my chest, so I tried to control my breathing. I pretended to be checking my phone when the door opened. My father's facial expression told me he wasn't in a good mood, and for a moment, I honestly thought he'd caught me.

"We're going to have to postpone our chat for another time. There are some issues at our Texas site, and I must go over there now and potentially fire some people. Why is it so difficult to find competent staff nowadays?"

I sighed, relieved I didn't have to endure his company for too long.

He may not have disclosed why he suddenly became interested in Cos Pharmaceuticals, but something—call it sixth sense or the knot in my stomach—told me the answer to that same question was in those documents.

We made our way to the dining room, finding Claudia patiently awaiting our arrival. My father wouldn't stay for lunch with us, and I felt terrible for her. I was sure she must have been excited to spend the afternoon sharing wedding ideas with me, but my plan was to lock myself in my room and go through every single document I had snapshots from until I found an answer—anything.

"I'm flying back to California tomorrow morning, so I guess I'll see you in a few weeks for Christmas?"

"Yes. And remember to get your tuxedo ready for the ball. There's no need to worry about the mask. Claudia got one for each of us shipped from Venezia."

With the wedding around the corner, Claudia and my father had opted to host a grand masquerade ball for New Year's Eve this year, so Zayn's and my presence were mandatory.

"When you're part of New York's elite society, you cannot plan a tacky bachelor or bachelorette party like some middle-class couple. Our positions hold grand responsibilities, so planning an elegant party is the best way to handle people's expectations. The masquerade ball is Claudia's idea. I personally hate it, but planning events makes her happy and keeps her busy."

Those were my father's words when I asked about the ball's purpose.

Charming.

"Sienna will be on the guest list. I just wanted to give you a heads-up," I casually informed him.

My father halted in the hallway, turning my way. A shift in his expression was noticeable before he answered, "Considering that we might end up working together, I suppose there's no harm in inviting her."

Though I hadn't invited her yet to the ball, I planned to. It'd be the perfect excuse to spend more time with her, something I had been craving more and more lately. Since we discovered that our letters had been intercepted all those years ago, my feelings for her had resurfaced.

You're a fool, Ander; those feelings never left.

But I wouldn't act on them. She was seeing Noah...or Zayn. I hated seeing her with them. Sometimes I wished I could go back to that party. If I could, I would make her mine.

Fuck it.

If I get another shot, she will be mine.

*   *   *

After two hours of googling financial terms, I realized I knew nothing about finances.

None.

Niente.

Nada.

I understood some of the content, but not enough to draw conclusions. Sienna would need help translating these, and that help wasn't coming from me. That was a fact.

I texted Sienna to let her know what I'd found.

Me

> Hey. I found something. *Pic of the folder*

Sienna

> WTF. What's inside?

Me

> There are several documents, but I'm not a finance expert, so I don't understand if there's something compromising here. Let me upload them to iCloud, and I'll send you the link.

Sienna

> Thanks Ander.

Me

> No worries. See you tomorrow? We can look at them together or find someone who can help.

Sienna

Yes. I'll be home by the time you arrive.
Safe flight.

Home. The fact that Sienna felt at home in my place made me smile. Speaking of home.

Me

Hey.

Zayn

Hey. How's NY?

Me

Same. Need something from here?

Zayn

Are you really texting me to ask if I need something from home?

Me

Not really. Have you talked to Noah?

Zayn

There's nothing to talk about.

Me

Don't be a dick. He's your friend, and you fucked the girl he likes in front of him.

Zayn

He shouldn't have come to the kitchen.

Me

Rolling eyes emoji

Zayn

Yes, I know. I'll talk to him.

THE PACT

(Zayn)

He was probably doing it on purpose to punish me. Twenty minutes. I had been waiting for Noah at The Patio, a local bar, for the past twenty *fucking* minutes. He left me on read for several hours before replying to my texts. He wouldn't pick up the phone either. A double blue tick that perfectly said, *"Fuck you, Zayn,"* without even saying it.

But I'd wait. I was patient.

Ten minutes later, Noah showed up. He wore gray sweats and a black T-shirt—zero point on effort—and his facial expression was as bitter as the IPA I was drinking.

"Hey, thanks for coming," I said.

"Sure, I had nothing better to do."

My eyes probably rolled to the back of my head. Noah getting angry was never a fun sight. He'd act like a thirteen-year-old every time.

"What did you want to talk about that was so important?" he asked.

"Really, man? You can't think about a single thing we need to talk about?"

Like a kid.

Every. Single. Time.

"I mean…if you want to apologize, I'm all ears."

"And what exactly should I be apologizing for?" I knew what I did wasn't right, but it wasn't wrong either. Sienna and Noah weren't exclusive, and although going for the girl my friend was interested in was a bit of a dick move, I really liked Sienna. And I met her first. But I never thought I'd see her again. Maybe if I could explain myself and he understood…

"OK. That was harsh. Listen, I won't apologize for what happened in Rye." The sound of the chair scraping against the floor made me jump. Noah was leaving the boat. "Hey, wait. Where are you going? I'm not done."

"If you think I'm going to stay here to listen to you talk about what amazing sex you're having with Sienna, you're delusional," he exclaimed.

"Noah. I'm not sleeping with Sienna." *Liar.* "Wait, man. I haven't finished my apology!" I shouted.

I'm not sure what made him stop. The fact that I said I wasn't having sex with her or that I was going to apologize.

"If that was the start of an apology, it's the worst one I've ever heard. You need to work on your skills, dude." Shaking his head, he returned to the barstool and placed his left arm on the counter.

I ordered him another IPA before I resumed my apology.

"Look. Let me say what I want to say, and then you can shout at me as much as you like, but we need to move forward somehow, Noah. I hate that we're not hanging out together and that you only talk to me when Ander is around."

He stayed silent, so I proceeded with my case.

"You know how much I liked the girl I met in New York, even before finding out that the girl was Sienna. And when I saw her at The Cave…shit, Noah, I knew that I couldn't throw away the chance to be with her again. I know that I'm selfish and an unreasonable bastard, but I'm obsessed with her. I can't stop thinking about her. But you're also my friend, and I don't want to lose you. I know I was a dick in Rye, that I didn't think of your feelings. Please tell me what to do, but don't tell me to stop chasing her because I won't promise you that. If she wants me, she can have me. All of me." I've never been a man of grand speeches, so this was a first. Since the moment I saw Sienna on Noah's birthday, I couldn't stop it. The feelings, the need to make her mine.

"Shit, Zayn. I knew you liked Sienna, but I never thought you felt that way about her. You've always been a player, so I assumed you were just thriving on the challenge."

Noah wasn't wrong. I'd always been a player, and Zayn, *the player*, was who Sienna met in Manhattan. However, to my surprise, I really enjoyed her company that night, the conversation, the jokes, her laugh, and the sex. *Fuck*. She was addictive. I don't know how many times I'd fucked my hand the past week just thinking about her tight pussy.

"I know, man. I don't know. I can't imagine how pissed you probably were when you found us in the kitchen." I hope he didn't see much because I would have seen red if it had been me. What a hypocrite…

Noah tittered and shook his head.

"Did I say something funny?" I was confused.

"If I tell you something, do you promise you won't use it against me?" he asked, chuckling.

I nodded.

Noah took a sip from his beer and continued. "In fact, I wasn't that pissed and that pissed me off."

Did I say confused?

"You may think I only saw a bit of the performance, but the truth is that I was there from the very beginning."

"WHAT?" I yelled. Almost everyone in the bar turned around to check where the shriek was coming from and why. I lowered my voice and asked him, "What do you mean you were there from the beginning?"

Noah sighed.

"I mean what I said. When I saw you two go at it…I just couldn't stop watching. My feet were glued to the floor, and if I'm frank, my cock was hard. Really hard. Hard to the point that I considered putting my hand inside my pants and jerking off from the shadows like a fucking voyeur."

I'd never seen Noah blush, but his pink cheeks gave him away. His beer was almost untouched.

"Let me get this straight. You've been mad at me this entire week when, in fact, seeing me and Sienna turned you on?"

"Yeah. Something like that. But I was pissed too. I'm still pissed. I also like Sienna a lot, and although I didn't have a chance to talk to her about exclusivity, you went behind my back and fucked her when I was under the same roof. It's not my fault that seeing you both turned me on. An unexpected side effect."

I appreciated Noah's honesty, but it was clear that we were unwilling to give up on Sienna.

"I guess we'll wait and see what she decides. I propose a truce and a pact. Whoever she picks, the other one won't get mad and blindside the chosen one. Deal?" I extended my hand.

"Deal," Noah replied, shaking my hand.

May the odds be in my favor.

* * *

When Noah and I arrived at the apartment, Ander and Sienna were perched on the kitchen peninsula, looking confused while reading several documents scattered on the counter.

"What are you guys doing?" I asked.

"Ander found some documents in his dad's office and took photos.

We're just going through them. Do you want to help us?"

We dug into every document for three hours, hoping to uncover helpful information. Ander had told us how he stumbled upon these papers after talking to his dad about the CEO position, but our efforts seemed useless without knowing what we were looking for.

"Look. It doesn't make sense," Ander blurted. "Some of these documents mention several lines of investigation with additional budget allocated to them, but when I look at the R&D pipeline, these aren't included." Ander had put aside several budget authorizations that apparently could not be found in the R&D report. "See? Here. Your dad signed these five documents, but when you look at the summary report, they're not mentioned," Ander commented while pointing at a document showing records of all Cos Pharmaceuticals' research projects from 2010 to 2015.

"Maybe these projects were stopped, and that's why they're not there," Noah stated while snatching four Budweiser cans from the fridge and handing them around.

"I thought about that too, but these other projects here say 'terminated,' so if they were stopped, it should say. They would be here." Ander kept flipping through the documents, but he couldn't spot any papers discussing the reasons behind those projects getting axed, assuming they were indeed terminated.

"Maybe you can ask your contact at Cos Pharma for any details. You should have access to that info." I glanced at Sienna, but she appeared to ignore my comment.

"Wait a minute. What the actual fuck?!" Sienna burst out, her eyebrows furrowing in confusion. "Why is Professor James Reed's name here?" Sienna gestured toward one of the budget allocation approvals that had caught Ander's attention. Under the section labeled "Research

Team Structure," it read "Research Assistant Dr. James Reed."

"Who's Professor James Reed?" Noah asked, but everyone ignored him.

"How do you know it's him? There must be thousands of James Reeds in the United States." Ander made a good point, so I grabbed my phone and quickly searched for Professor Reed's profile on the Stanford University website. It only took me a few clicks to find what I wanted.

"It is. Check this out," I said while showing my phone screen to the group. Every single lecturer at Stanford had a profile under the Staff section with details about their professional career and merits. It was a long shot, but the information was there. From 2013 until 2016, Professor James Reed worked at Cos Pharmaceuticals. After that, he was employed as an assistant professor at Columbia University in New York before being offered a position at Stanford this year.

"Shit." Sienna sighed. "If he worked for my dad, how come he's never mentioned that to me?" We didn't have an answer for her, so we just stayed quiet. "I guess I need to have a conversation with him tomorrow. I'll speak with Peter, too, but I think including the CFO in the call would be best. He should know if there was a budget allocation toward these projects. He has been in the company for longer than I remember, so I'm sure he worked for my father around these dates."

At least we now had a plan in place. Perhaps Professor Reed could share valuable insights from his time at Cos Pharma. I only worried this lead would turn out to be a dead end.

TOO MANY SECRETS

(Sienna)

We spent the rest of the evening discussing what I should say when confronting Professor Reed. Part of me wanted to storm into his office and challenge him about not revealing his connection to my father, but Ander was right. If I approached him too aggressively, there was a chance he would shut down and refuse to share any information at all.

"I'm tired, guys. I'm going to bed," I announced, standing up from the kitchen stool.

"Can I have a word with you, Sienna?" Noah asked before I had a chance to leave the room. "In private." Noah followed me to my room and closed the door behind him. He stood there, arms crossed over his chest, while I sat at the end of my bed, nervously patting my hands on my legs. I had a feeling about what he wanted to talk about, but I kept quiet and gave him a moment to gather his thoughts.

"I just wanted to tell you that I had a chat with Zayn, and we've cleared the air between us. So it's all good."

The last thing I wanted was to cause any bad blood between Zayn and Noah, so part of me was glad things were right again between them.

"I'm happy to hear that."

Noah uncrossed his arms and closed the distance between us as he sat beside me. I averted my gaze to my hands, idly toying with the hem of my dress. He lifted his right hand and locked my hair behind my ear. The contact made my skin burn. Noah noticed the blush creeping into my cheeks and softly chuckled.

"Noah…" I breathed while turning to face him. "I know you and Zayn want an answer from me, but I'm not ready to give you one yet. Honestly, you know how much I like you, but choosing you means losing Zayn, and I don't want that. I know I'm very selfish for wanting you both, but I'm trying to be honest. Sorry if my indecision hurts you both. It's not intentional; that is why I haven't decided yet, and I don't know if I can make one. I don't want to hurt any of you."

Noah kept quiet for a few seconds before he spoke. "I know… we'll give you more space if that's what you want. I just wanted to tell you that I haven't changed my mind. I want you, Sienna. Badly. You're incredible. You're smart, funny, sweet, and fucking gorgeous. Believe me when I say all I want right now is to rip off your clothes and fuck you right here, but I'll hold myself back from doing anything stupid like kissing you."

Noah dropped his gaze to my lips.

I wanted him. But I also wanted Zayn. "Thank you for understanding, Noah."

"Good night, princess." Noah kissed my cheek before he left my room. That night, I dreamed about Zayn and Noah and how good it would feel if I could have them both.

* * *

I found myself rooted in front of Professor Reed's office, my gaze tilting upward to the ceiling. My heart raced, and my palms felt clammy as I gathered the courage to knock on his door. After a deep, steadying breath, I turned my attention back to the door, raising my hand to deliver two hesitant knocks.

"Yes? Please come in." He seemed surprised to see me. I closed the door and stood at the entrance of his office. "What a nice surprise. Please sit. What can I do for you?" he asked, waving his hands toward one of the chairs.

"I don't know where to start, so I guess I'll just let it out."

Professor Reed arched a single eyebrow, evidently caught off guard by my statement.

"Why didn't you say you worked for my father?"

He reclined back on his chair, linking his hands together in front of him.

"I didn't think it mattered. Why do you ask?" His face showed no expression.

"I came across some documents, and your name was on one of them." I didn't want to mention what kind of documents, at least not until I had a chance to speak with Peter and Michael.

"Well, yes. I worked at Cos Pharmaceuticals for several years, but they made my team redundant, so I took the opportunity for a career change." I could sense he wasn't telling me everything, so I tried pulling more answers from him.

"Redundant? Why?" I asked.

"Budget restrictions, I guess. They said they had to size down the R&D department, so I was let go."

"You could have said something when you realized who I was. Why didn't you?" Professor Reed looked to his left and took a long breath before responding.

"I thought you might be tired of hearing everyone expressing their condolences, and I didn't want to contribute to that weight by sharing mine. It didn't seem necessary." There was a long silence before he continued talking, not so subtly changing the subject. "Have you heard from the police department?"

I briefed him on the most recent developments in the investigation. Officer Johnson, the investigator assigned to my case, had made some headway, although everything at this point was still speculative.

"I hope they catch the culprit soon. I don't want one of my best students getting distracted or worse."

"I hope so, too. Anyway, thanks for your time, Professor."

"No need to thank me. My door is always open for you."

I walked out of his office with a weird feeling. Chatting with him stirred up bitter memories from last summer and the struggle to keep moving forward. I wanted to make the right call about William Scott, and my gut told me there might be more to his sudden interest in the company. So I was determined to dig deeper and figure things out before making my decision. Maybe he had some leverage, which was why he held those confidential documents. It would be easier if he'd just come clean about why he left the company, but when it came to Mr. Scott, simplicity was never part of the equation.

* * *

"Hi, Peter. Hi, Michael. Thank you for taking the time to speak with me."

After I left Professor Reed's office last week, I emailed the CFO and COO at Cos Pharmaceuticals to schedule a meeting. I was sitting in Zayn and Ander's living room with my laptop in front of me, my screen displaying two exhausted faces on Zoom.

"Hi, Sienna. Gosh, you've grown up!" Michael exclaimed. "I'm glad to hear from you. Peter here has told me you're now in college. Congratulations on being accepted at Stanford. Your father would be very proud."

My stomach churned at the mention of my dad, but I managed to push down the bitter taste rising in my mouth and forced a hesitant smile.

"Thank you for your kind words, Michael," I responded.

"You didn't say much in your email. What is it you wanted to talk about?" Peter was always straight to the point, and I really appreciated it this time. I had no desire to give Michael yet another opportunity to offer his condolences. His sympathy had already been abundantly shared during the funeral, and I was eager to avoid revisiting that day.

"Yes. So...okay. I stumbled upon a set of documents that reference extra budget allocations for five R&D projects, all of which were approved by my father. Strangely, these particular projects weren't included in the summarized report, which accounted for all of the therapies in our R&D pipeline. Can you send me further details on these? I'll share their INNs and project codes with you to make them easier to identify. I've pasted the info in the chat."

A couple of minutes later, Peter broke the silence. "Where did you find these documents?" His tone was sharp.

"It doesn't matter. Do you know something about it?" Both men were clearly uncomfortable with my inquiry.

"Has William said anything to you?" The mere mention of his name sent shivers down my spine.

"Peter. I won't ask you again. Do YOU know something about this?"

He paused for a moment before Michael jumped into the conversation.

"Tell her, Peter. She needs to know, especially since William expressed his interest in re-joining the company."

Michael's words caught me by surprise, yet I remained silent and tried looking indifferent to their words. They clearly knew something I didn't. Whatever it was, it seemed troubling enough to worry them.

I tried to pull my best *I-already-know* face so they would continue talking.

With a heavy sigh, Peter said, "Six years ago, Michael found several discrepancies in some of our monthly financial reports. When he raised his concerns with your father and William, your father brushed it off and requested him to keep it under wraps. Just to clarify, these reports indicated that substantial sums of money that were originally designated for specific R&D projects had been redirected to an offshore account. A few weeks later, William handed in his resignation. When I confronted William, he didn't say much. He just said that he had a disagreement with your father and didn't wish to continue working with him. About a week later, your father made a considerable contribution, covering the missing amount from our accounts, and did so as a silent investor. He also made it clear that we were to keep all this information to ourselves."

"What are you implying?" My head spun with the information as I tried to piece everything together.

"Sienna, your father was the signatory of those documents. I suppose William confronted him about it. From what William told me a few weeks back when he proposed his candidacy, it looked like they had a heated argument, which ultimately led to his departure from the company. Michael attempted to persuade me that the right course of action was to involve the authorities and report the embezzlement of private funds. However, having known your father for a considerable period of time, I couldn't bring myself to believe he would engage in such conduct. Since the money was eventually returned, I managed to convince Michael that the best approach was to write it off and move forward, hoping this information wouldn't come out. Cos Pharmaceuticals helps millions of patients with their drug developments. Calling the authorities would have meant dissolving the company, damaging the trust of health authorities worldwide, or causing significant delays in bringing new therapies to the market."

A wave of dread washed over me. Peter's words were like a punch in the gut, and I struggled to come to terms with them. I didn't want to accept the idea that my dad could be involved in something so terrible, but there was a strange logic to it. William's abrupt departure from the company and the ensuing fallout, which resulted in my dad forbidding me from seeing Ander, had always puzzled me. What if my dad wasn't the one who didn't want me to see Ander? What if William asked my father to distance himself from their family due to his actions? My mind swirled with questions, and I felt overwhelmed, not knowing where to begin seeking answers.

"Anyway, after we announced your new position as the major shareholder, William approached us and expressed his interest in being considered for the CEO position."

I hesitated, but I needed to know.

"Are you implying that he may have evidence and is leveraging it to secure his return to the company?" I asked.

"I can't say with absolute certainty. He hasn't brought it up, but the timing definitely raises some suspicions," Peter remarked.

He was spot-on. Why now? I asked myself. After all, my dad's passing might have created an opportunity for him.

All these secrets, all this lying—it was really getting to me. Being left in the dark about something so big was just infuriating. My dad could've easily fed me some excuse, but instead, he chose silence and cut off all contact with Ander. And my mom? She just went along with it, with no sympathy whatsoever, especially after all those months of me pouring my heart out to her about Ander not replying to my letters. Peter should've filled me in on this as soon as I took over the company and William... William and his damn schemes.

Just give me a fucking break.

"Peter, tell Mr. Scott to come to our offices. Give him some dates and time slots, and I'll be there. I'll only give you an answer after I've confronted him. I wanna see if he's playing us. Let's hope he's honest with me. Otherwise, he can go and fuck himself. I don't want any more secrets. And that applies to the both of you, too." With that statement, I ended the call.

I rose abruptly from my chair, my hand instinctively reaching for the flower vase on the table before me. Without much thought, I threw it forcefully against the wall just as Ander entered the apartment. The crash echoed through the room, mirroring the surge of emotions I could no longer contain. I collapsed onto the floor, a torrent of tears streaming down my cheeks. Ander crossed the room in a few strides and knelt in front of me. He grasped my shoulders and pulled me into a close, comforting hug.

"What's wrong?" His words came in a gentle, caring tone. I tried talking between sobs, but the anger and disappointment were too strong for my words to make any sense. Ander lifted me and walked me to the couch. He held me without saying anything while my tears left a trail of black mascara on his T-shirt.

"I'm so sorry, Ander," I blurted.

"Don't worry about the vase," he responded, gently stroking my hair.

"No, I don't mean the vase. I'm so sorry. About everything. It's all my family's fault." I couldn't stand it. Because of my dad, Ander and I never talked to each other again. He was the reason his father hated me so much, to the point of intercepting my letters.

"What do you mean?"

"I just spoke with Peter and Michael, the COO and CFO at Cos

Pharma." I paused, attempting to stifle my sobs. "They told me that my dad might have redirected specific R&D funds into an offshore account by fabricating certain documents."

"Holy shit."

"I know. I suspect your father confronted mine and left the company to avoid being involved in any scandal. I believe that's why my dad forbade me from seeing you and sent me off to Europe."

"Fuck. I guess it makes sense."

"What makes sense?" I asked.

"What my dad told you on Thanksgiving. That he didn't want to taint the memory of your father with stories from the past."

"I'm so sorry," I repeated between sobs.

I felt utterly drained. Everything came crashing upon me. My parents' death, moving to a different state, the fraud, my mixed feelings for Zayn and Noah, the regret of losing Ander...it was all too much.

I nestled into his embrace but continued to cry until my sobs gradually subsided, and the world around me faded into darkness.

*   *   *

When I opened my eyes, I was welcomed with more darkness. The moonlight through the window was the only thing shedding any light. I glanced around briefly without moving. Somehow, in my sleep, Ander and I had shifted, and we were both now lying on the couch, my body pressed to his side and my head nestled between his neck and chest. His smell was captivating and masculine, with earthy and citrus notes. I could feel his breathing on my temple and the rise and fall of his chest with my hand. His right arm was around my back, and his hand gently rested on my hip. I can't remember the last time someone held me like this. It felt...*safe*.

After a few minutes of savoring this peaceful moment, Ander

broke the silence.

"Hey, how are you feeling?"

"Honestly? I don't know." My head was still resting on his shoulder, and I tried my best to avoid looking at him. I was hurt and embarrassed. It was hard to digest that my dad's actions had pushed Ander's father to leave the company he helped build. I was furious and disappointed. "I'm so sorry, Ander. If it wasn't for my father…" Before I was able to finish my sentence, Ander grabbed my chin and lifted my face toward his.

"You don't have to apologize for your father's mistakes."

"It's just… I wish I could go back in time. I wish I'd made different choices and tried harder to stay in touch with you. It's not just my father's fault that I lost you," I said with a hint of regret in my voice. Ander remained silent, his eyes scanning my face as his hand cradled my cheek and his thumb gently brushed against it.

"I'm here. You never truly lost me." Ander leaned closer, his lips brushing mine tentatively. It was a gentle kiss, like the one we once shared surrounded by trees. But my emotions were heightened, and all I wanted was to be consumed by his kiss.

As if hearing my thoughts, he parted his lips and softly trailed his tongue along my lower lip, eliciting a moan from me. I opened my mouth, delicately meeting his tongue with mine. Ander groaned, igniting a surge of lust in my chest that traveled to the apex of my thighs. He deepened the kiss. It was unhurried but passionate. Our tongues danced together as my lips sensually moved against his. Grabbing a handful of his dark blond hair, I got lost in the moment, only to be interrupted a few seconds later by the jingling of keys at the front door.

I abruptly ended the kiss, my heart still pounding in my chest as a surge of anxiety washed over me at the thought of Zayn catching us.

I quickly stood and ran to the bathroom, closing the door behind me and pressing my back against it. I could hear them talking, but I stayed hidden until a soft knock on the door startled me.

"Are you okay, Sienna?" Ander's worried voice reached my ears.

"Yes. I'm okay. I just need a minute." I walked toward the bathroom sink, placed both hands on the marble counter, and tried to calm my breathing. As if things weren't complicated enough after hooking up with both Noah and Zayn, that kiss only added to the confusion.

What the hell were you thinking?

I cautiously cracked open the bathroom door to see if anyone was outside, then ran to my room. Quickly grabbing my phone from the bedside table, I unplugged it from the charger and opened a new message.

Me
SOS. SOS. SOS.

Maggie
What's wrong?

Me
I fucked up.

Maggie
I'm calling you.

Me
No. I can't talk right now. OMG. Ander and I just kissed!!!! What do I do????

Maggie
WTF?!! When? How? Is he a good kisser? Shall I come over?

Me
No, please. Let's meet tomorrow morning for coffee. I'll tell you everything.

Maggie

Thumbs-up emoji. Starbucks at 9?

Me

See u there.

I stayed in my room for the rest of the evening although I knew I would eventually need to confront Ander.

We shouldn't have kissed, and that thought troubled me. As much as I wanted to erase what had just happened between us, all I could think about was how much I wanted to do it again.

BE GRATEFUL

(Sienna)

"Two gingerbread lattes with skimmed milk, please. No sugar." After placing our order, Maggie and I sat at our usual table at the local Starbucks. I hadn't yet mentioned anything that had happened the day before, and Maggie didn't prod me to share any details the moment we met at the counter. I barely slept last night, tossing and turning in my bed, unable to stop my mind from revisiting my kiss with Ander. It felt right but also wrong at the same time. I left the apartment before anyone else woke up just to avoid an uncomfortable encounter with my temporary roommates.

"Are you just gonna stay quiet the entire morning, or are you gonna start spilling the tea?" Maggie asked.

I rolled my eyes.

"Start talking."

I sighed.

"We were lying on the sofa, and we kissed, but Zayn came home, and I panicked. I ran and hid in the bathroom and then in my room."

"Who kissed who first?"

"He initiated the kiss, but I didn't stop him. Oh God, I'm such a slut."

"Yes, you are. But who cares?" Maggie said, gesturing with her hand in the air and shrugging her shoulders.

"It's just...everything's so fucking complicated. First, I fucked Zayn in New York, and I enjoyed every second of it. We immediately connected at the bar, and the conversation was super easy; he told me about his family drama, and I told him about mine. It was pure chemistry from the beginning. But it was supposed to be a one-night stand.

"Then I met Noah. He's so fucking gorgeous... on the inside and on the outside. He's so smart and so much fun to be around. He has this possessive and wild side in bed that drives me crazy. He's 100% a pleasure dom, and he doesn't even know it."

"Mmm. I'd like to circle back to this conversation later, but please continue," Maggie added.

"And Ander...I don't know what to tell you. He was my best friend and my first kiss. There's so much history that I can't ignore...What I never expected was the fucking plot twist of all of them being best friends. Listen, living in that apartment is becoming an occupational hazard."

"Yes. The universe does have a fucked-up sense of humor, but sometimes the humor is dark; believe me. Be grateful that its sense of humor sent your way three guys with big dick energy. I mean, you could write a book about it. I would call it *Siennerella's Journey: Finding the Right Fit for her Cooch.*" Maggie chuckled at her own joke.

I threw my paper napkin at her, which only made her laugh louder.

I placed my elbows on the table and rested my chin between my palms.

"The thing is, I grew up reading about princesses and castles and finding your Prince Charming—your one true love. But I want to be with all of them. Am I crazy for wanting more?"

Maggie took a sip of her coffee and responded, "You're one lucky bitch. You know that, right?"

Was I? I was now in a difficult position. Should I tell Zayn and

Noah that Ander and I kissed? It would lead to another argument between them, without a doubt. Also, I wasn't even sure about how things were between Ander and me, so I questioned whether speaking up was the most sensible thing to do. I knew there was a pending conversation between us, but I wasn't prepared for it just yet. I needed more time to think about my feelings, or everyone involved in this mess, my mess, would end up getting hurt. Things had escalated beyond what I had anticipated.

"That's one way of putting things. What would you do if you were in my situation?"

"Me? I would sleep with the three of them. Period. *Carpe diem, tempus fugit,* and all that bullshit. It's better to apologize than live with regrets."

I cracked a laugh. "You're insane." Maggie knew how to lighten my mood, and I appreciated her efforts to always make me laugh in the most uncomfortable situations. "Talking about regrets, there's something else I need to tell you. But promise me you won't tell a soul."

"I won't. I'm great at keeping secrets," she responded, so I told her what I had discovered about my father.

"Fucking hell, woman. And you say you're gonna confront Ander's dad? It sounds like he's an intimidating man," she exclaimed, shaking her head.

I was scared to face him, but if I wanted to give Peter an answer about the CEO position, I had to talk to him. Otherwise, a part of me would feel like I was betraying my father.

"When are you talking to him?"

"Peter will call me when the meeting has been scheduled in our New York headquarters, probably in the next couple of weeks, before Christmas.

"Speaking of Christmas, have you figured out your holiday plans?" I asked her.

I hadn't given it much thought, but since this would be my first Christmas without my parents, I'd been delaying thinking about my options. However, one thing was clear. I didn't want to spend the holidays alone at Moore Manor.

"I haven't made any plans," Maggie answered. "And you? Are you spending the holidays with Sarah?"

"I would have loved to, but her dad was invited to Shanghai by one of his investors, and I can't go with them. It's a shame. I was looking forward to seeing her. I'll have to wait until spring break to travel there."

I knew Maggie didn't have any family, so maybe I could convince her to spend the holidays with me.

"Would you like to come with me to New York?"

Her face lit up, and Maggie gave me the biggest grin ever.

"I'd love to! Are you sure you don't mind?"

I grabbed and squeezed her hand and said, "Of course, I don't mind. I'd rather be with you than spend the holidays buried in champagne and alone in an empty manor."

Returning the squeeze to my hand, she retrieved her phone from the table and began planning. Most of her ideas centered on hitting Christmas markets, shopping, and sipping eggnog in front of the fireplace while playing board games.

By the time we left Starbucks, my holiday agenda was already full of all the activities Maggie had planned.

* * *

I arrived at the apartment an hour later, hoping I'd be able to avoid Ander for a few more hours. Apparently, I wasn't the luckiest bitch after all.

Ander sat on the couch, furiously typing away on his phone. He turned his head as I shut the front door, locking eyes with me. I started to walk toward my bedroom when Ander called my name.

"Yes?" My response sounded sharper than I had intended.

"Can we talk for a second?" he asked.

I stood in the hallway, shifting my weight from one foot to another and holding my purse as if it could protect me from this conversation.

"What do you want to talk about?" My tone caught him off guard, and his expression shifted to one of disappointment.

"About last night…" Before he could continue, I stopped him. The last thing I wanted was to hear how much he regretted kissing me out of pity.

"There is nothing to talk about. I was emotional, and you just tried to comfort me. I get it, so don't worry, I won't tell Zayn and Noah. I won't make things more uncomfortable than they already are."

Ander stood, but I took several steps back when he tried to close the distance between us. He noticed and stopped in his tracks.

"Is that what you want?"

I could hear the hurt in his voice, but I couldn't stand being the reason for them to fall apart.

Bros before hoes, right?

Zayn and Noah didn't talk to each other for weeks, and it really sucked to know that I was the reason they avoided each other.

"Yes. It's best if we never talk about that kiss. As a matter of fact, it didn't happen." Saying those words felt like swallowing a bitter pill, but they had to be said. That kiss was everything I would have hoped for a long time ago, but now things were too complicated between us.

His expression turned cold.

"Got it," he responded and turned away without saying another word.

Once I was alone in my room, I lay on my bed and cried myself to sleep.

THE POSITION IS YOURS

(Sienna)

One week before Christmas Day, Maggie and I flew to New York. She buzzed with excitement during the whole trip, acting like a kid in a candy store. I'd splurged on first-class tickets, and she made the most of it, constantly asking for champagne and munching on all the fancy food from the in-flight menu. Meanwhile, I couldn't manage to eat a thing. I was anxious about meeting William and confronting him about the circumstances surrounding his exit from Cos Pharmaceuticals.

We hopped in an Uber straight from JFK airport to Cos Pharma offices. Maggie wasted no time and checked in our luggage at the reception before embarking on a shopping spree that would keep her occupied until my meeting with William concluded.

New York City was in full-on Christmas mode. The streets bustled with tourists and last-minute shoppers. I'd already sorted out gifts for Maggie, Zayn, Noah, and Ander, so at least that was already covered. As we were saying our goodbyes last night, I extended my Christmas wishes to the guys and assured them I'd find some time in the new year to get together and swap presents before our classes resumed. For the past few days, I had kept my interactions with Ander to a minimum, keeping my distance as much as possible. I wouldn't be able to stop myself if he were to kiss me again, and that wasn't an option.

Just a couple of steps past the threshold of our office building, beads of sweat formed on my forehead. I had crafted my speech to the tiniest detail and practiced it a hundred times over, yet as I approached the main reception area, every carefully memorized word suddenly vanished from my mind like smoke in the wind.

"Good morning, Miss Moore. Mr. Scott is waiting for you. Would you like me to bring you some coffee? Maybe some pastries?" Just what my racing heart needed: caffeine.

"No, thank you."

Handing over my coat and purse, I squared my shoulders and straightened my posture, trying to present myself as a poised and confident businesswoman. With a newfound—but completely fake—determination, I strode toward the glass room where William awaited me.

"Good morning, Sienna. You look lovely."

I narrowed my eyes. William had never given me a compliment about my looks, so I assumed he was attempting to butter me up or perhaps testing the waters in some way.

"Thank you," I politely responded. "Not only for the compliment but for coming to our offices on such short notice. I know the week before Christmas is busy in this line of business."

He smiled and waved his hand, inviting me to take a seat in front of him.

"So to what do I owe this pleasure? I doubt it's just to wish me a Merry Christmas. A card would have sufficed for that."

I don't know what it was about him that always made me feel small when I was around him, but I tried not to show the effect his words had on me.

"As you well know, I'm already aware of your *sudden* interest in rejoining our wonderful team, so I just wanted to have the opportunity to discuss the position with you and ask you why you think you're the best candidate."

He shifted in his chair and ran his right hand through his ash-blond hair, releasing a chuckle.

"Sienna. Cut the bullshit. I know why you called me in, so get to the point. No need to beat around the bush."

I released a long breath before I spoke. "I know why you left the company."

"Do you now?" he said, lifting both eyebrows.

"Yes, I know. But I want to hear it directly from you. And I want the whole truth. I'll know if you're lying to me."

"I doubt it. I'm a great poker player, but if you want the truth, the truth you shall have." He reached for the carafe of water resting on the table, handling it with deliberate care. He poured a glass of water for both of us, taking his time in the process. His sipping was so unhurried that it almost felt like he was competing for a Guinness World Record in the category of the slowest water drinker. My left eye began to twitch.

"Six years ago, Michael approached both your father and me regarding some financial irregularities he'd uncovered. Your father appeared to have forged documents and redirected funds allocated for certain projects into an offshore account in Panama. As you may already be aware, these projects turned out to be nonexistent."

William's gaze shifted nervously from side to side, and he couldn't resist fidgeting with his watch every few seconds. I thought to myself that it was the first time I'd seen William anxious, but with everything at stake for him, I could imagine keeping his composure must have been difficult.

"When I confronted your father, he explained that your family faced severe financial difficulties. He claimed to have made some successful investments and intended to return the money before anyone noticed. In short, he swore that he would return the money, but our trust was irrevocably shattered, so I presented your father with my resignation a couple of weeks later. Because of our years of friendship, he implored me to keep the matter confidential. Apparently, Michael and Peter had already agreed to sweep it under the rug as long as the money was returned. That marked the end of our friendship."

His version mirrored the narrative that Michael and Peter had previously shared with me, and once again, I found myself profoundly disturbed by my father's actions.

"Why didn't you go to the authorities about my father? You had the option to do so. You could have kept your position at Cos Pharma, perhaps even becoming the sole shareholder." I knew William enough to know that he didn't engage in acts of charity solely for altruistic reasons. It always baffled me how two individuals with such contrasting personalities could be such good friends. He, after all, was an egocentric, selfish bastard with a God complex, whereas my father was a man of steadfast principles. I guess I was wrong after all.

"Did you know your father and I became friends in high school? After graduating, we went to Stanford, just like you, and our friendship strengthened. We once were more than friends; he was my family, my brother. He was the one who introduced me to my former wife, Nora. I owed him a lot, so that was my way of repaying him. But after that, we were done; he said he wasn't resigning, so I did. He could have come to me, and I would have gladly helped him."

His words hit deeper than I had expected, to the extent that I found myself feeling sympathy for the man seated across from me. He gave up his dream; after all, Cos Pharma was as much his creation as it was my father's.

"Do you have any more questions?"

"Why now? Why do you want back in?" I asked him.

"Come on, Sienna, you've known me for quite some time. Do you honestly believe I would have returned while your father still ran the company? Not a chance, even in a hundred years. His unfortunate death provided an opportunity to come back, and I have a business mind. I'm genuinely sorry for your loss, but I must be honest. After all, Cos Pharma was as much mine as it was his."

I pinched the bridge of my nose with my fingers in an attempt to bring some relief to the impending migraine. I still had some more questions, so I continued with my interrogation.

"Why did you throw away the letters I sent to Ander?"

William rubbed a hand down his face before he answered.

"I was angry, and after leaving the company, my mood changed. As you're aware, Nora divorced me, and regrettably, your letters arrived during some of the darkest days of my life. I threw them away and unjustly punished you and Ander for your father's and my own errors. It was unfair, and for that, I do apologize."

His words didn't change the fact that his and my own father's actions had caused me to lose my best friend, but oddly, they did bring some kind of closure. I had made up my mind. I just hoped I wasn't making a big mistake.

"The position is yours."

"Excuse me?"

Was William not anticipating my response this quickly, or was he deaf?

"I said that the position is yours. Don't make me regret it, William.

I'll communicate my decision to the board this afternoon. Accept this as an early Christmas present."

I dragged the chair backward with the intention of getting up and out of that fish tank, but before I could stand, William said, "What are you doing for the holidays? Are you staying at Moore Manor?"

I nodded.

Why did he care?

"Why don't you spend the holidays with us? I'm sure Ander would be thrilled to spend some time with you."

I doubted that.

"In fact, why don't you stay until after New Year's Eve? Claudia has planned a decadent party, and I'd like to have you there. It could be like a fresh start for both of us. What do you say?"

"I would need to ask your son, and I've brought a girlfriend from college with me, so it's not just me you'd be inviting over to your home." I didn't want to sound like I was blurting excuses, but I worried that Ander wouldn't be pleased to see me.

"The more, the merrier. Initially, I believed it might have been just a phase, but he likes you. Claudia will also be pleased to have other women around."

William was clearly extending an olive branch, and I didn't want to start our new business venture by rejecting his proposal.

"If you insist, we would love to join you. Thank you for the invitation."

He clasped both hands together, pleased with my acceptance.

"Fantastic. The party is 'Venetian Summer Night,' black tie etiquette is required, so please bring an evening gown. Claudia shipped extra masks from Italy in case she changed her outfit at the last minute, so I'm sure she won't mind lending you a couple of them. Let me know if you want me to send a car to pick you up."

The sudden change in his attitude gave me whiplash, but when I left that office, I felt like a huge weight had been lifted off my shoulders.

HOE HOE HOE! MERRY CHRISTMAS

(Sienna)

"Do you think the massive house is a juxtaposition to his small dick?"

I couldn't help but roll my eyes as Maggie and I got out of the Uber that had just brought us to Scott Manor.

"I need you on your best behavior, Maggie, so please, hold your tongue. I know you have a dark humor, but these people don't know you like I do."

Maggie put a hand on my shoulder and squeezed it.

"Jesus, take a chill pill. I was joking." She paused. "He clearly has a small dick."

We walked toward the main door with our luggage. I wasn't sure what to bring or how many options were considered acceptable. Maggie had it easy; she only had to place everything back into her suitcase and zip it shut. As for me, I spent the entire morning going through my walk-in closet, trying to figure out what to pack. I needed to pack both formal and casual clothing, including an evening gown for the New Year's Eve gala. Maggie borrowed one of my dresses. She didn't care that it was a bit short for her. In fact, she saw it as the ideal opportunity to borrow a pair of Louboutin from my collection and show them off.

"I think I brought too many things. Ander and Zayn will think I'm moving in with their parents." I was panicking. I ended up bringing a big suitcase, a small suitcase, and my large Dior book tote bag. I knew it was too much, but a girl needed options.

A few seconds after I pressed the ring bell, the door opened, and a man with silver hair and a strong build—probably in his fifties—greeted us.

"Good afternoon," the man said. "You must be Miss Moore. Please, come in. Mr. Scott mentioned we were expecting you. I'm Gordon, the butler. May I have your coats and your luggage?"

"They have a butler?" Maggie whispered so I could only hear her.

"Thank you, Gordon. Yes, and please call me Sienna. This is Maggie Towerby, a friend from college."

"Welcome, miss. Mr. Scott requested that I escort you to your rooms and allow you time to relax. Dinner will be served at seven o'clock. Please allow me to guide you to your accommodations." Gordon indicated that we should leave our luggage downstairs, reassuring us that he would promptly bring our belongings up once we settled into our rooms.

"Are Ander and Zayn at home?" I asked him while he guided us to the upper level.

"Yes, they are home. I believe Mr. Scott is in his room, but Mr. Siegel left not long ago to buy some last-minute presents in the city."

I was nervous to see Ander. We hadn't spoken since my meeting with his father at our offices, and I wasn't sure if he knew I'd offered him the CEO position in the company.

I was assigned the same room I'd been in when I came during Thanksgiving, so as soon as Gordon left to show Maggie where she would sleep for the next few days, I walked out of my room and crossed the hallway to Ander's door. I could hear the creak of his bed.

I knocked on the door twice.

The first thing I noticed when the door swung open was a shirtless Ander. My eyes traveled down his chest toward his perfectly sculpted abs and stopped at the delicious happy trail between his stomach and the hem of his sweatpants. I probably spent too many seconds ogling him, only to be disturbed when the sound of him clearing his throat reached my ears.

"Are you checking me out?"

I could feel the heat spreading through my face. I dropped my eyes so he wouldn't realize how flustered I was. Since our kiss, things had been a bit awkward between us.

"I just wanted to say hi. Hi."

Seriously, Sienna? Hi?

"Can I talk to you for a sec?" I timidly asked.

"Sure, come in." I crossed the threshold, and Ander shut the door behind me. I walked toward the window and turned around to face him.

"Have you talked to your father?"

Ander walked to a chest of drawers against the wall on the opposite side of the room and pulled a white T-shirt with long sleeves out of one of the drawers. I was disappointed, not going to lie. I would have preferred it if he had remained shirtless. He was nice to look at.

"Yes, I did. He mentioned you've agreed to give him the position. What made you change your mind?"

I noticed some hesitation in his tone and wondered if he disapproved of my decision.

"Everyone deserves a second chance, and he confirmed everything Michael and Peter said. I have no reason to think he has ulterior motives."

"My father always has ulterior motives, Sienna. Trust me."

My eyes followed the stack of books and movies lining one of his walls. I recognized some of them from the countless hours I spent at Scott's residence as a child. One piqued my curiosity, so I picked up the DVD from one of the shelves—*Mean Girls*.

"You were obsessed with that movie. I still remember how you wouldn't stop using the sentence '*that's so fetch*' for a full month. You bugged me all the time."

I burst out laughing.

"That's why you liked calling me *bug*." I sighed. "I can't believe you remember that."

"I remember everything, *bug*."

"Do you remember what you said in those letters you wrote to me?" I asked.

"Sienna…" He stood behind me while my fingers traced the DVD cover in an attempt to avoid looking at him.

"I want to know, please," I insisted. I needed to know.

He sighed.

"I would write about my days here, in Rye. About how much I fucking missed you. About the last time I saw you."

The day we kissed.

I turned to face him. He was looking down at me. His eyes were full of something—sadness…maybe regret.

"If you'd known that we wouldn't see each other again for six years, would you have made a different choice that day?" My dad used to say that you shouldn't ask questions if the truth was too hard to handle, and I was terrified of hearing something that would break my heart all over again. Maybe I shouldn't have said that question out loud.

"Yes."

I could hear my heart shattering into pieces. Sensing my discomfort, Ander lifted his hand, held my face gently, and said, "If I could go back, I wouldn't let you get on that bus."

Ander's mouth was suddenly on mine. This time, his kiss was not gentle like the other day at his apartment. He shoved me into the bookshelves, and I let out a sharp hiss as pain shot through my spine from the force with which he slammed me against it. I was too turned on to care. I dropped the DVD with the impact. I grabbed his T-shirt with my hands, pulling him as close to me as possible while both of his hands grabbed my face. Every corner of my skin burned with need. And I needed him. I wanted him to touch me everywhere, to feel his body on mine.

I could feel his erection pressed against my lower stomach, and my body instinctively began to move, searching for any form of friction or relief from the deep ache I felt within me.

"Fuck, Sienna. You drive me crazy," he said between kisses.

"I hope it is a good kind of crazy."

Ander lifted me and guided me to circle my legs around his waist. His hands pressed my body against his, his hard length rubbing against the thin fabric of my leggings and thong. I locked my ankles behind him to push him closer, and Ander made a deep, growling sound that mirrored the moan that escaped my lips. One of his hands traveled underneath my sweater until his fingers pinched my nipple.

"Oh my God," I cried out. My head fell back, and I arched my back when he deliberately did it again. My underwear was soaked, and he had barely touched me.

Ander moved us toward his bed and laid me on my back as he climbed on top of me. We stayed in the same position, but he lifted my sweater and the top I wore until he could access my red bra. He pushed it down, not caring about unclasping it, and brought his mouth to one of my breasts. The heat of his mouth, the wetness of his tongue…he licked my nipple and sucked it in such a delicious way that my body began to tremble. He moved to my other breast, but this time, his right hand moved inside my leggings until he pushed his middle finger between my folds.

"Fuck," he breathed as he sucked my other nipple again. "You're soaked, Sienna."

"Please," I begged as I ran my fingers through his soft hair.

"Tell me what you want, love."

"I want you, Ander. I need you inside me."

Someone suddenly knocked on the door three times. Ander quickly removed his hand from my throbbing pussy and covered my chest with my sweater. He was clearly concerned that someone could burst into the room and find me half naked.

On the contrary, I was furious.

"Ander, your butler said this is your room. Sorry to bother you, but have you seen Sienna? She's not in her room."

Fucking Maggie...

Ander looked at me, leaving it up to me to decide whether I wanted to respond.

"Yes, Maggie. I'm here. Give me a minute. I need to finish my conversation with Ander. I'll be in your room in five." I couldn't hear Maggie's footsteps walking away from Ander's bedroom door, so I held off for a few seconds before saying anything to Ander.

I softly kissed him after I put my bra back in place.

"I need to go," I said.

"Sorry, I couldn't help myself." He looked remorseful. I knew he was referring to my Zayn and Noah predicament, but I didn't want Ander to feel guilty for his actions. I had also displayed a lack of self-control, so we were both responsible for what had happened. And I knew I should feel guilty for adding an extra layer of complication to my life, but with Ander, whatever was happening between us felt right. Deep down, as much as I wanted to brush my feelings for him aside, I knew this would eventually happen, especially after the moment we shared at his apartment.

"Don't. Please don't ruin it. I enjoyed every second of it, Ander." I tenderly caressed his cheek, locking my gaze with his. I could easily get lost in the depths of his blue eyes.

"I understand you have feelings for Zayn and Noah, but it's just… I can't help it. Every moment I'm near you, I want to kiss you, to feel you. I probably shouldn't be saying this, especially since Zayn and Noah are my closest friends. And it's even more complicated since Zayn will soon become my stepbrother."

His declaration caused my heart to skip a beat. I couldn't count the nights I'd yearned to hear those words from him or how many times I had cried myself to sleep in Sarah's dorm, missing him. He once was my best friend, my first kiss, but then we became strangers. And now, he was right here, standing in front of me. Zayn and Noah were also present, not physically in the room but occupying my thoughts. The whole situation was messed up. It felt like my heart was splitting into three pieces, and I had no idea how to prevent them from tearing it apart completely.

"Every time something big happened to me, like when I got into Stanford, I wanted to tell you about it. After all these years, I still felt your absence in my life. I'm not sure what the future holds, but one thing is certain: I want you to be a part of it, no matter what," I confessed.

Ander kissed me once more. I couldn't get enough of his kisses.

We stood at his door, my hand on the doorknob.

"Let's enjoy Christmas for now. Noah's coming on the 27th to spend a few days with us, so maybe all of us can talk and figure things out," he suggested. "See you at dinner?"

"Yes. I'll see you at dinner." I leaned in and gently kissed his lips before making my way to Maggie's room.

I didn't even have a chance to knock before Maggie swung the door open, her grin stretching from ear to ear, much like the Grinch.

"Well, well, well. Or should I say Hoe Hoe Hoe, Merry Christmas? It only took you, what, thirty minutes? I bet on before midnight, but I underestimated you."

My cheeks turned red, and I felt the heat radiating across my face. "Shut up, Maggie."

"Oh baby," she said with a smirk. "You know I won't."

* * *

"Tell me. What's the deal with the three musketeers?"

We still had a couple of hours until we had to get ready for dinner, so Maggie and I reclined on the bed, resting on our sides and facing each other. I placed one hand underneath my cheek and sighed.

"This is a mess. I don't even know what's wrong with me. I shouldn't be pining for three men, especially when they are best friends. What does this situation say about me?" Maggie went to open her mouth, and I stopped her. "You know what? Don't tell me. I have an idea of what you must think about me..."

"No, you don't," she retorted. "You're human, and I don't believe in soulmates. I know you like all three of them for very different reasons. I'm not going to judge you, and you know it." Her words gave me some level of reassurance. "In fact," she continued, "I kind of admire you. I wished I had the same confidence to be so open about my sexuality, but..." Her expression turned somber.

"But what?" I pushed her.

"This conversation is too heavy for my liking."

I wondered what could have possibly happened to Maggie and why she wanted to cut the conversation short. Was she bullied in high school? Did someone mine her confidence when it came to sex?

"You know you can tell me anything. It'll stay between us, I promise."

She paused momentarily, contemplating whether she wanted to open up to me. Then she rolled onto her back, her eyes fixed on the ceiling and her lips forming a thin line.

"I want to share a story with you, but I need you to promise me that you won't breathe a word of it to anyone, especially not the guys. I don't want them to see me as a broken toy."

Her statement left me feeling uneasy.

"My dad, Robert, took care of me after my mother passed away following her two-year battle with breast cancer. My dad had a good job. He worked in research; that's one of the reasons I took an interest in science, but the money we had barely covered the mortgage, my school expenses, and the healthcare bills she left behind. I wasn't fully aware of our financial struggles, but that changed when my dad was laid off from the lab. It was a tough period, and he turned to drinking, which created a vicious cycle. I thought things couldn't get worse, but I couldn't have been more wrong." Maggie's eyes looked glassy. She blinked, and a single tear trickled down her temple, disappearing beneath her blond hair. "As I told you when we met, he committed suicide."

Her story turned my stomach, and the idea of a younger Maggie feeling helpless and alone made me feel sick.

"You know, I had no other family apart from my father, so I essentially became another orphan entering the foster care system. I transitioned between different foster families for a year, but things took a turn when I was eventually placed with the Millers.

"What I'm going to share with you… I'm not looking for sympathy… I haven't told anyone in all these years, so please, Sienna…" She turned her face toward me. "Please don't say anything, just listen to me."

I remained silent as she shifted her gaze back to the ceiling and took a few deep breaths to regain her composure.

"Carl Miller, my foster dad, practically ignored me for the first couple of months. But one night, something changed. He came to my room in the middle of the night and…" Her voice quivered, and more tears started to flow uncontrollably.

"Oh, Maggie." I pushed myself up from the bed and reached her with my arms. I hugged her tightly. Maggie wept inconsolably, and I remained in the same holding position until her sobs gradually quieted down. I couldn't imagine the pain she must have felt every time she relived those moments.

Who could do those things to a child?

"How long?" I asked.

"Too long. When I turned sixteen, I took a job and started the legal process to emancipate from them, my legal guardians at that point. Carl and his wife, who I'm sure knew what was happening behind closed doors, never opposed throughout the process. That's why I have intimacy issues, in addition to others. I go to therapy once a week. It helps, but I don't think anyone recovers from something like that. Some days, all I want to do is curl up in bed and cry. Other days, I want to die, and other days, I want to make them pay." Her voice became increasingly enraged toward the end of her statement, but I couldn't blame her.

"Thank you for sharing your story with me, Maggie. It must have been tough for you. You know I'm here for you, now and always. So if you ever have one of those days when all you want to do is curl up in your bed and cry, call me. Especially if you're flooded with dark thoughts. I promise I'll be there in no time, and we can cry together. You're not alone, Maggie."

Maggie squeezed me tighter, and we hung on like that until there was a soft knock on the door, and Ander's voice came through, saying, "Dinner will be ready in half an hour."

WHAT DO YOU MEAN?

(Sienna)

Maggie chose not to join us for dinner last night. Instead, she remained in her room, and I completely understood. Revisiting those years must have been a truly harrowing experience. Today, however, she behaved like everything was fine, and our conversation never happened.

While Ander and Zayn played basketball in the backyard, Maggie and I spent the entire morning baking ginger and chocolate chip cookies with Rosita. I was watching them from the kitchen window, shirtless, all sweaty, and their muscles shining in the sunlight. Even though it hadn't snowed in a week and December was warmer than usual, it was still winter. I didn't know if they were brave or simply stupid. Of course, they ignored Claudia's advice and kept goofing around with their bare torsos, which was seriously distracting. In fact, I'd been so distracted while retrieving a tray from the oven with our third batch that I now had a minor burn on my left wrist.

Every time I stared at the kitchen island, I remembered the time I was sitting on top of it with Zayn between my legs, fucking me hard on the counter.

Rosita had only left to enter the pantry room when Maggie turned to face me and teased, "You're blushing and dribbling all over the cookies, and we know it's not the only thing that's getting moist around here.'"

I punched her on her upper arm to make her stop.

"Rosita is going to hear you! Shut your big fat mouth!" I whispered.

The housekeeper returned carrying more flour and another pack of chocolate chips. It didn't seem she'd heard Maggie's comment.

"Have you got all your presents wrapped? I only bought a present for you, so I hope the guys don't mind. I didn't get them anything. I initially thought we were spending the holidays alone, and honestly, I have a limited budget, so don't expect anything fancy." Maggie didn't know, but I'd bought her something that would blow her mind. I didn't care what she got me. The only thing I really wanted was to see her face on Christmas morning.

"Yes, I have them all wrapped and ready. Including yours," I responded, and her face lit up.

"I'm genuinely excited this year. I've spent the past couple of Christmases alone, and it's been four years since my last one with my dad."

Her comment made my heart ache. Nobody should spend these days alone, and especially not Maggie.

At that moment, I decided to throw a Christmathon party for her. It was a fantastic idea, *thankyouverymuch*, especially since Ander and I used to do it every year. The concept had evolved in the past two thanks to Sarah's input, but the new changes made Christmathon even better. It was an upgrade.

"I'm gonna make this Christmas rock for you, and I have a plan."

"Do you? Oh God…please. What is it?"

"Christmathon!" I lifted my arms without realizing they were covered in flour.

Maggie laughed while I coughed and asked me between giggles, "Christ…what?"

"So...Ander and I watched many Christmas movies as kids, and we called it 'Christmathon.' Our parents used to celebrate the holidays together, but when I left for Switzerland and we stopped hanging out, I would watch them on my own or with Sarah. She came up with this cool idea two years ago for our 'Christmathon' sessions. We'd pick a particular word for each movie we watched. Whenever a character in the movie said that word, we'd take a shot. She sneaked into our principal's office and stole a bottle of whiskey the first year, then grabbed a bottle of vodka last year. We should do it when Noah's here. Everyone gets to pick their poison and snacks. It'll be fun." My voice squeaked at the end. I was so excited.

"If it involves alcohol, I'm in."

We continued working on the next batch of cookies while "All I Want for Christmas Is You" by Mariah Carey played in the background.

An hour later, Zayn and Ander walked into the kitchen. Rosita was helping us with the cleanup, and the final batch was cooling down on the counter. Zayn tried to pick one from the tray, but I was able to slap his hand away before he snatched a chocolate chip cookie. He gifted me with one of his characteristic smirks.

"Ouch. You're very protective over your cookies."

"Yes, I am. They are for tomorrow, so you'll have to wait," I exclaimed.

Ander came out of the laundry room, holding two hand towels and throwing one to Zayn.

"What are your plans for today? We could resume your self-defense training in the gym downstairs," Zayn suggested.

We had been training on and off for the last few weeks, although this time, we kept the sessions professional and our clothes on.

"Yes, that'd be great. I haven't heard from the stalker lately, but it doesn't hurt to be prepared if they show up again..." It had been a few weeks since they threatened me with a knife, but I was worried that they would corner me when I was alone and helpless. At least I wanted to be ready if it happened again.

"Get changed. I'll see you downstairs in ten."

*   *   *

I could hear "Suffering" by Melrose Avenue blasting through the speakers as I descended the steps to the basement, which was cleverly divided into three distinct sections, each serving a different purpose. To the left was a cozy little kitchenette with a dark wooden table positioned at its center. A massive L-shaped leather sofa stretched out directly across from the kitchenette, facing an impressive 85-inch TV. On the right-hand side was a dedicated workout area. The presence of weights, dumbbells, exercise mats, and other modern equipment gave the space a fitness-friendly atmosphere. The room screamed *man cave*.

"Hey there." I made my way toward the mats, where Zayn was currently stretching. With each movement, his shorts and T-shirt clung to his body, and I wondered how good it would feel to have another one-on-one like that time at The Dragon Den.

Focus.

I caught Zayn smirking at my ogling. I'd been doing that a lot lately.

"Let's begin with a warm-up before diving into the training. It's important to avoid straining your muscles," Zayn advised, demonstrating the correct stretching techniques. He then guided me through the tactics we'd discussed in our previous training sessions.

For the next couple of hours, we reviewed the things I should improve and practiced counteracting attacks when they came from different angles.

I was lying on my back, staring at the ceiling, as I attempted to slow my breathing and relax. He'd been exceptionally quiet during our training. He wasn't very talkative, but his silence felt different this time.

"Where's your mind at? You're very quiet today."

"It's nothing." He sighed.

"You know you can talk to me about anything, right?"

He stayed pensive for a few seconds before speaking.

"It's this time of the year. It always makes me moody."

"Is it because you miss your father?"

He nodded. It was an obvious question. The night we met, he told me about his father's passing.

"I get it. It's my first Christmas without my parents. It's weird, especially spending the holidays in this house. Did you know I used to spend every Christmas Day with the Scotts until I was twelve?"

"What was it like?"

I bit my bottom lip, and my eyes dropped to the floor.

"Some of my best memories happened in this house," I confessed.

He searched my face, trying to find something. Regret, maybe? What could it have been but never was?

"What happened between you two?"

Too much was what I wanted to say.

"I think somewhere down the line, we became more than friends, but after what happened between my dad and William, my father made it his mission to forbid me from seeing Ander. While I was in Switzerland, we tried to stay in touch through letters, but...let's say the mail got lost before they reached their destination." I changed the subject. "Tell me more about your father. What was your relationship like?" I wanted to know more about Zayn and what made him, well, him. He always carried this *I don't give a fuck* attitude about himself, but the truth was that I began to witness a side of him that I never expected to see. He was full of passion and cared about the people he loved.

"He was the best man I've ever known. He would come to every single tournament and take me fishing on the weekends. My mom absolutely adored him. That's why I struggled to understand what she saw in William or how she could be ready to settle down with another man so quickly."

"She seems happy."

"I think so too. I stopped overanalyzing it when I realized my attitude was negatively affecting her. The last thing I want is to have the only parent I have left resenting me."

He'd never been so honest with me, and I appreciated that he was opening up to me on such a delicate subject.

"She loves you, Zayn. I can see that much."

Zayn gently raised his hand, tucking away a stray strand of hair that had slipped from my ponytail behind my ear. The gesture was so sweet and caring that my body shifted toward his until his palm touched my face, and his thumb stroked my flushed cheeks with light movements.

"Have I ever told you how beautiful you are, Sienna?"

My blush deepened, but it wasn't because of the workout this time.

"When you say those things, it's hard to resist you," I admitted.

"Believe me, it's taking me a lot of restraint not to bend you over the sofa right now and fuck you senseless."

My pussy throbbed. I hadn't had sex since Thanksgiving, and my body was now betraying me. Four weeks was a long time when I was constantly surrounded by the hottest guys I'd ever hooked up with in my life. Maggie said I was a lucky bitch, but my conscience was working overtime. No matter how I looked at it, any decision I made would hurt someone.

"What do YOU want, Sienna? Forget about what I want and what Noah wants."

And what Ander wants…

He saw what was going through my mind.

"I wish it were that simple," I answered.

"It is. We have talked about death and grieving. A little talk about your feelings and what you want is light conversation at this point." He chuckled.

Could I be totally honest with him? Would he think I was a little slut for all these thoughts I had in my head about having sex with them? Maybe at the same time? I was already carrying a significant weight of guilt for not mourning my parents in the way society deemed appropriate. The truth was that my heart still ached from the loss. However, these guys had unexpectedly entered my life amid this emotional chaos. Their presence, how they seemed to care about me, had breathed new life into my world, offering a glimmer of hope within the shadow of my grief.

"Don't judge me, okay?"

"Never."

I took a deep breath before saying, "I really like you and Noah." For now, I opted to exclude Ander from the conversation, as managing the situation with two candidates in the running was challenging enough. "Not only because of the way you make me feel…physically. I mean, the sex has been amazing, no complaints here, but the way you are, too, especially around me. You show me that you care about me, about my well-being…keeping me safe. I can't think about a scenario where I choose one and not the other…so I've been wondering what it would be like…you know… to be with both of you."

Zayn's eyes widened.

I knew it. I shouldn't have opened my mouth.

"What do you mean by 'the both of us'? At the same time?"

A grin slowly appeared on his face. I nudged him away with my shoulder, hoping to prevent his smug expression from leading to any teasing or jokes.

"You know what I mean, asshole. Yes."

"Interesting choice of words."

I smacked his arm and exclaimed, "Stop it."

Zayn wouldn't stop looking at me funny, and I found it difficult to maintain eye contact because I felt incredibly embarrassed after confessing my fantasies to him. I stood. After tightening my ponytail, I cast a glance over my shoulder.

"You're impossible," I muttered before adding, "I'll see you at dinner."

My footsteps echoed as I hurried upstairs.

CHRISTMATHON

(Sienna)

"Ho Ho Ho, Merry Christmas!"

I woke up to someone bouncing on my bed, and that someone was Maggie.

"Ugh, it's only eight thirty, Maggie. We are not seven anymore. I went to bed only a few hours ago."

After a delicious dinner with the Scotts, the Siegels, and Maggie, we spent the rest of the evening talking in the living room and playing cards. Everyone except for William, who apparently had to prepare some paperwork that needed to be ready before the 26th.

Before heading off to spend Christmas with her family, Rosita thoughtfully prepared a batch of homemade hot chocolate for us. Claudia entertained us with stories about baby Zayn as we sipped our mugs. He didn't seem too thrilled when she mentioned his old fear of the dark and how her late husband had signed him up to learn martial arts so he could learn how to fend off the imaginary monsters that lurked in the shadows under his bed. It was a great night. It reminded me of those nights when I was a child, and my dad would spend hours listening to me playing the piano while my mom prepared dinner.

Maggie's loud cries snapped me back to reality.

"Sienna, c'mon! I'm too excited to wait in my room for you to wake up. Don't you want to open your presents?"

I couldn't bring myself to lie to her. I'd spent the entire week pondering what Zayn and Ander might have picked out for me. During our time at Stanford, they'd casually mentioned that they'd gotten me a gift, but I honestly hadn't built up any expectations.

With a groan, I peeled my bed sheets away and made my way to the bathroom connected to my bedroom, where I brushed my teeth and washed my face. Going through the clothes that hung in the wardrobe, I searched for a cozy outfit. I settled for a pair of blue jeans, a simple white T-shirt, my beloved Converse sneakers, and a festive Christmas sweater Sarah had sent me from Camden Market. It said, "Dear Santa. Define Good." I loved it.

We headed downstairs, Maggie still bouncing at my side like a little puppy. As I descended the steps, the warm scent of burning wood and the tempting smell of chocolate cookies began to tickle my senses. Upon entering the living room, my jaw practically hit the floor. While I had already seen the beautifully decorated Christmas tree that Rosita and Claudia had put together, I was surprised by the multitude of presents scattered across the floor, the festive garlands adorning the marble fireplace, and the array of ornaments thoughtfully placed throughout the room. The transformation was nothing short of magical. Zayn, Claudia, and Ander were seated on the floor, sipping coffee and indulging in the cookies Maggie and I had baked the day before. William lounged comfortably in a leather wing chair, reading The New York Times.

"Oh my God! It looks amazing."

"It really does, doesn't it? The boys here wanted to make this day extra special for you and Maggie, understanding how much you've both been through in recent months. Isn't it cute?"

Claudia's comment took me by surprise. *Cute* didn't even begin to describe the overwhelming emotion I was experiencing, realizing they went above and beyond for us. There were even stockings with our names hanging from one of the bookshelves!

"Who wants to open their presents first?" Claudia cheered, clapping both hands together.

We took turns opening our presents. Maggie had gifted me a personalized mug with a Starbucks logo that said, "I like my men like my coffee. Hot." I didn't say anything about the word *men*, but I noticed the corner of her mouth starting to curve upward as I glanced in her direction.

Funny.

"Now my turn." I stretched out my arms, holding a box, and reached it toward Maggie. As soon as she tore away the wrapping paper, her eyes widened in surprise.

"You're fucking kidding me, right?"

When Maggie opened the brown box and peeked inside the red bag, she whimpered, "Oh my God, oh my God. You got me a pair of fucking Louboutin?"

I knew how much she loved my shoe collection, and money had never been a problem for me. What she offered me was more valuable than any pair of shoes I could buy her. So I bought her the So Kate 120 patent-leather pumps in black. She kept eyeing mine every time she came to my apartment, so when I started planning my Christmas shopping list, I had no doubts I would buy them for her.

"I can't believe you bought me my first pair of designer shoes… and they are fucking Louboutin!" She launched herself at me, knocking the air out of my lungs as my back hit the carpet.

"My turn!" Zayn exclaimed. "Here." He handed me a small velvet box.

"I hope it's not an engagement ring," Ander commented.

Zayn snorted, and although I knew Ander was teasing, I found myself unexpectedly drawn to the idea of Zayn proposing on one knee. My stomach did a double backflip.

Within the crimson velvet box rested a golden necklace with a locket pendant. The necklace concealed two pictures, one on each side: my dad and my mom. I tried to swallow a sob that got caught in my throat.

"Zayn…" I couldn't speak. Tears pricked my eyes. This beautiful man was not only good at listening and sex, but he also had a beautiful soul and remarkable gift-giving skills. "It's beautiful. I…I love it." I turned to face him and gently placed a kiss on his cheek, lingering for a few seconds longer than necessary.

"Okay. Now mine." Ander stood and took a box from under the tree, placing it in front of me. "I hope you like it as much as I did when I put it together."

I frowned, unsure of what he meant. Was it a DIY present?

I opened the box.

As soon as I realized what it contained, I gasped in surprise. Inside, I found a *Pride & Prejudice* DVD Special Collection, a pink hoodie with the phrase "Most ardently," Hershey's Milk Chocolate Bars (my favorite), and various other items that stirred memories of our shared childhood. Yet two items stood out among the rest within that box. There was a stack of letters, four, neatly bundled with jute twine, accompanied by a note that read, "To read on January 1st. You need to know the past to understand the present and face the future. With love, Ander." Those two words—*with love*—sent my heart racing. Trying not to make eye contact with him, I picked up the other object that had piqued my interest. A young Sienna and Ander gazed back at me when

I flipped over the frame. I vividly recalled that trip to Hawaii in the summer of 2008. I was missing my front teeth, and Ander couldn't resist poking fun at me during the entire trip. I gently traced my fingers over the photograph. In the picture, he carried me on his back along the shoreline in Maui. I crawled on my hands and knees to where he was seated, planted a tender kiss on his cheek, and whispered in his ear, ensuring our words were for our ears alone, "Thank you, Ander. You're my Christmas miracle, and I'm never letting you go." Then I retreated, locking eyes with him briefly before we resumed unwrapping our presents.

* * *

It was snowing.

I sat outside, protected by a thick blanket wrapped around me, cradling a hot latte in my hands. I always loved Rye during the winter season. It looked magical.

At last, everything was quiet, and I enjoyed the simple pleasure of listening to the snowflakes fall. All morning, trucks came and went, bringing furniture and stuff to decorate the New Year's party salon.

I reached into my sweater, pulled out the locket, and opened it. Zayn had printed two pictures from my Instagram account so I could always carry my parents with me. It had been one of my favorite presents ever.

The sound of a vehicle pulled me back to reality. I smiled when I noticed a Ford F-150 coming into view.

Noah.

Ander had confirmed with him that he would be joining us for a few days before the party. Noah quickly exited the rental car, retrieving a suitcase from the trunk, and then hurried toward the entrance, where I stood waiting.

"I've missed you, princess," he confessed.

Placing my coffee mug on the bench, I outstretched my arms, and an excited Noah lifted me into the air, spinning me around.

There was an indescribable feeling of completeness, knowing that all three of them would be under the same roof. It was hard to put into words, but my heart overflowed with happiness now that Noah was here with us, with me.

"I've missed you too, golden boy," I replied as Noah brushed my hair aside and tenderly kissed my neck, sending a wave of butterflies dancing in my belly.

"How was Christmas?"

"I had an amazing time. If you had been here, it would have been perfect. How's your family?"

Noah put me down but quickly grabbed my hand, interlacing our fingers.

"They're good. My parents had some friends over. Nothing formal, which was great, and my *obaachan* came over from Tokyo. I dropped her this morning at DCA before driving here."

"Who's your *obaachan*? And you drove all the way from Washington? You must be exhausted, Noah! It's a long drive…come, let me help you with the luggage." I attempted to grab the suitcase, but Noah pushed it farther away from my reach.

"*Obaachan* means grandma in Japanese, and I'm far from tired," he mentioned, using the hand that held mine to push me closer to him. Noah lowered his face until his lips were mere inches from mine. His gaze dropped to my mouth, and he asked, "Do I need to show you how far from tired I am?"

I hoped that the redness in my cheeks and nose from the cold would conceal the blush that slowly spread up my neck.

Confirmed.

I was horny as fuck and trapped in a house filled with gorgeous men.

"Let's go inside, princess, but before that…can you explain to me what the fuck is 'Christmathon' and why Maggie has been texting me nonstop about it for the past forty-eight hours?"

* * *

"I say we take a shot every time someone says Kevin." Maggie's suggestion was practically a suicide attempt.

"Do you know how many times they mention his name? No. We can't choose Kevin, or we'll end up in the ER department with alcohol poisoning," Ander exclaimed.

He was right. We'd watched *Home Alone 2* over a hundred times as kids, and there was no way we would listen to Maggie's suggestions.

"I have an idea," I interrupted. "I suggest we take a shot every time someone says New York. It's fitting, don't you think?"

We were camped in Zayn's room. Maggie sat on a gray bean bag while the guys lounged on the bed, surrounded by countless pillows and popcorn bags nestled between their legs. I laid on the bed on my side, supporting my head with my hand and keeping a dark gray throw blanket covering my legs. Zayn's room was slightly smaller than Ander's, but the decor was entirely different. Ander's aesthetic was preppier, with blues and grays dominating the color scheme, whereas Zayn's room exuded a dark, enigmatic, and sexier vibe. The walls were covered with posters featuring some of his favorite groups, such as Thirty Seconds to Mars, My Chemical Romance, Korn, Fall Out Boy, and Good Charlotte. A king-size bed with an iron frame and white bed sheets sat in the middle of the room. Books and vinyl records were scattered across the floor, and another black bean bag occupied a corner. On the opposite side of the room were shelves loaded with trophies, presumably earned during his time competing in jujitsu. Next to Maggie, who had declared herself the referee, was a tray with tequila, lemon, and salt.

Four hours and two movies later, we were officially drunk.

Maggie had fallen asleep on the floor braced to a fluffy pillow, and judging by Ander's deep breathing in my lap, he was out cold, too. He had this peaceful expression on his face, and I couldn't help but feel the temptation to trace the lines of his nose, jaw, and lips with my fingers. However, I refrained from doing so just in case Noah and Zayn read too much into the situation.

"Do you think we should wake him up?" I asked the boys. I didn't want to disrupt his sleep, but it was already three o'clock in the morning, and I knew he had planned to wake up early the following day.

"We should also wake Maggie up." Zayn stood and knelt before her. "She's going to complain about her back tomorrow if we let her sleep on the floor. I mean, the rug is comfortable, but not that much." He nudged her. "Wake up and go to bed, blondie."

Suddenly, Maggie jumped from the floor and knocked Zayn down, causing Ander to jolt up from my lap at the sound of Zayn's yelp.

"Don't touch me!" Maggie screamed.

"Jesus…Maggie, it's alright. It's me, Zayn." Zayn spoke gently to reassure her.

Maggie glanced around, and a faint blush tinted her cheeks. Her sudden reaction embarrassed her, but I knew why she had reacted that way. Zayn didn't.

"Sorry, Zayn. I was having a nightmare," Maggie apologized.

Zayn nervously rubbed the back of his neck with his hand, avoiding Maggie's gaze as he looked at the wall.

"Don't worry about it. I'm sorry if I scared you," he apologized.

Ander broke the awkwardness and yawned.

"I think I'm going to bed," he announced. He stretched his arms, turned to Zayn, and asked, "Court, nine o'clock?" Zayn nodded. "Are you going to bed, Sienna?"

"I think I'm going to stay and finish watching *Last Christmas* with the guys," I responded. I've been a fan of Emilia Clarke since the premiere of *Game of Thrones*, so as soon as the movie was released, it immediately found its place on the Christmathon list.

"I'm going to bed too. Good night, guys," Maggie said as she approached the door.

Once Maggie and Ander retreated to their rooms, Zayn, Noah, and I returned to the bed and pulled the comforter over ourselves. I was sandwiched between them, with Zayn's leg touching mine beneath the sheets and Noah's fingers tracing circles on my right arm. My breathing picked up, but I blamed it on the alcohol.

"Do you think I'm more attractive than Henry Golding? He's technically half Malaysian, not Japanese, but I'm curious where I stand on your beauty scale."

I burst into laughter. That was one of the things I truly liked about Noah. His sense of humor and his knack for making random comments at the most unexpected moments were among my favorite things.

I shifted to look at him, and my gaze fell to his lips. He was undeniably handsome. Telling him he was better looking than Henry would only feed his already inflated ego. But I did it anyway.

"He has nothing on you. You're one of the most beautiful men I've ever seen, Noah, and you have a killer body."

Noah smiled, and my heart melted.

"One of them?" he retorted. "Who are the other ones?"

"Am I one of them?" Zayn asked.

"I'm not sure. Do you think you've earned that spot?" I joked.

Zayn swiftly turned toward me and began tickling my sides.

"Nooo, noooo, please, stop," I pleaded, attempting to stifle my laughter as best as I could, not wanting to wake up the whole household. However, it became pretty challenging when Noah decided to join in, grabbing my wrists and aiding his friend in the playful torment. With all the tickling and fighting, Zayn ended up between my legs with both hands on each side of my head. I could feel my heart beating with such intensity that I thought it would come out of my chest.

Thud. Thud. Thud.

Out of nowhere, Zayn leaned in and kissed me. It took barely a couple of seconds for my brain to register what he had done, but the moment I opened my mouth and felt his tongue touch mine, I forgot we had an audience and kissed him back. I wanted to touch his arms, his shoulders, but I couldn't. Noah held me down, pinning my hands on each side of my face.

"Zayn, stop…Noah…we can't," I said, turning my face and pulling away from the kiss. I suddenly panicked at the thought of Noah's potential anger toward us.

He glanced at me and then directed his gaze to Noah, who was kneeling on the bed just behind my head.

"I don't think he minds. In fact, I think watching us turns him on," Zayn stated.

"What?" I exclaimed.

"What the fuck, man! That was between *you* and *me*. You promised."

I wiggled my way out from between them until I stood at the foot of the bed.

"Care to explain?"

Zayn looked at Noah, then back at me and exhaled.

Noah looked resigned.

"Do you remember when Noah caught us downstairs in the kitchen, you know...fucking? Let's say he was there, hiding in the shadows, watching us the whole time."

"What do you mean by *the whole time*?" I blinked rapidly, attempting to process what Zayn had just confessed.

"I didn't intend to watch the entire thing," Noah chimed in. "Don't get me wrong; I was pissed. But it turned out that watching you two also turned me on. So there you have it. Now you know. Happy?" Noah directed his response to Zayn.

Zayn rose from the bed and came closer to me. When he stood in front of me, he cupped my face with both hands.

"I've been dying to kiss you for the past four days, and I don't think I can spend one more second on that bed with you if I don't claim your lips. I don't fucking care if Noah wants to watch."

The kiss was so powerful that I thought it would consume me. A moan left my mouth as Zayn moved one of his hands to grip my hair, tilting my head backward. The position gave him better access to my neck, so he started kissing, biting, and licking that sweet spot below my ear. I gripped his T-shirt with such force that my knuckles turned white. "I think someone doesn't want to watch anymore."

I opened my eyes, which I hadn't realized I had closed at some point, and attempted to push myself away from Zayn. However, he spun me around so that my back was against his chest. I worried that we had crossed a line that could jeopardize the friendship I had forged with Noah, but, to my surprise, Noah stood before me. His eyes had darkened, and his face bore an expression that seemed to oscillate between desire and anguish.

"Hold her hands."

Zayn complied with Noah's order and held my hands behind my back.

"What are you doing?" I clenched my legs with anticipation. I didn't have to check to know that my underwear was probably soaked.

"The question is, what do you want me to do?" Noah teased.

I opened and closed my mouth like a fish twice because I was embarrassed to say out loud the things that came to mind.

"Do you want me to leave so you can have fun with him, or do you want me to stay too?" Noah insisted.

"I...I..."

Zayn dropped his mouth to my ear and whispered, "Remember what you told me the other day? It doesn't have to be a fantasy. Just say the word."

"Please," I begged.

"Please, what, Sienna?" Noah continued, "Use your words and tell us what you want."

I pushed my body backward until I felt Zayn's hard cock pressed against my ass.

"Please, stay. I want you both."

"Good girl."

A shiver traveled down my spine in response to Zayn's praise. Noah stepped closer and brought his mouth to mine until our lips were so close that I could practically feel his breath.

"If at any point you want to stop, just say it. Okay?"

"Okay."

My hands were sweaty, and the anticipation was killing me. I had never done something like this before, but I remembered when I found out they had shared a girl, maybe several, in the past. The thought of them kissing and touching another girl made me fucking furious.

Noah dropped to his knees without breaking eye contact.

He tugged his fingers underneath the elastic band of my leggings and very slowly pushed them down, along with my underwear, until I was completely exposed.

"So fucking beautiful," he said.

I lifted both feet, one at a time, until I was free of them. Noah picked them up and tossed them on one of the bean bags.

"I've been dying to eat this pussy for weeks. Believe me when I say that by the time we're done with you, you won't be able to remember your name and will only know how to scream ours."

Before I had a chance to respond to Noah, he buried his face between my legs and started circling the apex of my thighs with his skillful tongue. While Noah continued to feast on me like a starving man, Zayn kissed, licked, and bit my neck. He linked my hands together until he was able to hold both with one of his and use the other to circle and pinch one of my nipples through my clothes. A lightning strike of pleasure traveled from my breast to my throbbing pussy.

"You like that, don't you? You enjoy being at our mercy, knowing that your body is ours to use."

"Yes," I breathed. "Touch me, Zayn. I want…I need you to touch me, too. So fucking much."

Zayn helped me out of the oversized top until I only wore my white lace bra.

"She's beautiful, isn't she?" Noah asked Zayn between each swirl of his tongue. "But she'll look more beautiful when that mouth of hers is around my cock while you fuck her raw."

Oh my God.

I almost came hearing those words coming from Noah's mouth. I was equally filled with lust and fear. I had been very sexually active since I lost my virginity almost three years ago, but I had never been with two guys at the same time. I worried that my nerves would betray me.

Zayn unclasped my bra and threw it on the floor. He stood behind me. I was unable to see what he was doing until I heard him undoing his belt and unzipping his jeans. A moment later, his hard length pressed against my lower back, and his hands cupped my breasts. Every inch of my skin was covered in goose bumps. It was too much—the feeling of Noah's tongue, the touch from Zayn's expert hands.

Noah pushed two fingers inside me and started pumping them in and out. At the same time, he sucked and licked with short strokes my clit. Every time he curved his fingers, he expertly touched that spot inside me that made my body shudder. I moved my hips back and forth, clenching and unclenching my muscles, seeking more pressure from Noah's mouth.

An intense pressure started to build up in my lower stomach, and my breathing became more erratic.

"That's it, Sienna. Come for us. Let us see how much you enjoy us playing with your body." Zayn's encouragement tipped me over the edge, and my vision blurred as I reached my climax. The orgasm hit me so hard, like a tidal wave, that Zayn had to cover my mouth with his hand so nobody heard my screams. Noah continued playing with his tongue until I couldn't take it anymore.

"Please stop…I can't," I softly whimpered, my words muffled by Zayn's hand.

He stood and kissed me so passionately that Zayn lost his balance and stepped back. I could taste my own arousal, and that turned me on more than I thought it would.

"Lie on the bed, Noah." Zayn's voice was deep and commanding.

Breaking off our kiss, Noah walked toward the bed. I was panting and knew they were far from being done.

"What are you going to do?" I asked Zayn.

"I'm going to do what Noah said. I'm going to fuck you hard while you suck his cock until you choke on it. Understood?"

"Man, I didn't know you were this bossy. It makes me hard." Noah laughed.

"Take your clothes off, Noah."

He immediately obliged and started to take off his sweatpants and T-shirt.

"Sienna, I want you on all fours on top of him, but don't touch him until I say so."

Noah lay down with the filthiest look on his face while he moved his hand up and down his hardness. I crawled on top of him until my face hovered over his waist, and my hands were placed on each side of his body. I could see the precum on the tip, and I craved to bring my mouth down and lick it, to taste his saltiness.

"Fuck, Sienna. I don't need to touch you to know how wet you are. I can see it from here," Zayn said.

The bed dipped behind me, and Zayn gripped all my hair with one hand.

"I want to see how you take Noah's cock in your mouth. I want you to start slowly until he cannot take it anymore, but if I tell you to stop, you stop. Got it?" Zayn yanked my head back by the hair.

"Yes," I hissed.

"If you don't, I'll personally punish you, and believe me, it won't be the kind of punishment you'll enjoy."

Noah cleared his throat before saying, "Are you done with all the threatening, Zayn? I'm dying over here."

"Sienna...show him how well you can take him."

When I circled Noah's length with my hand and brought my mouth to the tip, he growled. I started slowly, just as Zayn had instructed me. I licked every inch with my tongue and applied enough pressure with each stroke of my hand to make him lift his ass from the bed. He clearly was dying for more, and I was happy to please. I pushed his dick to the back of my throat, choking on it until tears pricked my eyes.

"Fuuuuuuck, your mouth feels like heaven." One of Noah's hands instinctively reached out to grasp my hair. Zayn let him hold my hair while I continued to swallow every inch of him. His hand pushed my head up and down until each thrust of his hips became more violent. I knew he was getting closer.

"Yes, that's it. Take my cock, Sienna. Let me fuck that beautiful mouth of yours and show me how much you like it."

Zayn slid his fingers alongside my slit, and I whimpered.

"I'm going to fuck this pussy now, so hold on tight to Noah, but don't stop sucking."

I felt Zayn slide his dick along my wetness until it was coated with my arousal. He pushed in the tip of his cock, and I moaned.

"Fucking hell, Sienna. You're so tight." Zayn pushed even farther, slowly stretching my walls until he was buried inside me up to the hilt. He carefully slid out and very slowly pushed his cock back inside me. He continued repeating the same motion, fucking me with low strokes, never breaking the rhythm.

"I've missed you," Zayn confessed. "Are you ready for more?" Zayn grabbed my hips, pausing for a few seconds before he slammed into me again, and again, and again, each thrust now more violent than the previous one. "God, you feel so good."

The noises that filled the room were obscene, a mix of our groans and moans mixed with the sound our bodies made each time they connected.

"Fuck, man. I think I'm gonna come," Noah said.

"Stop, Sienna. We're not done yet."

I released Noah and turned to look at Zayn. His jaw clenched, and his tattooed chest glistened with sweat. He'd never looked more beautiful.

Zayn slowed his movements, and with an authoritative tone, he asked, "Do you trust me?"

I didn't have to think twice.

"Yes," I answered.

"Good. This is what's going to happen." Zayn licked his right thumb, pressed it against my ass, and added, "I want you to ride Noah while I take your ass."

My eyes widened.

Zayn saw my hesitation.

"Have you done anal before?" he asked.

"Ehm, yes. But not while someone else was already fucking me."

Zayn slowly pushed his finger inside, and I shivered.

"I can't promise it won't hurt at the beginning, but I can promise you that you will enjoy it. Like Noah said, just say the word if you want to stop."

I trusted both. Zayn and Noah would never do anything to hurt me, and the excitement from taking them both simultaneously was strong enough for me to nod.

"Say it," he commanded with the deep tone of his voice, and my pussy clenched around his shaft. "Say how much you want us to fuck you at the same time. How much you want to be ours."

"Yes," I panted, "I want you both to fuck me. Make me yours."

In one quick movement, Zayn jumped from the bed and went straight to his bedside table. He opened the first drawer and took a tube of lube from the back.

"Come up here, princess. Show me how much you love riding my cock," Noah demanded.

I moved up until I was practically sitting on his lap. I placed one hand on his chest and guided his length to my folds. I slowly sank down, savoring every inch of his flesh. His jaw tightened as he gazed at me with pure lust and adoration. Once it was in, I started riding him with a steady pace, making sure I rubbed my clit with his body with every hip movement.

"Noah," I moaned, "touch me, please." Noah lunged upward and covered my nipple with his mouth, sucking and licking while I continued to seek my own pleasure with his cock.

"Are you ready, babe?" Zayn asked.

The coldness from the lube contrasted with how hot my skin felt. I was ready to combust. Zayn gently coated my back entrance and then used his other hand to push me farther onto Noah's body.

"Don't move until I tell you to. That goes for you, too, Noah."

Noah gave him a salute, which made me snort.

When I felt Zayn's tip pushing against my ass, my entire body trembled. I was tense, so as Zayn stretched me, I closed my eyes and pinched my brows together. Noah noticed how anxious I was, so he held my face between his soft hands and gently kissed me.

"Breathe," he whispered against my lips.

I took deep breaths until Zayn pushed against the resistance and was completely buried.

"Fuuuck. Hold still. I need a second. Otherwise, the party will be over too soon…her ass is so tight, man."

I welcomed the pause to catch my breath.

"You've never looked more beautiful," Noah added.

When Zayn began to move, Noah also did. They swiftly fell into a rhythm, and when one slid out, the other immediately thrust in. My body started to tremble, and sweat covered every inch of it. It was all too much. I felt too full with both impaling me on their cocks. My pussy clenched every time Zayn slammed his hips forward, pounding into me.

"Oh God, don't stop. I'm gonna come," I cried.

"Come for us, princess," Noah commanded. "Let us hear you scream our names while we fill you with our cum."

And I detonated.

Describing the orgasm as the best I'd ever had would be an understatement. I cried out, my nails digging deeper into Noah's chest as I clenched my thighs.

"I'm so close," Zayn exclaimed.

They kept moving in unison until Noah's and Zayn's release followed my own a few seconds later.

I dropped down until I pressed my forehead against Noah's and smiled.

"Fuck. I can't believe we did that."

I glanced over my shoulder at Zayn. His dark hair looked all damp with sweat, half covering his eyes. He gently pulled out, followed by Noah, their seed dripping down my legs.

I lay on the bed beside Noah, my heart racing a thousand miles per hour. Zayn came back from the en suite bathroom with a wet cloth and pushed it between my legs to quickly clean me up.

"Fuck me, that was wild," Noah said while I placed my head on his chest, resting my arm around his waist and my leg over his thigh. "Are you okay?" Noah kissed my hair while he stroked my arm. I immediately melted into his touch and took a deep breath.

"I'm more than okay," I responded. "I don't think I've ever had an orgasm that intense in my life."

"You're welcome," Noah boasted.

Zayn crawled into bed and pushed the covers over our naked bodies. He cuddled me from behind, spooning me while peppering the back of my neck and shoulders with sweet little kisses.

I had reached heaven.

As I lay in bed, I could feel the gentle pull of sleep tugging at my consciousness. The softness of the sheets and the warmth of their bodies made my eyelids grow heavier. The world around me began to fade away. But just before I dozed off, the image of Ander's face unexpectedly surfaced in my mind. My chest tightened, and I wondered how wonderful life would be if he were also mine.

LIKE YOU MEAN IT

(Ander)

After one long shower, two painkillers, and a gallon of water later, I started to feel like myself again. Last night, I drank way too much tequila, but there was nothing quite like playing some basketball to help sweat the alcohol out of your system. I grabbed a pair of shorts and a long-sleeved T-shirt and quickly dressed before heading toward Zayn's room.

I knocked twice before calling out his name.

"Zayn, c'mon. Let's go shoot some hoops."

There was no answer. They'd probably stayed up until late drinking and watching the movie, so I imagined he was possibly knocked out cold. After waiting a few minutes, I decided to try the doorknob. It was unlocked.

When I opened the door, I froze. It felt like all the blood in my body rushed to my feet.

Noah, Zayn, and Sienna were underneath the bed covers, which only covered their legs. They were naked. Noah spooned Sienna, who lay across Zayn's chest.

"What the fuck?!" The moment I yelled those words, Sienna woke up. When her eyes connected with mine, she gasped.

I was livid, and by the look on Sienna's face, she could tell. I turned around and stomped to my bedroom without sparing another look at them.

They had fucked.

The three of them.

"Wait!"

I heard Sienna calling me, but I didn't want to talk to her. I was enraged. I was furious with her for giving me hope that there was more to us than a friendship, at them for touching her in ways I wished I could, and at myself for falling for her once more.

"Ander, please. Wait."

When I reached my door, I looked at her from the corner of my eye. She was trying to wrap herself in a blanket as she hurried down the hallway.

"I don't want to talk to you. Go back to the room."

"Please, let me explain."

I walked inside my bedroom and pushed the door, but Sienna pushed it with her hand before I could close it. I gave up and walked toward the windows. I couldn't look at her—not like this. I knew that if I opened my mouth, I would say things I would probably regret later, so I kept my lips shut.

"I'm sorry you had to see that. I never wanted you to see us like this. I was going to explain it to you today. I was going to tell you."

"TELL ME WHAT?" I shouted while I spun around to face her. "That you've been fucking both of them behind my back? That you played me the other day?"

God.

She looked gorgeous just with that blanket on and her messed-up morning hair.

"That's not fair. You know that's not true. You're saying that just to hurt me."

I closed the distance between us and dropped my head until my eyes were leveled with hers.

"Yes, you've been playing with me. You wanna fuck them? Be my guest. But I'm done. You and I are done." I ground my teeth together until my jaw hurt. She was heaving, her gaze continually shifting between my eyes as if she were trying to guess if I was telling the truth and contemplating her next move at the same time.

"But I'm not done with you."

She dropped the blanket.

When she crashed her lips to mine, I cracked.

I grabbed her by the throat, applying enough pressure to choke her without cutting off her air.

"Don't fucking test me, Sienna." I looked down at her, taking in her pointed nipples, the smooth curve of her breasts, and her firm stomach. How many times had I imagined her like this? Completely bare and at my mercy. "I have very little self-control at the moment, and I can't promise I'll be gentle," I growled.

She bit her lower lip and looked at me with sultry eyes.

"I don't want gentle. Please, Ander, fuck me like you mean it."

I made her walk backward, still holding her by the throat, until her ass hit the sofa in the middle of the room.

I lowered my mouth and whispered in her ear, "I'm gonna fuck you until your body can't take it anymore. You're gonna come so hard and so loud that the entire house will know who you belong to. You're gonna scream my name until your voice is hoarse, and the only thing you can do is call for God. And you're gonna take it, and you're gonna like it."

Sienna was so shocked that she remained there, silent, staring at me with those fuck-me eyes. So I kissed her with all the bottled-up rage and desire that coursed through my veins. I pushed my tongue inside her mouth, devouring her like my life began and ended with her. She wrapped her arms around my neck as she deepened the kiss.

"Turn around and hold on to the sofa," I commanded.

When she was bent over, I traced my hand along her spine until my hand reached her ass, and I spanked her.

SPANK.

"Fuck!" she yelped.

"That's for fucking Noah and Zayn."

SPANK.

"That's for pushing me to my limit. For taunting me."

SPANK.

"Oh God!" This time, her yelp was followed by a moan.

I caressed her red and swollen ass cheek and said, "That's for showing up to my room completely naked with that tiny blanket."

"Please, Ander," she begged. "I need you so badly."

I dropped to my knees, and before she realized what I was doing, I angled my mouth and licked her soaking pussy.

"Ander," she breathed.

I loved hearing my name on her lips when I knew I was the one causing her pleasure.

"You taste like fucking heaven. Let me hear you scream my name again."

I pushed my tongue inside her pussy and then sucked hard on her clit until she was practically grinding against my mouth. I changed between long strokes and quick ones just with the tip of my tongue.

"Oh God, Ander, oh God. Yes, keep doing that. Don't stop."

She didn't have to tell me fucking twice. I buried my face in her pretty little cunt until her legs started to shake. But I wasn't done yet. No. This girl who had come back to my life like a storm would soon discover what she had been missing all these years. I couldn't wait to show her how much I craved her with my cock.

"We're just getting started." I stood and pushed my shorts and briefs down until my cock sprang free. I had never been this hard in my life. I pumped it twice before I rubbed the head between her glistening center. She whimpered at the anticipation. I placed the tip at her entrance and warned her, "I told you I wouldn't be gentle." With one hard thrust, I buried myself inside her pussy.

"Fuck! Fuck! You're too big; it hurts."

She was probably sore from last night, but I didn't fucking care. A little bit of pain was what she deserved for playing with my feelings.

"You can take it, Sienna. Now move and show me how much you want my cock."

Sienna held the sofa tighter until her knuckles turned white and then pushed her ass back and forth, back and forth. But it was too slow for my liking. After all, I had promised her rough. I grabbed her by the hips and began to slam into her like a possessed man.

"Look." *Thrust.* "What." *Thrust.* "You've." *Thrust.* "Done." *Thrust.* "To." *Thrust.* "Me." *Thrust.*

She was so tight that it didn't matter that I had masturbated in the shower that morning, thinking about her mouth wrapped around my dick.

She tried to cover her moans with a hand over her mouth, so I grabbed her again by the throat and choked her. I could feel her pulse under my fingers. When her breathing got shallow, I moved one of my hands to circle her clit.

"Come for me. Show me how much you enjoy it when I fuck you like my little whore."

The moment I released her neck and the blood ran back to her head, I pinched her clit and slapped her ass. Her climax hit her so hard that her screams and the way she clenched around my cock tipped me over the edge.

"Fuck," I cried as I released myself inside her, filling her up to the brim.

The moment she dropped her head to the backrest, I pulled out, put my dick inside my clothes, and took the blanket from the floor. When she stood, I threw it at her.

I was still mad—at her and at myself for being so weak. She was playing with the three of us, but I had fallen for her so hard that I couldn't deny her—to possess her.

Snagging the blanket in midair, she furrowed her brows.

"What are you doing?" Sienna asked.

The mental picture of them in bed flooded my thoughts once more. I couldn't allow her to have this hold on me because in every scenario that infested my mind, she ended up picking Zayn or Noah but never me. I knew that one way or another, she would be the end of our friendship. And I would never allow that to happen. She left once. She could do it again, but my heart wouldn't survive this time. Especially not now, after I just had a taste of her.

I started pacing toward the bedroom door when she pleaded, "Don't do this, please. Don't do this to us."

I held the door open and looked at her naked body one last time.

"There never was an *us*."

I NEED YOU

(Sienna)

It'd been four days.

Four never-ending days since Ander and I had sex.

He'd been avoiding me, and all my efforts to reach out had been unsuccessful. The distance between us was growing to the point that it was agonizing. I feared that we had crossed a point of no return.

There never was an us.

Those words kept repeating in my head like a broken record.

I thought that, finally, we were facing the feelings we had been dancing around for the past few months, but I guessed I was wrong. He was angry with me for sleeping with Noah and Zayn, and every inch of my body felt the depth of his possessiveness with each thrust. My pussy was sore the following two days after having my first threesome and then being fucked by Ander the following morning. Even my ass still looked red from all that spanking. And I loved it. But when he uttered those words, my heart shattered into a million pieces.

For the past three days, I stayed in Zayn's room with him and Noah, but we'd limited our interactions to kissing and cuddling. I was in a sour mood, and Ander's silence drove me crazy. I believed they noticed the change between us although they hadn't asked me why I'd kept it to myself. I didn't know what Ander had told them, but based on the way they didn't want to address the elephant in the room, I bet he hadn't said a word.

It was three o'clock, and today was the "Venetian Summer Night" New Year's Eve party. Chaos flooded the house since eight o'clock this morning as men and women scurried about, arranging furniture, flowers, lights, and candles. Claudia hired a makeup artist and a hairstylist for Maggie and me. It was a lovely gesture, and although I liked doing my own hair and makeup, it was nice to feel like we were getting ready for a red carpet event.

"You've been very quiet. Is everything alright?" Maggie asked before taking a sip of her latte. Her head was overloaded with curlers, and her makeup was already done.

"It's nothing. You don't need to worry."

"But I do," she retorted.

I let out a long sigh and set my ginger latte on the table.

"It's complicated. Ander and I had a fight a few days ago, and he hasn't talked to me since then."

She contemplated her answer for a few seconds before she replied. "Yeah, I noticed. I was waiting for you to say something. In fact, Noah asked me if I knew what it was about. They also have no clue what's going on." Maggie placed her coffee on the table and continued. "I wouldn't worry too much if I were you, though. He's in love with you. Give him some time, and he'll come around."

I snorted.

"He's not in love with me."

"You're fucking blind, Sienna. He's madly in love with you, and everyone can see it. Haven't you noticed the way he looks at you like you were a goddess sent from Mount Olympus? Like he wants to pounce on you but at the same time make you the mother of his children?"

I'm pretty sure my laughter could be heard from Manhattan.

"You're delusional."

"Maybe I am," she responded. "But not about this. Are you gonna talk to him tonight?" Maggie took her silk robe off and slipped into the dress she borrowed. She turned around and asked me to zip it.

"I don't know. It's been days since our argument, and I'm not sure I can let another day go by. I don't want to start the year like this."

Maggie sat on a chair and put on her new Louboutin shoes.

"Is it just a fight, or did something else happen?"

I didn't know if Maggie was just very observant or I simply had to work on my poker face, but she consistently managed to read everyone's emotions very easily. I stayed silent.

Maggie stood, placed a hand on her hips, and said, "Look. It's none of my business...I know. But you need to face your feelings and stop playing games with them. It's not fair to them. They aren't just some fuckboys from Ibiza. They're your friends, and you need to take responsibility for your actions."

"Wow. That's quite the lecture before closing out the year."

Maggie looked pissed, and I didn't understand why my situation with the guys affected her so much, especially as she had encouraged me to hook up with all three, but I guessed she was just trying to avoid an implosion of catastrophic proportions.

"Okay. I'll talk to Ander tonight," I replied.

"Good."

* * *

I quickly checked myself in the mirror before heading out. I wore a floor-length, long-sleeved burgundy velvet dress, an off-the-shoulders style with a thigh-high slit on the right, and my favorite pair of Jimmy

Choo golden sandals. As for the jewelry, I kept it simple. I wore some small golden earrings and the pendant Zayn gave me for Christmas. My makeup looked natural, except for my choice of lipstick—a shade of burgundy that perfectly matched the color of my dress.

Someone knocked on the door just as I finished putting my Venetian golden mask on.

"One second," I shouted.

When I opened the door, my heart stopped. Zayn leaned on the doorframe wearing a tux. My mouth dropped. His mask was black and golden, and although it covered half of his face, the glimmer in his eyes still shone through.

"You look…" He cleared his throat before continuing. "You're the most beautiful woman I've ever seen, Sienna. That dress…that dress would look way better around your waist while you sit on my face. What do you say?"

I hit his arm and slightly pushed him.

"We don't have time for that. We're gonna be late!"

"That's a shame, but I have a few ideas about how I want to start the year. I want to start it with a bang, if you know what I mean." Zayn winked at me, but I ignored his comment and moved around him to walk toward the stairs. Before I reached the first step, Zayn grabbed my arm and stopped me.

"Allow me." He offered me his arm and one of his sweetest smiles. I couldn't resist every time the light came through the bad-boy facade. He could fool everyone, but I knew that behind those tattoos was a beautiful, sensitive soul.

"Lead the way," I said, linking my arm through his.

As we stepped into the ballroom, I came to a halt. I stood there, speechless, with my jaw on the floor. It wasn't a big room by any means, but the way it had been decorated made you feel you were in the Italian Renaissance. Crystal chandeliers hung from the ceiling, casting a soft, warm glow upon the room. Along the walls, Claudia had managed to place intricate tapestries in deep burgundy and royal purple, creating an illusion of opulence.

I quickly glanced around the room and saw Noah and Maggie chatting at the other end.

"Look, Noah and Maggie are over there," I pointed out.

As we moved deeper into the ballroom, I caught the scent of freshly cut flowers. I recognized the aroma of lilies, magnolias, and orange blossoms instantly. I had spent a couple of springs in Seville, where the aroma of orange blossoms permeates every street during that time of the year.

The moment Noah saw me, his eyes darkened.

"You look stunning, Sienna. Come here." Noah wrapped his arm around my waist, pulling me close to his side, and gently placed a kiss on the corner of my lips.

"Have you seen Ander?" I asked them.

"Yes. He's around here somewhere," Maggie replied. "Have you talked to him yet?"

"No. But I intend to."

"I don't know what's going on between you guys. Would you mind sharing it with the group?" Noah squeezed my middle.

"Let me talk to him first," I said, scanning the faces around me until I made eye contact with William, who stood next to the bar. He gestured with his hand for me to join him. "I need to have a word with Ander's father. I'll be back." I proceeded to walk over to where William stood with a couple in their mid-forties.

"I hope you're enjoying the party," he said, kissing my cheek.

"Let me introduce you to Lorena and Patrick. They are old friends of mine who also knew your parents."

"It's lovely to meet you. You look so much like your mom," the woman, Lorena, said.

The mention of my parents felt like an icy hand had gripped my heart. My chest tightened, and a heavy weight settled upon my shoulders. It was as though the air in the room had thickened, making breathing difficult. Memories of my parents flooded my mind, vivid and poignant, and I could feel their absence like an ache deep in my soul. I was going to start a new year without them in my life, and that was a hard pill to swallow.

The words hung in the air, heavy and tangible, casting a shadow over the conversation. I struggled to maintain my composure, to hide the raw vulnerability that threatened to spill over. I knew she didn't mean to make me feel uncomfortable by any means, but the mention of them had uncovered a well of grief that I thought I was handling well. Apparently not.

"Thank you. That's very kind of you. She was a beautiful woman."

"And so are you," Lorena responded.

"Have you seen Ander?" I looked around, but I didn't see him.

"I believe he's helping Claudia with something. Lorena, Patrick… do you mind if I have a word with Sienna in private?"

"Of course. It was a pleasure meeting you. Enjoy the party."

Once the couple was far enough away not to overhear us, William leaned in and said, "Peter sent me the contract, and I went ahead and signed it this afternoon. But before I say anything in my speech, I just wanted to ensure you're okay if I announced it tonight."

"Of course. I don't see the issue."

"Great. I know that I've already said it, but thank you. It feels great to be back at Cos Pharma."

"No problem, just…don't make me regret my decision, okay?" I still had some reservations, but I was also aware of my father's wrongdoing. William deserved to be back.

"I won't."

"Hey, girl." Maggie came behind me. "You look thirsty. Shall we get something to drink?"

"Champagne?" William asked.

Maggie and I both nodded. William turned around and placed our drink orders.

"I wanted to give you a heads-up," she warned, gesturing toward the opposite corner of the room. "I spotted Ander over there. He's in conversation with a cougar who cannot keep her hands to herself. It seems like he could use a bit of rescuing." Maggie noticed my hesitation. "Go. I'll bring you the champagne."

My friend was right; that woman kept touching Ander's arm and chest and laughing like he was the funniest person in the world.

Bitch.

Was I jealous? Maybe.

"What's so funny?" I deadpanned. The woman turned to look at me, and I noticed her slightly sneering back at me.

"Nothing. And you're…?"

I extended my hand and said, "Sienna, Ander's friend."

"I'm Charlotte, but my friends call me Charlie."

"I'd normally say it's a pleasure meeting you, *Charlotte*, but that wouldn't be entirely true," I remarked. Her fake, plastic smile vanished as I continued. "I need to have a word with Ander, so if you'll excuse us…" My eyes briefly caught the glint of a wedding ring on her left hand. "I'm sure your husband must be looking for you. Or maybe not," I added dryly. Without uttering a word, she walked away, though I could have sworn I heard her calling me a whore.

"What was that about?" Ander asked.

"Nothing. She was all over you, and I noticed you seemed uncomfortable, so I thought I'd step in."

"So it wasn't because you were jealous?"

Just then, a glass of champagne magically appeared in front of me.

"William sent this over for you," Maggie chimed in. "I'll leave you two to chat. Come find me when you're done." She smiled at Ander and strolled back to join Noah and Zayn.

I took a sip, hoping it would bolster my confidence.

"Listen. I know you're upset, but you haven't even glanced in my direction in the past few days, and I cannot bear it anymore. Please, Ander. Talk to me."

"What do you want me to say?"

"I don't know. But say something. After what happened the other morning, I thought we had finally crossed the line we had been dancing around for the past few months. You know how I feel about you, and I get that it was a shock seeing me naked with both of them, but it doesn't change how I feel about you."

"It's not that simple. I don't like being a second plate, especially if I'm the third course."

I downed a generous gulp of champagne. Perhaps with a touch of alcohol in my system, I could summon the courage to say everything that was on my mind.

"You're not just some casual fuck, Ander. But I can't deny that I have feelings for them. You're well aware of that. I'm not sure what the answer is, but please, don't shut me out."

"So basically, you're just going to keep fucking them, right? And

I have to be okay with that. It's either that or I lose you again. Is that what you're saying?"

"It's not only about sex, Ander. Not with you and not with them. My feelings for you are not any lesser because I also have feelings for them. I…I…" My vision blurred at the edges, and the sounds around me seemed to drift into the distance. I lost my balance, my coordination failing me, but Ander swiftly wrapped an arm around me, steadying me against his chest. The empty glass slipped from my hand and shattered into a multitude of tiny fragments as it met the floor, prompting the nearby crowd to turn and see what had happened.

"How many glasses of champagne have you had?" he asked.

I couldn't think straight; my breath grew shallow and labored, and it became an effort to draw in each successive gulp of air. A wave of nausea hit me so hard that, for a moment, I feared I might vomit all over Ander's tuxedo.

"Only one."

"Shit, your pupils. Have you taken any drugs?" Ander's concern escalated with each passing moment.

"I…I duon't dooo thaet shhh…shit." My tongue felt sluggish, and I couldn't articulate clear words.

"Fuck. Help! HELP! Someone call an ambulance!"

"What's wrong with her?"

I could hear voices around me but was too weak to open my eyes.

"I don't know," Ander responded.

I could feel the pulse in my temples quicken, and a weird sensation began to wash over me, like a rising tide of darkness slowly overtaking my consciousness.

"Come back to me, Sienna, please. Open your eyes, love. I need you."

My senses dimmed, and the final clear thought that flickered through my mind was the unsettling notion that I hadn't been brave enough to express my true feelings, and now, I might never get the chance to confess that I was completely, utterly, and irrevocably in love with the three of them.

A DRAMATIC TURN OF EVENTS

(Sienna)

"She's waking up."

I slowly opened my eyes, and the sterile white ceiling of a hospital room greeted me. My throat felt raw and scratchy, as if I had swallowed a handful of sandpaper. I tried to clear my throat, but it only intensified the discomfort. The room seemed unfamiliar, and confusion settled in as I tried to piece together how I'd ended up here.

My lips were parched, and I desperately needed water.

"Water."

"Here," Ander said as he placed a plastic cup with a straw closer to my mouth. "Just small sips, or you'll get sick."

Zayn, Noah, and William stood at the foot of the bed.

My movements were slow, and my limbs felt heavy. Panic started to creep in as I realized that I couldn't remember what had led me to this hospital bed. I tried to recall the events leading up to this moment, but my thoughts felt muddled, like a puzzle with missing pieces. The faint beeping of monitors nearby added to my disorientation. I knew I needed answers, but my immediate priority was quenching my intense thirst.

"You scared the shit out of us, princess. How are you feeling?"

"Like I've been hit by a train." I chuckled, but my laughter quickly dissolved into a fit of coughing.

Why does my throat hurt this badly?

"Oh, we've been freaking out over here, but sure, go ahead and laugh it up," Zayn fired back.

"Sorry. What happened?" I asked.

"What's the last thing you remember?" Ander asked. He was seated on the bed. Once he set the plastic cup on the nightstand, he took my hand in his.

"I...I...remember talking to you. You were upset. The next thing I remember was you begging me to open my eyes."

Ander's lips tightened as he squeezed my hand.

"Someone tried to kill you," Noah explained.

"What?" I exclaimed, confused. *Why? Who? How?* I had too many questions and zero answers. I couldn't remember a single thing.

"Someone spiked your champagne with barbiturates, and you suffered from an overdose. You were lucky that it was almost New Year's Eve, and the roads were empty—the ambulance arrived fifteen minutes before you went into cardiac arrest." Zayn filled me in with details on how those minutes went by. "The police want to speak to you, but we've told them you need rest before giving a statement."

"But I don't have a clue about what happened or who could've done it."

"We do," Noah chimed in.

"Huh? You know?" I asked, a sense of worry creeping in.

"The stalker. We found a note and a black dahlia in your room," he said, making my head spin and my body shake.

"Don't worry, love. We have it all handled." Ander said, reaching out to softly touch my cheek. I leaned on his hand, finding comfort in his touch.

"I've been in touch with a private security firm, and they'll contact you sometime this week to set up your protection for when you're back at Stanford. Until then, we'll be on watch, always keeping you in sight," William reassured me.

"You should get some rest," Ander insisted.

"I feel fine. I'm tired, but it's okay." I turned my head to Noah and asked him, "What did the note say?"

"Here." Noah retrieved a piece of paper from his pocket and passed it to me. Careful not to pull out the IV in the back of my left hand, I reached for the note and unfolded it.

Sometimes revenge tastes like poison.

"The police have reviewed the security camera footage at my house. However, a significant number of people, including guests and staff, came and went that day. It might take them a while to narrow down a full list of potential suspects," William said.

"Do they have any?"

"Me, to begin with. They interviewed all the waitstaff from the party and the alcohol supplier company. But honestly, it could have been anyone," William remarked.

"They're also questioning Maggie as we speak," Zayn added.

"Let's leave the police to do their job. I'll let them know you're awake, but I'll ask them to give you more time to wake up. Don't talk to them unless there's a lawyer present with you, okay?"

"Thank you, William."

"Boys, Sienna needs some rest, and you need to eat something," William advised as he gently squeezed Noah's and Zayn's shoulders. He then motioned with his head, indicating to Ander that he should leave the room.

"Actually, I'd like to speak with Sienna. I'll call you when I leave the hospital, but text me where you're going for food, and I'll meet you there."

"Okay, man. Get some rest, princess. We'll come by later," Noah stated.

He waved his hand, but Zayn came closer and gently kissed my forehead, saying, "See you later, babe."

"Thank you, guys," I responded.

Noah and Zayn grabbed their backpacks and left the room with William.

The silence stretched for a few minutes, and I used the opportunity to drink more water.

"I don't even know where to start," Ander admitted, his hand rubbing his tired face. He looked wiped out, and I wondered how much sleep he had managed since I arrived at the hospital.

"Well, how about you tell me how long I've been unconscious?" I suggested.

"You've been in the ICU for a couple of days, but once they got you stable, they moved you to the regular ward."

"So it's…"

"January fourth. Yep."

"Wow. And to think that my parents were worried last year because I slept through January first." I chuckled.

"Sienna, I thought I'd lost you." I glanced at Ander and noticed tears streaming down his cheeks. "I thought I'd never see or kiss you again, and that thought consumed me the past few days."

I cupped Ander's face with both hands, gently wiping away the tears streaking his cheeks with my thumbs.

"Shhh, I'm okay now. I'm here with you, and I'm not going anywhere."

Ander held the wrist that didn't have the IV line and confessed, "I don't care, Sienna. I've been thinking about it, and I don't fucking care. I don't care if you also have feelings for Noah and Zayn. When I thought you might not make it, it tore me apart. I was fucking scared. I can't picture my life without you, and I can't deny it any longer, Sienna. I'm in love with you. You have no idea how much I fucking love you. I'll gladly take any piece of your heart you're willing to give me. You're mine, and I'm yours."

He softly kissed me. My heart burned with all the things I wanted to say, but I didn't have the will to break that kiss. Each gentle stroke of his tongue brought me back to life, and I met every single one with all the love I knew resided in my heart.

"I love you, Ander," I replied between kisses. "I was already in love with you the first time we kissed. I've told you before—I'm yours."

Our kiss was interrupted by three knocks on the door.

I tried to calm my breathing before Ander asked whoever was on the other side to come in.

"Sorry for disturbing you, Miss Moore," a nurse said. "But the police insist that they need to talk to you."

"No problem. Tell them to come in." I tugged the bed sheets a little higher, ensuring they now covered my chest, as I quickly realized that I was wearing a very thin gown, and my nipples now peaked through the fabric after that kiss.

A moment later, two men dressed in dark suits entered the room.

"Miss Moore, please accept our apologies for disturbing you," said the taller law enforcement officer. He presented his badge before offering a handshake. "I'm Detective Cortes, and this is Agent Miller from the FBI."

"FBI?" I asked.

"Yes. Detective Cortes believes there could be a link between the threats you've been receiving back at Stanford University and your attempted murder. Officer Johnson, who is leading your case and a good friend, called me."

"Do you mind if we ask you a few questions?" Detective Cortes pressed.

I glanced at Ander. I told William I would only talk to the cops with a lawyer present, but I didn't see the issue. At the end of the day, I was the victim.

"Sure."

Detective Cortes retrieved a notepad and a pen from the inside pocket of his jacket.

"Miss Moore, how many threatening notes have you received so far?"

"Five, if you consider the one they left at Scott Manor," I answered.

"When did you start receiving those threatening notes?"

"Hmm. It was a few days after my friend Noah's birthday. That would be around the third week of October."

The detective noted the date down.

"Do you even have anything new to ask? Your buddy over there should have all the info on those first four notes," Ander sneered, his patience wearing thin.

"Watch your tone, boy." The detective turned to me again. "Are you aware of any threats ever made against your family? Did your parents ever tell you if they also received any notes?"

"What does this have to do with my parents?"

"Please answer the question, Miss Moore," Agent Miller insisted.

"No. If they did, they never told me. Why are you asking me this? Did someone threaten my parents?"

"Could you grant us a moment, young man?" Detective Cortes asked as he approached my bedside. His body language underwent a noticeable change, and his jaw clenched visibly.

"If you have anything to say to me, you can say it in front of him," I stated.

Ander folded his arms and thrust out his chest. The detective appeared uneasy and briefly glanced at the FBI agent before giving a hesitant nod.

"Very well," he replied, pausing to return his notepad to the inner pocket of his jacket. "Yesterday, when I spoke with Agent Miller, he brought up a call from the National Transportation Safety Board that his colleague Officer Johnson had received two days ago. The NTSB gathers on-site data to establish the likely cause of each civil aviation accident in the US, but I assume you were already informed about the ongoing investigation into your parents' accident. Given that your sedation was being discontinued today, I thought it best to hear it from us before the final report was ready for public release next week."

Time seemed to slow down, stretching the seconds into agonizing minutes as I braced myself for the impact.

"What does the report say?" I asked.

Ander draped his arm around my shoulders in a protective gesture. This time, Agent Miller spoke.

"Miss Moore, the NTSB has determined that the mechanical system's software was hacked. Your parents' deaths were not the result of an accident."

I brought my hands to my mouth and gasped.

"Your parents were murdered, and we have now classified the case as a homicide."

THE CABIN

(Noah)

"What's going on in that head of yours, princess?"

Sienna had been very quiet for the past two days. She thought no one had noticed, but every time she slipped into the hospital bathroom, I could hear her sobs from the other side of the door. It was really frustrating to see her hurting like this and not be able to do anything about it.

"I was thinking about this song. He's right, you know...Lewis Capaldi. I kinda wish I'd said something different on the day they headed to Cabo."

I hadn't realized that "Before You Go" by Lewis Capaldi was playing on the radio. Zayn moved between the car seats until he was able to reach for the radio and change stations.

"Sorry. I wasn't paying attention. Do you want me to turn the radio off?" I asked.

Sienna sat in the passenger's seat, and her gaze was fixed upon the dense rows of trees lining the winding road ahead. We were heading to my parents' cabin in the Santa Cruz mountains, where we would spend the rest of the week until our classes resumed. Ander's dad thought it was a great idea to get her out of the house and get some fresh air.

Zayn and Ander were sitting in the back of the car with Maggie in the middle. She fell asleep the instant she stepped into the rented car at the airport. Her caveman-like snores filled the car for most of the trip, so I put the radio on because they were driving me crazy. How could someone who looked like a Barbie snore like a freight train?

Maggie and William were now excluded as suspects. The FBI discovered that one of the bartenders working behind the bar wasn't part of the company Claudia had hired. According to Agent Miller, he'd used a fake ID to gain access to the premises, making him the prime suspect. However, the challenge was that everyone wore masks, and the video quality was poor, complicating the investigation.

"No, it's fine. I wasn't listening to the radio until that song came up."

"What would you have said?" I asked.

"You know, I've been thinking about that for months now, and every time I end up at the same point—I was a total jerk. They didn't deserve all that hate I dished out, but I guess my judgment was pretty messed up thanks to all that built-up resentment." She turned to me, tears welling up in her eyes. "I would've told them that I loved them."

As we approached our destination, the car's tires crunched over the gravel road, the rhythmic hum of the engine echoing through the serene forest. The towering trees created a lush green canopy overhead, casting shadows on the narrow path ahead.

Twenty minutes later, after exiting the highway, we finally arrived at the secluded cabin. It was my mom's favorite place when she wanted to get away from the chaotic life in Washington. It stood nestled among the trees, its wooden facade blending with the natural surroundings.

As I switched off the engine, the soft rustling of leaves in the breeze welcomed us. The fragrance of pine needles permeated the air.

"How frequently do you come to this place? It's beautiful," Sienna said as she exited the car and scanned the entire property.

"Unfortunately, not as often as I'd like. My mom adores this place, but her busy schedule doesn't allow us to visit as much as I'd want to. Anyway, let's have the guys handle the luggage while I give you a tour," I offered, reaching out my hand, and Sienna took it without a moment's hesitation. I pulled the keys out of my front pocket and opened the main door.

Beep. Beep. Beep.

I disconnected the alarm and placed my keys, wallet, and mobile phone on the kitchen counter.

Sienna's eyes widened the moment she stepped in and slowly pivoted to take in the spacious open entrance.

"Oh, wow. It's huge!"

"That's what she said."

Sienna snickered and gently slapped my arm, but I was glad I could bring a smile to her face despite everything she'd gone through.

"This is the living room and the open-plan kitchen. We don't keep any food in the house in case any animals break in, but later, I'll go with Ander or Zayn to the closest town to get some groceries and drinks."

Sienna walked around the room, taking in all the small details, from the plush sofas to the stone fireplace. A grand wooden table separated the living room from the kitchen, and nature-inspired artwork adorned the walls. The warm, earthy tones of the kitchen's wooden cabinetry and the gleaming granite countertops added a touch of modernity while maintaining the cabin's rustic character.

"There is a small bathroom over there," I said, pointing my finger to the end of the hallway. "And this is my mother's office." I swung the door open and welcomed Sienna inside. What I liked the most about this room were the massive bookshelves that stretched up to the ceiling. Reading had become a passion of mine, especially since I borrowed one of my mom's books last year—*Den of Vipers*. It was a bit surprising to think my mother enjoyed that genre, but those books were surprisingly enlightening and educational.

"What's in there?" she said, signaling with her head to the massive armory cabinet.

"My father likes to hunt. That cabinet is where he keeps his rifles and a couple of revolvers."

"Do you hunt too?" she curiously asked.

"I've only gone a couple of times with him. My mom is pro-guns, but I don't like them. It used to be locked when I was a child, but since she installed a new high-level security system, she has kept it open, and the office closed. If someone breaks in, we would immediately know."

I shut the office door as we made our way toward the staircase. There were four bedrooms, all located on the second floor.

"There's only four bedrooms…" Sienna observed.

"You can sleep with me if you want. Or not…" The corner of my mouth twitched with amusement as Sienna rolled her eyes. "But let's not worry about that now. We can assign rooms after dinner." I didn't push further on the sleeping arrangement because I wasn't sure where we stood. Ander had told us while she was in the ICU that they'd slept together the morning after our wild night, which was the reason he and Sienna hadn't talked in days. Apparently, he went mental when he found us sleeping naked in Zayn's bed, but their argument turned out to be just a warm-up act before they eventually ended up tearing their clothes off. I thought it would piss me off to imagine them together, but I knew they had history, and them being together seemed like the obvious finale to the incredible mess we had created. It was all kind of fucked up, and now I wondered if Zayn and I had only been a distraction.

The idea of losing her was like a painful jab in my chest. I couldn't get her out of my mind, continuously craving her, feeling an intense urge to keep her safe and make her smile. I couldn't help but be drawn to her whenever she was around, much like how the moon orbited around the Earth or like a moth to the light. I had tried for a long time to play it all as mere entertainment, a fun ride, the thrill of the hunt, and all that. The reality was that Sienna Moore had become my whole world, and now I had to contemplate a different possibility: that she and Ander might ultimately find their way to each other, leaving Zayn and me as nothing more than a story she'd share with her friends during a game of bridge at the golf club.

When we reached the bottom of the stairs, all our luggage had been brought in.

"Thank you for bringing my bag inside, guys." Sienna thanked them.

"No worries, babe," Zayn responded. "Do you like the house?"

"Yes, it's beautiful. I guess you've been here before, right?" Sienna accepted a glass of water that Maggie had poured for her.

"Yes, we've been a couple of times since we met last year. It's a short trip from Stanford." Ander placed his backpack on the couch and took out an iPhone charger. "Noah, what do you want us to do about the food? Do you want us to go into town before I take my jacket off?"

"Actually, yes. That'd be awesome."

"Do you want me to come with you?" Maggie asked.

"No, it's fine. Just send me a text with anything you want, and we'll buy it."

While Zayn and Ander left to buy us food, I showed Maggie the house and asked her to pick a room.

"All of them are very similar, except for the bigger primary bedroom, which has a walk-in closet, but all of them have their own bathroom, so you won't have to share the space with us."

"Where are you going to sleep, Sienna?" Maggie asked her friend.

"I haven't thought about it." Sienna nervously nibbled on her lower lip while casting a shy glance in my direction.

"I'm happy to share my room with Zayn or Ander, so you have your own," I suggested.

"You can stay with me." Maggie knew that choosing a room could make Sienna feel like she was choosing one of us, but after what happened on New Year's Eve, I only wanted Sienna to be safe and happy. I would sleep on the couch downstairs if she asked me.

"I think that's a good idea, Maggie."

I tried not to look disappointed because a small part of me was looking forward to waking up next to Sienna's beautiful face every morning.

I still had a week to convince her, though.

ENOUGH WITH THE WORDS

(Sienna)

"I'm so sorry that I have to leave."

Yesterday, Maggie received a phone call from the Stanford University Administration about some issues with her scholarship. She panicked, so I booked her an Uber back to campus.

Giving her a tight hug, I responded, "You don't need to apologize, Maggie. I know how important that scholarship is for you, so keep me posted as soon as you know what the hell is happening, okay?" I stepped back, keeping my hands on her shoulders. "And if there's anything we can do, please tell us. You're a boss bitch and all of that, but you're not less independent because you lean on your friends every now and then."

"Okay, mom," she replied while rolling her eyes.

Noah placed her luggage in the trunk and said, "Call us when you get there."

"I will."

After bidding farewell to the others, Maggie hopped into the car and waved through the window.

"Well, it's just the four of us now. So…what do you want to do, Sienna?" Noah smirked at me; he was such a goof sometimes.

"Why don't we cook something nice and play some board games? Let's chill a bit; I'm exhausted from all that hiking you're forcing us to do," I said.

Noah opened his mouth and put his hand on his chest.

"Excuse me?" he said like he was offended. "You wound me. I haven't forced anyone to come with me. You clearly wanted to show off that perfect ass by wearing those leggings. So don't blame it on me. You obviously came with your own agenda."

"Which was…?"

"Tempting us, babe. Why do you think we kept letting you lead the hike?" Zayn answered with a grin.

An hour later, with our bellies full of delicious ravioli pasta cooked by Zayn, we sat on the carpeted floor in the middle of the living room. Noah cut several pieces of chocolate cake so we could eat them in front of the cozy fireplace. I lay on my back with my head propped against one of the sofas as I accepted a plate from Noah, which I carefully placed on my lap.

"What game do you want to play?" I asked.

"Not Monopoly, that's for sure," Zayn exclaimed while sitting cross-legged in front of me. "Last time we played, Noah got upset and spent an entire week avoiding Ander's calls. He's super competitive."

"I'm not," Noah replied. "I just don't like when people cheat."

"What about UNO?" I asked.

"Do you enjoy violence, Sienna? Otherwise, I don't know why you'd suggest such a thing," Ander responded, moving his head from side to side.

"I have an idea."

We all looked at Noah, waiting for him to speak.

He lifted a finger. "Truth or dare."

"What are we, twelve?" Zayn laughed.

"Are you worried we're gonna find something you don't want us to find out? We know you have yellow pajamas with Minions all over it. We don't need a stupid game to find out you're a teddy bear at heart," Ander stated.

Ander had lived with Zayn for months now, so I was sure he knew many things about him that I could ask about during the game. I couldn't hold my laughter.

"Minions? How cute, Zayn. Okay, I'm in, but if you don't answer and want to avoid the dare, a piece of clothing must go," I added.

"Uhhhhh. I like it. You go first, princess. Truth or dare?" Noah asked me.

"Dare."

"Brave girl…" Ander whispered.

Noah ran his hand through his hair before speaking.

"Okay. I have a good one. I challenge you to share what you like most about each one of us."

"That's an easy one. Zayn, I like how protective you are and the passion you put into everything you do. Noah, I like your confidence and your sense of humor. Even in my lowest moments, you always know how to make me laugh. And Ander, these months in the lab have shown me how smart you are and how driven you are in every aspect of your life."

"You overlooked pointing out my good looks, but I'll let it slide since you've just been discharged from the hospital," Noah responded.

"That's very kind of you," I said with a straight face.

"Okay, now it's your turn to ask, Sienna," Ander added, taking a bite of his chocolate cake.

"Zayn. Truth or dare?" I challenged.

"Truth," he responded.

I took a few moments to brainstorm ideas until the perfect one came to mind.

"What's your biggest turn-on?"

"That little sound you make just before you're about to come."

The room went dead silent.

Is it me, or does the room suddenly feel too hot?

"Yeah, I can see that," Noah said while laughing.

Ander clenched his jaw.

"Okay. My turn," Zayn exclaimed. "Ander, truth or dare?"

"Dare."

"I dare you to kiss Sienna in front of us for two minutes. But I'm not talking about a peck on the lips. I wanna see you with her, and I bet Noah wouldn't mind either."

"You cannot keep your fucking mouth shut, can you?" Noah exclaimed.

Ander gazed at me, silently asking for permission.

"It's okay, Ander," I encouraged him.

He placed his plate on the coffee table and then crawled all the way to where I was sitting. He stopped only a few inches from my mouth, and I took a deep breath. The anticipation was killing me. I had thought about kissing Ander a thousand times since we hooked up, and now that he was piercing me with his blue eyes, all I could think about was that a kiss would never be enough. Ander put his hand on the back of my neck and pulled me toward him until our lips met. I closed my eyes instinctively and surrendered myself to his consuming kiss. I opened my mouth, inviting Ander's tongue to play with mine. It was a slow kiss, but it burned every corner of my soul until my body was fully ignited. I couldn't contain this hunger, an insatiable feeling slowly taking over my sanity. A moan escaped my mouth, and Ander dropped the hand that held my head to pinch one of my nipples. My moan grew louder, and our kiss deepened. I didn't need to touch my underwear to know I was completely soaked. I could feel my arousal between my thighs.

"Two minutes," Zayn stated.

When Ander broke the kiss, I was panting, and my heart raced a thousand miles per hour. The bulge in Ander's pants was an indication that he was as turned on as I was.

"That was sexy as fuck," Noah breathed.

Ander crawled back to his place without breaking eye contact. His eyes were full of lust and promises.

"Noah. Your turn. Truth or dare?" he asked.

Noah put a piece of chocolate cake in his mouth and replied, "Truth."

Ander bit his bottom lip and asked, "Weren't you jealous seeing Zayn and Sienna together?"

Noah paused for a moment before responding to Ander's question.

"Yes, I was. But only at the beginning. Then I realized I was more pissed at not being involved than anything else. It was so fucking hot seeing them together…and then we shared that night, the three of us, and it was perfect. It's by far the best sex I've ever had. Does my answer bring you any comfort?"

"What do you mean?" Ander asked, confused.

"You can't stay away from her, but you're worried that you won't mean as much to her as we do. Am I wrong?"

My eyes kept bouncing between Ander and Noah. You could cut the tension with a knife, and it was obvious that this was the first time they'd had this honest conversation. Noah clearly wanted to rip the Band-Aid off.

"I already lost her once. I don't think my heart could handle losing her again."

I put my cake down and stood. I walked toward Ander and stopped in front of him. I lowered myself to his lap, straddling his legs, and both my hands held his beautiful face. I stayed there for a few seconds, memorizing every hue of his irises, his plump lips, the perfection of his nose. I brought my mouth down and kissed him, but it wasn't like our previous kiss. This kiss was gentle and full of love and adoration. I broke the kiss and planted my forehead against his.

"You'll never lose me, Ander. My love is not finite. What I have with you, Noah, and Zayn is so fucking special...but it has taken me time to come to terms with it. I was raised in a conservative household, so it was hard for me to accept that it was okay to give myself entirely—body and soul—not to one but three men. I was super confused in the beginning, worried that I would fuck up your friendship because that's the last thing I wanted to do. But here we are, and I don't regret anything that has happened between the four of us. You're mine, and I'm yours, but I'm also Zayn's and Noah's, and they're also mine. Will you be okay with that?"

Ander stayed silent for what felt like an eternity.

"Please, say something," I begged.

"Enough with the words," he breathed as his mouth came crashing to mine. He firmly held my face in his hands and kissed me with such intensity that, for a moment, it seemed like he was demonstrating his possessiveness and reluctance to share me with his closest friends. But then he abruptly stopped kissing me, turned his face to Noah and Zayn, and said, "What are you doing, guys? I'm gonna need help undressing her, so move."

My mouth dropped to the floor, and Ander smirked at me. Two seconds later, Noah lifted my arms and took my sweater off me.

"I thought you'd never ask," Noah admitted.

As soon as I was only wearing my bra, Zayn started trailing kisses from my left shoulder to that spot beneath my earlobe that weakened my knees. I closed my eyes to focus on the sensation.

Is this really happening?

"Open your eyes, Sienna," Ander ordered. "I wanna see how much you're enjoying this. I wanna look at your face when you come and you beg us to stop because you can't take it anymore. Understood?"

I nodded.

"Stand up."

Zayn and Noah moved so I could get off from Ander's lap. When I stood, Ander knelt in front of me and dragged down my leggings and then my underwear. Without needing further instructions, Zayn unclasped my bra. Once he removed my clothes, Ander stood in front of me.

These three gorgeous men surrounded me as if I were prey, and they were ready to pounce. They shared a look, and without uttering a word, they slowly undressed before me. I'd never been to a striptease show, but I doubted it would get better than this. Their bodies were a work of art. All of them.

Ander held my hand and guided me to one of the sofas. He sat down and asked me to sit on top of him but with my back against his chest.

"I wanna see what you see. I wanna feel how your body moves," he whispered in my ear while he kicked his feet between mine and spread my legs farther. I felt exposed, but the hunger in Noah's and Zayn's eyes made me feel powerful. These beautiful men were at my mercy, willing to do whatever it took to pleasure me.

"I bet you wanna have a taste, Noah. Why don't you show *our* girl how well we can play together?" Ander added with a gravelly voice.

"Abso-fucking-lutely." Noah dropped to his knees in front of me, slowly moving his hands from my ankles, my knees, alongside the inside of my thighs, until the thumb from his right hand slowly traced my slit. "I bet you won't be able to stay put once I start flicking here with my tongue," Noah said, slowly rubbing circles on my clit.

My body moved at its own volition, my hips swaying back and forth.

"Say it," Noah said. "Tell me how much you want me to eat your pussy."

"Please, Noah," I begged.

"Please, what?" he insisted.

"Please, make me come on your face."

"That's my girl." Noah dropped his mouth and slowly licked my slit. His tongue moved with a controlled rhythm, building up the heat until my ass couldn't stop grinding on Ander's hard cock. My eyes locked on Zayn, who stood behind Noah, clearly enjoying the show.

"Look at you, love. You don't understand the power you have over us." Ander's hands explored every inch of my skin. He licked his thumbs and started playing with my nipples while Noah kept licking and sucking my bundle of nerves.

"Zayn, I need you," I breathed between my moans.

Zayn moved toward the sofa and sat next to me. I gently grabbed his engorged dick with my right hand and started pumping him as he came closer, covering one of my breasts with his mouth. It was all too much, too many sensations all at once. My legs started shaking uncontrollably. I could feel the heat building in my lower abdomen.

"Oh my God. I'm gonna come. Please, don't stop. Keep doing that."

Noah followed through until I reached my climax. I shut my eyes so hard that I could see tiny sparks everywhere, and my screams filled the room. However, Noah didn't stop; he kept licking and sucking, extending my orgasms until the intensity of it became unbearable, and I had to physically stop him by using my left hand to push his face away.

"Hope you're ready because we've just started." Ander grabbed my waist and held me until I stood on my feet, but when I thought he was going to ask me to move, he placed the head of his cock at my entrance with one hand while he pushed me downward with the other one to take all of him in one thrust.

"Fuck!" I hissed.

"That's it. Take my cock, Sienna. You're such a good girl for me," he praised as he moved his hips up and down.

I bent slightly over his legs so I could ride him.

"Noah, Zayn. Come here," I demanded. "I need to taste you both so fucking much." They both stood in front of me, but Zayn was the first one to pull my hair and push his cock inside my mouth. He tasted so good. I fisted Noah's length with one hand and Zayn with the other one while I played him with my tongue. I licked away the precum, and with one swift movement, Zayn pushed his hardness to the back of my throat until I gagged.

"Fuck yes. Keep going. Show me how much you love sucking my cock," he growled.

I kept licking Zayn until Noah turned me to face him.

"Someone's jealous," I muttered.

"Jealous? You have a smart mouth; let me put it to better use." Noah's fingers grabbed me by the throat as he pushed into my mouth. "Oh God. Just like that. Keep sucking, princess."

Meanwhile, Ander kept thrusting into me while I almost struggled to breathe. He picked up the pace, and when he started circling my clit, I came undone. Ecstasy flooded my veins, but Ander didn't stop when he felt my walls contracting. Once I came down from the high, he turned me around so I could straddle him.

Ander looked over my shoulder and said, "That's two orgasms: one for Noah and one for me. It only seems fair that Zayn now gets a taste of Sienna's ass and gives her a third one. What do you say, *brother*? Let's show her how well we take care of family business."

Ander spread some of my juices around my ass so it could lubricate the area and pushed a finger inside. After a minute or two of pumping one finger in and out, he added a second one while he sucked one of my nipples. I didn't understand how my body could react so much after two orgasms, but I guessed it was because I was obsessed with these boys, and I'd never get enough of them.

Once I relaxed enough and my hips started moving back and forth, Ander pushed the tip of his length between my folds, and I slowly lowered myself until it was buried to the hilt.

"Stay still. Zayn, come here," Ander instructed. He lay down, and I pushed myself on top of him until my breasts touched his chest, giving Zayn better access.

The moment I felt Zayn's cock, I tensed. Ander must have felt it because he grabbed my face with both hands and slowly kissed me.

"Relax. You can do it," he reassured me.

"The other time, I was a bit drunk and less nervous," I replied, nibbling on my lower lip.

"Let me distract you then," he responded. "Remember when I saw you the first time at the freshers' party? I couldn't believe how beautiful you were. Never in my wildest dreams did I imagine that the little girl I remembered would turn into this goddess."

I moaned as Zayn started to push the head of his cock inside my ass.

"Fuck, it's so tight. Don't you move, Ander, or I swear to God I'm gonna blow my load before the fun starts," Zayn warned.

Ander continued saying, "Remember when I saw you arriving at the

VIP area during Noah's birthday? Your cheeks were flushed, and I knew you had probably fucked him in one of the alcoves or the bathroom. And when Zayn said you were the 'Manhattan' girl…I was so fucking jealous…That night I fucked my hand in the shower while I imagined myself punishing you for wanting another man who wasn't me."

"How did you punish me in your fantasy?" I moaned.

Zayn was almost all the way in.

"I imagined you tied up to my bed and using your body for my own pleasure, edging you so hard that you would cry for my cock to fuck you into oblivion."

The moment Zayn started thrusting into my ass and Ander moved his hips, I forgot how to breathe.

"That's it, babe," Zayn said, placing one hand on my hip and grabbing my hair with his other fist. "Feel us both fucking your doubts away. Let us worship you the way you deserve."

"Princess, I know you're kind of busy now, but I need your mouth," Noah admitted. He came to stand next to my face, kneeling on the sofa. Taking my chin, he pushed his thickness into my mouth. "Now swirl your tongue around my cock and suck."

I could not concentrate. Zayn and Ander moved in sync, pounding into me with abandon. Their moans filled my ears as all my problems dissolved like melted ice. At that moment, nothing mattered. There was no grief, no responsibilities, no fear of being targeted. It was just us. Pure and raw desire.

"Look at you, Sienna. Look what you've done to us," Noah growled.

"You're ours as much as we are yours," Ander added.

"Fuck, it's too much. I'm gonna…" Zayn rasped before he released his cum inside me, his movements slowing while Ander continued with his steady pace.

The moment Zayn removed himself, Noah took his dick out of my mouth and moved behind me.

"You've lost your chance to give her that third orgasm, Zayn. It's now my turn, princess. I've been looking forward to fucking your ass since I met you."

Lust consumed my body, and goose bumps covered my skin as Noah entered me from behind. The sound of his skin slapping against mine drove me mad. That sound was such a turn-on.

"Holy shit. I can feel your cum still inside her."

"I can't take it anymore," I moaned.

"Yes, you can. You take us so well, love." Ander continued with his merciless thrusts until everything became blurry, and we both reached our climax at the same time. My inner walls contracted until I became a wanton mess, sweat rolling down my back and forehead.

"Fuuuuuck!" Noah's grip on my hips tightened as he also finished inside me. I could feel his and Zayn's cum—and probably mine, too—leaking down my thigh. I collapsed on top of Ander while he drew circles on my back with his fingertips and planted a kiss on top of my head. I needed a moment to pull myself back together.

Zayn and Noah sat next to us, one on each side. Zayn placed a hand on my thigh while Noah carefully put a strand of my hair behind my ear. I loved their need to touch me anytime they were close to me.

"That was insane," I said as my breathing slowed to match Ander's heartbeat's rhythm.

My feelings for them were crystal clear. It wasn't like a light bulb moment; it was more like a gradual dawning. It began the moment I started noticing all these little things—the way their smile could turn even the gloomiest day into sunshine, how their laughs were the sweetest melody I had ever heard, and how I genuinely looked forward to every moment I got to spend with them. During the past couple of days, I would catch myself daydreaming. And now, looking into their eyes, I could see a future filled with shared adventures, late-night conversations, and happiness. True happiness.

What we had found was something truly special.

Any doubts I had dissipated as my consciousness drifted away. I loved these boys with all my heart, and whatever the future held, I knew I wanted them to be part of it. They were mine as much as I belonged to them.

"I love you guys."

"I love you too, princess." Noah gently placed a kiss on my head.

"Me too. You own my fucking heart, babe," Zayn responded as he gently ran his fingers along my cheek.

"You already know how much I love you, Sienna," Ander replied. "Now rest. We'll give you an hour before we destroy your pussy and your ass again."

"WHAT?!"

091499

(Sienna)

We spent the remainder of the winter break secluded in Noah's house. Most of the time we were naked with our limbs tangled with the bed sheets. At some point, I thought I was gonna have a stroke after so many orgasms. They fucked me everywhere in the house in every imaginable position.

I wished we could have stayed longer in our little cocoon, but after the news about my parents' murder spread in the tabloids, I took a flight to New York.

I hadn't touched any of my parents' stuff after their funeral, mainly because I couldn't physically enter their room and my father's office. Those two bedrooms still smelled like them. Every time I opened the door, I would have an anxiety attack and immediately close it again. This time, I promised myself I'd be strong for them. Maybe there was a clue somewhere in Moore Manor pointing toward the culprit.

What if they had received threatening notes like me?

My father was smart. If he had felt threatened at some point, I'm sure he would have saved enough evidence for my mom or me to find.

My phone pinged.

Maggie
> Morning. When are you back?

Me
> On Sunday. I'm in NY.

Maggie
> NY? I thought you were with the boys…
> Is everything okay?

Me
> I just came to see if I could find any evidence in my dad's office. Maybe he kept something in the house if they were being threatened.

> At least, that's what the FBI believes. They'll search my house tomorrow morning, but I wanna have a look around myself first.

Maggie
> I wish I were there with you to hug you. I would have helped you search the house.

Me
> Thank you, but I need to do this on my own.

Maggie
> I get it.

> Call me if you need anything xxx

Once I arrived home, Mrs. Bishop welcomed me and brought my luggage to my bedroom, but I went straight to my father's office. I only had a few hours before the FBI barged into my house, and I needed to know if the people targeting me had anything to do with my parents' deaths.

What if they believed I was also going with them to Cabo?

What if they planned to kill the three of us all along?

I was supposed to be on that flight but couldn't stomach spending a week alone with them. My mom hoped that I'd change my mind, so she insisted on keeping my name on the passengers' list. "Just in case," she kept saying to me. Maybe they thought I'd be on that plane.

Goose bumps covered my skin.

I walked down the hall until I reached my dad's office. I took a deep breath and opened the door. The moment I stood behind his desk, it hit me—a hint of musk, Cohiba cigars, and whiskey. A lump formed in my throat, and tears coated my eyes. I missed my dad. All I could think about as I stared at the two chairs facing his seat was how many times I lashed at them for sending me to Europe. If I could go back in time, I'd tell that naive girl to leave the resentment aside and tell them one last time how much she really loved them.

I sat on my dad's chair and opened the first drawer. I took everything out and started going through every item and piece of paper.

* * *

Four hours later, I'd already searched half of his office, so I moved on to the bookshelves and checked book by book. I had already watched too many episodes of *CSI*, movies, and murder documentaries to know that some books could hide more than beautiful stories.

I smiled when I found some of our family photo albums. I didn't remember the last time I'd seen photographs of my parents when they were younger, and I was a baby. There were pictures of my first few birthdays, holidays in South Africa, and school plays. I laughed when I found a picture of Ander and me. We probably were around seven and eight years old, smiling at the camera, dressed like cowboys, and holding hands. I took a picture and sent it to the guys in our group message.

Me

Look what I found *LMAO emoji*

Noah

Please tell me that boy is Ander *emoji with heart eyes*

Ander

Where the fuck did you find that?

I remember that day. You cried because I shot you, and you kept sobbing while screaming to your parents that you were dead and I wouldn't play with a ghost.

Me

You always found a way to piss me off.

Zayn

Does that costume still fit you? I know someone you could ride with it.

Me

rolling eyes emoji Seriously, Zayn? I show you a childhood photo, and all you can think about is me riding your dick?

Zayn

Maybe I can put you on your four *wink emoji*

Noah

Count me in.

Ander

Any luck with the search?

Me

No.

> But I'll keep going until I've checked
> everywhere. I miss you all.

Noah

> We miss you too. Come back to us. We
> need you.

My heart warmed with his words. How did I get so lucky to have the three of them in my life?

Me

> I'll be there on Sunday evening.

Noah

> Make sure you rest these couple of days
> because the moment we see you, you
> won't get any sleep *peach emoji* *cat
> emoji* *eggplant emoji* *drops emoji*
> *tongue emoji*

I laughed as I put my phone away in my pocket and continued with the task at hand.

I removed every book and flipped through the pages, expecting a note to drop, but when I placed a couple of books back on the shelf, I noticed something metallic on the wall.

A safe.

My parents never told me they had one. But why would they?

I removed every book from the shelf and looked for the manufacturer's name. I typed the name on my mobile browser and checked different pages to familiarize myself with the type of safe. Based on the manufacturer's official website, it could either be a four or six-digit code. However, given that six held sentimental significance for my dad due to my mum's birthday, which fell on June 6th, 1976, I opted to take a guess. I grabbed a notepad from the desk and sat down on the floor. Before I attempted to try my luck, I guessed brainstorming a bit would not be such a bad idea. I wrote down his birthday, my birthday, and my mom's birthday, but something told me that those would be an obvious combination for someone to figure out.

I tried a couple of combinations with no luck until something clicked in my head. I quickly stood, dropping the notepad as I walked with determination toward the safe.

091499.

The day my dad and William founded Cos Pharmaceuticals.

Bingo.

The safe opened.

I got so excited that I started jumping and crying at the same time.

I took everything out, except for a gun that I decided to leave inside the safe: a small box—slightly smaller than a shoebox—a couple of diamond necklaces from my mom that I recognized, a few Treasury notes, and some cash.

I took the box back to my dad's desk and opened it. There were a few folded documents, some envelopes tied together with a thin manila rope, and a few notes joined with a paperclip and a photo. I turned over the photo. A younger version of my dad stared back at me. He looked happy, his arm around William's shoulders. Another man was in the photo with a white coat who I didn't recognize and a man in his twenties who looked familiar. I narrowed my eyes until it hit me.

Professor James Reed.

WHAT.THE.ACTUAL.FUCK.

I mean, he did say he worked at Cos Pharma for a brief period when I told him about the documents Ander found in his dad's home office, but he never mentioned being this close to my dad. Why would he lie to me? They must have been close, even friends. Otherwise, why would my dad keep this photo?

I put the photo aside and grabbed the folded documents. They were printouts of what looked like financial movements, money coming in and out. The document at hand appeared to be a personal bank statement originating from an offshore account in Panama. However, there was no name associated with the account. A few particular movements on the statement were marked with a yellow highlighter, indicating significant deposits made from an account with the initials W.A.S.

I remember Michael and William mentioning that my dad would send money to an offshore account in Panama, and I wondered if these were the bank statements that proved it. But why would my dad keep something that could incriminate him?

I moved on and picked up the stack of envelopes. The moment I checked who sent those letters, my blood pressure rose.

Alexander Scott.

I turned them around, and there it was: my name, written in terrible calligraphy. These were the letters Ander wrote to me.

All of them.

Twelve letters.

I didn't realize I was crying until one tear fell on top of the first envelope. I opened the first one with trembling hands and mentally prepared myself, but it didn't matter how much I worked on my breathing...I knew his words would probably pierce my heart.

Dear Sienna,

I can't believe you're gone.

My dad told me that writing you a letter was a waste of energy, but I don't agree with him. You were never and will never be a waste of my time.

I know you only left a week ago, but a lot has happened since then.

My parents have been arguing a lot in the last week to the point that I think my mom is going to leave my dad. She threatened him last night to file for divorce. If that happens, I wanna live with my mom. I hate my father.

Silvia asked me to say hi. She came with Connor and Gareth two days ago, and we watched a movie in my room. When she saw the DVD on my bedside table, she wanted to watch Pride & Prejudice, but I told her there was only one girl I would watch that movie with. Guess who?

How is your new school? Do you have a TV in your room? Do you share it?

I've checked the place out online, and it looks super cool. Have you made any friends yet? I want to read all about it.

I can't stop thinking about you.

I miss you.

I want to kiss you again.

Yours,

Ander

PS Do you have a new phone? I have texted you, but you're not receiving my messages.

I was sure I looked like a mess reading Ander's letter. Also, fucking Silvia. I bet she was happy that I was out of the picture. I always suspected she had a crush on him, but I got my confirmation when I saw her arms around Ander's neck in his swimming pool the following summer. I should have drowned the bitch when I had the opportunity.

I removed the paper clip from the notes, but one flew down to the floor. I picked up the piece of paper and placed it on the table.

I gasped.

I know what you did, and you will pay for it.

I picked another note.

I lost everything because of you.

Another note.

You can't hide behind your money. I'll fucking destroy you.

There were at least seven notes. I opened the gallery on my phone and searched for the pictures I had taken from the notes my stalker had sent to me.

Same font, same way of tracing the "y." The same person who threatened my father and probably killed him and my mom was also threatening me and possibly trying to murder me, too.

I put everything inside the box and charged to my room to pick up my luggage.

"Change of plans, Mrs. Bishop. I'm flying back to California tonight," I shouted while running upstairs. "Can you call an Uber?"

THE USB

(Sienna)

It was the beginning of the new year, but I was already exhausted. It was the second flight I had taken in the past twenty-four hours, and knowing it would take me another forty minutes to reach Ander's and Zayn's apartment didn't help.

I knew the guys weren't home. Noah got tickets for the three of them to watch the Los Angeles Lakers vs. Boston Celtics, so considering that I was supposed to be in New York, they planned to spend the weekend in Santa Monica.

I missed them so much.

Maggie offered to spend the night with me at the apartment. I needed my friend more than ever after what I had discovered back at my house in Port Chester. I was convinced that whoever murdered my parents had also tried to eliminate me during the New Year's Eve party. But why? The notes implied that their deaths were some kind of payback, so what if my father pissed someone really dangerous off? All the documents and mementos in that box pointed to the same thing—William was involved in some way. I was sure of that. Maybe I could call him tomorrow and ask about the other man in the photo or about my dad's relationship with Professor Reed.

By the time I arrived at the apartment, it was already ten o'clock. Maggie stood in front of the building, hands in her pockets and a scarf bigger than her covering her neck and shoulders. Her perky nose looked red, probably from the cold.

"Hey girl, I missed you," she said, hugging me tight.

"Same. Let's go inside. It's freezing."

When we entered the apartment, I went straight to my room. Maggie followed me, helping me carry my luggage and tote bag. She placed everything next to the door and dropped her ass on top of the bed.

"You said it was an emergency. What happened? Did you fight with the guys?" she asked, furrowing her brows.

"No, no. Nothing like that. We're good. Actually," I said, biting my lower lip. "We are really good. If you know what I mean." I smiled.

"Such a lucky whore. Seriously, I hate you." The amusement dropped from her voice. I stiffened at the way she said it, but then she burst out laughing, and I joined her. "I'm joking. I'm glad you finally followed my advice and went with the flow."

"What advice? You told me to stop playing with their feelings?"

"Yes, I did. To play with their dicks. And you understood the assignment." She grinned.

"I want to show you something. I'm not sure what it means, but I think I'm getting closer to the truth of what happened to my parents."

The air became thicker, and Maggie shifted uncomfortably on my bed.

"Look." I opened my tote bag and took out the wooden box. I placed everything on top of the bed, including the box: the bank statements, Ander's letters, the threatening notes, and the photograph. "Look at the photograph. Do you recognize someone in there?"

She looked at the photo, and her eyes widened.

"Nooooo. Where did you find this?"

I took the photograph from her and poked it with my finger.

"I don't know why, but he lied to my face. He said he had worked for my father, but Reed never mentioned they were that close. I don't know who this man with the white coat is, but maybe William knows. I'm calling him tomorrow."

"Do you think that's wise? What if he's involved somehow in all this mess?" She sounded concerned.

"I need to know."

"And what are these?" Maggie questioned as she picked up the letters and the notes.

"These are the letters Ander sent me when I moved to Switzerland. My father intercepted them. And those"—I paused—"my father received those. It's the same handwriting from the notes I received from my stalker. Whoever kept sending me black dahlias with a note and tried to poison me at the party is behind my parents' death. I'm convinced they tried to kill me, too, but didn't succeed."

Maggie ground her teeth, the muscles in her jaw tightening.

"I can't believe this is happening," she stated.

"Me neither. By the way, I haven't asked you if you've already had dinner. Are you hungry? We can order something." I dropped on the bed next to Maggie without realizing that the wooden box was too close to the edge of the bed.

Thump.

The box hit the floor, resulting in a loose piece of wood. A sinking feeling settled in my stomach, not due to any damage I had caused. It was the sight of the USB drive that had tumbled out, glistening amid the plush carpet.

"What's that?" Maggie asked.

I picked up the USB from the floor and inspected it.

"No idea. I guess there was a hidden compartment inside the box that I hadn't noticed before." I went straight to my luggage and grabbed my laptop. I plugged in the USB drive. There was only a file, a .mov video.

"Why do I have the feeling that this is not a homemade porn movie made by your parents?" Maggie joked although she clearly looked uncomfortable.

"Only one way to find out." I took a deep breath and double-clicked the file.

It took me a few minutes to recognize the room on the screen. There was a wooden table, big windows, and a sofa in the corner of the room. I had slept on that sofa countless times while my father worked. It was his old office in New York.

My father's face suddenly covered the screen, and Maggie and I jumped. It looked like he was placing the camera at the right angle before he sat on his chair and opened his laptop.

Why was he filming himself working?

Please, I don't want my mom to show up wearing a Burberry trench or something like that.

I couldn't hear a thing, so I turned up the volume.

A knock. It was subtle.

"Come in." My father's voice was loud and clear. I tried to swallow the lump in my throat. *God, how much I missed his voice.* I immediately recognized the two men who entered the room—the man in the picture with the white coat and William Scott.

"Thank you for coming. Please, close the door."

My dad stood, walked around the desk, and leaned on one of the corners of the table while facing the two men.

"You know why I called you both, right?" my dad asked.

"I have no idea, boss," the man with the white coat replied, shrugging his shoulders. He appeared to be in his late forties to early fifties, sporting a blend of dark blond and salt-and-pepper hair and gentle creases encircling his eyes. He stood taller than William.

"Shut up, Bob," William blurted. "Stop wasting our time, Edward. If you have something to say, fucking say it. I know why you've summoned us. I'm not a fucking fool." William's tone was cold and detached although he looked angry.

"Are you sure about that? Because only a fool would do what you've done and expect not to be caught." My father took a printed document from his desk and slowly walked toward William. Once he stood in front of him, he presented the piece of paper. William forcefully snatched it from my father's hands and stepped away before he looked at it.

"Where did you get this?" William asked with a hint of surprise and, I would guess, fear in his voice.

"Don't try to deny it, William. I know you've been diverting money from Cos Pharma to an offshore account in Panama with Bob's help. I just want you to explain why someone I have considered my brother since high school felt the need to forge my signature and put everything we've built in jeopardy."

I gulped.

"You wouldn't understand."

My father closed the distance between them and responded, "Try me."

William dropped his head and rubbed his eyes.

"I lost a poker game a few months ago, and let's just say that the individuals to whom I owed the money were far from understanding. They've been threatening my family, and I didn't know what to do. These individuals are dangerous. I didn't want this situation to impact you or your family by association."

"How much money?" my dad asked.

William sat on the corner sofa, his forearms resting on his knees. He looked up and said, "One point three million."

"And you didn't have enough money saved to pay this debt?" my dad questioned.

"I haven't been very lucky lately," William retorted.

"Fucking hell, William. Are you telling me you've blown all your savings? Your kid's trust fund?"

William nodded.

"Does your wife know?"

"No. I would like to keep it that way."

"You're in no position to make any demands, William." My father sat behind his desk once again. "Why didn't you come to me first? I would have helped you."

"It was a lot of money, and I thought I could solve the issue before anyone noticed. I just needed one lucky game, and everything would be fixed."

"You sound like an addict, William. Just one more game, one more hit. And I doubt one is ever going to be enough. Am I wrong? I've checked the amounts you've been transferring to your account, and based on what you owed, you should have been able to pay that debt months ago. What happened, William? Because from where I stand, I bet you kept gambling the funds away." My father turned his face and directed his next words to Bob. "Why did you play into all of this? I've known you for years. This isn't you. What did William have on you?"

William immediately replied, "I didn't…"

"Shut your mouth, William. I'm not talking to you," my dad yelled with a finger pointing at him.

Bob was visibly shaken, and his face drained of all color.

"Medical bills. You know my wife was sick for two years before she passed away, but some of the treatments she received weren't covered under my employment insurance. We're drowning in debt, and William promised me a percentage in exchange for falsifying some documents," Bob explained.

"This is a fucking mess." My dad leaned back in his seat and pulled his hair with both hands. "I can't trust you anymore, Bob. You may go to your office and take all your things. You're fired, effect immediately."

"I understand." Bob appeared defeated, his shoulders sagging under the burden of the repercussions of his actions.

"I don't want to draw attention to the situation, so please don't make a scene on your way out, or I'll be forced to call security. I believe that after so many years working at Cos Pharma, you'd like to leave with an ounce of dignity."

"I know it doesn't change anything, but I'm really sorry, Edward," Bob expressed.

"You're right. It doesn't." My dad's words cut through the air with a sharp and icy edge, leaving no doubt about the lack of compassion in his tone. It brought back memories of those countless times when he would engage in heated arguments with me, critiquing my life choices and behavior. The familiarity of the situation hit me like a painful déjà vu, only this time, it wasn't me who was on the receiving end of his unrelenting disapproval.

Bob turned around and left the office without muttering another word.

Maggie and I kept our eyes glued to the screen the entire time, but my attention shifted toward her when I listened to her sigh. Her lips were tightly pressed together, and her eyes appeared misty.

My father spoke once more, and my attention quickly returned to the screen.

"I can't fire you, William, but I have enough proof to drown you and your family with charges of embezzlement, fraud, and forgery. It won't look pretty, and I'd rather leave Nora and Alexander out of this. They shouldn't be paying for your sins."

"What are you suggesting? You want me to resign?" He scoffed.

"This is my only offer, so think carefully before you speak. You will sell your shares to me and make it look like a mutual decision—tell the world you want to pursue a new solo venture or that we had irreconcilable differences when it came to Cos Pharma's future. My offer will be fair and give you enough money to cover your debt and build something independently. If you want to blow all the money in underground poker games, be my guest, but the moment you're out, I don't fucking care. In exchange, I'll make sure this event gets buried and never comes to light, but you and I are over. We'll not be partners, and we'll not be friends. I want your family to stay away from mine. Is that clear?"

William's nostrils flared as he glared at my dad.

"Do you really think I'd just give up my position and shares? Remember, it's your signature on those documents, Edward. It'd only take one call from me to get you in hot water with some of those charges you just mentioned."

"Maybe you're right, but I have evidence that it's your name on that account in Latin America."

Suddenly, it clicked.

W.A.S.

William Archibald Scott.

The documents that my father had kept in the box were the evidence that William was the one stealing the money. Was he behind their murders? Is that the reason my dad kept those statements with the threatening notes?

"You should be grateful, William. Don't be mistaken by my kindness; if I go down, you're coming with me."

The recording stopped.

Maggie and I stayed silent for a moment, but my urge to voice my inner thoughts made me speak out loud.

"It was never my father." A single tear fell down my cheek, but I soon captured it with my fingers. "William and Bob were the ones who committed fraud and maybe even killed my parents." I ended the sentence with a whimper.

"Look, let's take a moment before jumping to conclusions."

"What conclusions, Maggie?" I stood and started to pace the room frantically. My breathing became more rapid and unstable. I could not breathe. "You've seen it and heard it with your own fucking eyes and ears!"

Maggie also stood and bridged the gap between us in two strides.

"I know, but I also think nobody should act on their impulses when they are as agitated as you are right now. Let me grab you a glass of water. Take deep breaths, and I'll be back in a second."

As soon as Maggie left the bedroom, I grabbed my phone and called Ander.

One ring.

Two rings.

Three rings.

Voicemail.

Shit.

A voice message should do.

"Ander, I know you're probably at the match, but I really need you right now. Please come back. I just found a video of your dad admitting to being the one who committed fraud, not mine. That's why he left the company. There's another person involved, someone named Bob, who assisted in forging some documents. I'm losing my mind, Ander. Please, I need you." I begged. "I plan to take this USB to the FBI, but I'd prefer it if you could come with me; after all, it's your dad we're talking about. Give me a call once you've heard this message."

I turned around and jumped.

"Fuck Maggie, you scared me. I've just sent a message to Ander asking him to come home. We need to show all the evidence to the FBI." I glanced downward, directing my gaze at her hand. "What are you doing with Zayn's trophy?"

"I'm sorry, Sienna, but I cannot allow you to do that."

I felt a sharp and intense pain in my head, but before I could register what was happening, everything went dark.

SO MUCH BLOOD

(Ander)

"Can you please go faster?"

What were the odds of us getting an Uber at the airport with the slowest driver in the whole country?

We had been trying to reach Sienna ever since I heard the message she left on my phone last night, but all our calls consistently went straight to her voicemail. We dialed her number on our way to the apartment, during our journey to the airport, before takeoff, and after we landed. To be honest, we were fucking worried; it wasn't like her to ghost us or ignore her phone for such a long period.

Each time I heard her voice, I felt sick to my stomach. She seemed incredibly distressed and frightened, and my only wish was to hold her close and reassure her that everything would turn out fine. Although I contemplated calling my father, I decided to wait until I heard everything Sienna had to share before confronting him.

"Calm down, Ander; I'm sure Sienna's fine. Maggie was spending the night with her, so I'm sure she's not alone, and there's a perfectly reasonable explanation as to why her phone is turned off." Zayn had tried his best to keep me grounded since we left Los Angeles with little success.

"Maybe she left her charger back in Port Chester and ran out of battery," Noah added.

"Then why hasn't she texted me or called me from Maggie's phone? What if something has happened to them? I should've gone to Port Chester with her."

"She wanted to go on her own. You did the right thing. We did," Zayn replied.

I knew he was right, but something was wrong. I could feel it.

We arrived at the apartment fifteen minutes later, and I almost jumped out of the car while it was still coming to a halt. Zayn and Noah stayed behind, paying our driver and taking care of the luggage as I called for the elevator.

"It won't arrive any faster."

I glanced to my right and managed a tight smile at Mrs. Green, one of my neighbors. She had evidently noticed my repeated pressing of the call button roughly twenty times in just fifteen seconds.

Ding.

The doors opened, and I rushed inside, followed by Mrs. Green, who stopped a couple of floors earlier than me. As soon as I stepped inside the apartment, I couldn't contain my anxiety, and I immediately called out for Sienna.

"Sienna! SIENNA! Are you here?" My heart was racing as I hurried into the living room, but she wasn't there. Without wasting a moment, I headed straight for her bedroom, all the while repeating, "Sienna, are you home?" The worry gnawed at me with every passing second, making each step feel heavier than the last. Her luggage sat in the room alongside her beloved tote bag. Her laptop was opened and resting on her bed.

"Is she in there?" Noah inquired from the hallway, but his words barely registered in my ears. My attention was fixated on the crimson stains that decorated the white comforter and spilled onto the floor. It was as if I were submerged underwater, and all external sounds had been muffled.

"Ander, Ander! Dammit, Ander!" Zayn seized my shoulders and jolted me back to reality.

"There's so much blood." Those were the only words I could muster before Zayn and Noah laid eyes on the pool of blood themselves.

"Oh, fuck." Zayn's eyes widened as he let go of me. "Mm-maybe there was an accident, and Maggie took Sienna to a hospital, right?"

"Maggie's phone is still off. I have DM'd her several times on her IG since we left LA, but she hasn't checked her socials either," I explained.

"I have a plan," Noah announced. "Ander, you and I will call all the Emergency Rooms from every damn clinic within a one-mile radius of this apartment. If there was an accident, Sienna or Maggie would have gone to the closest one. We'll ask for Sienna Moore and Maggie or Margaret Towerby. Zayn, do you still have the number of the girl you fucked from Administration last year?"

"Yes, why?"

"Call her, use your charm, and get Maggie's dorm and her room number. Now."

*   *   *

I had already tried five different clinics without success. We continued attempting to reach Sienna on her phone, but both her and Maggie's phones remained switched off. Maggie hadn't yet seen my DMs.

Noah sounded more desperate with each phone call. The more time passed, and the more I thought about the blood in her room, the more certain I became that the stalker was behind this. That they came when both were alone. I straightened my spine and reminded myself that I couldn't afford my thoughts to go down that path. It was a dangerous one. A path where all I could see was red. A path where I could imagine myself burning the whole world to get my girl back. *Our girl.*

"Guys," Zayn called us from the kitchen island. "Guys!"

"Okay. Thanks for checking." Noah ended the call and lifted his head to look at Zayn. "What? I was on a call, dickhead."

"I've just had a conversation with Emily from administration. She went through their database and couldn't locate any student matching the names Maggie, Margaret, Margarita, Marjorie, or Margot Towerby. She explored all possible combinations and found only one other Towerby, Dominic Towerby. So I can only consider three possibilities: one, Maggie has a cock between her legs, and she has successfully hidden this fact from us for months; two, she may have lied about her real name; and three, she's not an enrolled student at Stanford. Considering how she dresses, my bets are with options two and three, and I don't like any of them."

"Why would she lie about her name or about being a student here?" I asked.

"What we should be asking ourselves is, why didn't Maggie or Sienna give us a call or leave a note if there was an accident?" Noah challenged.

Noah was right.

For once, I wished I were one of those overly protective boyfriends who install location-tracking apps on their girlfriend's phones.

Wait a minute.

"Hold on! My keys… where are my keys?" I dashed toward the console table in the entry hall, and when I discovered it was empty, I rushed into Sienna's room to inspect her bags. Zayn and Noah followed me, wearing puzzled expressions.

"Did you leave your keys in the Uber?" Noah inquired.

"No, Sienna's keys, the ones I gave her." I went back to the living room and picked up my phone from the coffee table. I opened the Find My app. "The keys I gave her have an Apple AirTag. If she has the keys with her, which I believe she does, we might be able to find her location." I clicked on the AirTag under Devices, and in one second, the map showed me its location: a property located near Los Gatos Creek Trail.

Noah looked over my shoulder and blurted, "What the fuck is she doing there?"

I locked my phone, glanced at both Noah and Zayn, and stated, "Get your car keys, Noah, we are going for a ride."

DON'T CALL ME LIZZIE

(Elizabeth)

6 months earlier

"Are you sure about this?"

"Stop asking me stupid questions. Of course, I'm sure. We've been planning this for months."

The scent of white gardenia and a hint of something citrusy permeated the air. It was making me nauseous. I looked around, and the only things I saw were corruption, pretty lies, and zero accountability. I was sitting inside Edward Moore's private jet; at least it belonged to him until tomorrow. After that, only metal, blood, and tears would be left.

The aircraft was compact but luxurious, with light oak furniture and beige leather seats, a minibar, and a complete bathroom with a built-in shower. It could accommodate up to six passengers, but right now, it was only me and the darkness that surrounded me. Only the soft light of my laptop illuminated the cabin.

"It's not a stupid question. I want to make sure you won't regret this, Lizzie; the moment the aircraft blows up, you'll become a serial killer by definition after murdering Carl. Will you be able to live with yourself after that?" he asked.

He had a point, but he, more than anyone else, understood the need for revenge. After all, Edward had also ruined his life.

"That's if they make a link between both 'accidents.' Which they won't.

"I've been able to overcome other things which also tainted my hands with blood. Believe me when I say that I'm granting them a merciful death. They'll be gone before realizing what's happening, and I'll get closure."

I stopped typing the malware code and upped the volume from my AirPods.

"Are you getting cold feet?" I questioned him.

"I'm not a psychopath, Lizzie. I sure have my doubts, but you know I won't be able to deny you anything, even if it means slaying your demons and fucking you in their blood."

"I love it when you talk dirty to me." The corner of my mouth lifted, and I smirked.

"How long until you're done?" he asked.

"Maybe another half hour. After that, I'll disappear for a couple of weeks, just in case. In the meantime, stick to the plan. Go back to your home in New York and act normal. I'll call you as soon as I can."

"Okay, Lizzie. Be careful."

"I will, and hey, one more thing. Don't call me Lizzie from now on. One single mistake and we'll go down like this plane. Got it?"

"Sure thing, Maggie. I love you."

"Love you too."

TARANTINO WOULD BE PROUD

(Sienna)

My head throbbed so hard I thought my skull might just split open from the pressure, and my mouth was so dry that my tongue was stuck to the roof of my mouth. *Why did my head hurt so much?*

Then I remembered.

The video.

The message to Ander.

Maggie.

The trophy.

MAGGIE...Maggie fucking hit me!

I tried screaming, but the only sounds I was able to make were unintelligible groans. No matter how hard I tried, my voice just wouldn't cooperate. I was seated in a chair, tightly bound with my hands secured to the armrests and my feet firmly tied to the chair's legs. I made an effort to free myself by wriggling and twisting, but the knots used to bind me were impressively sturdy and refused to budge.

"Well, well, well. Her Royal Highness is finally awake."

I opened my eyes slightly until my sight adapted to the brightness of the room. It took some time for everything to come into focus, but the moment it happened, I saw her. Maggie. She stood in front of me, leaning on a kitchen counter with her arms and legs crossed and a sinister smile that would haunt me forever.

I quickly scanned the room, but I didn't recognize the place. It looked like any other apartment; nothing special about it.

"Where am I?" I asked through quiet sobs. Maggie's only response was a look of pure and utter confusion.

"Let me get this clear. You wake up tied up to a chair after your *bestie* hits you and drags you to the middle of fucking nowhere, and your first question is, where am I?" she exclaimed, pressing her fingers against her temples. "What they see in you, I cannot understand, but a hole is a hole, and apparently, you're very good at letting them fill you up."

She looked like my friend Maggie, but her tone and her words were those of a stranger. *Who is this girl?*

"Why are you doing this?"

"There you go. See? You are capable of asking smart questions, then." She pushed herself away from the counter and slowly walked toward me with the confidence of a predator stalking their prey. She then crouched until her face was level with mine. "I guess it's story time, so let me tell you one. Spoiler alert. It doesn't have a happy ending, at least not for you."

She stood and walked backward a couple of steps just to gain some distance.

"Once upon a time, there was a girl who lost her mother to cancer. Her dad, a great man with the kindest heart, worked in research, but his salary and insurance would not cover the cost of his wife's treatment. The day she passed away, he not only received her ashes in a metallic urn but a medical bill he couldn't afford to pay. His child was cold and hungry all the time, frequently eating at her dad's office cafeteria or showering in their facilities because it was free. She sometimes would see a girl wandering around those offices who would usually complain about not getting the latest dress or ballerina shoes from Dior. She was an entitled bitch."

My eyes closed just for a moment, but they were opened again the moment I felt the sting of a slap on my face.

"I AM NOT DONE TALKING!" Maggie screamed. She was enraged. "Where were we? Oh, yes…" She continued. "One day, his dad was fired from his job, and nobody would employ him, so he started drinking away his sorrows. He got so depressed that the only exit he saw was to commit suicide. The daughter received a small sum of money from the insurance, a goodbye letter from her dad, and a ticket to Horrorville. I'm sure you can recall the story I shared with you, can't you? The one about the boogeyman who would lurk in the shadows and come into the girl's room at night."

Tears coated my cheeks.

"Yes, I remember," I whimpered.

"Good. The girl wanted to escape her nightmares so badly that she considered following in her dad's steps. But one day, she reunited with an old friend who became her knight in shining armor. You see…the knight had also lost everything he'd accomplished at the hands of the same evil man who had fired her dad. He helped her kill the boogeyman and gave her a purpose: seeking revenge. And here we are."

Could it be true? Did William and Maggie plan my parents' death together? I tried to recall every conversation, every meeting with him, every smile. They both had access to my drink on New Year's Eve and Maggie to my apartment.

"Did you and William kill my parents?" My body and voice trembled, and a cold sweat covered my skin. I felt nauseous.

"You haven't been paying attention, Sienna."

The cabin door opened, and a tall figure entered the space.

"You." My eyes widened, and my stomach dropped.

"Hello, Sienna. You've missed a few sessions at the lab, but I guess it doesn't matter now…does it?"

*   *   *

One moment, Professor James Reed was shutting the cabin door, and the next, Maggie jumped into his arms, her legs encircling his waist. I might as well have been invisible because she kissed him like he was the only air her lungs needed, and he pressed her body against his while he moaned in her mouth and held her by her ass.

I was going to be sick.

"I missed you, love," Maggie said.

"I missed you too, Lizzie."

Wait a minute. Lizzie?

"Who's Lizzie?" I blurted.

Maggie released herself from James's embrace and placed her feet on the ground.

"Apologies. I haven't introduced myself properly. Elizabeth Price, but my friends call me Lizzie. You can call me Elizabeth."

"So your dad was Bob Price?"

"Bingo," she responded with a hint of amusement. For her, this was a fucking game. Lizzie whispered something to James before she slipped into one of the rooms. I used the opportunity to convince James to free me.

"James, please. Let me go. You don't have to do this," I pleaded.

James crossed his arms in front of his chest and stared at me, with his upper lip curled, as if I was the most disgusting being in the entire world.

"Please, James. She's going to kill me."

"Not yet. I want to have some fun first," Lizzie remarked as she entered the living room again. She held a small black leather pouch, which she placed on top of the kitchen counter. James blocked my line of view, so I couldn't see what she was doing, but the moment she turned around, my eyes focused on the scalpel she held in her right hand. "Babe, do you think our Princess's blood is blue or red?"

"HELP!" I cried out, feeling my lungs nearing exhaustion and my already sore throat growing worse. I wouldn't die like this. I refused to. Ander, Zayn, and Noah would come looking for me, but how could I expect them to find me when I had no idea of our whereabouts?

"Cry and scream all you want; nobody's going to hear your pleas, bitch."

With the scalpel in her hand, she circled me.

"Mmm. Where should I begin? Any suggestions, love?"

"It's your choice, baby. I'm sure you've already thought about a thousand ways of making it hurt." James leaned on the wall next to the cabin entrance. He had his arms crossed and checked his watch, looking bored.

"Well, I think I'd like to mark her beautiful skin first. Leave a present if someone ever retrieves her decomposing body from the lake."

I gulped.

"Please, Maggie...I mean Lizzie. Don't do this. You're my friend."

"For you, I'm Elizabeth. You haven't earned the right to call me Lizzie. And no. Maybe you're fucking stupid. Maybe I hit you too hard. But let me make one thing clear: if you haven't got the memo yet, we were never friends. I just stayed close enough and gained your trust with only one purpose. Finding an opportunity to make you suffer."

Tears clouded my eyes.

"But why? I haven't done anything to you."

"Your father did, and I paid the consequences. You'll pay for all those months of abuse, and I'll enjoy every second of it. You were supposed to be on that plane, but I miscalculated your relationship with your family. I made a mistake. It won't happen again."

"They'll eventually find out it was you who killed them!" I yelled.

Lizzie started to laugh until it turned hysterical.

"That's the beauty of our plan. I've left breadcrumbs so that your death leads back to William. He'll go to jail for your parents' murder, and I'll make sure that when your body is found, it traces back to him, too."

"How?" I asked.

She placed her hand inside her pocket and removed a small envelope.

"I took some hair from his bathroom when we were in Rye. James will make sure to leave some bruises on your body, too. He's also left-handed like dearest William. That, in addition to an email he sent you threatening you—which I deleted from your laptop—should be enough proof to convince a public jury."

"He never sent me an email," I replied.

"You're fucking thick. I did. I hacked his laptop. It was easier than hacking your parents' plane," she retorted.

Tears flowed freely from my eyes.

"Now, now. Where were we? Oh yes." Lizzie placed the scalpel on my arm and pushed it until my skin broke, and I started bleeding. I thrashed on the chair, screaming, as she attempted to scribble something.

"James. Hold her still. She's making a mess of my beautiful writing."

Reed grabbed my neck with his left hand and dug his fingers, crushing my windpipe.

"Stay still, bitch. I won't ask you again," Lizzie threatened.

She continued making cuts until she stepped back and said, "Done."

He released my neck, and I breathed until my lungs expanded. I looked at my bloodied arm. It hurt like a bitch. The words were jagged, but I could clearly read the message.

Whore.

"You can't torture her too much, Lizzie. We've talked about this. We need to make it look like a crime of passion, not one based on torture," James argued.

"I know...I know. You and your fucking logic are killing my vibe." She sighed. "Let me grab the Swiss knife I took from William's office." Lizzie turned to me and added, "I thought about it for a long time, but I finally decided I'm gonna stab you exactly fifty-two times, like the number of times Carl raped me. Isn't it poetic?"

Think, Sienna, think.

Looking around, I realized my chair was just like the others in the living room—cheap and easy to break. I assumed that Lizzie or James had picked this spot in a hurry without even caring about the furniture.

Before she left the room, I dropped my head back.

"I'm not feeling well." I did my best to appear sick without making it too dramatic. My eyes rolled back, and I let a bit of drool dribble down my chin. I was hoping all those drama classes from back when I was fifteen would finally come in handy. "Mmmnot...eling...well. Mmmmy h...ed."

"How hard did you hit her, baby? Did you give her a concussion?" James asked Lizzie. He came closer and pressed two fingers to my neck to feel my pulse.

"Su...mmmmyck James," I whispered.

"What did you say?"

James's ear came closer to my face, and I softly murmured, "Suck my dick, James." I parted my lips and lunged directly at his neck, desperate for a diversion. One that only the sight of blood could offer. My teeth sank into his carotid artery with a savage determination, applying so much pressure that my mouth was instantly flooded with his crimson life force.

"FUUUUUUUUUUCK!" James punched the side of my face until I relaxed my jaw. I would probably die today, but the bastard would come with me to hell.

"JAMES!" Lizzie immediately ran to James's arms, quickly putting pressure on his neck, while his legs gave out, and he sank to the floor. "James, please. Don't you dare close your eyes!"

I smiled like a fucking psycho, probably with all my mouth and teeth covered in James's blood. My heart pounded from the rush of adrenaline. Without thinking, I used my feet to push myself off the wooden floor and threw myself to the ground. Everything felt like slow motion until I heard the wood crack under me.

Lizzie lifted her head and screamed, "I'M GOING TO FUCKING KILL YOU!"

I was lucky she'd tied each leg separately because I needed to run the fuck out of her way. My hands were still bound to my back, but I quickly managed to maneuver them to the front, gingerly passing them over my leg.

Thank you, Pilates classes.

James's hushed sobs echoed like a haunting melody. Lizzie hesitated for a fleeting moment, realization crashing over her. He was dying, and there was nothing she could do about it.

"You bitch!" She lunged at me and grabbed me by my hair before I had a chance to stand. I found myself pinned against the wall, my face colliding with one of the picture frames hanging there. In response, I instinctively elbowed her in the face. The blow made her gasp and release my hair, giving me a moment to catch my breath. She stumbled backward, her nose bleeding. Lizzie shook her head and brought her fingers to her nose to check if it was broken. I took the opening to run to the kitchen area, but she jumped on my back, and we fell backward. Swiftly, she positioned her forearm against my throat, applying pressure while her legs encircled my waist as her feet exerted pressure on my pelvis. Her right elbow nestled beneath my chin, and her left hand gripped the back of my neck. Desperately, I attempted to pry her hands away, but I couldn't free myself from her hold. I was choking. I couldn't draw a single breath into my constricted lungs, and with each passing second, the burning sensation only intensified.

It was said that your life flashed before your eyes in the moments before death. That you could watch your days unfold like a movie reel, both the highs and lows, the good and the bad ones. But for me, all I could see were five things: my parents clapping for me from the audience after my debut piano recital, Zayn's devastating smile as we cooked together, Noah kissing me good morning every time I spent the night with him, Ander whispering *"I love you"* when he believed I was sleeping in his arms, and the scalpel that Elizabeth fucking Price had dropped on the floor next to James's now dead body.

*   *   *

I'm not fucking dying today!

Lizzie had me in a pretty tight hold, but I lucked out with the best jujitsu teacher around. He had taught me the rear naked choke, and I was about to show off what I had learned. I was determined to survive.

I reached behind my head with both my hands until I could scrape the back of my neck and was able to get ahold of Lizzie's hand.

"I'll break your neck like a toothpick!" Lizzie screamed.

As soon as I had full hold of her left arm and pushed it away, she responded by squeezing tighter with her right arm, but I didn't care. She was just where I wanted her without realizing it. I wriggled and squirmed until I had enough space to give her a headbutt right on the nose. This time, her nose bled as she screamed in pain. I pushed myself forward and crawled toward James.

"You're gonna regret that, bitch!" she yelled.

My face felt all sticky and gross with blood and sweat mixed, and my heart beat like crazy. Every move I made was like dragging myself through mud, but I kept going. It was like being in a nightmare you can't wake up from, just trying to get away any way I could.

Lizzie gripped my hair again and pulled me backward.

"Get the fuck away from me!" I shouted.

I spun around, my fist connecting with her cheek with a solid thump.

"Ahh!" Lizzie shrieked.

An intense pain shot from my knuckles to my elbow, but I couldn't let the pain cloud my mind. I had to survive.

As I straightened up, I caught sight of a vase on the nearby table. Without a second thought, I grabbed it. I swung it with all the force I could muster.

Lizzie saw me coming and covered her face and head with her arms. The vase collided with her left arm, shattering on impact.

She soon retaliated.

A swift kick to my stomach knocked the wind out of me as I fell backward. I gasped for breath, feeling the rage boiling inside me. Lizzie pinned me down and clasped her hands around my throat.

"You're like a fucking cockroach that never dies. Just. Fucking. Die." She continued strangling me, her fingers pressing into my soft flesh with a terrifying determination while I struggled for air.

My hand swept across the surface of the floor, fingers searching until they brushed against the cool metal handle of the scalpel. Grasping it tightly, I quickly move my arm, plunging the sharp blade into the side of Lizzie's throat. Reacting instinctively, Lizzie yanked the scalpel out, tossed it away, and immediately gripped her neck with both hands, trying desperately to stem the flow of blood that poured through her fingers.

The air was filled with the thick, metallic scent of spilled blood.

A look of shock and realization flashed across her face as her pupils expanded in fear and disbelief.

She knew it.

I knew it.

There was no way to undo what I'd just done.

Her body hit the floor as I pushed her off me.

I went into survival mode and knew that it had come down to either me or her making it out of here alive. There was no other way out, but the feeling of victory and relief quickly shifted to guilt once I realized I had taken not just one but two lives.

Sitting on the floor, I cradled her lifeless body in my arms as I rocked back and forth.

"I'm sorry. I'm so sorry." Tears streamed down my face like a river, mixing with James's and Lizzie's blood. I couldn't recall ever crying this intensely before, but I'd kept my emotions locked away for far too long. At that moment, I wasn't entirely sure to whom I was offering my apologies. After all, Lizzie and James were responsible for my parents' deaths. However, one part of me mourned the loss of my college best friend—the countless nights we spent chatting about everything and nothing, the wild parties where we danced until dawn, and the girl who never judged me when I confessed to her that I was in love with three different guys.

My cries were filled with agony, a pain so deep and dark that it threatened to infest every corner of my soul.

WE ARE GOING HOME

(Sienna)

I don't know how long I sat there, cradling Lizzie in my arms, with my gaze fixed on nothing in particular and my mind lost in a daydream. That was until the house lit up with blue and red lights. Shortly after that, someone shouted from the opposite side of the main door.

"Police! Open up!"

Before I knew it, the front door slammed open, and two cops with guns barged in.

I opened my mouth and immediately closed it. I was covered in blood, my knuckles white after so long holding tight onto Lizzie's sweater. My vision blurred with tears as one of the police officers pointed his gun at me while the other one secured the perimeter.

"Miss, I'm gonna need you to put your hands up and slowly step away from her?"

"I didn't mean to. They were going to kill me," I cried.

"Miss, I won't repeat myself. Put your hands up and step away from the girl."

I followed the officer's orders. I stood and put my hands up with my palms facing him. They were shaking and covered in blood.

So much blood.

"All clear!" the second officer yelled from the opposite side of the cabin.

"Don't move," he ordered, still pointing his gun at me. He knelt and checked Lizzie's vitals first, and then James'. Then, he took his radio out and spoke to the hand unit. "Dispatch, this is Officer Larsen, Badge number 467112, Unit 57. I need backup at 12 Alma Bridge Road, near Los Gatos Creek Trail. Requesting one unit to respond. We have two 10-7s on the scene, and I'm gonna need an EMS. Code 3."

"Officer Larsen, this is dispatch. Copy that. One backup unit is needed at 12 Alma Bridge Road, near Los Gatos Trail. You have requested an EMS and have two 10-7s on the scene—code 3. Your backup unit is en route to your location, arrival thirteen minutes. Keep us updated on the situation," a woman spoke through the radio.

"While we wait for backup to arrive, why don't you tell me your name?"

"My name is Sienna Moore," I responded, still holding my hands up.

"Okay, Sienna, can you explain to me what happened here?"

* * *

I was sitting inside the ambulance when I heard the screams.

The paramedics had already examined my head wound, disinfected and stitched the cuts from my arm, and cleaned the few lacerations I got from the ropes. I also had scratches from the fight with Lizzie, and my neck and face were a canvas of bruises. Still, I regarded them with pride, seeing them as badges of honor.

I didn't care about the scars on my body.

I had survived.

"Sienna! SIENNA!"

I raised my head upon hearing my name spoken by the familiar voice.

A police officer blocked Zayn's access to the cabin with a hand pressed on his chest.

"Sorry, kid, but you can't go inside. It's a crime scene," the police officer informed him.

"What the fuck!? I'm the one who called you. Let me in, you sonofabitch; my girlfriend is in there!"

"Zayn? Zayn!" I kept calling his name while I ran toward him. As soon as our bodies made contact, he engulfed me in his arms—one around my waist while his other hand cradled my head against his muscular chest. A moment later, Noah and Ander joined the group.

"We were worried sick. What happened?" Noah asked, stroking my hair while I buried my face in Zayn's chest. Their smell and warmth grounded me.

An hour ago, I was so sure I would die in this cabin that the fear of not seeing and being with them again made me do something I never thought I was capable of.

"I killed them. I killed them." That was all I could mumble between sobs as they held me together. Without them, my knees would have probably hit the floor by now; I was just wiped out. My heart was still pounding, and I shivered as the adrenaline wore off. I didn't even realize Ander had moved away from our group hug until I saw him chatting with Officer Larsen out of the corner of my eye. That was when I asked the guys to give me a little room to catch my breath.

Ander nodded to the police officer, and after a quick handshake, he went to speak with another officer who had arrived with the backup. Officer Larsen, on the other hand, turned his attention to me.

"Miss Moore," he began, "the paramedics are ready to transport you to the hospital. They need to address your wounds and run a few tests to ensure there's no internal bleeding or concussion." Suddenly, Officer Larsen was interrupted by an incoming phone call. "I'll need to take this; Agent Miller is calling me," he said, glancing at the caller ID. "I'll need you to come by the station tomorrow morning to give an official statement and answer some additional questions, but for now, you're free to go," he added, gesturing to the paramedics. "Excuse me," he concluded, turning away and heading toward the cabin, where Lizzie and James lay under a white sheet.

"Thank you, Officer," I responded. I turned my face to Noah and Zayn and added, "He said Agent Miller was calling him?"

Noah tucked a piece of hair behind my ear and replied, "When we spotted blood in the apartment and couldn't reach you because your phone was off, we got worried. That's when we decided to contact Agent Miller and told him that we suspected the stalker might have hurt you. We also shared your location with him."

"How did you know where I was?" I asked.

"Your keys. You probably haven't noticed, but your key ring is an Apple Tag. You were lucky that James and Maggie, or shall I say, Lizzie, had iPhones but had left them in the car," Ander chimed in once he rejoined our group. "He called us back before we got here to tell us that the police had arrived at the location and that you were safe. He also told us there were two casualties, James Reed and Elizabeth Price, whom you had identified as Maggie Towerby."

Even before he spoke, I could feel Zayn's eyes scanning every inch of my body, looking for injuries.

"You're covered in blood. Did they hurt you?" he asked, his voice tinged with rising anger.

"Yes, they did. But this blood is not mine."

Zayn and Noah raised their eyebrows and looked at each other before looking back at me with puzzled expressions.

"I'll explain everything later," I promised.

One of the paramedics, a petite woman in her thirties, approached us from the ambulance.

"Miss Moore, please follow me. We're taking you to the hospital now."

"I'll come with you in the ambulance," Zayn stated.

"I think it's better if I go alone and meet you all there. It doesn't feel right to leave Noah and Ander behind, and they only allow one person with me," I replied.

"Which hospital are you taking her to?" Noah asked her.

"We're taking her to Stanford University Medical Center," she answered.

"I'll see you there, guys." I placed a gentle kiss on Noah's, Ander's, and Zayn's lips before I followed the paramedic.

She tilted her head slightly as she lowered it, giving me a curious look before offering a timid smile. I replied to her by pressing my lips together and shrugging my shoulders.

Girl, you wouldn't believe me if I told you.

* * *

The drugs the doctors had given me worked wonders. They determined that I didn't have any internal bleeding and only suffered from a mild concussion. X-rays were taken due to my complaint about my right hand, but fortunately, there were no broken bones. Just a sprained wrist, which was now nicely wrapped in a bandage. I had to return in two weeks to have the stitches removed from my arm, but the only instructions they gave me were to rest and take strong painkillers.

I sat perched on the edge of a hospital bed, my feet dangling, hands resting atop my legs. As I awaited my discharge papers, the boys entered the hospital room.

"Are you feeling better, babe?" Zayn asked.

They all seemed concerned, and despite my reassurances between each test that I was fine, they continued to touch my arm and shoulder as if seeking reassurance of my presence. That I was alive.

"Yes, I think so," I responded with a strained smile.

Ander gently touched the back of my neck, his fingers tracing tiny circles on my skin.

"What the hell happened, love?" he asked.

I took a deep breath and then spilled the whole story, starting from when I found the USB drive, getting hit with Zayn's trophy, and ending with the showdown I had with Lizzie. I didn't hold back any details as I filled them in on everything.

"Fuck. How come we never noticed anything?" Noah snarled.

"I guess her acting was worthy of an Oscar from the Academy…" I mocked, but there was no amusement in my voice. "You should have seen her eyes. It was like looking at a completely different person."

"Well, I'm not sure if it's the best thing to say right now, but I'm fucking proud of you." Zayn grabbed my face and kissed me like I was his lifeline and worried that I would disappear the moment he stopped kissing me.

"I had the best self-defense teacher," I whispered against his lips.

"You fought like the queen you are, Sienna." Noah turned my face and kissed me, too, but his kiss was gentle, his tongue caressing mine.

I had never felt more loved than at this moment…but something else was missing. I longed for one final kiss from the boy who now stood a few feet away from me, his hands tucked in his pockets and his eyes clouded with concern. I cautiously stepped down from the bed and closed the distance between us.

I placed my hand on his cheek. "Look at me, Ander," I pleaded. Ander turned his head until our eyes connected. "Are you alright?" I whispered.

"I should be asking you that question, not the other way around."

"I'm fine, Ander," I promised.

"But I'm not. It's all my dad's fault. If it wasn't for him, none of this would've happened. I wouldn't have forgiven myself if Mag…

Lizzie or James…" His voice caught, tears pouring down his cheeks. Ander took a deep breath and closed his eyes, his face leaning toward my hand to seek comfort in my presence. "I thought we lost you."

"I said, look at me."

He gently opened his beautiful ocean-blue eyes.

"I'm truly okay, so let's stop thinking about the what-ifs. You, Zayn, and Noah are the loves of my life, and when I thought I might not see you again, your love gave me the strength to keep going, to fight. Your father made mistakes…yes. But he is not the one who killed my parents or hurt me. And I would never judge you by your father's mistakes. Ever. I love you, Ander. So fucking much." I leaned in and kissed him. It was a passionate, desperate, soul-consuming kiss. One of those kisses that you could feel in the depths of your bones. A kiss full of promises. Promises of a brand-new future together.

Just the four of us.

Ander interrupted our kiss, swiftly intertwined his fingers with mine, and led me toward the room door. Glancing back, I saw Zayn and Noah following us.

"Where are we going?" I asked him.

Ander gazed at me, offering a smile that warmed my heart.

"Home, my love. We are going home."

EPILOGUE
NEW BEGINNINGS

(Sienna)

7 months later

My skin felt so hot, beads of sweat rolled down the valley between my breasts while I was lying on my back.

"I'm gonna have a shower and head to the city center. I have an appointment for a facial. Are you sure you don't wanna come with me?" Sarah insisted.

"No, I'm good. Besides, the boys should arrive in two hours, and I want to be here when they show up."

Classes finished two weeks ago, so as soon as I was able to tie up a few things in New York with Peter, I packed my bags and took a flight to Spain. Sarah had booked an amazing villa in Ibiza, and for the past week, all I had done was sunbathe topless by the pool, drink *tinto de verano*, and visit local shops. Sarah had gone partying almost every night, but I missed Zayn, Ander, and Noah so much that all I wanted to do every night was to put *Pride & Prejudice* on my laptop and curl in bed with a pint of ice cream.

"I love you, darling, but you need to drop that sour face. You've been mopey and dragging your feet around the house like a bloody ghost. I know you miss them, but cheer up."

"Okay. I got it, Sergeant Afolami." I rolled my eyes.

Sarah narrowed her eyes at me. "Don't be an ass."

"I know…" I sighed. "Sorry for being the worst company ever."

Sarah sat at the end of my sunbed and grabbed one of my hands in hers.

"You know I love you. You've gone through a lot in the past twelve months, and I'm just worried about you. When you called me and told me about what happened, I almost dropped dead in shock. But I hope that this event with your professor and Maggie or Lizzie—or whatever the name of that cunt was—made you realize one thing." Her face was dead serious.

"What thing?" I asked.

Sarah looked me straight in the eyes and confessed, "That I'm your best friend, and you should not trust any whore who wants to take my place."

We both erupted into laughter, and I tugged Sarah down and hugged her. She was a great support after what happened a few months ago. As soon as I called her and broke the news, Sarah took the first flight to me. Since then, we've been texting or FaceTiming each other almost every day. She was extremely worried about me and my mental health, so she pushed me to get an appointment with a therapist to help me with all the trauma I had experienced since my parents' murder.

"Mmm. Noah was right. You do have nice tits." She giggled while rubbing her chest with mine.

I pushed her away and kicked her with my feet until her ass fell on the floor.

"Fucking pervert. Go and enjoy your facial, but don't forget we're having dinner at Can Berri Vell tonight at eight o'clock."

"I won't. By the way, have you heard anything from your lawyer?"

"Yes, Mr. Lehman called me this morning. The investigation was finalized two days ago, and William's lawyer was able to demonstrate that the statute of limitations for embezzlement in New York had run out, so the judge dismissed the case."

"Aren't you upset that he's gonna walk away without facing any consequences?" Sarah questioned.

"A bit but mostly, I feel pity for him. His ambition and greed made him lose his best friend, his company, and now his fiancée. Ander has been avoiding his calls, but I've told him he doesn't have to do it for me. It's his dad after all."

"So what's gonna happen to Zayn and his mom?"

"Claudia is living in my house in Port Chester, and I've opened an account for them so they can use my card until the authorities unfreeze their accounts. Hopefully, this will give them a sense of normalcy until then," I said.

Sarah placed a hand on my chest. "You have a heart of gold, Sienna."

I exhaled.

"For a second, I thought you were gonna make a move on me," I deadpanned.

Sarah responded by slapping my left tit.

"You wish." Sarah stood and placed her sunglasses on. "See you later, darling. Enjoy the peace and quiet while it lasts."

* * *

I put my AirPods on and closed my eyes.

I was absolutely in love with everything Ibiza had to offer. The food was amazing, the people were friendly, and the secluded *calas* where you could relax and soak up nature were outstanding. The vibrant nightlife and the warm Mediterranean sun were just the cherry on top.

My week here had been a blast, and even though I had followed a completely different routine compared to last year, I didn't miss my previous empty life of endless parties and casual flings. Everything was perfect, but one thing was missing. Well, actually, three.

"I Put A Spell On You" by Annie Lennox played on my phone when I sensed a shadow casting over my face.

Strange. I didn't remember seeing any clouds in the sky a few minutes ago.

When I opened my eyes, a tall figure wearing a black T-shirt that accentuated his tattooed arms and jeans blocked the sun.

"Zayn!" I tried standing, but someone pushed my shoulders down on the sunbed from behind. I bent my neck and smiled when I noticed Noah towering over me. "Noah," I beamed. "You're early." I was sure I had a stupid smile plastered on my face, but I was so happy to see them.

"Why are you naked, Sienna? Anyone could see you like this?" The voice came from my left, but I'd know that voice anywhere.

"Who's going to see me? I'm just by myself," I retorted.

Ander came into view, wearing casual chino trousers and a white linen button-down. He looked edible.

"Anyone. The gardener, the pool guy, Sarah's next conquest, a neighbor asking for a pinch of salt or eggs," he responded.

"Don't be ridiculous, Ander. Nobody's gonna see me naked; this is a secluded villa."

I tried standing again, but Noah had a strong hold on me.

"Hey, let me stand! I want to hug you. I've missed you."

Zayn's eyes darkened.

"We've missed you too, babe." Zayn bent over and placed both his hands on my ankles. He slowly pushed my legs apart until they were off on each side of the sunbed and my feet on the ground. He then crouched down and tugged at the ties of my swimsuit bottom as he locked eyes with me.

"What do you think you're doing?" I asked with a husky voice.

"Unwrapping our welcome gift. Lift your ass."

My breathing picked up as he removed the small red piece of swimwear and threw it on top of another sunbed.

"Mmmm. I can smell your arousal from here. Noah, hold her hands," Zayn commanded.

Noah grabbed both my wrists and placed them over my head. Zayn parted my legs wider, trailing kisses and biting the inside of my thighs.

"Have you been a good girl while we've been away, Sienna?" Ander asked.

I could only nod, mouth opened, while my eyes focused on Zayn's movements. My pointed nipples ached to be touched, and goose bumps exploded on every inch of my skin.

Zayn traced his fingers on my slit and stopped when he reached my bundle of nerves. He circled my clit in torturous movements, his mouth inching closer to my heated core.

"Fuck, Zayn, are you trying to kill me?" I breathed.

Ander dropped down and covered one of my breasts with his lips. I couldn't contain my moans as he sucked my nipple. He rolled and pinched the other one with his index finger and thumb as Zayn played with my slick center.

"Oh my God," I moaned, raising my pelvis as I sought more pressure from Zayn's hands.

"Zayn, is she wet?" Noah asked.

"She's soaking, man," Zayn responded. "Tell me what you want, Sienna."

"I want more."

"I need you to be more specific, babe."

"Please, I need you to lick my pussy."

"Anything else?" Noah asked.

"Yes, I need you all. I need you to fuck me. I need you to own me, to fill me with your cum."

"I love your filthy mouth," Zayn replied.

I complained with a grunt when Zayn removed his fingers, but a moment later, he replaced them with his lips and tongue. He licked and sucked my clit, while Ander continued to play with my nipples. My body was completely at their mercy, and I loved every second of it. They picked up the pace, and I could feel my arousal coating my inner thighs and Zayn's face.

"That mouth is begging to be fucked," Noah stated. He released my hands, and I immediately gripped Zayn's onyx hair with my right hand, pushing his face closer and moving my hips as I rode his face.

"Open your mouth," Noah ordered as he straddled my shoulders and pushed the tip of his hard cock between my lips.

I obeyed and opened my mouth, relaxing my jaw so he could fuck my mouth as he wished. Noah pushed his throbbing length to the back of my throat until I gagged.

"That's it, Sienna. Do you like sucking my cock, princess?"

I hummed and nodded as Noah continued to fuck my mouth hard and fast, tears coating the corner of my eyes.

I couldn't see Zayn with Noah now blocking my line of vision. But I did feel Zayn's fingers pushing through my folds and curling inside me while he flicked his tongue with an untamed rhythm.

Pressure built up in my lower stomach, and all I could do was moan around Noah's shaft.

Everything became blurry as my climax took control of my entire body, and I cried from the intensity of my release. Zayn continued to lick my pussy until I came down from my orgasm, and the world around me came back into focus.

Noah removed himself from my mouth, lay down on the sunbed next to mine, and said, "Come here. We're not done yet."

Zayn helped me stand, my legs still shaking, while Ander got something out of Noah's backpack and threw it at him.

"I'm gonna fuck that ass while Zayn fucks your pussy. Here," Noah said, holding my hand and helping me straddle him. "Your back to me, princess. I want Zayn and Ander to see your face when you come for us." Noah squeezed the bottle of lube that Ander had passed on to him and coated his dick with a generous amount, then circled some more around the ring of my ass. He placed the tip of his cock on my back entrance and slightly pushed. "Relax your muscles. You're in control, Sienna. We have time, so don't push too much if it hurts; do it slowly and let my cock adjust inside you."

I did as Noah said, placing both of my hands on his thighs to control my movement. Inch by inch, I lowered down until Noah's cock was fully inside my ass, stretching me in a way I had not experienced before.

"Fuck me, you're tight, princess," Noah grunted. "Zayn, you better come here and start fucking her now because I don't know how long I'm gonna last. I was almost a goner with her mouth."

Zayn unbuttoned his jeans and lowered them until they hit the ground around his ankles, and his cock sprang free. He was as hard as a rock, the thick veins protruding along his hardness and his head glistening with precum. He pushed my torso back until I was lying down on top of Noah while he leaned on top of me, holding his body up with one arm. In one firm but quick movement, Zayn pushed himself inside me, and all the air left my lungs. It hurt, but it was the kind of sweet pain I'd gladly take any day.

"You feel so good," Zayn growled.

They both fucked me senseless, cursing under their breaths until my voice was hoarse from all the screaming.

Ander stood next to us, his chinos already gone and his right hand pumping his cock at the same tempo as Zayn and Noah fucked me. It was the most erotic sight I had ever seen.

"Open your mouth, love."

I opened my mouth and stuck out my tongue. Ander placed the tip on it as he continued stroking his cock relentlessly.

"I'm gonna…" Before he finished his sentence, Ander exploded his load in my mouth, my face, and on my lips. I drank every drop of his saltiness and licked my lips while he cursed under his breath,

"Fuck…I love that wicked mouth of yours."

The sound of our sweaty bodies slapping against each other was one of my biggest turn-ons. Zayn and Noah continued to fuck me like two madmen until Zayn hit that sweet spot inside me that made my toes curl. I squeezed my eyes as I came hard with an orgasm more intense than my first one. My walls contracted around them, my whole body bursting like an erupting volcano.

"Fuck, I'm close too," Noah groaned. "Oh my fucking God…" I felt Noah's dick throb inside me before Zayn followed him over the edge.

"Fucking hell, babe. I love how your pussy strangles my cock when you come."

I was a shaking mess.

We stayed in the same position for a couple of minutes, letting our heavy breathing settle down.

Zayn helped me stand while Ander cleaned me up with a beach towel.

"That was a nice welcome," Noah teased.

Ander circled his arms around my waist and gently kissed my swollen lips.

"I missed you guys," I confessed. My heart was filled with so much happiness that I thought it would burst into a million sparkling pieces.

"Not as much as we've missed you." Zayn zipped his jeans and planted a sweet kiss on my shoulder.

I often wondered how things would've turned out if I hadn't crossed paths with these three beautiful men. They had made such a huge impact on my life in a very short period of time, and it was now hard to picture where I'd be without them.

They owned my heart, my body, and my soul.

I'd gladly give all my money away as long as I could live like this for the rest of my days.

And as I gazed upon them, I knew—without a doubt—they were everything I wanted and needed.

AUTHOR NOTE

Thank you so much for reading my debut novel, *Deadly Secrets*.

If you've enjoyed the book, I would greatly appreciate it if you could leave a review on Amazon and Goodreads.

I wrote a brief prequel detailing Sienna's and Ander's relationship when they were young, recounting the day Edward and Marie announced they had enrolled Sienna in a boarding school in Switzerland and the subsequent drop-off at the school. To access this bonus content, you can visit https://amacostaauthor.com/my-book.

Also, for those who are curious about the letters Ander sent to Sienna when she moved to Switzerland... would you like to read the last one? The one where Ander poured his heart out and told her she'd broken his heart? If that's a "Hell, yes!" please visit https://amacostaauthor.com/my-book to access this bonus content.

If you're interested in staying updated on my upcoming dark mafia romance series, Raising The Stakes trilogy featuring *Hunter*, *Wolf*, and *Rogue*, consider signing up to my S-Crew Team at https://amacostaauthor.com/s-crew-team for exclusive updates and news.

ACKNOWLEDGMENTS

A massive thank you to everyone who picked up my debut novel and decided to give it a shot. I really hope you've enjoyed reading this story as much as I enjoyed writing it. Honestly, I never thought I'd publish a book, but the support from this fantastic book community has kept me going till the end.

To my loving and amazing husband, thank you for listening to me read every scene, even the filthiest ones, so that I could have your opinion. I just want you to know that my book boyfriends have nothing on you. You are a dream come true, and I love you so fiercely that one life won't be enough.

Mom, dad…I want to apologize (not really) for some of the content—which I hope you do not read. Ever. You took me to Sunday service every week and sent me to a catholic school so I would be raised like a good girl. I can reassure you that I am. At least, that's what my husband tells me. And to my extended family (my own and the acquired one), you've always supported and encouraged me in every life decision. I just wanted you to know that I felt your support and love throughout this incredible journey.

To my friends, thank you for your unwavering patience in listening to me ramble on about my steamy books and asking about my progress on my novel. This genre may not be your cup of tea, but you have listened to and supported me all these months. A special mention goes to Antonio Jimenez, who guided me in using financial terms in the book appropriately, and Dani Mena, who always gave me helpful advice on marketing my book online. I'm so lucky to have so many talented friends!

To my alpha reader and niece, Marina. I couldn't have asked for a better person to read this story for the first time. Your work as an alpha reader was impeccable, and the messages you kept sending me, along with your constructive feedback, were the funniest shit ever. I hope writing this book made me the coolest auntie…although maybe I won the title of the most perturbed one. Don't tell me, and please don't translate any of the spicy scenes to your father.

To my beta readers, Hristina, Kai, Josie, Sneha, Brittany, and authors C.H. Maddington and Amelia Spencer. You have no idea how much I appreciate that you took the time to read my novel and provide comments and suggestions. In my humble opinion, our time is, after love, the most precious thing we can offer to someone, and you gave me yours voluntarily. You pushed me to do better, to write better. Thank you, thank you, thank you for being by my side. It meant the world to me that you signed up when I am no one in the publishing world.

To my cover designer Jani. The day I stumbled upon one of your drawings on Pinterest, I knew you were the perfect artist to design the cover I had in mind. To Jenny, my line and copy editor. Thank you for making my writing shine.

And my last acknowledgment (and probably the most important) goes to my big sister, Pilar. I hope you're proud of me. You always were my biggest cheerleader and pushed me to do better. I would have loved to share this journey with you, but I know you're still with me, lifting me up and holding my hand whenever I feel scared or anxious. I fucking miss you.

ABOUT THE AUTHOR

A.M. Acosta is a Spanish romance author from Sevilla, Andalusia.

She's a pharmacist by training and a passionate reader of fantasy and dark romance novels, so much so that her friends often wonder how she finds time for reading amidst her busy extracurricular activities. She enjoys writing, playing padel tennis, scuba diving, socializing with friends, traveling worldwide, and finding new dining spots with her husband.

A.M. Acosta is a self-confessed foodie, and her obsession? Japanese ramen, hands down.

She's also the kind of person who wears her heart on her sleeve, labeling herself as a hopeless romantic, a bit of a control freak, and someone who never gives up, no matter what life throws her way.

Having called four different countries home, she's currently based in Dubai.

Follow her on social media!

- TikTok, Instagram, and Threads @author.amacosta
- Facebook https://www.facebook.com/groups/amacostaauthor
- Website https://amacostaauthor.com
- Email amacosta.author@outlook.com

Printed in the USA
CPSIA information can be obtained
at www.ICGtesting.com
LVHW050541210624
783605LV00006B/58

9 788409 615797